A CHARME

D0052019

PIES AND

Prejudice

ELLERY ADAMS

New York Times
Bestselling Author of
the Books by the Bay
Mysteries

**First in a "delicious, delightful,
and deadly new series."**
—Jenn McKinlay, *New York Times* bestselling
author of the Cupcake Bakery Mysteries

BERKLEY
PRIME
CRIME

$7.99 U.S.
$9.99 CAN

S EAN

ISBN 978-0-425-25140-9

9 780425 251409

5 0 7 9 9

Pies and Prejudice

"Enchanting! The Charmed Pie Shoppe has cast its spell on me! Ellery Adams brings the South to life with the LeFaye women of Havenwood. This new series is as sweet and tangy as a warm Georgia peach pie."

—Krista Davis, author of the Domestic Diva Mysteries

A Deadly Cliché

"A very well-written mystery with interesting and surprising characters and a great setting. Readers will feel as if they are in Oyster Bay." —*The Mystery Reader*

"This series is one I hope to follow for a long time, full of fast-paced mysteries, budding romances, and good friends. An excellent combination!" —*The Romance Readers Connection*

A Killer Plot

"Ellery Adams's debut novel, *A Killer Plot*, is not only a great read, but a visceral experience . . . Visit Oyster Bay and you'll long to return again and again."

—Lorna Barrett, *New York Times* bestselling author of the Booktown Mysteries

"Adams's plot is indeed killer, her writing would make her the star of any support group, and her characters—especially Olivia and her standard poodle, Captain Haviland—are a diverse, intelligent bunch. *A Killer Plot* is a perfect excuse to go coastal."

—*Richmond Times-Dispatch*

"A fantastic start to a new series . . . With new friendships, possible romance(s), and promises of great things to come, *A Killer Plot* is one book you don't want to be caught dead missing."

—*The Best Reviews*

"[An] exciting new killer of a series . . . It's one of those 'don't bug me, I'm reading' books you're going to savor from the first page to the last." —*Feathered Quill Book Reviews*

Pies and Prejudice

Ellery Adams

BERKLEY PRIME CRIME, NEW YORK

THE BERKLEY PUBLISHING GROUP
Published by the Penguin Group
Penguin Group (USA) Inc.
375 Hudson Street, New York, New York 10014, USA

Penguin Group (Canada), 90 Eglinton Avenue East, Suite 700, Toronto, Ontario M4P 2Y3, Canada
(a division of Pearson Penguin Canada Inc.) • Penguin Books Ltd., 80 Strand, London WC2R 0RL,
England • Penguin Group Ireland, 25 St. Stephen's Green, Dublin 2, Ireland (a division of Penguin
Books Ltd.) • Penguin Group (Australia), 250 Camberwell Road, Camberwell, Victoria 3124, Australia
(a division of Pearson Australia Group Pty. Ltd.) • Penguin Books India Pvt. Ltd., 11 Community
Centre, Panchsheel Park, New Delhi—110 017, India • Penguin Group (NZ), 67 Apollo Drive,
Rosedale, Auckland 0632, New Zealand (a division of Pearson New Zealand Ltd.) • Penguin Books
(South Africa) (Pty.) Ltd., 24 Sturdee Avenue, Rosebank, Johannesburg 2196, South Africa

Penguin Books Ltd., Registered Offices: 80 Strand, London WC2R 0RL, England

This is a work of fiction. Names, characters, places, and incidents either are the product of the author's
imagination or are used fictitiously, and any resemblance to actual persons, living or dead, business
establishments, events, or locales is entirely coincidental. The publisher does not have any control over
and does not assume any responsibility for author or third-party websites or their content.

PUBLISHER'S NOTE: The recipes contained in this book are to be followed exactly
as written. The publisher is not responsible for your specific health or allergy needs
that may require medical supervision. The publisher is not responsible for
any adverse reactions to the recipes contained in this book.

PIES AND PREJUDICE

A Berkley Prime Crime Book / published by arrangement with the author

PUBLISHING HISTORY
Berkley Prime Crime mass-market edition / July 2012

Copyright © 2012 by Ellery Adams.
Excerpt from *Peach Pies and Alibis* by Ellery Adams copyright © 2012 by Ellery Adams.
Cover illustration by Julia Green.
Cover design by Diana Kolsky.
Interior text design by Laura K. Corless.

ISBN: 978-0-425-25140-9

BERKLEY® PRIME CRIME
Berkley Prime Crime Books are published by The Berkley Publishing Group,
a division of Penguin Group (USA) Inc.,
375 Hudson Street, New York, New York 10014.
BERKLEY® PRIME CRIME and the PRIME CRIME logo are trademarks of
Penguin Group (USA) Inc.

PRINTED IN THE UNITED STATES OF AMERICA

10 9 8 7 6 5

For Leann and Lorraine:

Friendship is the breathing rose,
with sweets in every fold.

—Oliver Wendell Holmes

Promises and piecrust are made to be broken.

—Jonathan Swift

Chapter 1

Ella Mae LeFaye Kitteridge slammed a ball of dough onto the countertop, sending a snowstorm of flour into the air. With angry fingers, she worked pinches of flour into the moist dough and then flattened it with her palm, her hazel eyes flashing a dangerous crocodile green.

"And then what happened?" asked a tiny woman sitting on a stool at a safe distance. She had eyes and hair the color of wet tree bark and always smelled of strawberries.

Smoothing a film of flour onto the surface of a scarred wooden rolling pin, Ella Mae paused in her work. "After class, I stopped by Whole Foods and bought organic lamb and an eggplant so ripe I could still smell the sunlight on its skin. All the way home, my mind was already in the kitchen, humming as I slid the Moroccan lamb pie into the oven, the pecans and maple syrup waiting to be made into dessert, Chewy gnawing on a bone instead of my new leather gloves."

"But you never made it to the kitchen. . . ." the pixielike woman prompted and bit into a red licorice twist, her expression a mixture of avid curiosity and genuine worry.

Ella Mae pressed the rolling pin against the dough, crushing it mercilessly, forcing it to thin and stretch, thin and stretch, her arm muscles made taut with the effort. When the dough was nearly translucent, she put the implement aside and gently lifted the buttery crust into a ceramic pie dish. She laid it down tenderly, as though putting a small child to bed.

Smoothing away minute wrinkles using the tip of her pinkie, she sighed, covering the dough with a breath of wretchedness. "I never made it to the apartment, Reba. I pressed the up button and waited for the elevator, but when it came . . ."

Ella Mae stopped speaking and pulled a mixing bowl filled with plump, freshly picked blueberries toward her. Closing her eyes, she scooped up the berries in her hand, inhaling their crisp, tart scent as they fell between her fingers into the pie pan. A single tear rolled down her cheek, dropping onto the last blueberry. It shimmered for a second, like a diamond catching a ray of sunlight, and the sparkle swept over the other berries like a wave of fairy dust. And then the glimmer disappeared as though it had never existed, like a star being rubbed away by the dawn.

The woman named Reba blinked in surprise. She leaned closer to the pie, shrugged dismissively, and took another bite of her red licorice twist.

Ella Mae drizzled the blueberries with a blend of lemon juice, lemon zest, cornstarch, sugar, and a touch of salt. Finally, she coated the glistening fruit with a crumb blend of butter, flour, oats, brown sugar, and cinnamon. She put the pie in the oven and turned back to Reba with a sigh. "I don't want to talk about it anymore."

Reba nodded and joined Ella Mae at the sink where she was washing her hands. "Why don't you mess about with your mama in the yard while this is cooking'? Maybe the two of you can catch up a bit."

Ella Mae gave a dry laugh. "Reba, *you're* the one who

raised me. You and my aunts. My mother was too busy with her garden teas and Derby parties and Junior League events. If I can't talk to you about what happened in New York, how will I find the words to tell *her*? She already thinks I'm a failure. Thirty-two, childless, and within the year I can add divorcée to that fine list of accomplishments."

"Listen, sugar. Those city folks don't need another bakery. But the good people of Havenwood, Georgia, do! A person can only stand so many sticky buns from the Piggly Wiggly. They go down the gullet like the *Titanic*." She curled an arm around Ella Mae's slim waist. "I remember the magic you used to work in this kitchen. You've always had a way with food, child. Why, just smell that pie! It's fillin' the whole room with—"

"Melancholy," stated a female voice in a low alto. A handsome woman in her late fifties removed a wide-brimmed straw hat trimmed with a pink and green plaid ribbon and patted a rebellious curl—black with filaments of silver—back into submission beneath her headband. Chewy, a young Jack Russell terrier, followed at her heels, his russet ears perked excitedly and a gardening glove secured between his jaws. He raced over to Ella Mae, caressed her with his black nose, and then trotted off to tear up the glove beneath the kitchen table.

Ella Mae put three mint leaves on the bottom of a tumbler and filled the glass with sun tea. Handing the beverage to her mother like a peace offering, she said, "You don't have to serve the pie to my aunts if you don't think it'll taste good."

"It will be an experience, I'm sure," Adelaide LeFaye stated cryptically. "And Reba's right. You have a gift when it comes to pastries. That's why I never understood why you took off with . . . with *that man* to go to New York. There are culinary schools in Atlanta, and I'm certain, especially in light of what happened, that we also have more *gentlemen* here in Georgia."

Curling her fists into tight, angry balls, Ella Mae tossed an ice cube into her mouth and started to crush it with her teeth—an old habit that had always irked her mother. "I haven't told you a single detail! I just got here and suddenly you know *exactly* what happened?"

Her mother shrugged. "It's written all over you, Ella Mae. You're too thin, your hair is dull, and your skin is sallow. You caught your man cheating and now you're questioning your value as a woman and wondering where you belong, where you fit in." She took a sip of tea. "I can answer that last question. Your place is in Havenwood, with your family. I spent the last six months having the carriage house turned into a charming little apartment. And guess when the last throw pillow was delivered by the decorator?"

"I don't know," Ella Mae answered sullenly.

"Yesterday," her mother remarked with a smug smile. "It was as if I knew you'd need a safe haven."

Ella Mae glanced at the oven timer and then filled a tumbler with crushed ice. "You make it sound like I need a place to recover from botched plastic surgery. For your information, my heart was broken! I pressed the button to call for the elevator, and when it came and the doors opened, there was my husband with the redheaded twins from five sixteen C."

"Sisters?" Reba breathed. *"Damn."*

Pulverizing ice between her molars, Ella Mae was lost in the unpleasant memory and Reba's comment didn't register. "I didn't recognize Sloan at first. I don't usually see him from an ass-in-the-air angle."

"Language, Ella Mae," her mother tut-tutted while Reba sniggered.

Her eyes flashing between a mottled green and brown, Ella Mae advanced on her mother. "My *husband* was screwing one sister and had his hand up the other one's skirt! Is *that* a nice, ladylike description?"

Reba put her hand on her chest. "Lord have mercy! Whatcha do?"

"I wanted to kill them. *All* of them," Ella Mae admitted, her rage ebbing away as suddenly as it had flared. "But the only weapon I had was Chewy. And what was I going to do? Send my terrier into the elevator to nibble them to death?" She shook her head in disgust. "No, I didn't want my dog to be tainted. If he touched any of them, I'd never want him to lick my face again!"

"Too bad you didn't have mace or somethin'," Reba mused. "Aren't you supposed to carry stuff in your purse when you live in a big city?"

Ella Mae couldn't help but laugh. "Reba. I traveled from our apartment to culinary school and back. I went to museums, boutiques, and ate at fabulous restaurants. Manhattan isn't some den of iniquity. It's a wonderful place. It's where I dreamed of opening my pie shop."

Reba turned on the oven light and peered at the baking pie. "If only you'd had *that* to toss in the elevator. Could you imagine the mess?"

She and Ella Mae exchanged smiles, but her mother's expression was stoic.

"I grabbed the only weapons I had on hand," Ella Mae continued her narrative. "A two-pound bag of flour, which I tore open and dumped on the six-legged beast, followed by a jumbo bottle of pure maple syrup. I then pelted them with an entire bag of pecan halves."

"Sounds like a new recipe for humble pie!" Reba shouted and hooted with laughter.

"I didn't stick around long enough to see what the building's super thought of the human tarts. I hit the elevator's alarm button just as he sat down at his desk in the lobby, grabbed Chewy, and ran." Ella Mae sank down on a stool, suddenly weary from having told the story whose finale spelled the end of her seven-year marriage to Sloan Kitteridge.

At that moment, the oven timer beeped. Ella Mae turned it off and opened the door, inviting a rush of heat and the scent of crisp dough and warm blueberries into the room. She imagined tendrils of sugar and cinnamon curling around her, coaxing the tension from her shoulders and taking her back to bike rides on dirt lanes and afternoons running barefoot through soft summer grass.

Ella Mae put the pie on the counter and all three women drew closer to it and to one another. Sparkles of sugar on the crumble's browned crust winked in the light, and for the first time since Ella Mae had come home, she found her mother looking quite pleased.

"Reba, be a dear and put the kettle on for tea. My sisters will be here shortly." She scrutinized Ella Mae's outfit of jeans and T-shirt and clearly found it wanting. "Are you going to freshen up before they arrive? I'm sure you want to make a good impression. After all, they haven't seen you for seven years."

Ella Mae examined the speckles of flour on her shirt and glared at her mother. She then turned and walked away, thinking, *And whose fault is that?*

Ella Mae's three aunts, Delia, Verena, and Cecilia, fluttered into her mother's house like a flock of colorful, noisy birds. Delia, a metal sculptor known as Dee to her family, spent most days dressed in overalls and wielding a blowtorch. In honor of her niece's return, she'd unbraided her long, auburn hair so that it fell in soft waves onto the straps of her gauzy floral sundress. She was the quietest of the four women and spoke in a soft, gentle voice. If Ella Mae made a pie to represent Dee, it would be a warm and comforting double-crust apple with a sweet surprise of raisins in the filling.

Verena, the eldest of the four sisters, was bright and bold as a cherry pie. She always wore outfits consisting of black and white pieces coupled with a vibrant accessory, so Ella Mae was unsurprised to see her aunt in a black skirt, white blouse, and an enormous necklace made of red coral. Verena was married to Buddy Hewitt, Havenwood's mayor, and spent her time serving on a host of town boards. She was the most gregarious of the sisters and tended to overeat, talk too loudly in church, and intimidate those who wouldn't back her latest charitable endeavors.

Then there was Cecilia, who went by Sissy. She dressed in flowing, pastel-hued garments and moved with the same grace as the young dancers at her school, The Havenwood School of the Arts. As she crossed the spacious entry hall to embrace Ella Mae, the hem of her orange sherbet skirt caressed the floor with a delicate whisper. Sissy's pie would be peanut butter chiffon. Light on the top but rich, sophisticated, and appropriately dramatic on the inside.

"We are *so* thrilled to have you back again!" After holding Ella Mae tightly, Sissy pushed her niece away and studied her. "Let me just drink in the sight of you. Oh." She turned to Verena. "Hasn't she *blossomed*?"

Sissy had a tendency to enunciate a single word of every sentence.

Verena put her hands on her hips and declared loudly. "You are a stunner, my dear! I have to admit, I'm jealous. I do recall when the four LeFaye sisters could walk into a room and the clocks would stop ticking for a full ten seconds, but the hands would fall right off the dial for you!"

Dee elbowed Verena. "You're exaggerating, Sister," she said in a near whisper. "We've never had the power to control time. If we did, I'd hit the pause button and catch up on the Davidsons' basset hound sculpture." She slipped past her sisters and gave Ella Mae a hug. "They lost their Radley over a month ago and I still haven't finished work on their canine angel. I can't seem to get his eyes right."

Sissy gave Dee a crooked smile. "Just think of Adelaide during freshman year when she drank *all* the spiked punch at the Confederate Ball. She had basset hound hangover face the next morning!"

The laughter of the women spilled into the empty air and

Ella Mae had the sensation of champagne bubbles popping around her. As they all moved into the living room, the light streaming through the windows shined a little brighter, making the sterling silver candlesticks and framed photos on the mantel glint like Christmas tree tinsel. Even her mother seemed to glow in the company of her siblings, and Ella Mae wondered if anyone had ever seen four such beautiful, gifted, and formidable sisters as the LeFayes.

It had been both wondrous and daunting to be reared by this collective of women. Though her mother and Verena had married, Verena never had children, and neither Dee nor Sissy had expressed a desire to marry or raise a family. Therefore, five women, including Reba, had served as Ella Mae's mothers, each of them teaching, guiding, and loving her until she'd left them behind for a good-looking man with a honeyed tongue.

Watching them now, Ella Mae was thankful that she'd kept in touch with her aunts during the seven years she was away, the seven years in which she and her mother didn't exchange a single word. They'd called her constantly during that first year in Manhattan, knowing she was lonely and that Sloan often worked late.

She'd tell them of the city's wonders while they'd update her on the doings in Havenwood. Ella Mae never asked after her mother, but her aunts always ended every conversation by saying, "And you know your mama sends her love, even if you don't hear her speaking the words."

At the time, Ella Mae believed Sloan's love was all that she'd needed. How wrong she had been.

Dee must have noticed the shadow hovering over Ella Mae's shoulder for she touched her niece on the elbow and gently steered her toward the sunroom where the table was set for afternoon tea. "Did you bake something?"

"Ella Mae volunteered to make us a pie." Her mother gestured regally toward the table covered with a gleaming white cloth and a silver urn bursting with bright yellow roses. Their petals shimmered in the light, reminding Ella Mae of the surface of a lemon tart.

"Adelaide!" Sissy gushed. "Is this your new Yellow Ribbon rose?"

When her sister nodded, Sissy leaned in to smell the bouquet. "Hmm, I smell homecomings and *happiness* and . . ." She inhaled deeply, her eyes closed. "Immeasurable relief."

Verena gave Sissy a bossy nudge. "The roses are lovely, Adelaide, but I am much more interested in finding out what Ella Mae learned in that fancy New York culinary school." She took a seat at the table. "Come on, girls! All I had for lunch was three fried chicken thighs, a pile of okra, and a biscuit oozing butter. I'm starved!"

The women giggled with mirth. Verena was notorious for her appetite. Unlike her sisters, who were slim and lithe as dancers, Verena had a solid build. She was by no means fat, but as the eldest and tallest of the LeFaye sisters, she seemed larger than life to most of Havenwood's populace. And when she was ready to eat, nothing could come between her and her meal.

Her mother served slices of Ella Mae's pie, deftly lifting precise wedges of the dessert onto cloud white plates. Watching her, Ella Mae decided that she'd be a rhubarb-raspberry tart a la mode—the filling forced into sweetness by a dram of whiskey and the acidic taste of the berries softened by a plump scoop of vanilla ice cream.

The sisters chatted away as they loaded their forks, but the moment they savored their first bite of tart blueberries blended with flaky dough and finishing with the crunch of the sweet crumble, the women fell silent.

Ella Mae twisted the linen napkin on her lap, her own pie untouched.

They don't like it, she thought, watching her aunts. Her mother hadn't served herself a slice, disappearing into the kitchen to get the tea instead.

Dee put her fork down and licked her blue-tinged lips. "Do you all remember Mack Davenport?" Her voice was so light and feathery that it nearly floated away. "That boy who lived down the street and moved away when I was in the third grade?"

Sissy and Verena nodded.

"I stole his baseball glove and slept with it under my pillow until high school," Dee continued dreamily. "Mack was my first crush."

Verena broke off a piece of crust and popped it into her mouth. She chewed, swallowed, and sighed wistfully. "I fell in love at church. John David Appleby. We sang in the children's choir together and he stood right behind me. His breath was like a cool peppermint on the back of my neck. Four years of imaginary candy-cane kisses. We never spoke a word, but he sang like an angel."

Sissy put her hand over her heart and sighed theatrically. "I kissed *my* first boy on a dock, watching fireworks reflect on the surface of Lake Havenwood. I thought I'd marry J. P. Littleton after that night, even though we were only *twelve*. I often wonder where he is now, what his life is like. . . ."

Ella Mae looked from one face to another, stunned at the transformation that had occurred around the tea table. The sisters' banter, light and airy as a cream puff, was gone, replaced by the blue tinge of heartache and regret.

"The pie," Dee whispered in awe. "It made those memories swim to the surface."

Verena and Sissy stared at their empty plates and then exchanged knowing glances.

"Were you thinking about Sloan when you baked this pie?" Verena demanded.

"Yes," Ella Mae answered.

Sissy put a hand over hers. "Tell us *exactly* what you felt."

Ella Mae hesitated and then whispered, "That I already

miss belonging to someone. That my chance for happily ever after has slipped away."

The yellow roses in the center of the table seemed to lose their luster as the three sisters studied their niece. No one noticed when her mother returned with the teapot.

"Verena? Dee? Sissy?" she cried, setting the pot so roughly onto the table that the urn toppled, scattering rose petals into the overturned porcelain cups. "Why are you crying?" She reached out to Dee, catching a teardrop on her index finger, and then raised the vibrant bead of moisture closer to her face, her eyes widening in astonishment. "And why are your tears blue?"

Dee dabbed at her face with her napkin and then, inexplicably, she smiled. "Not blue, Adelaide. Indigo. They're the shade of blueberries. Blueberries and heartache."

Sissy and Verena reached into their purses, popped open compacts, and examined their own stained cheeks.

"How marvelous!" Verena declared with a joyful laugh while Sissy looked thoughtful.

Grinning mischievously, Sissy grabbed her niece by the hand and gave it an excited squeeze. "Ella Mae, I have a *proposition* for you, my darling."

Chapter 2

Ella Mae came to Havenwood with two sets of clothes. She'd arrived on her mother's doorstep wearing a pair of black slacks, a sleeveless silk tank top, and a pair of sandals. She had Chewy's leash in one hand and a duffel bag containing the food-encrusted clothing that she'd worn that day in culinary class in the other. Now her jeans, black T-shirt, and socks had been washed and folded into a neat pile on the wing chair of the guest room. Her mother had loaned her a white cotton nightgown, which Reba fanned out on the bed just as she'd done when Ella Mae was a girl. This was the extent of her current wardrobe.

The feel of the nightgown, coupled with the lavender scent of the guest room's floral sheets, helped pull Ella Mae from a fractured dream involving a pair of naked redheads baking pies in her mother's kitchen. Rolling onto her side, Ella Mae blinked the dream away by kissing Chewy on his nose. She accepted an affectionate face washing in return and then headed into the bathroom for a shower.

Inside the steam-filled stall, Ella Mae thought back on

yesterday's bizarre reunion with her aunts. How could the pie have caused a discoloration of their tears? Perhaps some unusual pesticide had tainted the blueberries. And why had her aunts been so delighted by the odd physical reaction? Sissy had barely cleaned her face before digging out her day planner, penciling Ella Mae in to handle the desserts for The Havenwood School of the Art's summer open house.

"I'm not serving blueberries, that's for damn sure," Ella Mae spoke to the fog-covered mirror in the bathroom. The air was muggy and close and she threw open a window to let it ooze outside. Wrapping herself in a towel, she went back to the bedroom, unfolded her jeans, and laid them out on the floor.

It was summertime in Havenwood. That meant average temperatures in the nineties with enough humidity to keep the damp hair on Ella Mae's neck from ever drying. Smiling in anticipation, she picked up Reba's fabric scissors and began to cut the legs off the jeans. She began at a conservative length, just above the knee and then, feeling brazen, sliced off a few more inches. The moment she tried on the jean shorts, she felt ten years younger.

She slid on her canvas Keds, which she'd also worn on her last day of culinary school, and drew her whiskey-colored hair into a high ponytail. She owned no makeup and had only her watch, a pair of diamond studs, and her wedding rings as accessories. She stuck the rings in the drawer of the nightstand and stared at them for a long moment, seeing how the gold and diamonds were rendered dull without the benefit of the light. Touching the bare skin of her ring finger, Ella Mae vowed to find a way to keep herself occupied so she wouldn't spend the day brooding over her broken marriage. She decided to begin by cooking bacon and eggs for herself and Chewy.

The kitchen was quiet. Reba didn't start her housekeeping duties until midmorning and her mother was a nocturnal creature. Last night, long after Ella Mae had fallen asleep with the lamp burning and the paperback copy of *To Kill a Mockingbird* from her high school freshmen English class splayed open on the quilt, she'd been awakened by the sound of mother padding around the house.

Ella Mae hadn't slept well. She'd tossed and turned, disturbed by the absence of noise. In Manhattan, she was accustomed to the constant cacophony of sound enveloping her apartment building. In Havenwood, the police and ambulance sirens, blaring taxicab horns, and the shouting, swearing, or singing of strangers was replaced by the gentle sawing of crickets and the resonating croaks of bullfrogs. It was a different symphony, lacking the dissonance to replicate an urban melody.

In the empty kitchen, the quiet continued to rattle her. She ate breakfast, read the newspaper, and drank a cup of coffee. Wrens and finches twittered outside the window and the drone of cicadas began to increase in volume as the sun rose higher in the milky blue sky. Sighing, Ella Mae found her gaze wandering to her unencumbered ring finger again and again. Slamming the paper shut, she jumped out of her chair.

"Let's go for a bike ride, Chewy," Ella Mae said and hastily loaded the dirty plates into the dishwasher. She then led the leaping, exuberant terrier into the garage. "It'll give me a chance to come up with a menu for Sissy's event."

Her bike was exactly where she'd left it, in the far corner behind the wheelbarrow. She cleaned it off with a wet rag, inflated the tires, and tried out the bell. She rang it three times, smiling at the merry trill, and settled Chewy in the roomy straw basket attached to the handlebars.

"Do not gnaw your seat," she admonished her grinning dog as she began to pedal, but there was no need to worry. Chewy took to bicycle riding instantaneously, his dark chocolate eyes glimmering with excitement, his tongue lolling from between gleaming white teeth. As they passed under a lane of ancient magnolia trees, the sunlight streamed through the branches.

She rode for a mile, turning from the residential road onto the dirt path leading to the swimming hole.

"I wore a bikini last time I was here," she told Chewy. "And when I jumped off the rope swing into the water, my top floated away. I about died when Hugh Dylan had to fetch it for me. He was the cutest boy in the entire school, but he never even looked at me until the one day I wanted to be invisible."

Chewy was too busy soaking in the sights and smells to listen to Ella Mae's remembrances. At eight months old he was still a puppy and, so far, had been exposed to greenery only at Central Park. Now there were trees and lush undergrowth as far as the eye could see. Squirrels teased him from the canopy, and everywhere he looked there were sticks. Hundred of sticks. Thousands of them.

Sensing his delight, Ella Mae rubbed his head. "We'll find you a fine stick at the swimming hole. You'll love getting your paws wet."

The pair faced forward as the bike tore downhill, wind whipping through Chewy's fur and lifting Ella Mae's ponytail into the air like a kite's tail.

When the ground leveled out, Ella Mae dismounted and leaned her bike against a tree. She told Chewy to jump out of the basket. Amazingly, he obeyed, running in circles around her ankles as she edged toward a clump of blackberry bushes concealing the edge of the rock and the fifty-foot drop to the cool water below.

Ella Mae heard a splash and, for some reason, felt as though she had invaded someone's privacy. The swimming hole was known to all the locals and she'd bathed in its waters hundreds of times, but her seven-year absence made her feel like an intruder and she quickly hid behind a tree, peeking around the rough bark to catch a glimpse of the swimmer.

She saw his head and shoulders first, bursting from the water with the power of a breaching whale. He held his muscular arms outward as if he might embrace the hillside above him, grab onto the billowy clouds, and pull the maize-colored sun from the sky. His hair was dark and clung to his neck in wet curls, and his broad back was rippled with muscles.

Unaware that he had an audience, the man flicked a coin high into the air and then watched as it fell into the deepest part of the swimming hole. Ella Mae saw the coin catch a sunbeam and wink once before it was swallowed by blue.

Chewy wagged his tail and raced down the path. Just as he let out an excited bark, the man dove under the water. Ella Mae followed her dog, keeping one eye on the uneven terrain and another on the surface, waiting for the man to come up for breath.

But he didn't come up for breath.

"Oh, Lord," she whispered, feeling her heart pound against her ribs. He'd been under for over a minute by the time she caught up to Chewy. He was sniffing a pile of clothes—khaki shorts and a Mountain Dew T-shirt—with gusto.

"Stop it," Ella Mae hissed, her fearful gaze on the water.

After another thirty seconds, she decided to dive in after the swimmer. She ran back up the hill, preparing to jump straight into the deepest part of the pool, when the man suddenly appeared fifteen feet away from where he'd gone under. Now he was near the narrow stretch of shore, breathing hard and smiling.

He dropped the coin onto a flat stone, water streaming down his chiseled and tanned torso. Ella Mae couldn't tear her gaze away. He was like a merman, slick and streamlined, powerfully built and ethereally handsome.

"Dante!" he called out, and Ella Mae crouched low, not wanting to be caught spying. She grabbed Chewy by the collar and pressed his muzzle to her chest and he bucked to break free, but at the moment, something very large crashed through the undergrowth on the opposite bank, drawing the attention of both Chewy and Ella Mae.

"Hey, boy!" The man stood, his arms opened to greet the

biggest dog Ella Mae had ever seen. He was white with black spots but was way too large to be a Dalmatian. With a resounding bark of joy, he jumped on his master and the two crashed into the water, the man's laughter floating up to Ella Mae.

She picked up Chewy and hurried to her bike. "We'll come back later," she promised her squirming terrier. "I don't have a swimsuit and I am *not* skinny-dipping with those two around."

Still, the image of the man emerging from the water made her skin tighten and burn as if she'd been out in the sun too long. To quell the desire she felt stirring in her blood, Ella Mae began to silently recite the ingredients in a pine nut tart crust.

Safely back on the rock ledge, she untied the plastic bag she'd wound around the handlebars of her bike before setting out and began to fill it with plump, juicy blackberries.

She was already envisioning the pie she'd make to mark this trip to the swimming hole. The crust would be of crushed graham crackers, to echo the sandy bank. Then, a layer of moist blackberries, to remind her of the dark waters. And on the top, a cloud of lemon chiffon to represent the summer day. She'd garnish the edges with small blackberries and mint leaves.

Unbidden, her mind strayed to the day she'd first met Sloan Kitteridge. Ella Mae had ridden her bike to Havenwood's roadside fruit stand to buy strawberries. Sloan was passing through town on his way to a company retreat at the lakeside resort when he spotted Ella Mae pedaling along. He was so caught up in the vision of this lovely girl with the long, tanned limbs, full lips, and hair floating out behind her like a ribbon of caramel, that he drove his rental car into a ditch.

Having stopped to see if the driver was injured, Ella Mae had taken one look at the handsome stranger and saw her ticket out of Havenwood. She'd gone away to college, of course, but had returned home only to take an assortment of unfulfilling jobs. She'd dated a few local men but had never fallen in love. Feeling trapped by her mother's silent but domineering presence, Ella Mae longed for escape, to have adventures like her archaeologist father—a man she'd never known. A man who'd died worlds away just a few days before her birth.

Ella Mae's turn for adventure had come when Sloan drove into that ditch. He exited the car and smiled at her as if the accident had been a gift. He'd taken her to lunch, then dinner, and stayed at the resort long after his retreat was over. When he returned to New York ten days later, Ella Mae went with him, leaving all she knew behind to follow the whims of her heart.

"And here I am again," she whispered to the trees. "Starting over." She popped a blackberry into her mouth and chewed, savoring its tart succulence. "I can still have a good life. I can make my own happiness."

Looping the bag of blackberries onto her right wrist, Ella Mae decided to focus on the tarts she'd bake for the open house instead of thinking about Sloan or the beautiful man from the swimming hole.

On the ride back to her mother's house, which was called Partridge Hill and had been in the LeFaye family for two centuries, Ella Mae decided to take a shortcut in order to get the berries safely into the kitchen before they spoiled. This meant riding on the lane bordering the Gaynors' property. Ella Mae would normally avoid this route, seeing as Loralyn Gaynor had been her enemy since the two girls were in kindergarten.

Ella Mae had no idea whether Loralyn still lived in Havenwood, but she pedaled as fast as she could past Rolling View, the Gaynors' sprawling estate. Her mother had once told Ella Mae that it had held another, less bucolic title in the past, but the Gaynor family had expunged that name when they'd begun raising thoroughbred racehorses.

"She's probably happily married with a perfect husband and a perfect house," Ella Mae stated petulantly to Chewy. "Two darling cherubim for children and a job . . . No, she wouldn't have a job, now would she? Loralyn was never fond of working. She cheated her way through school and hired someone to write her college application essays. She'll have a housekeeper and a gardener and will spend her free time playing tennis and getting her hair done."

Ella Mae glanced nervously at the circular driveway leading up to the large brick Georgian, but there was no sign of life in the manicured front yard.

"That's a relief." Ella Mae turned away from the house. "Loralyn's the last person I'd want to run into. She'd do anything in her power to make my life even more of a living hell than it is now."

Chewy just looked at her from his perch in the bike basket.

"Oh, you don't even want to know how much I hated that girl. She pulled my hair on the bus, crushed my Girl Scout cookies with a brick, told the teachers I'd pinched her or copied off her or said curse words, put worms in my food, and stole the heart of the only boy I'd ever loved. She was evil then and I bet she's just as wicked now."

Distracted, Ella Mae drove over a large stone and nearly crashed into the split-rail fence. Chewy whined and shot her an accusing look.

"I'm sorry, sweetie. See what happens when I think about that girl? She doesn't even have to be here to do me harm."

Chewy gave a little sniff.

"You're right, I'm being silly." Ella Mae ruffled her dog's ears. "Loralyn is probably a million miles away from Havenwood and can't lift a finger against me. It's nice to think that my childhood bully is busy making someone else's life miserable."

Ella Mae began pedaling again, humming a little as she headed for home.

Chapter 3

Ella Mae had given Reba the pie she'd made with the wild blackberries. Reba told her the following morning that it was the best thing she'd ever eaten.

"Any, um, side effects?" Ella Mae had asked, trying to disguise her anxiety by focusing on stripping the sagging petals from an arrangement of her mother's apricot-hued roses.

Reba, who had been filling a pitcher with tea bags and water, looked up and chuckled. "Only if you count me watching *Dirty Dancing* followed by *Top Gun* followed by *Legends of the Fall*. I was so hot for a man last night I almost ordered a pizza just so I could jump the delivery boy!" She shook her head in befuddlement. "Don't know if it was the pie or my hormones, but there was so much steam comin' off my body last night that it went out through the chimney and made my neighbors think I'd started a fire in June!"

Reba's story had made Ella Mae wonder. Had her animalistic attraction to the beautiful stranger from the swimming hole been infused into the pie? Had it burrowed into the crevices of the blackberries or melted into the sugar crystals of the lemon chiffon?

"Ridiculous," she'd muttered and dismissed the idea.

Now, two days later, she stood in the gleaming kitchen of The Havenwood School of the Arts, preparing to bake eight-dozen individual tarts to serve at the school's open house for prospective parents and students. She'd decided to make three different tarts. The first would be a fruit tart of fresh peaches resting on a bed of almond filling; the second, chocolate pecan with a chocolate cookie crust; and for the third, she planned to bake a lemon tart with a short-bread crust.

Early that morning, Sissy had unlocked the school's kitchen and showed Ella Mae where the cooking utensils were kept. The pair had bought the bulk of the supplies for the open house the day before at the Costco in Kennesaw, but Ella Mae had insisted on acquiring peaches and lemons from the local farm stand.

She was ready to begin her first professional job as a baker. Having never had the chance to complete an externship during culinary school, Ella Mae hadn't actually made any products for members of the public. She'd baked for her husband and her friends, but never for strangers.

Still, she felt she'd been preparing for this day since she was a child. Ella Mae had helped Reba cook ever since she could reach the counter with the help of a step stool. Even in the unfamiliar kitchen of Sissy's school, Ella Mae was at home. The chilled dough had been transported to the walk-in refrigerator, the peaches and lemons were waiting to be prepped, and the sounds of "Alla Hornpipe" from Handel's *Water Music* tripped into the kitchen from one of the practice rooms down the hall.

Sissy swept into the kitchen just as Ella Mae was tying on her apron. She looked as though she had much to do and didn't want to linger long.

"Do you have everything you need?"

Ella Mae nodded. "I do, thanks. I'm just a little nervous. Everything I've made has been for my culinary class. This is the real deal."

"That it is, but you were *born* to do this." Sissy paused. "Come with me for a minute."

"Let me preheat the ovens first."

Sissy waited until the dual commercial ovens had been programmed and then led her niece to the practice room filled with Handel's upbeat composition.

"Look at the dancers," Sissy ordered. "Tell me what you see."

Six girls, slender as willow branches, were practicing the dance they'd perform for the prospective parents that afternoon. Ella Mae watched them bend and stretch as though they had no bones in their bodies. Each movement was graceful and fluid, flowing into the next like waves curling into the shore. But what was the most transfixing was the rapture on the girls' faces. Their eyes were distant, as though the dance had transported them from the room, lifting their souls into the air where they could become one with the music.

"I see inspiration," Ella Mae told her aunt.

Sissy smiled, pleased. "Yes. Picture these girls as you bake today and *your* work will be inspired too."

Ella Mae did just that. The notes from Handel's compilation kept her company as she boiled the peaches and then slipped them from their skins like a woman shrugging off a thin coat. She hummed while pouring crushed almonds, flour, melted butter, sugar, and eggs into the industrial mixer. Later, after spooning the rich chocolate pecan filling into tiny tart pans lined with cookie crusts, Ella Mae twirled around and around in front of the ovens, her wooden spoon raised like a conductor's baton.

Gone were all thoughts of Sloan or of how strange it felt to wake up alone in the guest bedroom bed in the carriage house or that Chewy had gnawed through her one and only purse last night.

She felt weightless, floating on warm, dough-scented currents.

When all the tarts were done, four of Sissy's current students arranged them on ceramic platters and carried them to tables on the enclosed veranda. The parents and prospective students would conclude their tour of the school by taking refreshments in the upholstered wicker chairs facing Lake Havenwood. By the time they reached the room, they were tired and hungry. Fans turned lazily overhead, greeting them with the tantalizing aroma of fresh, warm pastry, and the visitors loaded their plates and retreated to chairs to sample one of Ella Mae's tarts.

Within minutes, the restrained and polite chatter increased in volume. A girl seated in the middle of the room began to sing the opening bars of "The Flower Duet" from the opera *Lakmé*. Unbidden, the girl at the next table joined her, their voices intertwining like jasmine vines.

Suddenly, two other girls rose and began to dance while a third opened her violin case and effortlessly accompanied the singers. Ella Mae caught Sissy's eye and was amazed to see that her aunt appeared calmly amused, as though spontaneous displays of artistic talent occurred at every open house.

Later, as Ella Mae tidied the kitchen, Sissy breezed in, her face glowing. She handed her niece an envelope stuffed with cash.

"This is more than we agreed on," Ella Mae protested.

Sissy waved her off. "I had to give you a commission. Every *single* family put down deposits to secure a place for their daughter before they left. We've never had a full enrollment prior to July first before. Thanks to you, I can actually enjoy the rest of my summer." She performed a celebratory pirouette.

"Well, I do need to buy a new wardrobe," Ella Mae said. "And Chewy tore my purse to shreds, so I'd better hit the shops while Reba's keeping an eye on him."

Sissy had just opened her mouth to comment when the shriek of an alarm bell echoed through the kitchen.

"What's going on?" Ella Mae shouted over the clamor.

"Someone pulled the fire alarm! Help me make sure everyone's clearing out of the building. I don't know if this is real or a hoax. *My* girls are too well mannered to set off the alarm as a prank, so I don't know what's happened!"

Hearing the worry in her aunt's voice, Ella Mae darted off toward the back veranda. Turning a corner, she tripped over the curled end of a rug and went sprawling. She grunted and eased herself up on all fours, the ringing of the alarm bells reverberating in her head.

"That was mighty ungraceful for someone involved in a school for the arts!" a sarcastic voice yelled near Ella Mae's ear.

Ella Mae turned and came face-to-face with her childhood nemesis, Loralyn Gaynor.

Her mouth stretched into a hundred-watt smile, Loralyn put out her hand to help Ella Mae to her feet. It was limp and useless as a dead fish. "Where are all the parents and precious progeny? Didn't get scared off by that little old bell, now did they?"

Rising indignantly to her feet, Ella Mae glowered at the stunning blonde she'd hated for most of her life. "Did y*ou* set off the alarm?"

Loralyn feigned shock, but a spark of malice glimmered in the iris of her eyes. "Puh-lease. I have better things to do with my time."

"Then what are you doing here?" Ella Mae watched her old enemy's face closely, searching for signs of mischief.

Mercifully, the alarm ceased as abruptly as it had begun.

"Ah, that's better," Loralyn said congenially. "I just stopped by to pick up a brochure for a neighbor's daughter. She sings like a parrot and dances like a marionette, so she should fit in here just fine." She fanned herself with the brochure, pivoting her hand so that Ella Mae couldn't help but notice the enormous diamond on her ring finger. "Oh, yes, congratulations *are* in order," she said though Ella Mae hadn't uttered a word. "Thank you very much. This happens to be lucky husband number three."

Ella Mae frowned. "And that's something to brag about? Did you poison the first two? Nag them to death?" She bit back a string of snide remarks. Why was she behaving like some catty teenager?

"Nothing that messy, cupcake," Loralyn answered with perfect civility. "I simply discovered that divorce could be quite lucrative. Men are so easy to manipulate. Hire a prostitute here or an underage cheerleader there and voilà! The money rolls into my bank account for years and years." Loralyn's eyes narrowed wickedly. "But that's not what happened in your case, now is it? I bet you actually loved your husband, didn't you? Poor Ella Mae. Couldn't you keep your man satisfied?"

This is what you get for provoking her, Ella Mae scolded herself. *But how did she find out about me so quickly?*

Loralyn pursed her lips, studying Ella Mae from head to toe. "You're still slim, I'll give you that, but judging from the unpleasant smell in the air, you didn't learn much at that fancy cooking school."

Ella Mae stood a fraction taller. "Someone should warn your fiancé about what a prize you are. Maybe I should volunteer."

Loralyn lowered her voice to a serpent-like hiss, her eyes flashing with anger. "You do *anything* to mess with my plans to fatten up my piggy bank and you'll be sorry. Trust me, I've dealt with slyer foxes than you without so much as chipping a nail." Recovering almost instantaneously, she pasted on a polite smile, turned, and wiggled her fingers over her shoulders. "Gotta run, darling. I just wanted to get a look at you, but now I have a wedding to plan and lots of pretty things to charge to my fiancé's credit card."

The *clip-clip* of her heels against the bare floor receded

and another set of footsteps, definitely male, stomped into the room from the opposite direction.

"Ma'am? Are you okay?"

Ella Mae swiveled to see a fireman standing just inside the doorway. She took in his molasses brown hair and sea blue eyes, the strong line of his jaw, and the set of his broad shoulders. Her mouth went dry and she heard Handel again, even though the music had been switched off long ago. She smelled cut grass, the damp sand at the water's edge, and blackberries.

Hugh Dylan! The merman from the swimming hole is Hugh Dylan! Ella Mae bit her lip, for here was the grown-up version of the boy she'd been in love with her entire girlhood.

The air between them crackled like a summer thunderstorm, and Ella Mae could swear that her blood was growing warmer, surging into her heart, threatening to ignite the oxygen in her lungs. Her skin burned softly as she looked into his eyes, wondering how she could be feeling such a sensation of heat and yet could think of nothing but secret pools of blue green water.

"Is there a fire?" she said, all thoughts of Loralyn Gaynor swept aside.

"False alarm," he answered in a voice as smooth as waves curling into the shore. "Are you a teacher here?"

She shook her head, disappointed that he didn't recognize her. "No. I came to make the tarts."

"I thought I smelled something amazing." Hugh smiled at her and waited for her to speak again, but she couldn't. Her tongue had gone flaccid, like a deflated birthday balloon.

The awkward silence stretched between them until the man finally gave an apologetic shrug, turned, and headed out the way he'd come.

Ella Mae didn't want him to leave, but she was angry with herself for falling to pieces over her girlhood crush only days after her husband had made a colossal fool of her.

Sissy appeared behind her niece before Hugh had the chance to vanish through the door at the opposite end of the hall. "Thank you!" she called.

He pivoted and gave Sissy a friendly wave, but his hand froze in the air as his glance slid to Ella Mae. He locked eyes with her, bowed briefly from the waist, and then walked off.

"My, my!" Sissy cooed. "Maybe there *was* a fire here today after all."

Ella Mae shook her head, but inside, she was reeling. *Hugh Dylan. The last time we met he was dating Loralyn and I lost my bikini top in the swimming hole. Hugh, my first crush.*

The merman who had coaxed her blood into a slow boil.

Swallowing to cover up her embarrassment, she said, "I think Loralyn Gaynor pulled the alarm. She was probably hoping to ruin your open house but showed up too late."

"Typical. The Gaynors are many things, but punctual has never been one of them." Laughing, Sissy took Ella Mae's elbow and the two women strolled through the halls to the front door. "That family has hated us for three centuries, but the rivalry sure keeps things lively around here."

"Who's her fiancé? Do you know?"

Sissy shrugged. "I didn't realize she'd hooked another one so soon, but you can be certain that he's older and richer than Loralyn. That girl's a walking cliché." Sissy shook her head in disdain and then pointed an authoritative index finger at her niece. "You just keep your distance, Ella Mae. You've got enough on your plate without messing with the likes of Loralyn Gaynor."

Ella Mae said nothing. Despite Sissy's warning, she felt inexplicably driven to discover the identity of Loralyn's next husband.

They collected their purses and headed outside into the stifling heat. "Before you go clothes shopping, I want to show you something," Sissy stated enigmatically. "Can you spare me *half* an hour?"

"Sure," Ella Mae agreed. "My calendar is pretty blank at this point."

They got into Sissy's car, which had been baking in the direct sun all day long. The moment Sissy picked up speed on the road leading into town, Ella Mae put her window down. Holding her hand out against the rush of air, she mulled over her financial situation. Both her credit cards and bank accounts bore Sloan's name. She could max out her credit card and withdraw as much cash as she needed for now, but eventually, the money would run out. Ella Mae needed to see a lawyer about her financial rights, but she suspected it wouldn't be long before she'd have to get a job, and the closest bakery was an hour away.

Maybe one of the area restaurants could use a pastry chef, she thought but then remembered she hadn't received her degree from culinary school. A sigh escaped from between her lips and was swept deeper into the car's cabin by the slap of incoming air.

"Your wheels are *spinning*," Sissy said and glanced over at her niece. "What are you thinking about?"

"Nothing pleasant. First of all, I need a lawyer. I want to get divorced as soon as I can. And I've got to get a job and train Chewy. He's still just a puppy and I haven't spent enough time with him. I think he only chews things to get attention." Ella Mae pushed a strand of hair from her face and closed the window.

Sissy slowed as they turned onto Emperor Street and began to search for a parking spot. Havenwood was busy most weekends, but during the summer it was packed with tourists. They filled the resort overlooking the lake's western shore, went hiking in the mountains, and patronized area shops. Today was no exception and Sissy had to circle the block between Fritillary and Swallowtail Avenue three times before she found a spot.

Gesturing for Ella Mae to follow, Sissy walked briskly through knots of strolling vacationers and made a right onto

Swallowtail Avenue. She stopped in front of a small cottage-style house that had been turned into a high-end children's boutique and teashop. A wooden plaque above the front door read The Mad Hatter and featured the eccentric haberdasher from *Alice in Wonderland*. According to the laminated menu taped over one of the panes, the teashop was open only for the use of little girls' parties, and the cost of each finger sandwich was as inflated as the Mad Hatter's over-sized head. Apparently, the locals had also found the prices too steep, for the shop had gone out of business. A sign from the nearby real estate office now hung in the middle of the large display window.

Ella Mae admired the shaded front porch and the tiny garden area dividing the small house from the brick building next door. The annuals planted in the flowerbeds had died from lack of water, but a robust climbing rose had worked its way up the gutter and spread itself along the roofline, creating a riot of hot pink blossoms that popped against the dark gray shingles.

"Cute, isn't it?" Sissy asked.

"Definitely." Ella Mae stared at the façade. "I'd paint it butter yellow with a pink raspberry door. Put a few café tables on the front porch and patio, and plant a matching rose vine on the other corner of the building. It could be really great."

Sissy seemed to be distracted by a blur of movement inside the vacant shop. Then, she smiled. "A really great *what*?"

Ella Mae shrugged. "I dunno. A coffee shop or a bakery."

"How about a pie shop?" Sissy suggested. "With a counter along that wall and pies for sale in a display case on the opposite side. Folks could have coffee and pie for breakfast, lunch, *and* dessert. You learned how to make savory pies, right?"

After reciting the names of some of her favorites, Ella Mae peered through the window again and was surprised to see Verena and Dee emerging from the store's back room. Grinning, Verena opened the front door and beckoned her in.

"What are you all up to?" Ella Mae asked upon entering.

Her aunts pasted on innocent expressions but said nothing. Ella Mae spun around slowly, imagining a chalkboard with daily specials, a Formica counter where patrons could linger over a slice of pie and a cup of coffee, small café tables inside and out, and a rotating display in the front window featuring the pies, tarts, quiches, and cobblers of the day.

"It's a nice fantasy," she said aloud. "But I don't have that kind of money."

Verena took a checkbook from her purse. "We're not exactly on par with Donald Trump, but if you take the four of us on as silent partners, we'll see a profit on our initial investment within a year. Any other objections?"

Ella Mae looked surprised. "Four? My mother knows about this?"

Dee held out a newspaper and said, "She showed us the ad."

"We'll have to act fast!" Verena bellowed. "This is prime retail space and I've heard that Loralyn Gaynor has asked her fiancé to buy it for her as an engagement gift. She wants to open her third nail salon but it's—"

"Your decision," Dee interjected softly. "You're the only one who can determine whether you're home for good or if you want to work things out with Sloan."

"The only thing I want to work on when it comes to my marriage is how fast I can get out of it!" Ella Mae declared hotly. "Come Monday morning, I want to be sitting in a lawyer's office planning my future as Ella Mae LeFaye. As of this moment, I'm ditching the name Kitteridge for good."

As Ella Mae spoke these words, the roses growing on the cottage opened their cups wider, releasing their sweet, heady fragrance into the air. Even the tight, young buds unfurled, stretching their blush-colored arms outward.

Dozens of monarch butterflies responded to the call of their scent, flitting around the vines in a flurry of black and orange.

The three LeFaye sisters exchanged satisfied smiles and then opened their arms to accept a grateful hug from their niece.

As the butterflies swarmed over the blooming roses, Ella Mae studied the reflection she saw in the glass of the display window. There was Aunt Dee with her long braid of auburn hair and denim overalls, Aunt Verena in a white dress with black polka dots and a pair of chartreuse pumps, and Sissy, who had the same whiskey brown curls as Ella Mae, but wore her hair cropped to the base of her neck. And then, on the other side of the glass, was her mother, her black hair billowing around her shoulders, her hazel eyes raised to the rooftop.

Ella Mae stepped outside and stood silently next to her mother.

"What do you think of the name, The Charmed Pie Shoppe?" she eventually asked, spelling out the last word.

Adelaide reached her left hand upward and a single rose petal floated into her palm. She handed the pink petal to her daughter. It smelled of spun sugar and the promise of things to come. "I think it's perfect, Ella Mae."

Chapter 4

Ella Mae woke at five thirty-three on Monday morning to the sound of her cell phone vibrating on the glass-topped nightstand. The moment she was yanked from a dream in which her child self was about to jump from a tire swing into a muddy puddle, the phone fell silent. Seconds later, it began buzzing violently again, skidding into the brass lamp base until Ella Mae scooped it up and examined the caller's number.

Sloan.

He'd left her a series of text messages overnight beginning with, "I know I screwed up, but where are you? Are you okay?"

"Of course I'm not okay!" Ella Mae hissed at the phone and then scrolled down the list. Sloan had texted her every few hours, begging her to respond to his concerns for her safety.

Chewy stirred at the foot of the bed, his paws twitching as he ran in his sleep. Ella Mae put a hand on his head, pausing to enjoy the warmth of his fur beneath her palm, and then got out of bed and walked over to the window. The sun was climbing over the horizon, breathing orange and pink into the eastern sky. Ella Mae watched as the light chased shadows from the garden and painted her reflection with a golden glow.

She smiled. Today was a day for changes. Aunt Verena planned to be at the real estate office at nine sharp to put in an offer on what Ella Mae hoped would become her very own pie shop. In the rose hue of dawn, it was easy to envision a brand-new life in Havenwood. A rich life. At that moment, it was possible to believe that she could fulfill her dream of running her own business, that people would come from all over Georgia to sample her pies.

Fully awake now, Ella Mae dressed in shorts and a T-shirt and tiptoed downstairs, a groggy terrier at her heels. The pair crept out the back door and walked down the long, sloping lawn toward the lake.

The dew-covered grass felt glorious beneath Ella Mae's bare feet. It had been years since she'd followed the path, but the feel of the cool flagstones under her toes and the sound of crickets and croaking frogs greeted her. The lake was diamond studded, and Ella Mae swept her gaze toward the east where the luxury hotel and spa stood atop a formidable hill like a medieval castle. Straight ahead, the homes of Havenwood's wealthiest families huddled together on the pricey parcels of land overlooking Lake Havenwood. The largest houses were at the bottom of the verdant hills and featured private docks and furnished boathouses bigger than Ella Mae's entire Manhattan apartment.

To the west was the business district, where Ella Mae hoped to soon join the ranks of the hard-working men and women who got up early each morning to unlock doors, switch on lights, and sweep sidewalks clean. She could already picture herself in her favorite cherry-print apron, watering urns filled with bright annuals as bluegrass music danced through the speakers mounted above the cash register. Pies and quiches would be baking in the double ovens, and the smell of buttery dough would be carried on the breeze to her fellow shopkeepers, causing them to lift their noses in anticipation.

"I'll start with breakfast and lunch service," she told Chewy, who was focused on a pair of mallards floating past the far edge of the neighbor's dock. "If things take off, I'll do some catering. Ladies' luncheons, wedding desserts, family dinners."

Hearing a familiar word, Chewy looked around, clearly hoping that his food bowl would suddenly appear nearby.

"I have so much to do! I'll have to design the layout, make a list of equipment, drive to the closest restaurant supplier, create a menu—"

Her list was interrupted by the buzz of her cell phone, which she'd absently slipped into the back pocket of her shorts. She read Sloan's latest text message. "Sweetheart, come home. Let's talk."

Ella Mae frowned. Sloan called her sweetheart only when he'd done something to upset her.

She sighed. As much as she wanted to, it was impossible for her to simply stop loving her husband. She couldn't just turn off her feelings by pressing an invisible button. Yet she knew that going back to her life in New York was out of the question. The door to the past had closed with the resounding thud of a bank vault. One day, she might be able to forgive Sloan for hurting her so deeply, but how could she ever trust him again?

Then and there, Ella Mae made a decision. Unless Sloan was willing to start over with her, to leave behind the city's temptations and live in his wife's territory, in Havenwood, then their marriage was over.

"I need to tell him that," she said. Treading on the rough wooden boards of the narrow wharf that extended into the lake's shallow water, she sat down at the end, her feet dangling in the water. She created small ripples with her toes and then dialed the number of the high-rise apartment she'd made into a home, a place of soft colors and comfortable furniture, of unique artwork and the scents of lavender and lemon. Her clothes were there. So were her photographs and recipe cards and beloved cookbook collection. She thought of the dozens of baking tools and costly spices neatly arranged in the small kitchen and of Chewy's favorite squeak toy. Would she ever see those things again?

"Sweetheart!" Sloan sounded terrible. His voice was thick with misery and fatigue. "You finally called! Where are you?"

Ella Mae fought to keep her voice steady. "I'm in Havenwood, Sloan. I took a bunch of cash from our savings account, bought a plane ticket and a dog carrier, and here I am."

"Havenwood?" He couldn't mask his astonishment. "But I thought you and your mother weren't on speaking terms."

"We are now. Somewhat. Reba and my aunts welcomed me with open arms. These are my people, Sloan." Ella Mae swallowed. She was unprepared for how hard it was to say what had to be said. "I don't want to talk about what happened. Ever. I'm not coming back to Manhattan. Our marriage is over. I'm filing for divorce."

"You can't just throw away seven years over *one* mistake! I love you." He sounded shocked and scared and angry all at once.

Ella Mae closed her eyes and tried to ignore the swell of sorrow washing over her body. "Maybe you do, Sloan, but I deserve a better love than you have to offer."

Her words lingered heavily, like a full thundercloud, forcing him into silence. Suddenly, the distance between the uptown skyscraper in New York City and the lakeside wharf in the mountains of northwest Georgia stretched far beyond its nine hundred miles.

"So that's it?" he whispered after a long pause.

"I'm staying in Havenwood," she answered firmly. "If you'd like to work things out, then come down here."

Sloan barked out a dry laugh. "What? You want me to leave my job? Our apartment? For how long?"

Ella Mae shrugged, even though she knew her husband couldn't see the movement. "For good."

Another laugh. "Come on, honey. I can't leave the city for a two-horse town. What would I do? Work in the local bank? Spend my evenings at church potlucks? Chitchat with the hicks in line at the post office? That's not me and it's not you either."

The ghost of a smile appeared on Ella Mae's face. "Actually, this place has always been a part of me. I just turned my back on it, but my roots are here. My family is here. And I'm going to open a pie shop here."

"Not with my money, you're not!" Sloan spat out and then immediately softened his tone. "Look, I'll give you the funds to start a bakery in Manhattan or . . . maybe the Bronx. Just come back, finish school, and let's get on with our lives."

Anger surged through Ella Mae. "You cheated on me, Sloan! You can't sweep something like that under the rug! Don't you get it? If you aren't going to prove that you'd do *anything* to win me back, then we're done. This is your *only* chance. I have an appointment with an attorney at ten."

"You can't ask me to give up my entire life at the snap of your fingers," he argued.

"Yes, I can! Do you think I could ever step foot in the lobby of our building again? Do you think I could *ever* ride that elevator? And *you*? The idea of you touching me, kissing me, makes me feel sick to my stomach. Do you think that's all just going to disappear because you said you were sorry?" She was yelling now. "It won't! You have to earn forgiveness, Sloan! You have to show me that you're worthy of a second chance!"

Sloan uttered an exasperated sigh. "This is going nowhere. Why don't you call me later, when you've calmed down a little? I can't talk any sense into you when you're acting like a hormone-crazed teenager."

An image of the young and lascivious redheaded twins entwined around Sloan's naked body flashed through Ella Mae's mind. "Oh, excuse me, but I thought that was *exactly* the age group that turned you on!" she shouted, snapped the phone closed, and hurled it into the lake.

Chewy barked and dove off the wharf, assuming Ella Mae had tossed a stick into the water for him to retrieve. He struck out in the direction of the splash, his mouth open in a smile of pleasure.

Ella Mae uttered a strangled sound that was part sob, part laugh and then raced to the shore to find her dog a real stick. The pair played in the shallows until Ella Mae's caffeine addiction drove her back to the house, a wet and happy terrier by her side.

Reba was in the kitchen, reading the Sunday paper as she sipped from her coffee cup. Her hair was in thin rollers and she had yet to apply her false eyelashes. The room smelled of strawberries. "You're up mighty early," she said.

"It's a big day. Real estate deals are going down, I'm filing for divorce, moving into the carriage house, and who knows what else." Ella Mae poured herself some coffee and joined Reba at the table. She could feel Reba's eyes on her, studying her.

"It's gonna be right hard to start over," she said, passing a carton of half-and-half to Ella Mae. "But you've got the guts and the heart to do it."

Nodding, Ella Mae grabbed Reba's hand and held it tightly, drawing strength from the smaller, pixielike woman she'd known since infancy.

"Your mama told me you'll be seein' August Templeton this mornin'. Now *that's* a man who looks every inch an esquire. The Templetons have handled the LeFaye family's legal matters for generations. August'll take good care of you." Reba smiled. "There are two things August is especially fond of: sweets and your aunt Delia. You can't give him Dee, but I reckon you can whip up somethin' tasty to take that nice lawyer." She peered at Ella Mae over the rim of her coffee cup. "Might convince him to give your case extra-special attention."

"Sounds like a fine idea." Ella Mae stood up and grabbed eggs, butter, and cream cheese from the refrigerator. She discovered a box of graham crackers in the pantry and began rooting through the cupboards, setting almonds, pure vanilla extract, and sugar onto the counter. She then programmed the oven and tied on one of Reba's aprons. "I'll make him a cheesecake tart. While I'm prepping the crust, why don't you tell me about August and Aunt Dee?"

Reba began flipping through manufacturer coupons, making a pile of those she wanted to keep and the ones she'd dump into the recycle bin. "There's no story really. August and Delia went to school together. She was a tall, quiet girl. Pretty as a summer's day. Even back then, she preferred to spend time with animals instead of people."

"And August?" Ella Mae asked over the growl of the food processor.

Waiting until the sugar, almond slivers, and graham crackers had been pulverized into fine crumbs, Reba said, "He was her opposite in every possible way! Short, round as a meatball, and allergic to everythin' and anythin'. If it had fur or petals, the boy would turn cherry red and his eyes and nose would leak like a drippin' tap."

Ella Mae pulled a face.

Reba laughed. "Make no mistake, August was a proper little gentleman. He carried a hanky and made fun of himself when he had one of his attacks. He was absolutely charmin' and everybody was fond of him. Still are. But no matter how hard he tried, he couldn't get Dee's attention."

After melting butter in the microwave, Ella Mae poured it into the food processor and pulsed the mixture until it was evenly moist. She then pressed the crumbs into a tart pan and placed the crust in the oven. "Poor guy. And he still carries a torch for her?"

"Olympic-sized," Reba said, neatly ripping out a coupon for paper towels.

Ella Mae spooned cream cheese and sugar into the bowl of the stand mixer. She then added eggs and vanilla and almond extract, only allowing the appliance to mix the contents until they were barely blended. Detaching the bowl, she scraped the sides with a spatula and paused, staring off into the distance.

She imagined her aunt as a lovely young woman dressed in jeans and a plain cotton shirt, her hair in the trademark braid. Reserved and gentle, Dee spent her time volunteering at the animal shelter, begging her mother to adopt yet another homeless kitten or puppy, and taking horseback riding lessons. Quiet and shy, she had been well liked but was the true introvert of the four sisters.

The oven timer chimed and Ella Mae removed the tart pan, inhaling the buttery, almond scent of the cookie crust. She glanced at Chewy, who was stretched out on the tiled floor, and felt a rush of tenderness for her dog. He had adjusted so well to their sudden move and had been such a comfort to her. Ella Mae realized with a jolt of happiness that her terrier hadn't devoured a single slipper or handbag for days. Still holding on to that warm sensation of affection, she poured the cheesecake filling into the pan and returned it to the oven.

"Was there ever anyone special in Aunt Dee's life?" she asked, reducing the oven's temperature so the tart wouldn't bake too quickly.

Reba kept her eyes fixed on the coupons. "That's not for me to say, honey. Delia likes to keep her romances close to the chest. Go on to your room now. I'll listen for the timer while you're gettin' gussied up."

Forty-five minutes later, Ella Mae was seated in August Templeton's office. Upon entering the reception area of the stately brick townhouse, she'd expected to be led into a dark, wood-paneled room lined with mahogany bookshelves and hunting prints, but her lawyer's space was quite surprisingly cozy. The walls were painted a mustard hue and decorated with black-and-white photographs of Havenwood's historic landmarks. August did possess the clichéd mammoth wood desk, but he didn't sit behind it, tenting his fingers and looking every inch the southern attorney he was. Instead, he joined Ella Mae in one of the comfortable leather club chairs at the far end of the room, which overlooked the courthouse through the office's large bay window.

August was impeccably tailored in a seersucker suit, bow tie, and pocket handkerchief. His bald head shone in the midmorning light as brightly as his polished loafers. After he'd taken her hand and gallantly pressed it between both of his own, he asked if she cared for any refreshment.

Declining the offer, Ella Mae settled into a chair and looked at August's round, dimpled face and his round, compact body and knew that she liked and trusted the fastidious little man. He reminded her of a southern Hercule Poirot.

"It pains me to see you after all this time under these unpleasant circumstances," August began and gestured at the tart Ella Mae had set on a nearby side table. "Especially when you come bearing gifts. I don't suppose you recall the last time we met. You were just a pigtailed girl when you accompanied your aunt Delia to my sister's house."

Thinking back, Ella Mae vaguely remembered helping Aunt Dee deliver a cat sculpture to a tearful woman living in a peach cottage on the outskirts of town. The woman, whose name escaped Ella Mae, had clearly loved two things, her cat and her flower garden, and had been heartbroken when her furry companion had succumbed to feline leukemia.

"Your sister had lost her cat," Ella Mae said solemnly, recalling how upset the woman had been.

August produced an indulgent smile. "Bethany was torn in two, but Delia turned Bethany's cat into a steel angel, and my sister began to recover from her sorrow. Now, my sister has three cats and a whole perennial garden built around

Delia's sculpture. I'll always be grateful to her for the kindness she showed Bethany that day."

A shadow of sadness had crept into August's brown eyes, and though it was in Ella Mae's nature to attempt to lighten the mood, she knew that her purpose in meeting with the dapper attorney would prevent her from doing so. "I feel like I'm in the middle of a grieving process too," she said. "I never saw myself as a divorcée. Divorce is something that happens to other people, not to devoted, reliable, sensible me. I thought things were good between Sloan and me, but it's over now." A lump formed in Ella Mae's throat. "I just don't know why I wasn't enough for him."

August patted her hand. "At the end of the day, you're only responsible for your own actions, my dear." He glanced at the notepad resting on his right thigh. "In your voice mail message you, ah, detailed your husband's infidelity and that you were a legal resident of New York state." He looked at her, his face kind and sincere. "Therefore, you must hire a New York attorney and file for divorce in that state."

"I am *not* going back there and I want you to represent me," Ella Mae stated firmly. "How can I file from Georgia?"

"You'll have to establish residency here, which will take about six months. But are you certain this is what you want to do? You may change your mind. Perhaps after the initial blow has faded . . ." Seeing the set of his client's lips, he trailed off. "Will this be a no-fault divorce?"

Ella Mae shrugged. "Probably, I gave Sloan a chance to fight for me, for us, but he declined. I don't believe he's truly sorry and that makes me think he'd cheat on me again. I'm assuming he'd relish the freedom to do as he pleases. All *I* want to do is move forward and find happiness here in Havenwood. My gut is telling me that this is where I'm supposed to be. It's like I left my dreams in a jar on a shelf in my childhood closet, and now I only need to reach up and open the lid so they can come true."

Emitting a wistful sigh, August clasped his hands. "What a lovely image. And if that is the case, may I speak on behalf of the entire town by saying that it is an honor and a delight to have you back." The lawyer beamed at her and then efficiently outlined the steps he would take to begin securing Ella Mae's liberty.

By the time Ella Mae left her attorney's office, it was lunchtime. Her mother and aunts planned to meet her at The Porch, a tiny, hole-in-the-wall barbecue restaurant favored by the locals.

Verena was seated at one of the dilapidated picnic tables out front when Ella Mae arrived on her bicycle. Seeing her niece, the robust woman gave a regal wave, as though Ella Mae were a courtier being granted approval to approach the queen's throne.

"You should be wearing a hat!" Verena's voice boomed over the sidewalk. "You're as pink as your mama's First Blush of Love rose."

Leaning the bike against a streetlamp, Ella Mae laughed. "I bet! It's been so long since I felt the full force of the Georgia sun on my skin." She took one of the paper napkins off the table and wiped her damp forehead. "How did things go this morning?"

Verena handed Ella Mae a menu. "Pick out what you'd like for lunch first. Dee and your mother are in line and Sissy should drift in any minute now."

Ella Mae took a quick glance at the laminated menu. "Fried catfish sandwich. Hope it's as good as I remember."

"It is, but I'm *ravenous*," Verena answered. "Had some god-awful fiber cereal for breakfast and was hungry again by ten. It's going to take both the pulled pork *and* the ribs to calm the beast today. I'll let the others know what you want, Ella Mae."

A few minutes later, Adelaide and Dee came out the restaurant's side door carrying plastic red trays piled with plates of barbecue and glasses of sweet tea. Dee put a serving of fried chicken, hush puppies, and slaw at the empty place at the table and shot Verena a quizzical look. "Where's Sissy?"

Verena shrugged, reaching for her sampler platter. She paused only long enough to arrange a napkin over her black-and-white floral skirt before attacking the baby back ribs with gusto.

"How did it go with August?" Ella Mae's mother asked.

"Getting divorced is more complicated than I'd hoped. I need to establish myself as a Georgia resident as soon as possible. In six months, I can fill out all the paperwork required to become single, but that wait is going to drive me crazy. It's bad enough that you're keeping me in suspense," Ella Mae said. "What happened at the Realtor's?"

Her mother sprinkled pepper on the inside of her bun and reassembled her own catfish sandwich. "We left an offer, signed the papers, and wished the agent a nice day. Now we wait. Apparently waiting is our theme today. Where is Sissy?" she asked impatiently.

At that moment, Ella Mae spied Sissy at the far end of the block. Dressed in a creamy linen blouse and a sage green skirt of crinkled cotton, she floated up the sidewalk in her long-legged graceful stride, creating an image of a magnolia blossom being whisked off the branch by a strong breeze.

"We've got *trouble*," she announced, squeezing Ella Mae's shoulder before taking a seat. "Loralyn Gaynor's fiancé made an offer on *our* pie shop site right after we left. Apparently, he's planning to buy it for her as an engagement gift. She'd like to open a deluxe nail salon—one that includes tanning beds."

Verena was aghast. "Tanning beds! We live in Havenwood, not South Beach! Can't she just put an addition onto one of her other nail salons?"

Ella Mae no longer felt like eating. "Who's her fiancé?"

"You could have knocked me over with a feather when

the agent told me, but Loralyn is engaged to Bradford Knox."
Sissy took a long sip of sweet tea.

Adelaide put down her sandwich and scrutinized her
sister. "Knox? Are you sure? Bradford isn't Loralyn's usual
kind of . . . prey. He's smart, savvy, and was utterly devoted
to his late wife. Why would he want to marry such an
overt—"

"Bloodsucker!" Verena bellowed.

"Phony?" Dee suggested quietly.

Shooting her sisters an impatient glance, Adelaide said,
"I was going to call her a gold digger, but I suppose your
adjectives are just as accurate."

"I remember hearing about Dr. and Mrs. Knox when I
was a teenager." Ella Mae pushed her plate aside and leaned
on her elbows in order to look at each of the women at the
table. "He was an equine vet and she ran a horse camp for
children with disabilities. Some of the kids in my school
used to volunteer there. What happened to her? To Mrs.
Knox?"

Sissy frowned. "Ovarian cancer. It happened about five
years ago and word has it that Bradford hasn't so much as
glanced at another woman since. He's a good-looking man
and has a successful practice, though I've heard that he sees
fewer and fewer patients these days."

"Only the wealthy ones," Dee said with a hint of accusation. "Thoroughbreds."

Verena shrugged and picked up a rib. "And why not? He's
almost seventy and he's worked his whole life. He can be
selective with his clientele now. But why wouldn't he be
equally selective about the second Mrs. Knox?"

Her mother shrugged, clearly ready to drop the subject.
"She must have something to offer."

Sissy let out a moan. "I do *not* want to think about what
that ill-mannered tramp has to offer. We all know it isn't a
sweet disposition or a kind heart." She shook her head, as
though regretting her choice of words. "Let's forget about

Loralyn. I've left a second bid, higher than her fiancé's, of course. By this time tomorrow, that darling little retail space will either belong to the LeFayes or to the future Mrs. Knox." •

Everyone began talking at once. Adelaide suggested they look for an alternate location for Ella Mae's pie shop, Verena recommended holding Bradford Knox hostage until the deal went through, and Sissy counseled patience.

Dee placed both hands flat on the table and her three sisters immediately fell silent and looked at her expectantly.

"I happen to know the seller," she said softly. "He's a client, actually."

Sissy clicked her tongue sympathetically. "He lost a pet?"

Dee nodded. "Yes, a cockatiel named Paco. I'm not finished with his sculpture yet—Paco's crest has been giving me trouble—but if I worked really hard this afternoon . . ."

Verena beamed at her sister. "You could deliver it tonight! And the man would be *so* moved by how you captured his precious bird's likeness in metal, he'd accept our offer without a second thought! You're a genius!"

Coloring slightly, Dee whispered, "I don't know . . . It feels wrong, to take advantage of the man's grief."

"Nonsense!" Verena shouted. "You're simply finishing the piece sooner rather than later, and your client is going to love it and cry over it and be healed by it. That wouldn't change no matter when it was delivered. You're giving your client what he needs now and helping your niece at the same time. Two good deeds in a single day! You've always been the most giving of the four of us, Dee."

Ella Mae looked intently at her aunt. "You don't have to do this, Aunt Delia."

Her mother lifted her plastic fork from a pile of slaw and waved it like a wand over Dee's head. "Go ahead and work your magic, Sis. There's a reason my daughter came back to Havenwood. I have a feeling the pie shop is an important part of her destiny."

The words sounded so formal and serious that Ella Mae

nearly burst out laughing, but her aunts were nodding in solemn agreement.

Suddenly, a wind sprang up from nowhere, ruffling the napkins and caressing the damp tendrils of Ella Mae's hair. It was redolent with aromas. Roses, crushed sage, baking bread, damp wood, chrysanthemums.

The scents were all familiar, tickling a memory hidden deep within Ella Mae's mind. Just as she attempted to grab hold of it, the strange breeze disappeared, leaving her aching to remember what she had once known.

"Everything all right, Ella Mae?" Sissy asked. "You look like you flitted off for a minute there."

"Oh, no, I'm done leaving," Ella Mae answered in a faraway voice. "There are parts of me that are just coming to life. It's like I've been asleep for a long time but am finally waking up."

A swallowtail butterfly landed on the edge of her bike basket and flapped his magnificent gold and black wings double-time, as though he had something urgent to impart. Then, a stray current whisked him up, up, at a frenzied pace. Ella Mae watched, until he became a small spot in the sky, racing toward the blue blur of the mountains above.

She followed the flight of the beautiful creature toward a place in the distant forest that seemed to be calling to her. Ella Mae watched, trying to make sense of the tugging sensation she felt inside, until the sun burned tears into her eyes and she was forced to look away.

Chapter 5

Ella Mae was back in her mother's kitchen, washing the tomatoes she'd bought from the roadside stand on the way home from lunch. The ancient farmer had been at the same location since Ella Mae was a child and she'd been delighted to see him clad in his customary denim overalls and straw hat, nose buried in a paperback as his customers perused crate after wooden crate of ripe and colorful fruits and vegetables.

Putting the tomatoes on a dish towel to dry, Ella Mae ventured into her mother's kitchen garden for fresh basil, amazed that the herbs were so verdant and robust beneath the unforgiving Georgia sun. Squatting by a row of bushy rosemary plants, she inhaled deeply.

An image of the pie shop rose in her mind, pastel and rose-covered as a fairy-tale cottage. Holding the vision in place, Ella Mae gently separated basil leaves from the largest plant, rubbing one of them until her touch coaxed forth its strong scent. It burst into the air, an invisible beanstalk of fragrance surging skyward.

Ella Mae hummed and re-entered the kitchen, where she removed the seeds from the tomatoes and cut them into bite-sized pieces. After chopping the fresh basil, she placed a portion of the herb along with the tomatoes and a sprinkle of salt and pepper into a dish lined with one of her Parmesan cheese piecrusts. Using Reba's favorite ceramic bowl, Ella Mae blended mayo, fresh-squeezed lemon juice, grated mozzarella cheese, and the remainder of the basil.

As her spatula created figure eights and curlicues in the creamy mixture, Ella Mae willed the seller of the property on Swallowtail Avenue to believe that Havenwood would benefit from having a pie shop. Closing her eyes, she poured this faith in the success of her venture into the pie and topped the tomatoes with the mayonnaise blend, calling forth the vision of milling, eager crowds lining up to purchase one of her creations.

Aunt Dee stopped by at five thirty, looking pale and limp.

"You put too much into those sculptures," Reba nagged after catching a glimpse of Dee's face. "You gotta hold a bit of yourself back."

Ella Mae's aunt didn't answer, accepting the tomato and basil pie with a sigh. Finally, she murmured, "This doesn't feel right. To sway this man with gifts."

Reba waved the notion off. "You're just catchin' flies with honey. The practice is as commonplace as a cold in these parts." Reba glanced at the clock and, with a satisfied grin, pulled the cork from a bottle of red wine on the counter. "Besides, Loralyn Gaynor doesn't care a fig about the folks of this town. You all do. Now buy the damned place so I can have my kitchen back. Ella Mae's done nothin' but stuff my freezer with dough and fruit since she showed up."

"That can't be all bad. It smells just like summer in here," Dee said, inhaling the aroma of cooked bread, tomato, and basil.

With a shake of her head, Reba said, "That ain't summer. It's what destiny smells like when you bend it to your will.

Now get your hide to the seller's place or destiny is gonna get bored and leave."

Dee complied. Ella Mae watched her aunt climb into her truck, which was covered with bumper stickers supporting a variety of animal shelters.

The rest of the evening passed with the slowness of dripping sap, but Dee's mission was clearly a success, for the next morning Aunt Verena's triumphant shouts were reverberating down the telephone line.

"We're under *contract!*" she bellowed the moment Ella Mae answered the phone. "And the seller's even agreed to a rushed closing. The property will belong to the LeFaye women by noon this Friday!"

Ella Mae, who had just returned from a strenuous bike ride, threw down the towel she'd used to mop off her wet face, picked up Chewy, kissed his black nose, and then held him in her arms as she twirled round and round her mother's kitchen. Infected by the excitement, Chewy yipped and licked Ella Mae's chin while Reba laughed in mirth.

"Put on something decent!" Verena ordered good-naturedly. "No cutoffs and T-shirts. Meet me at the bank at ten. We have a number of financial issues to sort out."

Quickly ironing a new pair of off-white slacks and an amber blouse, Ella Mae slipped on a pair of bronze-hued sandals and examined herself in the mirror.

The ruddy brown of the blouse brought the filaments of auburn and copper in her hair to life. Her skin had turned from northern pale to a salubrious pink, and her eyes, filled with the promise of her new future, sparkled with threads of gold.

"You're as pretty as a Georgia peach!" Reba declared as Ella Mae came downstairs carrying a pair of grocery bags. "Are you movin' into the guest house today?"

Ella Mae nodded. "It's time. But don't worry, I'll come over every morning for a visit."

Reba puckered her lips, sending a burst of strawberry

scent into the air. "I won't be here when you get up, sugar-
plum. I'll still be fast asleep wearin' my rollers and my
aromatherapy blindfold."

"I won't be baking anything for weeks, Reba. We have
to remodel first."

Shrugging, Reba walked Ella Mae to the back door. "All
I'm sayin' is that you'd best start gettin' yourself on a sched-
ule. The roosters won't even be stirrin' when your alarm
goes off, but you gotta get your body used to wakin' up before
dawn. Bake a bunch of pies now and stick 'em in the freezer.
You never know how many contractors will need a little
butterin' up."

Ella Mae admitted that this was wise advice and then
gestured at her newly pressed pants. "If I ride my bike into
town . . ."

"I'll drive you. I've gotta do some banking myself." She
grinned. "And I'm in the mood for a sucker. A green one. I
don't know what they put in the dye, but those green ones
are the best. Taste a wee bit like cough syrup and cotton candy
mixed together."

"Ugh." Ella Mae laughed. "You can't beat the yellow
ones. They taste like a day at the beach."

Reba drove like a seventeen-year-old boy. She roared
down the roads in her mammoth Buick, radio blasting, kicking up tornadoes of dust. She adopted the overly confident
motorist's practice of rolling stops and pretended to be completely unaware of the stick on her steering column that
would activate her turn signal.

They reached the bank with plenty of time to spare. Ella
Mae felt a little queasy, and her knuckles were bleached white
from gripping the handle as Reba swerved around an elderly
man edging the nose of his station wagon into the street.

"Just how many moving violations do you have?" Ella
Mae asked the diminutive woman sitting beside her.

Pulling up to the drive-through teller lane adjacent the
bank, Reba missed scratching the paint off her side mirror

on the building's red brick by centimeters. "Honey, I've flirted my way outta more tickets that you can imagine."

While Reba conducted her business with the jocular and chatty teller, Ella Mae rolled down her window in hopes of inviting a wisp of fresh air into the Buick's stifling cabin. Reba had long rebelled against air-conditioning, claiming that Freon clogged the lungs.

She took her sweet time filling out her deposit slip, too busy exchanging gossip with the teller to realize that Ella Mae was wilting and that a long line was forming behind her car.

The growl of a diesel pickup truck pulling out of the teller lane to the right of the Buick caught Ella Mae's attention. She watched as a large white Mercedes sedan took the truck's place. The luxury car gleamed in the morning light like a polished opal and Ella Mae briefly wondered who was on the other side of the tinted window.

As though sensing a shift in the air, Reba abruptly stopped talking and swiveled her head to the side in order to check out the Mercedes.

"Knox," she said, clearly intrigued. "Last time I saw him, he was drivin' a beat-up Suburban. He's sure come up in the world."

Bradford Knox had eased down his dark window and was thrusting a freckled arm out of a form-fitting suit coat in order to grasp the plastic transfer tube. As Knox shifted in his seat, straining to reach the tube, his herringbone blazer bunched up at the neck. With his severely receded hairline, pronounced nose, and thick neck protruding from the crinkled suit jacket, Loralyn's fiancé bore a close resemblance to a box turtle.

Catching Ella Mae's eye, he smiled, conveying his embarrassment over having to struggle so hard to grab hold of the tube. She smiled back. No matter how close she got to those tubes, it was always a strain to close her fingers around the slippery plastic. She gave the older gentleman a sympathetic nod, and in this brief exchange, Ella Mae decided that Bradford Knox was a likeable fellow, regardless of the car he drove or the woman he had chosen to marry.

Her congenial feelings toward Loralyn's senior citizen suitor were reinforced by the courteousness with which he addressed the bank teller. Reba had finally signed her deposit slip but had yet to place it in the metal drawer, so now both of the drive-through lanes were thoroughly congested by a pair of chatty customers. Amazingly, no one in line seemed to mind. There were no honks or shouts or threatening raps against the window. Ella Mae reflected that had this holdup occurred in Manhattan, it was likely that someone would have already suffered bodily harm.

"I forgot how good it feels to slow down," she whispered to the sunshine bathing her forearm. She listened to the birdsong coming from the magnificent magnolia shading the bank's parking lot and marveled at the dinner-plate size of the tree's white blossoms. Ella Mae was jarred from the tranquil moment by the abrupt clanging of the fire station's alarm bell.

A baying from Knox's passenger seat echoed the alarm, and Ella Mae leaned forward to catch a glimpse of an aged bloodhound, snout raised to the roof, howling his mournful tune. The wail of a passing fire truck momentarily prevented any further conversation between the tellers and their customers, and everyone froze, waiting for the sound to decrease in volume.

Ella Mae started to laugh. She found the bloodhound's throaty song and the passions with which he bayed both funny and endearing. Bradford Knox smiled even wider and then put a comforting hand on the glossy fur of his dog's left shoulder. Their shared mirth quickly dissipated when the rear window slid down to reveal the glowering face of Loralyn Gaynor.

"You are *not* going to get that property away from me!" she shouted angrily over the siren's clamor.

Startled, Ella Mae gestured at the front of Knox's car. "Does your fiancé enjoy his dog's company more than yours?"

Loralyn glowered. "I refuse to sit on that seat. It's covered in disgusting dog hair. Besides, I like being driven around. It befits someone of my status. Now, as I was saying, that property is mine!"

Ella Mae leaned farther out the window and tried to think of something to say that would assuage Loralyn's ire. "The bid's already been accepted. Let it go. I'm sure your fiancé will buy you something equally amazing as a wedding gift. He seems like a nice guy."

Bradford Knox didn't hear this exchange as he was doing his best to cajole the bloodhound into crooning out the passenger window but the dog turned the opposite direction and howled right into Bradford's ear.

"You'll be sorry you messed with me!" Loralyn spat. "If you go through with your plans, I'll make sure your business fails. I'll tell people I found bugs in your food. Or hair. Maybe even a fingernail!"

"Oh, grow up!" Ella Mae cried. "Don't you ever get tired of being a bully?"

Whipping off her designer sunglasses, Loralyn's eyes narrowed with hostility. "You took what was rightfully mine and I am *not* going to let this go! I own two nail salons, Little Miss Betty Crocker, so it'll be all too easy to find something *unsavory* to put into a cherry pie or a chocolate tart."

"You wouldn't dare," Ella Mae growled loudly.

Loralyn grinned a wolfish grin. "I *would*! I'm tired of you LeFayes trying to steal my family's thunder! You're not our equals. Never have been and never will be. Your aunt Delia is beyond flaky, Verena is a pig, Sissy is a drama queen, and your mother is an arrogant, rose-snipping bitch!"

Ella Mae inhaled sharply and glanced at Reba to see whether she'd heard this string of insults, but Reba had her head out of the window and was yelling to the bank teller through the speaker. Ella Mae caught the phrases "she didn't!" and "wait until her husband finds out!" before turning back to her childhood nemesis.

"I refuse to respond to your baiting, Loralyn. I'm going to open my shop and you'll have to deal with it!" She was sorely tempted to stick out her tongue and wiggle her fingers behind her ears like a triumphant five-year-old.

Loralyn laughed and the sound gave Ella Mae goose bumps. There was no joy in her laughter. It was a harsh, grating noise like the scrape of a fork against metal. "You're a fool, Ella Mae." She smoothed back a stray hair and glanced around to see whether anyone could possibly hear her over the cacophony created by the alarm and the bloodhound. "I've seen you riding your mutt around in your bike basket. It would be *such* a shame if he got loose and met with an accident. He's such a *tiny*, little thing. So fragile." She raised her brows suggestively.

Ella Mae felt the temperature of her body rise, the pink skin of her cheeks darkening to a shade of rhubarb. Infusing her voice with all the menace she could muster, she mixed her age-old hatred for Loralyn with the ripe anger Sloan had ignited in her, she opened her mouth and cried, "Stay away from my dog *and* my family! If you don't, Lord help me, I will KILL YOU!"

Two things occurred seconds before Ella Mae's threat was launched from her throat into the heavy Georgian air. The siren abruptly ceased and Loralyn raised her window, cutting off the end of Ella Mae's words with the precision and finality of a guillotine's blade.

In what now seemed like deafening silence, her shout assaulted Bradford Knox instead, slamming into him like a prizefighter's right hook. His eyes widened and he put his hand over his heart, as though to ward off a second blow. Reba's chatter was forgotten and the juicy tidbits of gossip coursing back and forth between the Buick and the bank teller dried up like a desert riverbed.

Ella Mae looked away from Knox to see the teller staring at her, openmouthed in astonishment. Behind the garrulous bank employee, a second teller and the branch manager looked at Ella Mae with a blend of shock and disapproval.

People in Havenwood simply did not behave in such a manner. Ella Mae knew that by high noon everyone in town would know what she'd said and that her lack of good manners would be blamed on too many years of city living.

It was with a sickening turn in her belly that she realized Reba still had her scarlet fingernail pressed against the bank window's speaker button. Ella Mae could see that the faces of the customers in line were all turned in her direction.

The silence was absolute.

"Reba," Ella whispered, gently pulling on the offending arm. The call button sprang back out and the teller's metal drawer slid closed. "Can we go?"

"But I didn't get my sucker!" Reba protested.

Sinking down in her seat, Ella Mae said, "I'll buy you a whole bag of suckers. Just get out of this drive-through!"

"You're gonna have to go inside anyway, darlin'. No avoidin' it. Make sure to get me a green sucker when you're done, ya hear? The ones at Piggly Wiggly don't taste the same."

Reba waved to the slack-jawed teller and gunned the car out of the lane, pulling to a stop at the bank's entrance with a screech of brakes. Ella Mae was tempted to sit and wait in the Buick's sweltering cabin until the current group of bank customers exited the building, but her future was waiting for her. It called to her, in a sweet voice that nonetheless demanded obedience, and she rushed to answer.

By the end of the next business week, the LeFaye women owned the property at 9 Swallowtail Avenue. To celebrate the closing, they decided to go out to dinner at Le Bleu, the elegant restaurant inside Lake Havenwood's luxury hotel. Reba had been invited too, but declined.

"I've got a date with a hot mailman," she'd explained to Ella Mae. "My regular carrier is about as sexy as an elephant seal, but he's recoverin' from foot surgery and the United States Postal Service saw fit to send me a James Dean look-alike. Sure, he's older and thicker in the waist than Jimmy D., but I sure like the spark of devilry I see in his eyes."

"Have a good time!" Ella Mae had called as Reba saun-tered out the door wearing a sequined miniskirt and flip-flops, her hair in a cloud of tight curls, and then silently wondered if she'd ever look forward to dating again.

That night, she slipped into a celery-hued wrap dress, pulled her wavy hair back into a neat twist, and tucked a gardenia blossom behind her left ear. Her mother was radi-ant in a turquoise dress and a stunning necklace of platinum beads. Her black hair tumbled down her shoulders, the strands of silver framing her face reflected the light from her necklace, and for a moment, standing beneath the pur-pling sky, she appeared far younger than her fifty-eight years.

Ella Mae's aunts were already seated at a table with a stunning view of Lake Havenwood when she and her mother strolled into the restaurant. Every head in the room turned to watch their progress.

Verena, attired in a black dress with a white jacket embel-lished by a fuchsia silk flower, shouted for champagne and the waiter hustled off to obey. Sissy wore a silk poet's blouse and several strings of pearls while Dee wriggled uncomfort-ably in a form-fitting dress made of yellow linen.

"Stop *fidgeting*," Sissy chided amiably. "You can't wear those overalls every day!"

Dee pulled on the tail of her braid and flashed a self-effacing smile. "I like all the pockets. It feels strange not to have gum or Life Savers or my phone on hand."

"Gum? You used those pockets to conceal your cigarettes back in high school," Adelaide teased.

"And *other* things," Sissy added with an enigmatic wink.

The waiter arrived carrying an ornate silver ice bucket on a tall stand. A second waiter held a tray of champagne flutes aloft and deftly placed a delicate crystal glass in front of each of the women at the table.

Verena waited until their glasses had been filled with the golden sparkling wine and then rose to her feet. "To The Charmed Pie Shoppe. May everyone who steps through its pink raspberry doors be changed by the experience!"

As Ella Mae raised her glass toward the center of the table, gently clinking rims with her mother and her aunts, an orb of light formed, like an immature planet within the center of their circle of glasses. It was too bright to look at directly, so Ella Mae averted her face. She'd done the same thing at the lake earlier, when the sun had reflected off the water's mirrored surface. But this light was more complex. It had the shadowy depth of a cut diamond and hovered in the air like a Fourth of July sparkler freed from its stick.

Ella Mae caught her breath in disbelief, the hairs on her arms standing on end as a feeling like an electrical current shot through her body. She felt infused with a rush of unadulterated power. It was intoxicating and frightening and yet she did not want the sensation to stop. Not ever.

What's happening? She wanted to speak but her thoughts refused to string together coherently. The white light turned her fingertips a glittering alabaster.

Then, one of her aunts retracted her glass to take a sip of the dry champagne, and just as suddenly as it had sprung out of the air, the light disappeared. Ella Mae nearly moaned in disappointment, but she was so thirsty that she closed her eyes and took a deep swallow of the sparkling wine, the image of the strange orb still etched on the dark canvas of her eyelids.

"So what will you do first, Ella Mae?" Verena asked as though nothing out of the ordinary had occurred.

Taking another substantial swallow of champagne, Ella Mae almost asked if anyone else had seen the supernatural glow but decided it must have been created by light ricocheting off the crystal glasses.

"I drove to a restaurant supply company in Fair Oaks and showed them my proposed floor plan." Blinking hard, she forced herself to focus by handing Verena a copy of the design she'd created on her mother's computer. "I thought I'd have to go to Atlanta, but these folks have everything I need."

"Do we have enough cash to cover the start-up costs?" her mother inquired as she closed her menu.

Ella Mae was about to answer when the waiter came to take their orders. When his leather pad was filled with an array of dishes, including cold avocado soup, grilled lobster, spinach and grapefruit salad, smoked salmon with mustard and dill, gazpacho, chicken with mushrooms and tarragon, and sun-dried tomato and pesto torta, Ella Mae answered her mother's question.

"Our budget covers everything except the cost of painting the exterior." She went on to explain the breakdown of expenditures.

Verena helped herself to a generous hunk of the baguette from the breadbasket and then added three pats of butter stamped with the hotel's crest onto her plate. She slathered the butter onto the warm crust and studied the pie shop's floor plan. "What's this here?"

Leaning forward, Ella Mae pointed at a square in the center of the kitchen area. "That's a pie press."

Sissy craned her neck so she could see the plans from across the table. "Ovens, double range, cooling shelves, dishwasher, sink with drainboards. Walk-in refrigerator and freezer in the rear corner. What's that smaller square next to the prep area?"

"A twenty-quart standing mixer. I'll probably use that piece of equipment the most," Ella Mae replied, accepting the breadbasket from Dee.

"May I?" Sissy reached for the second page of plans. "Ah, the front room—complete with display cases, espresso machine, soda dispenser, cash register, rotating window display, and café tables. I can *almost* see it in my mind's eye."

Dee pointed to a room set off down a narrow hallway at the far left. "Just one restroom?"

Ella Mae nodded. "If there were two, we'd lose too much floor space. We need every inch for people who want to dine indoors. I'll have tables on the patio as well, but during the winter and in the worst of the summer's humidity, folks will want to be inside."

The women exchanged opinions about color schemes as the attentive waiter served them chilled soup or salad. Ella Mae paused before driving the tines of her fork into a soft grapefruit wedge on her spinach salad. She felt a wave of contentment sweep over her. In the soft light of the dining room, with the din of quiet conversation settling around her shoulders like a silk shawl and the glimmering expanse of the lake beyond the window, all felt right with the world.

She watched the beautiful faces of her mother and her aunts as they argued over whether the laminate on the table-tops should be of a marigold or plum or periwinkle hue, and wanted to hold this moment in her heart forever, to lock it away for a time when she would need to cling to a treasured memory—one that could burn through a veil of sorrow and recreate a gilded flash of pure happiness.

Even the slight stiffness her mother displayed whenever she spoke could not tarnish Ella Mae's belief that she'd been destined to return to Havenwood. She hoped, in time, to be as comfortable in her mother's company as she was in the company of her beloved aunts.

Perhaps I *need to make more of an effort,* she thought, recalling how her mother had gone out of her way to make the carriage house especially inviting. Every few days, Ella Mae came home from a meeting with the restaurant supply company, the contractor, or August Templeton to find a bouquet of colorful blooms from her mother's garden arranged in a silver vase in the small kitchen.

The heady scent of her mother's roses mingled with fronds of fresh greens, lacing the air with a feminine perfume that Ella Mae had always associated with her mother.

As a child, she'd waited breathlessly each night for her mother's good-night kiss. She would tiptoe in the room, her white nightgown glowing in the moonlight, and kiss Ella Mae's cheek. Stroking her daughter's hair, she'd whisper, "I love you more than all the petals in my garden," and instead of being envious, the signature of the thousands of roses in the yard would embrace mother and child in a burst of enchanting scent.

Each night, Ella would fall asleep with the feel of that kiss on her skin and the smell of a wonderland of flowers on her pillow. Envisioning her mother entering the carriage house to plump the sofa cushions and deliberate over where to place her latest arrangement made Ella Mae smile. The roses had replaced the good-night kiss, but the perfume was as tender and magical as ever.

"Mom," she said, leaning to the side as the waiter cleared away her salad plate. "I was wondering if you'd be willing to design the patio garden. No one in Havenwood has your touch when it comes to growing things."

"Not in all of Georgia!" Verena declared enthusiastically.

Sissy was bobbing her head in agreement. "Not *just* the design. She's got to be in charge of the planting too. The flowers will bloom in triple-time to please you, Adelaide."

Ella Mae found her aunt's statement peculiar but easily forgot it when presented with an entrée of porcini-crusted filet mignon topped with a molded dollop of herb butter. She inhaled the salty aroma of chives, tarragon, and garlic rising from the melting butter and watched as an assortment of artistic and fragrant dishes were set in front of the other women.

Her mother cut a piece of her salmon and dipped it into a drizzle of creamy dill sauce. "I believe I could manage a patio garden for you." Her reply was brief, but the look of pleasure in her eyes provided the response Ella Mae had been seeking.

The LeFayes dined like queens, sipping champagne and offering one another tastes of their exquisite entrees. For dessert, they ate pomegranate sorbet garnished with fresh mint leaves. They chewed the leaves before leaving the table to cleanse their palates and then instinctively linked arms on their way out of the restaurant.

"If I hadn't eaten so much, I'd be drunk!" Verena exclaimed with a loud laugh.

Dee hiccupped and then let loose a giggle. "I think I *am* a bit drunk."

"Good thing *I'm* driving," Sissy said and jiggled the car keys. "Would you look at that moon?" She glanced at Adelaide. "This is your kind of night, Sister."

Verena paused to admire the glowing face of the full moon. "We'd better get on home. I haven't stayed out 'til eleven for years! Buddy will think I'm a burglar. He'll either call the cops when I try to sneak in through the garage or shoot me dead with his shotgun."

"I hope it's the former and not the latter," Adelaide said with a wink.

Ella Mae smiled at her mother and aunts, hoping her face could manage to convey her gratitude. "Thank you. All of you. For having such faith in me."

"You're a LeFaye," her mother stated with a proud tilt of the chin. "And that means—"

"That we've had faith in you since the day you were born," Sissy finished the thought and the merry band dispersed. The women went to bed with full bellies and light hearts, unaware of the shadows that would be revealed by the coming dawn.

Chapter 6

Ella Mae was jarred from sleep by the sound of knocking. Without fully waking, she wondered if she was hearing the clank of the old pipes in the guest cottage, but as the noise persisted, she realized that its source was that of a demanding pounding of a fist. Someone was at the front door.

With a growl, Chewy leapt off the bed in a flash of brown and white fur. Ella Mae heard the click of his nails on the stairs, his agitated barks bouncing off the slumbering walls and floors of the silent cottage like gunfire, and Ella Mae could almost hear the aged pine boards groan in protest as she jumped out of bed.

Ella Mae slipped a University of Georgia sweatshirt over her head where it fell protectively over the upper half of her gauzy white nightgown. Eschewing slippers, she hurried downstairs in her bare feet and peered through the glass panes of the front door.

In the gray-tinged half-light of the burgeoning morning, Ella Mae could tell that the uniformed man on the other side of the door was a cop. His stance was impatient and he continued to knock even as Ella Mae fumbled with the lock, terrified to open the door and invite this policeman into her small, cozy home.

What else would she be letting in once the deadbolt was turned and the heavy wood door swung inward? What dire words would come from the lawman's mouth at this ungodly hour? Had Reba or one of her aunts been in an accident? Was someone hurt? Dead?

Ella Mae put her hand on the knob, her fingers lingering on the cool brass. From this moment, there would be no turning back. Whatever pain the turning of this knob would bring, it had to be turned.

Holding Chewy by the metal-studded collar Reba had bought for him, Ella Mae opened the door.

"Yes?" she asked and winced, waiting for the hammer to fall.

"Are you Ms. Ella Mae LeFaye Kitteridge?"

She nodded. "It's just LeFaye now. What's happened?"

The officer looked her up and down and Ella Mae had the distinct feeling that the table lamp in the narrow entrance hall had given her nightgown the transparency of onion skin and that the slightly overweight, ruddy-faced police officer standing on her welcome mat was checking out her toned legs from ankle to hip. Tugging the sweatshirt lower, she repeated her question.

Blinking, the officer lifted a pair of unreadable eyes to her face. "Ma'am, I'm going to need you to get dressed and come with me to the station. We have some questions to ask you about an incident that occurred two hours ago."

"What incident?" Ella Mae felt anger growing in her chest, unfolding like a red rose under the summer sun. "I'm not going anywhere without more information." Her years as a New Yorker had taught her a thing or two about standing up for herself. "And while you're giving me an explanation, how about showing me some ID?"

The officer frowned but produced his badge and held it

out for her inspection. "Officer Jon Hardy, ma'am." He waited for Ella Mae to nod and then pocketed the badge. "A man was killed tonight and we have reason to believe you can shed some light on the matter. This is not a request, ma'am. I can cuff you and escort you through the station in your nightdress, or you can quickly change your clothes and come along of your own free will. Which one's it going to be?"

"What man?" Ella Mae insisted, gathering her squirming, snarling terrier into her arms.

Hardy hesitated. "A Bradford Knox of Little Kentucky."

Ella Mae couldn't help it. Her eyes opened wide in surprise. *"What?"*

"So you know him." Hardy made it clear that his remark was a statement, not a question.

"I know *of* him. We've never met."

Hardy took a step forward, forcing Ella Mae to retreat deeper into the house. "Plenty of time to talk through the details when we get to town. You've got five minutes. And, ma'am?" He pointed at Chewy. "Leave the dog here."

Upstairs, it was nearly impossible for Ella Mae to obey Hardy's commands. She wasn't being deliberately rebellious as she stared at the meager selection of clothes hanging in her bedroom closet, but the news that Bradford Knox had been killed and that the police believed she knew something about his death had rendered her immobile.

"Bradford Knox?" she addressed her limited wardrobe of comfortable T-shirts, form-fitting pants, and a pair of flirty sundresses. "Why would the police have anything to ask *me*?" She automatically slid on her favorite jeans, a chocolate brown T-shirt, and her Keds. Chilled by the strangeness of the situation, she put the UGA sweatshirt back on and ran a brush through her hair. Fastening it into a loose ponytail, she grabbed her watch and hurried down the stairs.

"One second." She gave Hardy an apologetic glance and

dumped a can of dog food into a bowl for Chewy. "If I don't leave him something, he'll tear my couch to shreds."

A flicker of amusement crossed Hardy's face. "You should send him to obedience classes at Canine to Five. My boxers went, and within a month, everything changed. No more marking their territory on my golf bag or my wife's favorite chair." The affection he felt for his dogs was extinguished as suddenly as it had flared. Opening the front door and gesturing for Ella Mae to step outside, Hardy was all business again. "This way, ma'am."

Taking another moment to kiss Chewy on the top of his head, Ella Mae grabbed her purse and cell phone and followed Officer Hardy to the police cruiser.

"I've never been in a cop car before," she said anxiously, wondering whether her mother was watching the scene unfold from her bedroom window, but the main house was dark and no figure appeared in the void between the curtains.

Sensing the reason for her hesitation, Hardy said, "You can call someone once your interview is over."

Ella Mae put her hand on the car's smooth roof and turned to Hardy with frightened eyes. "Am I under arrest?"

Hardy offered a noncommittal grunt. "You're considered a person of interest."

Nodding, she got into the backseat of the car. "I wanted to be well-known in this town because of my culinary skills. This is not the kind of 'interest' I was looking for."

Hardy closed the door on her words.

Two hours later, August Templeton joined her in the police department's conference room. He handed her coffee in a Hardee's takeout cup and a sausage, egg, and cheese biscuit wrapped in wax paper.

"God bless you. I couldn't drink the stuff they offered me." Ella Mae poured a little cream in the coffee and took a grateful sip. The drink warmed her belly and the familiar scent gave her comfort. Unwrapping the breakfast sandwich, she popped a small piece of buttery biscuit into her mouth. "If this is my last meal, it's a damn fine one. Thank you."

August smiled. "It's not quite that dire, Ms. LeFaye, despite the fact that the men and women of the Havenwood police force are quite beside themselves over this case. There hasn't been a suspicious death here since 1918, and now they've got a combined murder *and* arson investigation on their idle hands. They're as shiny-eyed as a child on Christmas morning!"

"I'm glad the cops are so excited, but they think I hit Bradford on the head with a rolling pin, locked him inside Loralyn's nail salon, and set the whole place on fire. I'm having a hard time sharing in their enjoyment."

Looking instantly abashed, August took Ella Mae's hand. "You're not under arrest. You've been asked to be available to assist the police with their inquiries. That means no jaunts to Paris, but being questioned does not necessarily mean that you'll be charged with a crime. There's simply no evidence to implicate you."

Ella Mae sagged in relief. "They didn't tell me a thing, August. Why *do* they suspect me?"

August cleared his throat and smoothed his perfectly pressed tie. "Several witnesses claimed that you threatened Doc Knox at the Peachtree Bank."

Groaning, Ella Mae put her face in her hands. "I wasn't talking to *him*. I was yelling at Loralyn Gaynor, but she put up the car window in the middle of my . . ." She trailed off, remembering the exact words she'd used.

"Threat?" August finished for her.

"Yes," Ella Mae admitted with regret. "But I had nothing against her fiancé. If anything, I felt sorry for the man. Why on earth would he want to marry such a cold, shallow, gold-digging bitch? Excuse my French."

August pursed his lips. "I don't remember learning that word in French class, but perhaps Mr. Knox was swayed by Ms. Gaynor's looks. She is quite a beauty."

"Sure, if you like Botoxed blondes. She's got more plastic holding her together than Legoland."

Raising his brows, August said nothing.

"You're right, that was ugly," Ella Mae mumbled contritely. "Loralyn is Hollywood gorgeous and her family name carries lots of weight in these parts, but I can't understand what the two of them had in common except for horses. The Gaynors run a horse farm and Bradford treats horses. Is that enough to base a marriage on?"

"A shared passion can be a powerful bond," August said wistfully, and Ella Mae sensed that he was referring to Delia. Reba had told her that August wrote big checks to area animal shelters each year as an anonymous donor. Delia received cards from these shelters detailing how the funds given in her honor were used to save sick or homeless animals.

Ella Mae decided that a love of horses still wasn't enough to sustain a marriage but didn't feel like arguing the point with August. She had more important questions to ask. "Am I the only person under suspicion? What about Loralyn? Maybe she and Bradford had a big fight? She's always been hot tempered and it *is* her nail salon. I couldn't have unlocked the front door, but she has keys to the place."

"Loralyn spent the night in Atlanta with three women from her college sorority. They got together to pick out bridesmaid dresses. Both the maître d' of the restaurant where they dined and the front desk clerk at the Ritz-Carlton recall Loralyn clearly." August gave Ella Mae a teasing grin. "Apparently, your childhood friend wore a black dress that showed a scandalous and, therefore, very memorable amount of décolletage."

Getting up from the table, Ella Mae tossed out the paper from her biscuit. She stopped in front of an oil painting of Lake Havenwood and stared at the depiction of the town's famous rowboat race. She hadn't been to the event for seven years but recalled how much fun it had been to watch. The painting's colorful boats skirting across a stretch of shining water forced her to consider that Bradford Knox had probably been attending the Row for Dough race for more than twenty years. Now he would never see it again.

"He seemed like a nice person," Ella Mae said, breathing her pity onto the glossy surface of the painting. "He had a kind face. I saw him in the driver's seat of his car at the bank and we exchanged a smile. That was all. But to think of someone striking him down and then leaving him in a burning building to die . . ." She fixed her gaze on a red balloon floating into a sky filled with cotton-ball clouds. "Who would do such a terrible thing to another human being?"

August stood and pushed his chair against the table. "It is an incredibly cruel and violent act. Someone was very, very angry."

"Loralyn said she would get me back for buying the property on Swallowtail Avenue," Ella Mae continued as though August hadn't spoken. "Did she point the finger at me?" She shook her head, nonplussed. "We obviously haven't outgrown our stupid childhood issues." Turning to face the attorney, she added, "I know it doesn't make any sense, but my dislike of her occurs almost at the cellular level. It's as if I've been programmed to be her enemy and vice versa."

"We are in charge of our own fate," was the attorney's rejoinder.

Someone rapped on the door and August opened it a crack. Ella Mae heard low murmurs from the hallway. August listened, nodded once, and then swung around and smiled at her. "Speaking of the future, let's get out of this stuffy room. You're free to leave, and I do believe you have a pie shop to open. If the rest of your treats are as heavenly as the tart you brought to my office, then you stand to make a fortune."

Ella Mae looked down at her hands, which still bore faint traces of fingerprint ink. She felt prickles of unease beneath the pads of her fingertips. "What if my prints are on the rolling pin? If it's a plain marble rolling pin, then someone could have switched it out with the one in my mother's kitchen. They're sold everywhere."

August opened the door wide and gestured for Ella Mae to leave the room first. "No sense worrying about information we don't have. I'm going to stand by you, Ms. LeFaye, no matter what happens."

"You believe me, then? That I had nothing to do with this horrible thing?" Ella Mae's eyes welled up with grateful tears. She felt as fragile and disconnected from the ground as the red balloon in the oil painting. If someone didn't grab hold of her, she'd surely float beyond reach. She could almost feel the air growing thinner, colder, as the earth dropped away beneath her.

"Steady now." August grabbed her by the elbow. "Of course I believe you. The LeFaye women are known for honesty." He gave her a sad, sweet grin. "Besides, your aunt Delia called and asked me to come here. While she was on the phone, she told me about the lovely meal you all shared together last night. She also mentioned how much you had to drink."

Remembering the flowing champagne, Ella Mae nodded like a child who'd devoured every cookie in the jar right before supper.

"It would have been quite a feat for you to have driven to town, lured Bradford Knox into the nail salon, hit him hard enough to knock him out, and then started a fire using a container full of gasoline," August continued. "However, it would be in your best interest for the police to come up with a more plausible suspect."

Ella Mae gave him a keen look. "Who benefits from Knox's death?"

August considered her question. "I'll try to discover which of my esteemed colleagues will be handling the estate. You might want to puzzle out who held a grudge against Mr. Knox. Because if you don't, and the prints on that rolling pin match yours, the police might not be over-

whelmingly inspired to chase down other leads. You're simply too convenient, Ms. LeFaye."

Releasing a sigh tinged with worry and fear, Ella Mae
said, "And here I thought my husband's infidelity was the
worst thing that could ever happen to me. I think being a
murder suspect trumps jilted wife any day."

Lacing her hand through his arm, August led Ella Mae
out of the station. "My dear, you're going to be the most
exciting thing to come out of New York City since bagels
and lox. Don't let this little incident derail your pie shop
plans. Your mama and aunts will help you sort this out, and
this humble barrister is at your beck and call." He gave a
brief bow, holding a palm against the swell of his belly as
he did so.

Right then and there, Ella Mae could have planted a
grateful kiss on the top of his bald head, but she held the
impulse in check. Instead, after declining his offer to drive
her home, she thanked him effusively. As he walked away,
his brisk, small steps calling to mind the image of a dapper
penguin, she vowed to ask Delia why she'd never given this
sweet, smart, and loyal gentleman the opportunity to
court her.

Ella Mae then turned directly into the path of the rising
sun and headed down Copper Avenue toward the smoldering
building that housed Perfectly Polished, one of Loralyn's
two nail salons.

The acrid smell of charred wood and melted plastic filled
the air, but Ella Mae was oblivious to both the unpleasant
odor and the orange cones set up across the intersection of
Emperor Street and Copper Avenue.

The tightly spaced cones were clearly meant to dissuade
pedestrians from approaching the scene, but Ella Mae
stepped over the line, drawn like a magnet to the blackened
structure partially obscured by a neon yellow fire truck.

Walking around the truck, she heard firemen calmly
shouting instructions to one another. They were no longer

spraying flames with water but were moving in and out of the ruined salon with crowbars and axes. The building's façade looked odd with its punched-in windows and missing door, like a child who had lost several teeth and now had a smile full of holes.

Ella Mae recognized Hugh Dylan immediately, even though he wore a helmet and she could see only his profile. He was squatting a few feet inside the doorway, examining something on the ground.

Hugh abruptly stopped what he was doing and looked up, meeting Ella Mae's gaze. It was as if he knew she was there before he saw her. Tucking a digital camera into the pocket of his jacket, he removed his helmet and marched over to her.

Ella Mae watched him draw near, fascinated by how his body moved, how his stride seemed light despite the heavy boots, how powerful his chest and shoulders appeared in the snug, navy blue fire department T-shirt, how the early light wove silver into his hair. His movements were fluid and full of strength and incredibly alluring.

"Ella Mae?" he asked hesitantly. "What are you doing here?"

She couldn't halt the smile that bloomed on her face. "So you remember me now?"

Hugh glanced at the ground. "When I saw you at your aunt's school, I thought it was you, but it'd been so long. . . ." His eyes found hers. They were a glistening, peacock blue, and Ella Mae believed she could stand there for the rest of her life and gaze into them. "You took me by surprise, but I hadn't expected you . . ." He shifted the helmet in his arms. "I wasn't prepared for how beautiful you became. I couldn't think of a single intelligent thing to say. You . . . stole my breath away."

Ella Mae felt all the heat from the burned wood rush into her and imagined she now glowed red and orange like the fire's embers. If she didn't look away from Hugh's blue stare, she was certain to turn into a pile of ash and be carried off by the wind. "It looks like the ribcage of a slain dragon," she said, pointing at the fallen beams that jutted skyward in ragged, black points.

Hugh followed her gaze. "Lots of burned buildings get that skeletal look. If this fire had gone unchecked for another hour or so, the whole thing would have just collapsed. It looks like air going out of a lung—that's how fast it happens."

Ella Mae caught sight of a policeman in conversation with another fireman and shrank back, finding cover around the corner of the enormous yellow truck. "How did this fire start?"

"Gasoline," Hugh replied. His brows were furrowed and Ella Mae knew he was probably wondering why she was acting so strangely. She didn't want him to hear her name in connection with this wreckage. Or to a murder. But if her prints were found on the rolling pin, everyone in Havenwood would know that she was a suspect.

"I never met Bradford Knox," she said. "I'd heard he was engaged to Loralyn Gaynor, but I didn't know him. Did you?"

The furrow deepened. "Not well, but I talked to him a few times over the last two years when I first got my business going. I needed advice from the area veterinarians and he was really helpful. A nice guy. His life shouldn't have ended the way it did."

"The police think I had something to do with this!" Ella Mae blurted out as though Hugh's last statement was an accusation. "But I didn't! I had no reason to harm Knox and I don't even own a car! How would I transport the gas? In my bike basket?" Her voice rose and her words tumbled forth. "How could I unlock the nail salon? Or lure Knox inside? Or hit him on the head when he wasn't looking?"

The fear she'd held in check broke free and Ella Mae began to cry. Pressing her shoulder blades against the truck, she slid down the warm metal until she ended up sitting on the steel running board.

Hugh took a seat beside her but said nothing. He waited in silence while she cried it out and then offered her a bottle of water.

"This will make you feel better," he promised, his gaze slightly guarded.

Ella Mae accepted the bottle, unscrewed the top, and drank. The water was cool and sweet in her throat. It smelled faintly of oranges, and when she closed her eyes and titled her head back to swallow, she imagined herself standing alongside a clear stream. The sounds of the firemen at work dropped away. She could hear only the gurgles and whispers of the pristine brook as it rushed through a sunny glade.

"Lord, that is the best water I've ever had," she said and examined the bottle. She did feel better. Lighter, revitalized, hopeful. "What brand is it?"

Ignoring the question, Hugh reclaimed the empty bottle. "Do you want to talk about this? I mean, I can't right now, but if you wanted to grab a cup of coffee tomorrow . . ."

Ella Mae felt a sudden longing to touch Hugh, to make certain that he was flesh and blood and not a figment of her imagination. Just one touch of his Mr. Darcy–like dark locks would prove that she was really sitting here, in an oasis of beauty and calm, before she had to return to the mess that was her life. "That would be nice. I'd really like to convince you that I had nothing to do with this."

"If you're an arsonist, then I'm an ax murderer." Hugh picked up his clipboard and turned his face back to the destroyed salon. "This fire was set in a hurry and it was sloppily done. Gas was splashed near the front door and the perpetrator or perpetrators used just enough to wreck the structure. The back room where Doc Knox was discovered was completely intact. Even the rolling pin we found was undamaged. Smoke killed Mr. Knox. The fire never reached him and, somehow, that gives me a little comfort." He gazed at the wreckage, his expression grim.

"I know what you mean. The thought of being burned alive . . ." Ella Mae swallowed the rest of the thought. "And the rolling pin didn't burn? Was it made of wood?"

"Marble, actually," Hugh answered. "My granny Glatt-felder had one just like it. She made the world's best shoofly pie. She was from a Pennsylvania Dutch community and could bake like no one else I've ever known."

Ella Mae pictured a big-boned woman with blond hair and blue eyes rolling out dough on a pine table, her cheeks flushed from the heat of a cast-iron stove. She could see her mixing ingredients in a yellow ware bowl, pausing only to wipe her strong hands on her apron and to give her beautiful grandson a taste of the filling. "Tell you what. If you provide the coffee, I'll bake something in honor of Granny Glatt-felder."

One of the other firemen called to Hugh and he instantly straightened and waved in acknowledgment, sending Ella Mae a subliminal message that he needed to go.

"I'll be working my other job tomorrow," he said quickly. "At Canine to Five. It's a doggie day care and grooming center on Satyr Lane. It's not very quiet. Someone's always barking."

She smiled. "Could I bring my dog along?"

"Sure. Dante, my Great Dane, is always looking for a new playmate." Apologetically, he began to move away from her, but Ella Mae felt a thread connecting them. It was a fragile thing, woven with fibers of curiosity and desire and a shared childhood, but it was there nonetheless.

As Hugh hustled into the building, Ella Mae wished that one day, after the pain of Sloan's betrayal had disappeared, that single thread would multiply to form hundreds of inter-laced strings, binding her to the man who smelled of dew-covered grass and had eyes like a secret Grecian cove.

"But not now," she murmured aloud in resignation. "I've got a husband to unload and a pie shop to open."

Walking past the truck toward the orange cones, Ella Mae turned to watch a wisp of gray smoke curl upward from the row of broken ceiling beams. Again, she thought of a dragon. This time, however, the creature did not resemble a charred skeleton, but a living beast, exhaling smoke and waiting in its ash-filled lair until it was ready to take wing.

Ella Mae shivered. There had been no dragon inside the nail salon, but something evil had left its signature behind. She wanted to distance herself from that evil, to be surrounded by the droning of bees and the industrious fluttering of butterflies, to feel the warm sunlight on her shoulders and hear the gravel of a garden's walking path crunch under her feet. She wanted to see flowers of every color. She wanted proof of life.

Ella Mae turned and began walking home. Home to Reba, to her mother, and to the roses.

Chapter 7

Ella Mae walked all the way home, a forty-minute hike. In the cool of her mother's kitchen, she stood in front of the sink and gulped down a tall glass of ice water. She then splashed her face with tap water and leaned over the counter, staring out the window at her mother's lush herb garden as droplets rolled down her skin and soaked into the fabric of her T-shirt.

Reba was out, leaving only a scent of strawberries behind. There were no other sounds within the house.

Ella Mae pulled on the pink rubber gloves Reba used when she cleaned pots and pans and then opened a deep drawer filled with an assortment of cooking tools.

Buried under two wooden spoons and a steel ladle was the marble rolling pin Ella Mae had used to make a dozen crusts since she returned to Havenwood. Placing it on a paper towel on the kitchen table, she sat down to give it a thorough inspection. The white marble looked just as she remembered when she'd last held the pin to make a tomato basil tart. The striations of pale gray running down the white surface were the same hue and the smooth hardwood handles were unblemished.

That gave Ella Mae pause. She doubted the implement was old, but Reba had surely used it many times before. Shouldn't the wooden handles show some sign of wear and tear?

Slipping the rolling pin in a large plastic bag, Ella Mae tucked it in a seldom-used cabinet and went outside in search of her mother. She found her in the lower garden, intently spraying a group of rose buses with something that smelled like eucalyptus. The roses, which had mango-colored petals, glistened in the light and seemed to lean toward her mother as she sang softly to them.

Chewy was there, too, fast asleep beneath a stone bench decorated with carved cherubim. Though he raised his head upon hearing Ella Mae's tread on the gravel path, he didn't get up to greet her. For some reason, his disinterest hurt her feelings. Had her mother replaced her in Chewy's affections?

Sitting down on the bench, Ella Mae put her hand underneath the seat to make contact with her terrier's smooth fur. He gave her fingers a compulsory lick and then returned to his nap.

Her mother set the spray bottle aside and mopped her forehead with a cotton hand towel. "I don't usually work at this time of the day, but I was getting restless waiting for August to call with a report. We couldn't imagine what the police wanted with you."

Ella Mae noted that her mother's handsome face looked pinched and weary in the noonday light.

Did worry for me cause that? she wondered, feeling her heart constrict at the thought. She'd wanted nothing more than to run home and be comforted by Reba and maybe even her mother, but now that the moment was at hand, Ella Mae felt uncomfortable.

"Do you make that spray?" she asked, changing the subject.

Something happened in her mother's hazel eyes. The concern she'd unveiled was quickly concealed again. "It's a mixture of eucalyptus oil, biodegradable dish soap, and water. I'm constantly waging war against aphids, and the garden center hasn't received my supply of ladybugs yet."

"That shade is beautiful," Ella Mae continued to focus on the flowers.

Her mother gave the grouping of bushes a fond glance. "It's called Maui Sunset." Her eyes swept the vast sun garden and its rainbow of blooms, and Ella Mae felt an age-old pang of jealousy. Her mother had always loved this garden and had spent so much of her time here, puttering among the roses. Throughout the winter months, her nose had been buried in seed catalogs and organic gardening magazines. Ella Mae was an only child, but she'd been competing with the roses for her mother's attention all her life.

It was all too easy to allow childhood pains to well up again, to silently question why her mother hadn't rushed down to the station to be at Ella Mae's side. Was her battle against garden pests so important that she couldn't at least have shown up in time to give her daughter a ride home?

Now, in this beautiful garden, Ella Mae thought of all the sporting events and recitals and plays her mother had missed over the years. Ella Mae curled her fists in anger, suddenly wishing she had the power to burn every petal into cinders.

"Where's Reba?" she asked, unable to keep her voice flat. Hurt pricked her words like a thorn.

"Come inside. Let's have a sandwich and some tea," her mother said by way of reply. Collecting her spray bottle and towel, she headed for the house. Chewy shot out from under the bench, smiling back and forth between the two women as if to say, "Lunch?"

His tail wagged even harder as they entered the kitchen. Ella Mae dug around in the refrigerator until she found the supply of sliced ham, cheddar cheese, and bread. She fixed sandwiches while her mother poured tea into tall glasses, cut half a lemon into thin slices, and pushed two into each glass.

"Tell me what happened this morning," she said after they'd eaten for a few minutes in silence. Chewy sat on his haunches at her feet, his long pink tongue hoping to lasso a morsel of ham.

Ella Mae scowled at her dog and then slipped him a bite of cheese under the table. Taking a deep breath, she told her mother all that had happened from the moment Officer Hardy showed up at the front door of the carriage house to what she'd learned from Hugh about the crime scene.

"I was going to ask Reba how long she's had her rolling pin," she added before her mother could speak. "It sounds like the pin used to knock Bradford out is just like the one I've been using, but I can't be sure."

Her mother laced her long fingers together and gazed pensively at her sandwich. "We never lock our doors. Anyone could have come inside and swapped rolling pins. But who would want to do that? And why?"

Ella Mae shrugged. "Loralyn Gaynor?"

A hissing sound escaped from her mother's lips, causing Chewy to raise his ears and grow stiff with alarm. "She wouldn't dare. True, her mother and I had words during this year's Garden Tour, but there's nothing new about our mutual dislike. Opal Gaynor and I have never gotten along. Like you and Loralyn, we were at odds all through school. Later, when the Gaynor's horse farm started producing champions, she used the money to influence crooked politicians and other white-collar thugs. All Opal Gaynor has ever cared about is money and power, and she delights in seeing those she considers beneath her suffer."

"Sounds just like Loralyn," Ella Mae said.

Tapping the pads of her thumbs together, her mother grew pensive. "Still, I don't think the Gaynors are behind this. The police have confirmed that Loralyn was in Atlanta and she had nothing to gain from her fiancé's death. He seems to have recently developed a very exclusive clientele and Loralyn is very fond of high society."

"She'll have to troll for another rich senior citizen," Ella Mae grumbled. "And if Loralyn isn't behind this, then who is? Who would do this to me?"

Her mother met her frantic gaze. "Perhaps it's not personal. Maybe someone at the bank overheard your threat and decided to use it to their advantage. I mean really, Ella Mae, what did you hope to accomplish by yelling at Loralyn like you were an angry drunk?"

"She was going to put nail clippings in my pies! She promised to ruin my shop before it could even get off the ground. She threatened *Chewy*." Ella Mae tossed her sandwich onto the plate. "I'm done with people thinking they can push me around!"

Her mother arched her brows. "Like Sloan?"

"Yes, like Sloan. And Loralyn. When I was growing up, she took every possible opportunity to bring me down. Why do you think I wanted to get out of this place?"

"Because of one girl? A childhood bully?" Her mother was incredulous. "Opal and I were like that, but I'd never let her have that much influence over my future."

Ella Mae shook her head. "I'd been cast in a role I didn't want to play for the rest of my life. I figured if I got as far away as possible I could reinvent myself. And I did." She sighed. "Now, just when I thought I could have a fresh start, I'm back in Havenwood's social sinkhole. Ella Mae LeFaye, pastry chef and murder suspect."

Her mother stood, stacked their sandwich plates, and placed them in the sink. She came back to the table but didn't resume her seat. "Then refuse to be pushed around. Refuse to be a murder suspect. Find out who killed Bradford Knox on your own."

Ella Mae nodded. As absurd as it sounded, her mother's advice felt right. "I will. I'll start by visiting Bradford's practice. I can bake his employees something." She glanced at Chewy and grinned shyly. "It's too bad I don't have a sick horse. But I'm new in town. I could pretend I thought Knox was a regular vet."

Looking strangely pleased, her mother opened a cabinet and pulled out a flower vase made of cobalt glass. "You make a pie and I'll put together an arrangement of my Fast Friends roses. Between the two of us, we'll have Knox's entire office confiding their deepest secrets to you."

With that, she put her wide-brimmed hat back on and left the kitchen. Ella Mae remained at the table, mulling over which pie to make. Seeing her mother pass beyond the patio doors, shears in one hand and a gathering basket in the other, Ella Mae felt a warmth bloom inside her chest. She scooped Chewy up from the floor and kissed him on the nose. "Is this what it takes to bring my mother and I together? A murder investigation?"

Chewy squirmed out of her arms and stood at attention in front of the refrigerator. Ignoring the plaintive look in his nutmeg eyes and the hopeful wag of his tail, Ella Mae opened the pantry and waited for inspiration to sweep over her. She'd expected it to be swayed by the smell of fresh peaches and warm honey, but today, its breath was redolent with the scent of chocolate.

Because time was of the essence, Ella Mae had to forgo a cream pie. It would take too long to chill. Fortunately, she had stocked up on several staples and had both pecan halves and chocolate waiting patiently on the shelves.

Ella Mae closed her eyes and pictured a frazzled office manager phoning clients to cancel Knox's appointments, having to explain to the few people who hadn't heard that the equine vet had passed away. Each call became more and more difficult as cries of dismay and words of condolence were heaped upon the woman.

"At least I hope it's a woman," Ella Mae murmured as she began to crush chocolate wafers over the bowl of the

food processor. "Because this pie will be so rich and choco-
laty that one bite should have her seeing me as an instant
confidante."

After pressing the cookie crumb mixture into a glass pie
dish, Ella Mae put it into the oven to bake and then began
work on the filling. She warmed a saucepan on the stovetop
and added a stick of butter, watching it spread into a puddle
of liquid gold. She then poured in corn syrup and white
sugar. Mixing the ingredients with a wooden spoon, she
closed her eyes and thought of the times she'd gone out for
coffee with her classmates from culinary school. When her
mind was awash with the sounds of remembered laughter,
comfortable banter, and the intimate exchange of aspirations
and fears, she set the pan aside to cool.

Ella Mae turned her attention to the large mixing bowl
on the counter. She expertly cracked four eggs into its shiny
metal basin and then beat them until they frothed and bubbled like a storm wave rushing onto the shore. After stirring
in vanilla and a pinch of salt, she paused, frowning.

"Something's missing," she said to the silent room.
"Music, for one thing." She pushed the play button on Reba's
CD player and was delighted to hear the opening strains of
"Long Time Gone" by the Dixie Chicks.

"Better," Ella Mae said as the beat burst into the room
with the energy of a hard rain. She drummed on the counter
with a pair of wooden spoons, singing along while Chewy
bounced up and down as if there were springs attached to
the bottom of his paws.

Ella Mae opened the bag of pecan halves and inhaled
their sweet, woodsy aroma. She hesitated before adding them
to the bowl. She was still overlooking an essential ingredient.

"Bourbon!" she exclaimed. That was what the filling
needed. An extra dose of richness to unite the pecans and
chocolate. Once she'd added a quarter cup of her mother's
Maker's Mark to the egg blend, she smiled with satisfaction.
Next, she stirred the cooled sugar mix into the bowl and

then added the pecans and chocolate. After a final stir, she spooned the filling into the cookie crumb crust, willing the pie to loosen the tongue of whoever sampled it.

An hour and a half later, with a warm bourbon chocolate pecan pie tucked in a nest of dishcloths, a vase of roses wedged into a box stuffed with newspaper, and Chewy whining in anxiety inside his pet carrier, Ella Mae eased her mother's Suburban out of the driveway and headed south.

Knox's practice was located two towns away in a burg named Little Kentucky. In the fifties, a family of horse breeders had relocated from the bluegrass state and established what would be the first of several well-known horse farms. Over time, Little Kentucky's reputation as an equine community grew and horse lovers from across the country had settled there.

The downtown area was small and tried to cater to both stable hands and upper-class farm owners. At one end of town there was a cluster of sad-looking cafés, bars, and discount stores. These reluctantly gave way to a grouping of posh boutiques and overpriced restaurants catering to the wealthy horse enthusiast.

Ella Mae had never cared for Little Kentucky. It was too insular for her tastes and she didn't speak horse. Like her aunt Dee, she was an animal lover, but she'd taken a nasty fall from an uppity mare when she was a girl and hadn't felt comfortable around the powerful creatures since. Loralyn Gaynor being the show champion of northern Georgia since toddlerhood had served as an additional deterrent to Ella Mae getting too interested in the equestrian world. She hoped only to remember enough terminology to ask the right questions of Knox's employees.

The Equine Center was a long, sprawling structure located down a narrow road called Saddle Brook Lane. Several rectangles of neat green fields divided by split-rail fences surrounded the building, and a mare with a wizened appearance moved to the end of the paddock as if to greet the Suburban.

Ella Mae alighted from the truck and was assaulted by the unmistakable odor of horse. It was a country smell and didn't bother her, but Chewy's nose was working double-time. He showed the whites of his eyes upon hearing the old mare snort a hello.

"It's all right, boy," Ella Mae cooed. "I'm sorry to use you like this, but I promise to buy you a nice bag of treats for being such a good sport."

Chewy's ears turned into twin mountain peaks upon hearing his favorite word. Ella Mae whispered encouragingly to him all the way to the front door. She juggled the pie, the flowers, and the carrier while wondering how she'd ever make it through the front door. Luckily, a woman holding a watering can suddenly appeared in the doorway.

"My, you've got your hands full," she said in a musical drawl. "I was just going out to give the ferns a drink, but they'll keep for a spell."

Ella Mae was relieved to find such an amiable individual from the onset. "Do you work here?"

The woman, who wore her gray brown hair in a tight ponytail, nodded. "I do, but we're not seeing patients today. I'm only open for folks in need of something from the pharmacy."

Feigning confusion, Ella Mae gestured at the carrier. "Oh, dear. I just moved here from New York and my little guy here has been acting kind of lethargic. He's barely touching his food, and for him, that's a big deal."

The woman, who was dressed in jeans and a white scrub top covered with designs of running foals, gave Ella Mae a perplexed look. "We're a horse vet, hon. Dr. Knox doesn't tend to dogs and cats. He only sees . . . saw . . ." Becoming flustered, she put her hands to her head and smoothed her already tidy hair. "I keep forgetting that he's gone."

Ella Mae put the carrier on the floor and took a step

toward the agitated woman. "Are you okay?" Without waiting for a response, she put the vase and pie on the counter dividing the waiting room from the office manager's area and removed the aluminum foil covering the pie. A current carrying browned pecans, warm chocolate, and baked crust encircled the woman in scrubs.

"I brought this in hopes of bribing Dr. Knox into seeing my dog, but I'd like you to have it instead," Ella Mae said softly. "I shouldn't have just showed up like this. It was impolite and I apologize."

Clearly influenced by Ella Mae's contrite demeanor, the woman's gaze flickered to the pie. "Don't worry about it, hon. I'm just a complete mess today, what with all that's happened. The world's gone crazy. Just crazy!" A sob rose in her throat and lodged there like a stone in a drainpipe.

Without a word, Ella Mae put her hand under the woman's elbow and steered her around the counter to a vacant rolling chair. "Why don't I cut you a piece of pie? You look like you haven't eaten for days." She pointed to a closed door at the back of the room. "Do you have a kitchen?"

The woman nodded and reached for the box of tissues on her desk. "Thank you."

Ella Mae found two plates, forks, and napkins in the third room on the left. She took a quick minute to walk down the wide hallway, noting that other doors were labeled with placards such as Imaging, Surgery, Reproduction Center, Ambulatory Center, and so on. Knox wasn't just a vet popping around to area farms to offer vaccinations and advice on injuries; he ran a state-of-the-art facility offering a number of specialized and undoubtedly very costly services.

"I'm Peggy, by the way," the woman said upon Ella Mae's return. She'd drawn the flowers closer and was touching the cantaloupe-colored petals.

Ella Mae introduced herself and then pointed at the carrier. "That's Charleston Chew. Chewy for short."

"You can let him out," Peggy offered after Ella Mae

handed her a generous wedge of pie. "He can't get into too much trouble."

Chewy shot out of the carrier and danced in between the women with relief. He then set about sniffing every square inch of the floor. "He is so precious!" Peggy exclaimed and then took a bite of pie. Her eyes went wide as the bourbon-tinged filling coated her tongue. Biting down on the soft, roasted pecans, she uttered a low moan. She chewed the second and third forkfuls with her eyes closed while Ella Mae waited patiently.

"Would you like to tell me what happened?" she asked when there was just a triangle of pie left on Peggy's plate. "You seem sad."

"I am. I really am. My boss, Dr. Knox, who was simply a lovely man, was killed. Some terrible person murdered him and now we don't know what's going to happen to the practice or how we'll manage without him." She made a sound between a hiccup and agonized sigh, put down her plate, and took Ella Mae's hand. "He treated us all like gold, and even though he left this place to Chandler—that's his son—it won't be the same. Dr. Knox was good with people *and* horses. You don't meet that kind of vet every day."

Ella Mae nodded as though she understood completely. "Is Dr. Knox's son an equine vet as well?"

"He is. He's . . . pretty good, but I've never warmed to him like I did to Brad—I mean, to his daddy. Chandler's had a chip on his shoulder because his daddy wouldn't make him a partner in the practice straight away, but he got worse when Dr. Knox started dating Ms. Gaynor. And the horses can tell that boy walks around with a knot of anger in his heart. They sense things about people."

"I used to go to school with Loralyn Gaynor," Ella Mae whispered. "We never did get along."

Peggy shrugged. "Everybody calls her a gold digger, but Dr. Knox was the one who'd be in a higher tax bracket after their marriage. You see, Ms. Gaynor was going to introduce him to all the top breeders and thoroughbred race farms. He'd have so much business that he planned to make Chandler an equal partner. Everyone was going to get their happily ever after. Well, almost everyone." A shadow surfaced in her eyes and Ella Mae couldn't help but wonder if Peggy had carried a torch for Bradford Knox. "But no one's going to be happy now. . . ." She reached out to stroke the embossed letters of Bradford's name on the clinic's business card and began to cry in earnest. Her fingers squeezed the card into a tight ball, her knuckles turning white with tension.

Is this grief or anger? Ella Mae wondered. Whichever emotion Peggy's hands were betraying, it was obvious that the office manager had had strong feelings for her employer.

And Loralyn? What would she have gotten out of the marriage? Ella Mae pondered this question while she watched Peggy. *When I saw her at the school, she didn't act like a woman in love. More like a woman with a strategy. Did she plan to help Knox build a lucrative practice and then file for divorce once her coffers were full?*

"Did Dr. Knox have any other children?" she asked Peggy to keep the conversation going.

Sniffling, Peggy nodded. "A daughter. Ashleigh. Now there's a gold digger for you. Divorced three times. Lives in a posh suburb in Atlanta and spends money like it grows on trees. She doesn't come to Little Kentucky much. We're all a bit too country for her tastes, but she and the good doctor talked on the phone all the time. She was the apple of his eye."

"Ashleigh sounds a bit like Loralyn. They both have a string of ex-husbands."

Peggy didn't reply. Instead, she opened her napkin and covered her face with it. Ella Mae couldn't decide whether she was drying her tears or trying to conceal a telling emotion.

Placing a second slice of pie on Peggy's empty plate, Ella Mae tried to think what else to ask. Either the dessert had loosened the office manager's tongue or her grief had freed her inhibitions to the point where she was confiding intimate details about her employer to a complete stranger.

"It's quite a shock to hear that Dr. Knox died . . . violently," Ella Mae said and looked nervously around the waiting area as if the perpetrator might be hiding behind one of the potted palms. "These parts are usually so peaceful. Did your Dr. Knox have enemies?"

While mechanically cutting off a triangle of pie, Peggy considered the question. "I suppose, but I couldn't name names. He was always sweet to me and I never heard him raise his voice or say a bad word behind anyone's back." She hesitated and seemed to be fighting against herself over saying anything more.

"Go on," Ella Mae prodded, her voice barely audible.

Peggy's lips seemed to part of their own accord, but her eyes glittered with anxiety when she spoke. "He's been acting secretive ever since we opened this facility last year. I don't know whether it's mortgaged to the eyeballs or not because I only handle the patient billings, but for the last six months or so Dr. Knox started coming in at night. He'd never done that before and said he came to check on post-op patients, but the next day, he'd be edgy as a thoroughbred in the starting stall. I knew he hadn't been here just for the horses. That had always been Chandler's job." She put her hands over her heart. "The night before he died, I left my cell phone here and came back to get it. Dr. Knox was in the back, arguing with someone."

"Who?" Ella Mae struggled to keep her voice mild.

"I couldn't tell if it was a man or a woman. I only heard a low, angry voice."

Ella Mae's pulse quickened. "Why were they arguing?"

"I couldn't hear what they were saying but I could tell that it was serious. I didn't stick around to find out because it was late and I was spooked by the doc's strange behavior. I know for certain now that he hadn't come in to check on his patients and I wish he could have trusted me with the truth, but it wasn't my place to ask questions." A fresh pool of tears filled her eyes. "Maybe I should have. If he'd confided in me, perhaps I could have helped him. If only he'd picked *me*."

After this statement, Peggy seemed to deflate. Putting her plate down, she went quiet and stared, glassy-eyed, out the window. Ella Mae knew that she'd gotten all she could out of the drained office manager. "Maybe you could use some help around here," she said halfheartedly. "I don't have a job yet and I love animals."

Giving her a feeble smile, Peggy shook her head. "I dunno. You'd have to meet with Chandler. Oh . . . I guess I need to call him Dr. Knox now." She looked so miserable that Ella Mae reached over and took her hand.

"It'll be okay. Your boss was lucky to have such a caring and loyal employee. A real friend. Just keep that in mind when you're feeling really low."

"Thank you, dear." With a little smile, Peggy held out Chandler Knox's business card. "Tomorrow's the funeral, so the office'll be closed, but you could call him the day after."

Ella Mae thanked Peggy, corralled Chewy back into his carrier, and left. Instead of heading home, she drove into town and parked in front of Little Kentucky's upscale clothing boutiques. She cracked the passenger window and poked her fingers into the carrier. "I'll only be a second. See that black dress in the window? If they have it in my size, I'm going to buy it. Mama's got a funeral to crash."

Chapter 8

Ella Mae was relieved that the memorial service for Bradford Knox didn't start until ten the next morning. After taking Chewy out for an early walk on the lakeside trail, she had plenty of time to swing by the pie shop and see how the remodeling was progressing.

Her mother had driven off in the Suburban, so Ella Mae had to borrow Reba's Buick. She had a harder time maneuvering this vehicle than she had her mother's SUV. Without the benefit of the truck's raised seat, Ella Mae felt like she was driving from the bottom of a pit. The engine was loud, the radio was crackly with static, and a rent in the seat fabric dug into the flesh of her right thigh. Still, Reba had driven the hefty sedan for over twenty years, and her scent—strawberries, licorice, and Aqua Net—circulated through the air vents.

"You're as bulky as a whale," Ella Mae told the Buick and gave up on her third attempt to parallel park the car on Swallowtail Avenue. She ended up pulling into the small delivery and refuse area behind the small cottage that was quickly being converted into The Charmed Pie Shoppe.

As Ella Mae turned off the engine, she saw Cyrus, the foreman, walk out of the cottage's back door carrying a rectangular piece of wood. Judging from the swell of the veins in his arms and neck, the wood was heavy. When Cyrus reached the trash receptacle behind the kitchen door, he rested his burden on the metal lip of the container and took a moment to catch his breath. Then, with a grunt Ella Mae could hear within the Buick's cabin, he shoved the wood into the vacuum. His face took on a look of satisfaction as a series of bangs echoed from inside the metal bin. Dusting off his hands, he strode purposefully back inside.

Ella Mae got out of the car and peered into the deep blue receptacle. The heavy piece of wood had somersaulted on its downward flight, coming to rest face up on a heap of broken plywood boards and shattered bits of laminate flooring. Ella Mae recognized it. It was the previous shop's sign, the one that had once hung above the front door, gazing possessively out to the street. Now, the words The Mad Hatter would call to no one save for the rodents and insects at the landfill.

At first, the sight saddened Ella Mae. What dreams had the previous owner invested into her business? She'd undoubtedly put just as much time and money into her shop as Ella Mae planned on devoting. It was all too easy to picture some woman poring over supply catalogues, placing every tiny tea table and china plate just so, and baking delicate little cakes for her pint-sized clientele.

As the months passed, she'd probably paced around her artfully arranged displays of beautiful children's ware and posh accessories and wondered why her shop wasn't teeming with customers. Ella Mae could imagine the advertisements in the newspaper, the sale signs taped to the window, and the worry multiplying in the silent store like an infestation of termites.

Eventually, the rent went unpaid, followed by unpleasant phone calls and letters filled with legalese. The shopkeeper had to vacate the premises after which the contents of the boutique and tearoom were auctioned and a shiny new sign, this one placed by an eager real estate agent, appeared on the front lawn.

A cloud crossed the sun's path, throwing the trash receptacle into shadow. The Mad Hatter's wide grin lost its comedic look. Pinching his teacup with his thumb and forefinger, the peculiar haberdasher bared his teeth at Ella Mae. She almost turned away but refused to be intimidated by a two-dimensional children's book character.

"I'm sorry," she told him and hoped that the sign Aunt Dee was making for the pie shop would not meet a similar fate.

Just then, the foreman reappeared in the doorway, a black garbage bag in his hand. "Good mornin', ma'am! Come on inside. Things are comin' together real nice. I can practically smell the pies cookin'."

"I'm going to make the very first ones for you and the crew," she promised. "Are you an apple pie man?"

"Yes, I am. Add a scoop of vanilla ice cream and I'll be a pig in mud. No cheese for me. I never did understand why folks wanna ruin a perfectly fine piece of pie."

Ella Mae watched as he tossed the bag directly onto the Mad Hatter's face. "Actually, I put the cheese in the crust. You should try it," she said, following Cyrus through the back door.

"Why not? You only live once," Cyrus replied affably.

Upon entering the kitchen, Ella Mae gasped in delight. "I can't believe how much you've gotten done! Do you ever sleep?"

Cyrus grinned. "We got your appliances yesterday right after we laid the floor. With the pipes and wiring already in place, it was light work to get them in." He gestured at the black-and-white tiles under their feet. "We've got some holes to patch before we put any paint on the walls, and Danny's gonna install the ceiling fixtures after lunch."

Ella Mae was speechless. The space was exactly how she'd pictured it on paper. The stainless steel appliances and new countertops were still ensconced in plastic sheeting, and every inch of the room was covered with drywall dust. Work boot prints made dirt-encrusted paths across the tile, but Ella Mae saw none of the mess.

She saw only gleaming surfaces and bright light. Instead of the buzz of hand drills and jigsaws, she heard the hum of the ovens and the industrious whir of the mixer. Freshly washed berries sat drying on the counter, sunlit sugar crystals converting them into garnets and rubies. Bluegrass songs piped through the mounted speakers, the mandolin and banjo notes infusing Ella Mae's movements with a zealous energy.

She could already feel the dough beneath her fingers. Just the thought of working in this bright kitchen made her heart swell with joy. It must have shown through her eyes for the workmen had all ceased their labors to stop and stare. And to smile.

"This is why we do what we do," Cyrus said, pleased. "And bein' paid in cash doesn't hurt either." Laughter burst from his chest and sprinkled onto the floor like a scattering of flour. The other men joined in and Ella Mae felt her happiness increasing, rising inside of her like mercury in a thermometer. The shop had been reborn through laughter and hard work and she felt a deep affinity for these men, for each black-and-white tile, for the appliances waiting to be brought to life.

A glance at her watch dampened her spirits. She couldn't stay much longer if she wanted to make Bradford Knox's memorial service.

"The display cases are due in tomorrow, right?" she asked Cyrus.

He nodded. "Yes, ma'am, and that means I need to know what color you want to put on the walls."

Removing a collection of paint swatches from her purse, Ella Mae handed him a strip containing five shades of brown. "I circled the winner. Café au lait. It'll look great with the floors."

"Coffee-colored paint, huh?" Cyrus took the swatch and held it against the closest wall. He squinted at it and then looked around the room. "I like it."

Ella Mae was relieved that he approved. She sensed that the foreman was not only a skilled craftsman, but had an innate gift for design as well. He understood what this shop needed. From additional electrical outlets to the style of sink in the customer restroom, he'd voiced an opinion on every detail. Ella Mae had expected to spend hours choosing materials and reviewing the budget, but Cyrus knew exactly what to buy and she trusted in his expertise.

Promising to return the next day with homemade treats for Cyrus and his crew, Ella Mae raced back to Partridge Hill. She took Chewy for a short walk, fed him, and changed into her black dress. She'd borrowed her mother's black dress hat and a pair of sunglasses with large lenses. Wrestling her hair into a knot at the base of her neck, she donned the hat and glasses in front of the mirror and smirked at her reflection. She looked like a two-legged beetle in the enormous black glasses and wide-brimmed hat. Yet she'd blend right in with the rest of the woman attending the service, because in rural Georgia, women still wore hats to church.

Reba returned from the Piggly Wiggly in the nick of time, staggering into the kitchen with an armload of groceries and a red licorice twist dangling from her mouth like a damp cigarette. She tossed the keys to the Buick onto the table.

"You look like Audrey Hepburn!" Reba declared, the words escaping through a narrow gap between licorice and lips.

Thanking her for the compliment, Ella Mae took a brown bag from Reba's hands. "Can I leave Chewy with you? I'll pick him up this afternoon before my . . . before I meet Hugh Dylan in town."

Reba bit down hard on her Twizzlers and scowled. "Do you think it's smart to be jumpin' in the datin' pool already?"

"Who said anything about dating?"

That earned her a snort. "You don't have coffee with a steamin'-hot fireman to talk about politics or religion. You sit there, your fingers dyin' to touch that hair of dark chocolate and willin' the buttons on his shirt to pop off one by one. You think about puttin' your hands on his rock-hard—"

"I'm going for him!" Ella Mae interjected, pointing at Chewy. "Hugh runs a doggie day care center and obedience school. I figured Chewy might benefit from a few classes."

Pulling a pack of licorice twists from the rhinestone-encrusted pocket of her denim skirt, Reba shook the candy at Ella Mae. "Really? So you didn't bake Hugh a *special* pie? You're just a concerned parent looking for the right school for your fur baby, huh? You haven't noticed that Hugh's sexy enough to have his own calendar or that he doesn't wear a weddin' ring? That he's so fine the birds fly lower in the sky just to get a closer look at him?"

Ella Mae hadn't listened beyond the word "pie." With all that had been going on, she hadn't had the opportunity to bake Hugh a shoofly pie. "Damn it," she muttered, ignoring the mischievous twinkle in Reba's dark brown eyes.

"Have a nice time!" Reba trilled as Ella Mae headed for the door.

It was only when the house fell away in the rearview mirror that she realized that it was rather odd for Reba to have wished her a good time. Then again, Reba was able to enjoy herself wherever she went. It was one of her most endearing qualities.

Ella Mae waited in the shaded parking lot of the United Methodist church until it seemed like the majority of the funeral attendees had passed through the polished oak doors. She slipped in to the gloomy accompaniment of the organ and selected a pew far in the rear of the sanctuary. She then slid all the way to the end of the row in order to gain a clear view of the front pew and the grieving family. Her gaze found Loralyn Gaynor.

If Reba thought Ella Mae looked like Audrey Hepburn, then Loralyn easily outshone her as a contemporary Grace Kelly. With her glossy blond hair carefully coiffed beneath a small but fashionable hat, her black gloves, and simple but elegant black suit accessorized by a single strand of pearls, Loralyn looked pale and beautiful. Every movement carried the smooth elegance of ballerina, from the dip of her chin as she accepted a whispered phrase of condolence or briefly took an offered hand, to the graceful manner with which she dabbed at her dry eyes with a delicate lace handkerchief.

Ella Mae imagined how Loralyn must have enjoyed walking down the aisle, knowing that she had a captive audience. She was so arrogant that she would have failed to recognize the irony of her solitary procession. A few months from now, she would have been marching on the red velvet runner wearing a Vera Wang wedding gown and clutching a bouquet of calla lilies in lieu of a cream-colored handkerchief. Now, she stood before her pew, her back as straight and stiff as a bride's. All eyes were upon her as they would have been during her autumn nuptials, but her face held no glow, no glimmer of happy expectation. Her groom was not waiting for her at the altar, but in the air-conditioned hearse stationed outside. It was the right stage, but the wrong play. Ella Mae felt a stirring of pity for her old enemy.

A sandy-haired man in his late thirties rose when Loralyn reached the front of the sanctuary and gave the pinched-faced strawberry blonde seated next to him a nudge, forcing her to make room for Bradford's fiancée. Ella Mae assumed from the pair's drawn features that she was looking at Chandler and Ashleigh Knox. Chandler gave Loralyn a polite nod but Ashleigh refused to even look at her.

The minister took his place in the pulpit as the last strains of the hymn rose lugubriously from the organ pipes toward the belfry. Ella Mae listened to the Scripture reading and the opening lines of the minister's message, but after a while, she began to shift restlessly in her seat, pivoting this way and that to take in every face in the chapel.

Was one of the mourners casting his or her eyes down out of piety or out of guilt? Had one of them worn sunglasses to obscure a gaze that was opaque with shame? Would the killer remain silent throughout the service out of respect or because he or she dared not speak, dared not risk words flowing forth lest their dark secret be released into the air. Was the murderer even present?

Ella Mae continued to study the occupants of the family pew. Chandler Knox, who was seated between Loralyn and Ashleigh, was boyishly handsome. When an elderly aunt took the pulpit to regale the mourners with anecdotes from Bradford's childhood, Chandler's cheeks softened into dimples and he smiled. Yet his body was stiff. He sat as erect as a soldier, as though he didn't dare relax control, and he grasped his Bible so tightly that the barn red cover buckled under his fingers. Ashleigh, whose face showed no traces of her father's affability or easy humor, glared at the aunt. She then craned her neck and turned her cold, angry gaze on anyone who dared to meet her eyes.

Toward the end of the service, Loralyn finally cast off her posture of remorse and sat back against the pew, opening her chest and breathing deeply. She stared unseeing at the ivy and daisy funeral wreaths and the copious arrangements of white daylilies, and Ella Mae wondered what was running through her mind. As the aunt descended from the lectern, Loralyn covertly looked over her shoulder, the handkerchief pressed delicately against her lips. She scanned the crowd, obviously seeking someone out.

As Ella Mae watched, the corner of Loralyn's mouth moved. It was a twitch, really, and lasted only a fraction of a second, but it registered pleasure. Leaning forward, Ella Mae tried to discern who'd elicited a crack in Loralyn's grief-stricken façade, but a woman in a hat decorated with a spray of black feathers blocked her view. At that moment, she bent down to retrieve an item from the floor and Ella Mae could see who had coaxed that spark of light in Loralyn's eyes. She was appalled to recognize the chiseled jaw line and wavy hair belonging to Hugh Dylan.

"What is he doing here?" Ella Mae murmured while everyone else recited a prayer aloud. "And why did Loralyn look at him like that?"

Suddenly, time rushed backward. The years peeled away like old paint to reveal a moment from Ella Mae's adolescence.

It was the first school dance of the season at Margaret Mitchell Junior High and the gym had been transformed from a cavern smelling of sweaty socks and mildew to an enchanted winter wonderland. Glittering paper snowflakes dangled on satin ribbon from the rafters. They concealed the basketball hoops and the championship pennants in a swirl of silver and white. The floor was covered in scraps of white confetti and the table linens were a dull silver. Even the windows had been frosted with washable paint.

Ella Mae walked beneath an arch of white and silver balloons, fearing the gaze of her classmates and yet longing for it as well. She was small-chested and bony, her scapulae protruding under the skin of her back, her childlike wrist barely able to support the weight of the corsage Reba had bought for her. And though she could not control her lack of curves, Ella Mae felt a touch of vanity over her hair. Normally a bramble of whiskey-colored curls, her mane had been straightened into a sleek French twist by a talented beautician who'd driven in from Atlanta at Ella Mae's request. She'd saved for months to pay for both her twilight blue dress and her hair sculpting, and for an instant, a breath in time, she felt like a princess.

There, beneath the arch of shimmering balloons, she could pause and drink in this moment of possibility. She looked the part. But would Hugh Dylan notice her? She had made this transformation for him. To finally make him really see her.

Hugh had been standing with a cluster of other boys on the far side of the gym when Ella Mae entered. He glanced her way and she could tell that he didn't recognize her at first, the slim girl with the straight hair and iridescent blue dress. She felt a rush of hope, of triumph. Surely, he'd ask her to dance, and once she was in his arms, they'd finally have a chance to talk. She'd be funny and smart and coy and graceful and he'd fall in love with her then and there. Surely, this was to be the night of her dreams.

But Ella Mae was wrong.

Seeing a potential rival, Loralyn had instantly detached herself from a cluster of giggling girls and walked, with the slow confidence of the queen of the popular crowd, to within inches of where Hugh stood. It was impossible not to follow her every movement. Against the backdrop of winter white and the lusterless pastels of the other girls' dresses, Loralyn drew every eye in her strapless black gown. Her long hair had been coaxed into soft waves, which fell down her tanned skin like a blond waterfall. Beyond her beauty, she possessed an air of sophistication that no other girl in the room possessed. Unlike Ella Mae, Loralyn was the kind of girl who made her own dreams come true.

Posing like a French model, she cast a coquettish look at her friends, opened a sequined Chanel clutch, and dropped its contents—a lipstick, bubble gum, a silver pen, and some money—onto the floor.

Hugh, the best-looking and most charismatic boy in school, darted forward to collect Loralyn's treasures. From then on, the two were inseparable. They'd dated all through junior high and high school. Loralyn constantly broke up with him and he repeatedly forgave her and took her back. It was as if she'd cast a spell over him that night in the gym.

Does she still have that kind of hold over him? Is there still something between them? Ella Mae wondered in dismay.

The rest of the service seemed interminable. Several people came forward to speak about Knox, but with the exception of the elderly aunt, all the stories were horse related and seemed to serve as excuses for a host of owners to brag about their latest victories at the track or the distinguished bloodlines of one of their studs. The only highlight occurred toward the end when Peggy, Bradford's devoted office manager, stood nervously before the crowd and began to sing "Ava Maria."

The notes, laden with Peggy's affection for her employer, caused a genuine sense of loss to settle onto everyone's shoulders like a heavy shawl. The poignant melody allowed blocked tears to flow, and by the time Peggy was done, a dozen people were blowing their noses and dabbing at moist cheeks. Ella Mae watched Peggy return somberly to her pew, where a man immediately put a comforting arm around her and whispered into her ear.

Other couples reached for one another, and Ella Mae felt a keen sense of loneliness at the sight. She could remember reaching for Sloan's hand at the last wedding ceremony they'd attended. When the groom kissed the bride, Ella Mae had clapped in shared joy, glowing with the knowledge her marriage was as strong as the day she'd added the name Kitteridge to her own.

"Stop it," she chided herself. Closing her eyes, she silently appealed to her Maker to heal her injured heart. When she opened them again, she felt calm and still. A few minutes shy of eleven o'clock, the service came to an end and the congregants filed out of the church to the accompaniment of yet another mournful hymn.

Ella Mae did not rise to follow. Instead, she studied every person who passed by her pew. Most of the faces were unfamiliar, but she quickly turned away when the people she recognized—Peggy, Hugh, Loralyn—headed for the exit. She continued to linger after the sanctuary had emptied, mulling over the fact that she'd learned nothing helpful beyond the assumption that Ashleigh disliked Loralyn. Hardly a motive for murdering her own father. If she were to commit a violent act against anyone, Loralyn would have been the more obvious victim.

As she reflected on Chandler's tense posture and the angry grip he'd had on his Bible, raised voices permeated the quiet.

"You idiot!" a woman shouted from the direction of the foyer. "I told you to rent a limo! I am *not* riding in the back of that ridiculous horse-drawn carriage. I'm in a black dress and it's June! That Amish-looking contraption might be fine for you and Daddy's white-trash fiancée, but *I* will not be seen in that thing."

"White trash?" Ella Mae heard Loralyn say. Her voice was dangerously calm. "You come from a line of farmers and schoolteachers. *My* family carries the pedigree around here. The Gaynors are one of the first families of Georgia. Your people probably came through Ellis Island carrying their belongings in a cloth bundle infested with lice."

Loralyn delivered the insult with the icy haughtiness of the Snow Queen, and even from where she remained seated in her pew, Ella Mae could hear Ashleigh spluttering with indignation. "I know your type. Tarts likes you are a dime a dozen in Atlanta. You were only using Daddy. You didn't love him and he didn't love you! He still kept Mama's picture in his wallet and he would kiss it when he thought no one was looking. What *was* between you? What kind of deal did you two have?" A pregnant pause. "Did you know about Daddy's scheme, Chandler? Are you in on it too?"

Laughing derisively, Loralyn said, "Chandler wouldn't understand what your daddy and I had planned any better than you would."

"Well, whatever you dragged him into got him killed!

I hope you're happy." The last word bubbled out as a sob. "No, I take that back. I hope you're absolutely miserable for the rest of your life. *You* did this. Because of *you*, the most generous man in the world died alone—tied up like some torture victim in a nail salon. A nail salon of all places!" Ashleigh began to cry louder, as if the feminine setting of her father's murder was too much for her to take.

Chandler cleared his throat. "That's enough. Show some respect," he commanded and Ella Mae was impressed by his composure. "Ashleigh, you will ride in the carriage as our father wished. 'Daddy' has written you enough checks over the years to have earned this one request." He hesitated. "As for you, Ms. Gaynor. We will get through this day by being courteous to one another. That is how we'll honor my father's memory, not by bickering inside a church. If there's any business you'd care to discuss tomorrow, you know where to find me. I'll be running the equine center from now on."

The two women had stayed quiet during Chandler's monologue, but now Loralyn uttered a light laugh. "I don't think we'll be seeing much of one another after today, Chandler. You see, your father and I had an understanding. A private one. It involved the racing circuit and certain investments and things I don't plan on divulging to you." Ella Mae heard Ashleigh begin to speak, but Loralyn wasn't finished. "As far as your daddy being the sweetest, most generous man in the world—think again, princess. Everyone's got something to hide and he was no exception. If he wasn't playing a dangerous game, then we wouldn't be wearing black today."

"It sounds like you might know who killed him. Do you?" Chandler asked and Ella Mae heard the anguish and desperation in his voice. Every cell in her body was on alert, her senses sharpened as she waited for Loralyn to answer.

"No," was all she said. "I told the police everything I could about your father and *my* fiancé. It's up to them to solve his murder."

Ashleigh made an unattractive snorting noise. She

undoubtedly thought Loralyn was lying. Ella Mae certainly thought so. "Why should you care? Now that Daddy's dead, you won't reap any benefits. You'll just walk away and look for your next husband, right?" Ashleigh's words were meant to sting, but they were unable to inflict an injury to Loralyn.

"You've pretty much summed it up," she replied callously. The sound of her heels clicking on the flagstones punctuated her cruel remark.

"I'd like to kill that bitch," Ashleigh hissed before Ella Mae heard Chandler shoo his sister outside.

After waiting a few minutes Ella Mae pushed open one of the heavy wooden doors and was surprised to find Hugh Dylan positioned on the other side. She stammered out a hello, but was immediately distracted by the sight of Officer Hardy leaning against a parked police car. Seeing Ella Mae, he jerked upright and began walking in her direction, his steely eyes fixed on her face.

"Ella Mae, what are you doing here?" Hugh spoke her name as though it were made of spun sugar. In his black suit, with his dark hair combed into neat waves, he looked just like a contemporary version of Mr. Darcy.

"Um, I just wanted to pay my respects. Like I told you the other day, I didn't know Mr. Knox, but I saw him the once and, well, he smiled at me like we were already friends." Hardy's rapid advance made her speak quickly, her words tumbling over each other. "And I wanted to show people that I'm innocent, that I'm sorry this horrible thing happened to Mr. Knox and to his family."

Hugh reached out to touch her on the elbow. "We can talk about that this afternoon. Are you still coming by?"

Ella Mae opened her mouth to speak, her body moving toward his hand, which had yet to make contact with her arm, but Hardy inserted himself in the narrow space between them. Hugh was forced to step backward and Ella Mae lost the comfort of his blue gaze.

"I'm afraid you're not going anywhere, Ms. LeFaye. Your prints matched those found on the murder weapon. I'm bringing you in."

Stunned, Ella Mae said nothing, allowing Hardy to take a firm hold of the arm Hugh had been reaching for seconds earlier.

Hugh called her name, but Ella Mae was too humiliated to answer or to even turn her head. At least the funeral entourage had cleared the parking lot so no one else could witness her disgrace.

"I didn't do it," she told Hardy in a panicked voice as he opened the car door and waited for her to get inside the police cruiser.

"You'll have plenty of time to convince me of that," he responded blandly and shut the door.

Ella Mae lifted her eyes to the steeple, which rose from the roof like a finger pointing at the cloudless summer sky. Sending forth a second prayer, more urgent than the one asking that her broken heart be healed, she stared skyward until the car pulled away from the curb and the steeple slid out of view.

Chapter 9

On this trip to the police station, Ella Mae was not shown to the relatively comfortable conference room with its oil painting of Lake Havenwood, but to a cold, stark interview room. As Hardy directed her to sit in a metal chair, she wondered who'd previously occupied the stiff seat. The worst criminals in the town of Havenwood were vandals and petty thieves. Occasionally, domestic disturbances erupted during the hottest midsummer nights, and every now and then, an alcohol-induced fistfight broke out in a local pub, but there hadn't been a murder within town limits in over one hundred years.

"That man waiting in the lobby. Is he a reporter?" Ella Mae asked Officer Hardy nervously.

Hardy moved to the wall closest to the door and then crossed his arms and spread his legs, adopting the authoritative stance of a drill sergeant. "He sure is. I'd stay clear of him if I were you. He's already taken way too many liberties describing this case."

Ella Mae swallowed. "Does the fact that he's waiting

to get a quote from me mean that I'm now officially a suspect?"

Before Hardy could answer, a second officer entered the room, introduced himself as Officer Jed Wells, and placed a recorder on the steel table in front of Ella Mae.

The sight of the recording device filled her with trepidation. "Am I under arrest?"

Wells settled down in the chair across from her and took a leisurely sip from an Atlanta Falcons coffee cup. "Should you be?" His tone was conversational, almost gentle in its inflection. "Did you kill Bradford Knox?"

"No," she replied immediately and then folded her hands on her lap, trying not to let fear cloud her judgment. "Since I wasn't read my rights, I am assuming that I'm not under arrest and I'd like my lawyer to be here if you're going to question me. Aren't I allowed one phone call?"

"We'll call Mr. Templeton for you." Wells nodded at Hardy, who promptly left the room. Ella Mae relaxed a little. Just knowing August would be by her side gave her hope. Perhaps she wouldn't have to swap her black dress for an orange jumpsuit after all.

At least I'd be warmer, she thought and pressed her cold hands together.

A wall clock, the room's only adornment, ticked steadily in the silence, which grew more uncomfortable as the minutes stretched out like a late-afternoon shadow. Ella Mae kept her eyes fixed on the clock's red second hand in order to avoid the casual scrutiny of Officer Wells. She rubbed her arms to keep the keep the gooseflesh from rising, but to no avail.

Hardy returned, carrying a plastic evidence bag containing a marble rolling pin. Without a word, he set it down on the table and then resumed his military posture near the door.

"Do you recognize this, Ms. LeFaye?" Wells inquired casually.

Ella Mae clamped her lips together and said nothing.

When August arrived moments later, he set down his briefcase, straightened his polka-dot bow tie, and proceeded to softly berate the policemen for trying to bully his client. Wells hung his head like a schoolboy caught pulling his classmate's pigtails.

"Ms. LeFaye will only answer questions because she wishes to cooperate. If, at any point, I believe her rights are being violated, I will terminate the interview." August glanced around the room and frowned. "This is a very unpleasant space. The conference room is drab enough, but this meat locker is right out of *Silence of the Lambs*. It's absolutely glacial in here. Are you trying to torture this poor lady into making a confession?"

Hardy made a noise that might have been a laugh or a grunt, but Wells recovered his decorum and placed a hand on the evidence bag. "This is why we wanted to talk to you today, Ms. LeFaye. What can you tell us about it?"

Ella Mae explained her theory that the rolling pin from her mother's house had been taken. "I put the replacement in a bag," she explained. "Maybe you can get the killer's prints off that one."

Wells looked dubious. "We'll send someone over to pick it up. Meanwhile, why don't you tell us exactly why you came back to Havenwood?"

The last thing Ella Mae wanted to do was air her dirty laundry in front of the two policemen, but she had no choice. She told them about Sloan's infidelity and her plans to open a pie shop on Swallowtail Avenue. Wells then asked her to describe her relationship to Loralyn Gaynor and to enlighten him about her reasons for behaving with such hostility toward Loralyn and her fiancé at Peachtree Bank.

Ella Mae told him everything, calmly responding to question after question until she felt like screaming. She could barely feel her fingertips, and her toes had gone numb in her strappy black pumps.

"I believe my client has told you all she knows," August said when Wells asked Ella Mae to describe her activities on the night Bradford Knox was murdered. "Now charge her with a crime or let her go so she can thaw while there's still some daylight left."

Wells was about to argue when there was a knock on the door. A female officer with an attractive heart-shaped face peered into the room and, seeing Hardy, gestured for him to step into the hall. Thirty seconds later, he ducked back inside and handed Wells a slip of paper.

The two officers exchanged unreadable glances.

"Gentlemen?" August held out his hands, palms up. "Are we excused?"

Wells nodded. "Apparently two witnesses have come forward claiming that Ms. LeFaye didn't leave her house after returning from her supper party at Le Bleu. They had a view of her place from eleven P.M. until dawn and said there was plenty of moonlight to see by. This pair swears they would have heard a twig snap, the night was so quiet." He frowned. "In my book, your alibi is still weak, but these folks have given you a reprieve for the time being."

Ella Mae's eyebrows rose. "Really? Who are they?"

August touched her lightly on the arm. "We'll leave the questions to the fine officers of the law, Ella Mae. I'd say that the account provided by these helpful witnesses should put you in the clear. Why don't you accompany me to my office? I have an update regarding a certain gentleman from New York."

What now? Ella Mae wondered in silent misery but followed August out of the interview room without protest. In the hall, she came face-to-face with a young couple holding hands and looking scared and yet fiercely determined.

Seeing Ella Mae, the young woman, who could barely be out of her teens, smiled and said, "You're the spitting image of your mama."

"I'm sorry, do I know you?" Ella Mae said.

The girl released her boyfriend's hand and offered it to Ella Mae. "I'm Kelly and this is Noel. We got engaged in your mama's rose garden the night that poor man was killed. That's why we're here. As soon as we heard that the police had brought you in, we knew we had to say something."

Ella Mae pressed Kelly's hand warmly. "I'm certainly grateful, but a little confused too. Were you and your fiancé in the garden the whole night?"

Pink roses bloomed over Kelly's cheeks and she glanced shyly at the floor. Noel put a protective arm around her narrow waist and nodded without a trace of embarrassment. "We'd asked your mama if it was all right for us to be there. See, it was a full moon and all the stars were out. I wanted to propose to Kelly on that old bench in the middle of the garden. I know it sounds weird, but I wanted to ask her at midnight, because that would be exactly a year after we had our first kiss."

"But I didn't get picked up by Officer Hardy until early morning," Ella Mae whispered.

Noel squeezed Kelly and grinned happily. "I know. After the most beautiful girl in the world agreed to be my wife, we sat on that bench and talked about everything. About what kind of wedding we wanted, the places we wanted to travel to, how many kids we'd have, what we'd name them. You know, the stuff that makes up a life."

Kelly's face glowed. "And we made promises to each other too. Never to go to bed angry, never to be afraid to speak the truth, and never to keep secrets from each other. Unless it was a good secret like a surprise party or something."

Faith in a bright and harmonious future shone out of the couple's eyes like starlight. Ella Mae realized with a jolt of sorrow that she had never looked like Kelly and Noel did now. Even when she'd stood before the full-length mirror in Sloan's Manhattan apartment to admire the silhouette she cut in her couture wedding gown, she hadn't been illuminated by a corona of love like this couple was. Perhaps the absence of family had reduced her radiance, or maybe, just maybe, she had never believed, as Kelly and Noel believed, that Sloan was her soul mate. She had loved him, but he had never been the other half to her whole. She saw that clearly now. Saw it and accepted it. Still, she did not want the rush of sadness she felt over this realization to show.

"It sounds like a perfect night," she told the young couple sincerely. "I remember the moon. It was magical."

Noel and Kelly exchanged a knowing glance and then Noel gave Ella Mae an exaggerated wink. "Yes, ma'am. Pure magic."

Ella Mae shook hands with the newly engaged couple again, thanked them for coming forward, and asked for their contact information. "I'd like to make you something to celebrate your engagement," she explained.

Just as Kelly was unzipping her purse to retrieve a slip of paper and a pen, Wells and Hardy appeared from inside the interview room. They looked displeased to find their witnesses in conversation with the woman they'd obviously begun to view as a likely suspect.

"We'll be sending an officer to your home to collect the other rolling pin," Wells reminded Ella Mae.

Sensing the shift in atmosphere, August promised to deliver his client to Partridge Hill as soon as they were done attending to an important legal matter. Giving Noel and Kelly one last smile of gratitude, Ella Mae followed August outside.

As August and Ella Mae slogged through the thick summer air, August assured her that the testimony of the young couple would do much to encourage the police to search elsewhere for Bradford Knox's killer.

"Don't get me wrong," Ella Mae responded. "I'm thrilled that they had a clear view of the guest cottage that night, but why did they choose my mother's garden? How would they even know what it looked like? You can't see the rear garden from the driveway and she never allows people back there during garden tours. She's always been strangely private about that part of the yard."

August held the door to his brick office building open. "Don't look a gift horse in the mouth, my dear. Fate has intervened on your behalf. Seems like it's about time too." He led her to the cozy seating area in his inner sanctum. "Speaking of gifts, your husband has sent you one." Handing her an envelope addressed to August Templeton, Esq. at 12 Red Admiral Street, Havenwood, Georgia, August told her to consider the contents carefully while he rustled up two glasses of sweet tea.

Perplexed, Ella Mae pulled a sheaf of paper free from its envelope, the latter having been slit open with the neat precision of a surgeon's scalpel. As she unfolded the letter, a check fluttered loose and fell onto her lap.

"Sweet Lord!" she exclaimed. The check, made out to her, was for the staggering amount of one hundred thousand dollars. Sloan's signature boldly declared itself from the bottom right-hand corner. The memo line was blank.

The check had been drawn from Sloan's personal account, an account he'd kept to himself. Ella Mae had no idea how much money was in there or how Sloan had accumulated this small fortune.

Staring at the neat line of zeroes her husband had penned inside the rectangular number box, Ella Mae shook her head. "What are you up to, Sloan?"

Without moving the check from her lap, she turned her attention to the letter. It had been typed on Sloan's corporate letterhead, and as Ella Mae glanced at the formal manner in which the date had been listed before her name, she couldn't help but wonder if Sloan's secretary had typed it or if he had actually composed it on his own computer. It read:

Dear Ella Mae,

I am sending you this letter through your attorney so that I can be certain you'll receive it. I don't care who reads it as long as it ends up in your hands.

Sweetheart, I miss you. I know you're hurt and angry. You have every reason to be. I've been thinking about your idea for us to start over again. It's a great idea, honey. I don't belong in Havenwood, but that doesn't mean that you and I don't belong together. We do. We're a good team, Ella Mae, and we were happy for seven years. We can be happy again. I know this for a fact. I'm so certain of this that I want you to take this money I'd set aside for our first house and use it to buy your pie shop. I know I can't force you to come back to New York, so open one in Georgia if you want. I only ask one thing in return. Don't pursue a divorce, okay? Give me six months to win you back. Give our marriage a chance. Take this to the bank, open your pie shop, and call me after your first day of business. Those lucky people in Havenwood won't know what hit them!

With all my love,
Sloan

Ella Mae dropped the letter on top of the check and pressed her fingers into her temples where a headache was stirring to life. She massaged the soft tissue lying against her skull like a blanket and reread the letter.

August returned carrying a pair of iced tea glasses. He handed one to Ella Mae and sat in the leather club chair across from hers. "In all my years, no one's ever written me a check with that many zeroes."

"It is a big check," Ella Mae agreed. "I don't know what to make of it, August. Sloan might truly be sorry for betraying my trust, and because he feels guilty, he's sending me this check so that I can fulfill my dreams." She took a sip of tea and examined several questionable lines in the letter. "But if he really wanted to give me a gift, there'd be no strings attached. This money comes with a condition. Cash the check and forget about the divorce."

"Only for six months. This is not a legal document, my dear. You can take that money to the bank and go ahead with the divorce without giving his offer a second glance." He studied his client for a moment and then leaned forward. "I don't know this fellow, Ella Mae, and Lord knows I don't want you to leave Havenwood, but I do believe you should take some time to give your husband's proposal some serious thought."

Though her first instinct was to put Sloan's check in the nearest shredder, Ella Mae decided to heed her attorney's advice. She wasn't interested in the money, though it would be nice to pay back her mother and aunts and be in no one's debt but the bank's, but she was interested in Sloan's unique attempt to get her attention. Why had he used money as a way to forestall the divorce? Why hadn't he simply flown down to Havenwood to plead his case in person? That would have made more of an impact than one hundred thousand dollars.

Folding the check into the letter, Ella Mae realized something else. August had yet to present her with a bill for his services. "I promise to think about it. In the meantime, I need to write you a check, don't I?"

August gave her a paternal smile, his round cheeks dimpling. He rose and scooped his car keys off his desk. "You don't owe me a cent. I didn't so much as fill out a form in the police station. I merely stood by your side as a friend of the family. If you decide to go through with the divorce, I'll charge you a modest fee to cover the cost of the thousands of trees we'll have to kill to obtain your emancipation. We lawyers are so very fond of paperwork."

Pausing at his secretary's desk, August informed the tidy, gray-haired woman that he was running out again to return Ella Mae to her car.

At the Methodist church, August pulled his Audi next to Reba's Buick. Putting his car in park, he turned to Ella Mae. "Go on home, dear. Whip up some magic in the kitchen and do some serious thinking. We might rush into love, but none of us should be in a rush to fall out of it."

Two things occurred to Ella Mae as the Buick churned up and down the hills around Lake Havenwood. The first was that she'd never fallen out of love with Hugh Dylan. That girlhood crush had been in hibernation during her marriage to Sloan Kitteridge, but it had survived intact none-theless. The second realization, which smothered this momentary thrill like an avalanche, was that she'd likely just ruined any chance she'd had of impressing Hugh. Instead of having an intimate conversation over coffee and pieces of shoofly pie with the man who might be the love of her life, she'd been unceremoniously hauled away in a police car.

Chapter 10

Back at home, Ella Mae changed out of her black dress and heels into white shorts and a bottle green T-shirt. Exhausted from the funeral, her involuntary trip to the police station, her visit to August's office, and the heat, she flopped on the antique sleigh bed that had belonged to her great-grandmother and closed her eyes. But she couldn't keep them shut. The presence of Sloan's letter on the nightstand sucked the tranquility from the air. It sent out vibrations, a rectangle of white noise, until Ella Mae stood up and crammed it into her pocket. She then crossed the stretch of garden dividing the guest cottage from the main house in search of her dog.

She found Chewy in the kitchen, snoozing in a dog bed made of red fabric, his belly and all four paws facing the ceiling. Upon closer inspection, Ella Mae realized that the bed was shaped like a Corvette convertible, complete with plush steering wheel and wiper blades. Only Reba would have purchased something so ridiculous.

Ella Mae also found her mother. She was seated at the kitchen table, sampling a generous wedge of one of the chocolate chess pies Ella Mae had placed in the freezer in the garage.

"I hope you don't mind." She waved a laden fork. "I'm famished. The salad I had for lunch clearly wasn't enough."

Ella Mae cut herself a sliver of pie, secretly delighted to have caught her mother eating one of her pies with such relish.

Without bothering to get a plate or utensils, Ella Mae tore off a strip of buttery, flaky crust and popped it into her mouth. "The strangest thing happened at the police station," she said after swallowing the comforting morsel.

Her mother, whose attention remained fixed on the pie, murmured an absent, "Oh?"

"I met Kelly and Noel. They're not the first couple to have spent the night in your back garden, are they?"

"What a strange question," her mother replied airily. "I'd have thought you had more pressing concerns right now."

Ella Mae leaned forward. "When I was a little girl, you used to wander around that circular path at night. And I remember other people being in that part of the garden too. A man, a woman, and you. I'd always thought I was dreaming, but it wasn't a dream, was it?"

With a shrug, her mother set down her fork. "It's a very romantic place, Ella Mae. Had you married someone else, you might have gotten engaged there too."

"But there are no flowers," Ella Mae protested. "Just a circular path of white stones and a rosebush I've never seen bloom."

An enigmatic smile crossed her mother's face. "Those are my Luna roses. They're very rare and only bloom by the light of the full or new moon. Perhaps you'll see them for yourself one day." She pushed a small bundle of paper across the table. "By the way, Reba wanted me to give this to you."

Ella Mae stared at her mother for a long moment, wanting to ask more questions about these strange nocturnal engagements, but she examined the stapled packet instead. It appeared to be a list of signatures photocopied from some sort of guest book.

"What it this?"

"The names of all the people who attended Bradford Knox's memorial service," her mother replied. "Reba knows the church secretary and was able to get the list in exchange for one of your sweet potato pies. Guess you'll have to restock the freezer before your grand opening."

Scanning the names, Ella Mae smiled. "Reba is a gem!"

"So am I!" Verena's voice boomed from the direction of the front door. She marched into the kitchen like a five-star general on parade and presented Ella Mae with a gift bag. "Ta-da!"

Ella Mae dug through layers of tissue to reveal a framed document bearing the town's seal. "The business license! I thought we'd have to wait another week."

"I have friends in high places!" Verena shouted boisterously. "And that's not all! My darling husband, our most esteemed mayor, has arranged for a ribbon-cutting ceremony a week from Saturday. Sissy's got a troupe of musicians lined up and I've called every journalist I know. Are you ready to be famous?"

Recalling the reporter waiting outside the police station earlier that day, Ella Mae sighed. "Yeah, as a murder suspect."

"That'll do!" Verena cried, undaunted. "All publicity is good publicity. Besides, August won't let this ridiculous finger-pointing continue." She paused and sent a fleeting glance at her sister. "Or do we need to get involved, Adelaide?"

"I don't think so. Ella Mae will sort everything out. In fact, I bet she already has a plan, don't you, dear?"

Surprised at her mother's intuitiveness, Ella Mae picked up the list and showed it to her aunt. "I know who to investigate now, but I'm going to need Aunt Delia's help."

"Grab your dog and get in my car!" Verena ordered.

"You'll melt quicker than an ice cream if you try to ride out to Dee's on that bike of yours. I hope you plan on buying a car before the summer's out. You need to conserve energy for all the enchanting fare you'll be whipping up in the kitchen!"

"And for your food handler's test," her mother added solemnly. "Aren't you taking it tomorrow?"

"I'm ready," Ella Mae answered. "As long as Cyrus is set for the pie shop's inspection, we should be able to open next Saturday."

Verena clapped her hands, startling Chewy into wakefulness. She scooped up the terrier and planted a loud kiss on his nose. He licked her chin multiple times before wriggling free.

"Throw your bike in the trunk, Ella Mae!" Verena commanded. "I can't dillydally this afternoon so you'll have to pedal home. I've got a Junior League meeting followed by a Preservation Society supper. Oh, I hope they're serving shrimp and grits again! Last time, I had two helpings followed by a tower of strawberry shortcake!" She chuckled merrily. "I don't think there's a woman alive who loves her food more than me!"

Inside Verena's white Cadillac, Chewy perched on Ella Mae's lap. With his head stuck out the half-open window and his hindquarters receiving the benefit of the Caddy's efficient air-conditioning, he was a very happy dog. Flecks of drool peppered Verena's passenger window but she didn't seem to care.

"He's such a darling!" she exclaimed. "I tell all my friends that my grandnephew here is smarter and more charming than all of their two-legged grandbabies!"

Ella Mae laughed. "Why didn't you and Uncle Buddy ever have kids?"

A shadow crossed her aunt's face. In a low voice, which sounded foreign coming from Verena, she said, "We wanted children, but something's wrong with my plumbing. Buddy was willing to adopt, but then you came along and filled up the empty space in my heart."

Too moved to reply, Ella Mae squeezed her aunt's arm and then leaned against the soft leather seat, her chin lifted toward the sunlight streaming through the pine branches overhead. She wanted to hold on to this moment, the warmth that spread through her chest, the feeling that came from being loved and cherished by her three aunts. Smiling, she rubbed Chewy's back and thought about how to convince Dee to go along with her plan.

Verena turned onto the narrow lane leading to Delia's house and studio and dropped her speed dramatically. "You can never tell when one of Dee's pack will dart out from the bushes," she said, peering into the dense greenery lining the road. "I don't even know how many creatures she's caring for these days. No wonder she has to charge a fortune for her sculptures!"

Stopping the Caddy in front of the tobacco-barn-turned-studio, Verena gave both Chewy and Ella Mae pecks on the cheek before driving off again. Ella Mae leaned her bike against Dee's mailbox and braced herself for the entourage of mixed-breed dogs to welcome her.

Four of them trotted around the corner of the barn, their tails wagging even as they issued a few cautionary barks. Chewy immediately exchanged friendly sniffs with each and every one of them. Two cats, a black longhair and a shorthaired orange tabby, were stretched out in the protective shade provided by a pair of lawn chairs. They opened their eyes into thin slits, examined Ella Mae and the new canine with disinterest, and then went back to their naps.

Both the front and back door to Dee's studio were shut up tight and Ella Mae knew that her aunt kept her beloved animals out of the barn because much of her work required her to use a blowtorch and band saw. Even now, as Ella Mae peeked into the picture window, she could see a shower of red and gold sparks leaping into the air and ricocheting off the concrete floor. A Beethoven symphony tried to escape through the glass panes, but the window held the melancholy violins in check. Dee never worked without Beethoven and had often told Ella Mae that the composer was the love of her life.

As Ella Mae watched, Dee retracted the blue flame of the blowtorch and slipped off her face mask. Tendrils of wet hair clung to her forehead and a sheen of sweat covered her skin, but she didn't seem to notice. Taking a step back, she scrutinized her sculpture with a critical eye and then withdrew a photograph of a Welsh sheepdog from the front pocket of her overalls. Kneeling before the metal version, which Ella Mae imagined was still warm from the lick of the blue flame, Dee put her right hand on the chest of the dog she'd created and held the photo of the flesh-and-blood version against her own heart with the other.

"What is she doing?" Ella Mae murmured, spellbound by the odd ritual taking place on the other side of the window.

Dee shut her eyes and began to move her lips. Suddenly, a shimmer of pearly light raced across the surface of the sheepdog's metal fur, and for a split second, he glowed with the same blinding whiteness as the orb Ella Mae had seen the night her aunts and mother had dined with her at Le Bleu.

And then it winked out as if someone had thrown a switch. One moment it was there. The next, it was gone.

Dee sank back onto a nearby stool, her shoulders sagging in fatigue. She was breathing heavily, her back expanding and deflating as she drew oxygen into her lungs.

Ella Mae knocked loudly on the studio's wide wooden door and waited for her aunt to slide it open.

"Why, Ella Mae." Dee produced a tired smile. "What a nice surprise." She glanced out into the yard. "Did you bring Chewy?"

"He's making friends."

Dee looked pleased. "Dogs are social creatures. You

should put him in a playgroup at Canine to Five. He'd get plenty of exercise and you won't have to worry about him when you're at the pie shop."

"I'm supposed to be having coffee with Hugh Dylan right now," Ella Mae answered gloomily. "Instead I was taken away from Bradford Knox's funeral in a cop car. That always impresses the men."

Dee gestured for Ella Mae to enter the studio. "I didn't realize you were interested in impressing him."

Ella Mae averted her eyes. "Before I met Sloan, I spent lots of time trying to get Hugh to notice me. I guess moving back here has got me picking up where I left off."

Dee laughed a deep, melodious sound like that of church bells heard from a distance. "Just make him a pie and he'll be yours."

Walking over to the sheepdog sculpture, Ella Mae reached out her hand and then hesitated. "May I?"

"Of course. It's not hot anymore."

Her fingertips brushed the wire whiskers and then moved to cup the smooth stainless steel of the dog's snout. Each of his marble eyes seemed to be infused with a single spark from the blowtorch. "I don't know how you do it, Aunt Delia. I've seen you make fish, cats, dogs, hamsters, lizards, birds, guinea pigs, and even a snake or two, and their eyes all have this glow, like they really see you."

With a nod, Dee gave the sheepdog an affectionate pat. "In a sense, they do. This guy will be a big comfort to his grieving family. The elements won't bother him and he'll still stand guard over their home for years to come. I've been told that he's going to be placed on their front porch. That's why I have him positioned like this."

"Like he can see the family coming up the walk," Ella Mae guessed. "He's smiling, his tail is wagging, and any second now he'd going to bound down the steps to greet them."

"Exactly." Dee turned away from the sheepdog with a

hint of reluctance. "Let's go into the house. I could use a glass of lemonade and something to eat. I think I forgot to have lunch today."

As Dee fixed herself a tuna fish sandwich, Ella Mae examined the piles of envelopes lining the kitchen counter with astonishment. "Are all of these requests for your work?"

Dee nodded.

"California, Kansas, Vermont, Canada, Bermuda." Ella Mae read off postmarks from all over the northern hemisphere. "How can you handle this many?"

"I can't." Dee sat down at her table and cast an apologetic glance at the envelopes before biting into her sandwich.

"Have you ever thought about hiring an assistant?"

Dee didn't answer right away. "It's not that simple, Ella Mae. There are only a few people who can do what I do. I met a similar artist at a symposium in England last year. She lives in France and is sought after by clients all across Europe." Dee got up, grabbed a bag of potato chips from the counter, and dumped a mound onto her plate. "And there's an older woman working in China. We're the only ones using our . . . method to create animal memorials."

"Couldn't you train someone? Take on an apprentice?"

Dee broke a chip in half and studied the fissure she'd created. "There was a time when that would have been the norm. But times have changed." She popped the pieces in her mouth and chewed. "Speaking of hired help, you're going to need an extra pair of hands in the pie shop. Are you putting an ad in *The Daily*?"

Ella Mae poured herself a glass of Dee's tangy lemonade. "I don't expect to be that busy."

"Then you are underestimating Verena's bullying power. She'll have every citizen in Havenwood at your grand opening or she'll find some way to have them fined, jailed, or publically disgraced." Dee put the tuna fish can on the floor. Two black-and-white kittens materialized from nowhere, licked the can clean, and scampered away again.

"I have a million little details to take care of before I can open, but first I need to figure out what happened to Bradford Knox. The police aren't going to cross me off their suspect list now that they've found my prints on the murder weapon." She hesitated. "That's why I came, Aunt Dee. I need your help." It was difficult to ask her aunt for assistance in the presence of hundreds of envelopes filled with the pleas of the hurt and grieving, but Ella Mae didn't know what else to do.

Dee saw her niece's guilty expression and knew precisely what troubled her. "I comfort as many as I can. You're family, Ella Mae. Tell me what you need."

Ella Mae showed her the list of names from the memorial service. "These are horse people. And you know what a tight group *they* are. Six families own the most prominent breeding farms in the region. The competition between them is fierce."

"But you'd never know it when they're together," Dee added.

"Bradford's office manager said that he'd been keeping strange hours at work. At the funeral, I overheard Loralyn mention a scheme that ended up costing her fiancé his life." Ella Mae jabbed at the list of names with her finger. "This scheme has got to have something to do with these horse breeders. And if Loralyn's involved, then money is at the heart of the matter."

Dee looked thoughtful. "Well, Dr. Knox was an equine vet and if he took these thoroughbreds as clients, then he might have been using illicit methods to keep them on the track. Those poor racehorses are run until they drop. Maybe he found a way to keep them going longer or faster or for more races—or whatever results those owners and trainers needed."

"That's what I was thinking!" Ella Mae felt relieved that her aunt hadn't dismissed her theory as being nothing but silly speculation. "My plan was to insinuate myself among this group by telling them that you're now offering horse sculptures. They could commemorate the finest champions of their stables and be the envy of their friends."

Waving her hands in dismissal, Dee's voice remained soft and gentle even as she shook her head in refusal. "I can't do horses. They're too big, Ella Mae."

"Just one, Aunt Dee. And not to scale. How about the size of the ones you see on the weather vanes at all of those horse farms?"

"It won't be the same. The finished product wouldn't carry that spark, that memory of life that all my pieces do. It wouldn't be a genuine Delia LeFaye sculpture." She sighed. "Besides, these people don't see their horses as pets or family members, but as an income source. I can't work for those kinds of people."

Ella Mae wasn't quite sure how to respond to her aunt's statement so she sipped lemonade and absently crunched on potato chips. The afternoon had turned languid. Heat settled on the tree limbs and rooftops and the sun stole the green from the leaves and grass. Both women gazed out the kitchen window at the yellow-tinged yard and sighed. The timing of their combined sigh caused laughter to bubble forth from their throats.

"I'll do it. For you. A single horse," Dee said, her grin disappearing. "With one condition."

"Anything."

Dee rose and handed Ella Mae the list of signatures. "I can only make a piece for someone who cherished their animal. You'll have to find a candidate who really loved their horse, even if that horse didn't make them a penny."

Ella Mae readily agreed.

"How will you break into their circle?" Dee asked.

"I'm going to try to get Chandler Knox to invite me to the Mint Julep Gala," Ella Mae replied. "And if he doesn't ask me, then I'll go anyway."

Dee looked thoughtful. "You're going to need a killer

dress. Don't buy anything. I might have something you can use."

After thanking her aunt, Ella Mae loaded Chewy into the bike basket and headed for home. She wanted nothing more than to scrub her hands, put an apron on, and plunge her fingers into a ball of homemade dough. She needed to make a pie so creamy, rich, and seductive that offering it to Chandler Knox would be the same as showing up at his office wearing a raincoat with nothing on underneath.

"I need to think about this one for a spell," Ella Mae told Chewy.

Skipper Drive, the road to Partridge Hill, passed by the entrance to a small community park where Ella Mae had spent hours reading library books in the shade of an ancient oak tree. A shallow stream traversed a rolling meadow pocked with dandelions, and walking paths crisscrossed the grass and disappeared into the nearby woods.

Resting the bike in the dry grass, Ella Mae sat down with her back against the oak's comforting trunk and ran her hands over the ridges and crevices of the bark. The leaves of the canopy shifted in welcome and she smiled, relaxing enough to be able to concentrate not only on Chandler's pie, but also on the stock she needed to build up before opening the shop next Saturday.

Chewy dashed after squirrels, his tail wagging so fast that it became a white smudge against the grass, and then splashed into the stream. Ella Mae joined him, kicking off her shoes and wading into the cool water. The mud squelched between her toes and filtered sunlight speckled her hair and shoulders.

"You love it here, don't you, boy?" she asked her dog, who responded with a full-body shake, covering her face with droplets of water.

Ella Mae laughed and then reached into her pocket for Sloan's letter. Her hands seemed to act of their own accord, folding the letter into sharp creases, tucking folds into one another, and folding again. She made a perfect little paper boat whose sails were embellished with words that no longer formed logical sentences. Ella Mae set the craft into the stream's lackadaisical current and watched until it bobbed past the oak and disappeared from view.

"We're not going back," she told Chewy and, to prove her conviction, tore Sloan's check into several pieces and deposited the fragments into the nearest trash bin. "I don't need a man to fulfill my dreams. I've got everything I need right here." She wiggled her ten fingers at her terrier.

She spent the long bike ride home considering Loralyn and her equestrian acquaintances. Once again, she wondered what scheme Loralyn had devised to make herself wealthier and how Bradford Knox fit into the plan.

A line from *Pride and Prejudice* floated into her mind.

" 'It is very often nothing but our own vanity that deceives us,' " she murmured. "Is that what's going on with me? Do I want Loralyn to be guilty of a crime so badly that I'm not seeing other possibilities?"

Ella Mae mused over this worrisome thought until she pulled into the garage. Chewy leapt out of the bike basket before she could come to a stop, barking to announce his hunger until Reba appeared at the back door with his dinner dish in her hand.

"Hugh Dylan called while you were traipsin' all over the county!" Reba shouted over the heads of the rosebushes. "Seems you stood him up this afternoon!"

Stunned, Ella Mae began to walk toward Reba, her heart beating faster with each step "He called? I didn't think—"

Reba set Chewy's bowl on the ground. "Stop hollerin' and get your . . ." She trailed off, her eyes narrowing and looked in the direction of the guest cottage. As she passed Ella Mae, she grabbed her by the elbow and spun her around.

"Why are you sniffing the air?" Ella Mae asked. "That's how Chewy looks whenever I cook bacon."

Reba was inhaling deep breaths through her nose. Her face had turned hard.

"Someone's here," she growled lowly and increased her pace.

A shiver crawled up the back of Ella Mae's neck. She was alarmed to find that she could no longer detect the scent of her mother's roses or Reba's signature aroma of strawberries. A block of thunderclouds had obscured the sun, and though this was a typical occurrence during summer afternoons, Ella Mae sensed a change in the atmosphere in the garden that was more significant than the impending rain.

Upon reaching the door of the guest cottage, Reba pointed at the paper object protruding from the brass mail slot.

"Do you know what that is?" she asked, her eyes darting wildly about.

Ella Mae couldn't reply. She moved forward slowly, as if she were slogging through snow, and reached out to grasp hold of the paper boat she'd released at the park twenty minutes ago.

It wasn't even damp.

"It can't be. . . ." she whispered and unfolded the letter in disbelief. Sloan's check had been tucked into one of the creases and Ella Mae examined it in astonishment. It had been taped together so neatly that at first glance, it appeared unblemished.

"Was that writin' on that there before?" Reba pointed at the words written in block letters on the back of Sloan's missive.

GO BACK WHERE YOU BELONG, it said.

Now it was Ella Mae's turn to send crazed glances around the garden, inside the garage, and toward the path leading to the lake. She crushed the letter in her hands and shouted into the darkening sky, "You just try to get me to leave! I belong here!"

Reba stood still as a stone, listening hard. "They're gone."

She reached out for the paper. "I'll take care of this. You keep your mind on pies."

Ella Mae curled her fingers into fists. "Someone feels threatened by me. This has to be connected to Knox's death." She looked at Reba. "Did the cops come for the rolling pin?"

"They sure did. Wouldn't even let me hand it to them, even though you had it all bagged up." Reba was relaxing her stiff posture. The muscles in her face loosened and her tone resumed its blend of sassiness and verve. "I'd have put up a struggle in the hopes of being handcuffed, but neither officer was decent lookin'. And that's saying somethin', considerin' how much I like a man in uniform."

Ella Mae couldn't help but smile, but then her eyes fell on the note in Reba's hand and her mouth compressed into a thin line. "Is Daddy's old gun collection in his office?"

Reba nodded. "Sure is. Your mama's mighty fond of those guns, though we don't clean them half as often as we should."

"Let's clean them right now," Ella Mae said, steel entering her voice. "Because I hope this creep comes sneaking around here again. Next time, I'll stick a shotgun barrel out the mail slot and see if he or *she* still wants to threaten me!"

Grinning, Reba took a packet of licorice twists out of her pocket and handed one to Ella Mae. "Now you're talkin' like a real Georgia gal."

Chapter 11

Ella Mae pulled up in front of the Equine Center and smoothed the wrinkles from her white cotton skirt. She'd paired the skirt with a low-cut garnet-colored blouse and open-toed sandals, hoping Chandler Knox would find her attractive enough to invite her into his inner sanctum. But first, she'd have to get past Peggy.

It was clear that Bradford Knox's practice was bustling despite his absence. Horses were being walked on leads in one paddock, a small troupe of thoroughbreds ran in carefree, lazy circles in the field adjacent to the barn, and the whinnies of contented animals blended with the soft morning light. To Ella Mae, the scene looked like the cover of a puzzle box. It begged to be captured, and she stood by her car for a moment, drinking in the tranquility.

Staff members moved about the grounds, oblivious to her presence. Those on foot carried bridles or plastic bins containing bandages and medicine while others zoomed about in John Deere utility vehicles towing trailers of feed or maintenance tools.

The roar of a tractor's engine in one of the rear fields broke the enchantment, and Ella Mae gathered the pair of buttermilk chess pies she'd baked at five A.M. and headed into the office. Peggy was behind her desk, a phone tucked between ear and shoulder as she jotted notes in an appointment book. She gave Ella Mae a welcoming smile and gestured for her to take a seat in the waiting area.

When she finished her conversation, Peggy stood up and pointed at the two pies. "Well, now, what have we got here?"

"Buttermilk chess. Fresh from the oven." Ella Mae peeled back an inch of aluminum foil and let the sugar-laced aroma of baked crust escape into the air. The invisible curls enveloped Peggy, hinting at a taste almost too sweet to bear, and the office manager closed her eyes in anticipatory bliss. "You really want a job, don't you?"

Ella Mae couldn't deceive this woman any longer. "In all honesty, I'm going to open a pie shop. However, I'd still love a moment of Dr. Knox's time. You see, my aunt is a renowned metal sculptor and she's holding a lottery of sorts to raise money for area animal shelters." She handed Peggy a color brochure displaying some of Dee's most remarkable pieces.

Peggy gasped. "Oh, my word. They're lovely!"

"Thank you. She'll be making her inaugural horse sculpture and I figured your boss, Chandler, could tell me how I could rub elbows with the equestrian crowd." Ella Mae lowered her voice. "I hear they're a tight-knit group."

"Close as cousins and just as catty," Peggy said with a smirk and picked up the second pie. "But it's you're lucky day because the doc's next client had to cancel. Let me pop back there and tell him that a pretty lady bearing gifts would like to see him." Her smile wavered for a moment. "It still feels mighty strange to call him Dr. Knox, but I reckon I need to get used to it."

Ella Mae waited for Peggy to leave before easing behind the counter and examining the appointment book. Several names appeared to have been scratched out, and she wondered if Bradford's clients lacked confidence in his replacement. There was also an invoice in Peggy's inbox bearing a yellow Post-it note and a large, red question mark. Glancing toward the door leading deeper into the clinic, Ella Mae risked a closer look at the invoice. Apparently, a company called Uraeus Pharmaceuticals sought twenty thousand dollars in payment for a shipment of anti-inflammatory supplies.

"Expensive medicine," Ella Mae murmured to herself and stepped away from the desk just as Peggy opened the door.

"Come on back! Dr. Knox is already working on his pie. He left home without breakfast this morning, and after taking one bite, he said he'd reschedule all of his clients if it was your wish." She pointed down the hall. "From the look on his face, I'd say he meant it too. Go on. Third door on the left."

Ella Mae walked down the wide corridor and came to a halt in front of Chandler's office. He was seated behind an impressive oak desk, upon which papers and patient charts were strewn untidily. He had his eyes closed and was licking his fork with obvious pleasure.

Unable to keep from grinning, Ella Mae asked, "Any good?"

Chandler jumped to his feet, the fork still clutched in his hand. He looked like a guilty child overindulging on cookies right before suppertime. "I wasn't exactly striking a professional pose, was I?" He gave her a little contrite smile and then pointed at the pie. "But this . . . it's beyond delicious. One taste and I was a kid again. Barefoot, toes in the sand, chewing on saltwater taffy. All my cares vanished. I couldn't stop eating. Who wouldn't want to feel like that in the middle of a workday?"

Ella Mae wondered how many burdens had fallen on Chandler's broad shoulders since his father's death. "It must be hard to have to fill your dad's shoes so suddenly," she said softly. "But I imagine it's also a great comfort to his clients to know that you'll be caring for their horses."

"Thank you. Um, Peggy told me your name and something about your artist aunt, but I'm afraid this pie has wiped my mind clear of intelligent thought, so how I can be of service?" He glanced at the pile of journals on the room's only spare chair and leapt forward to remove them, knocking another stack of paperwork from the top of his desk onto the floor.

Laughing, Chandler and Ella Mae both dropped to their knees and began to collect patient charts and magazines. Chandler said. "Don't look at this as a reflection of my skills as a vet, okay?"

Nodding, Ella Mae handed him the latest issue of *Thoroughbred Times*. "Are these your clients? Famous racehorses?"

The glint of amusement vanished from Chandler's eyes. "Just a few. My father handled most of the top-notch racers and I'm still trying to win them over. The owners aren't partial to change, and the trainers are even worse, but I'm making some headway."

Ella Mae handed him the brochure of Dee's sculptures. "I'm hoping to mingle with the racing set in order to raise money for our area's animal shelters, but I'm not sure how to break into their circle. Even though I grew up a few towns away, I'm not a horse enthusiast," she added apologetically.

"Don't worry, I won't take you out back and shoot you," Chandler said, looking over the brochure with interest. "These are incredible. I had a dog named Butterfinger who could have been this guy's twin." He pointed at one of Dee's most famous pieces, a golden retriever leaping in the air to catch a Frisbee. "I still miss that big, drooling hairball. He was the best dog a boy ever had."

Emotions flitted across Chandler's face as he studied the photograph of the sculpture. His wistful expression made him look young and vulnerable, and Ella Mae felt a twinge of conscience for using a man who'd just lost his father to gain access to the elite equestrian crowd. And yet, a murderer was on the loose, and who wouldn't want to see that killer apprehended more than Chandler Knox?

"I read about the Mint Julep Gala in *The Havenwood Daily*," she said brightly, hoping to chase away the shadow of memory and that her lack of subtly wouldn't put Chandler off. "Are you going?"

At the mention of the exclusive fête, Chandler perked up. "Yes, and it would be the perfect place to spread the word about your aunt's work." He came around his desk to return the brochure. There was a moment of awkward silence as he cast a glance of unveiled longing at the buttermilk pie. He then studied Ella Mae with a similar hunger, and she felt her cheeks growing warm. "Would you like to be my date?"

Ella Mae told herself that neither Chandler's boyish charm nor his all-American good looks influenced her decision. She told herself that she wasn't interested in men and therefore had not noticed the streaks of gold in his sandy hair, the glimmers of caramel in his large brown eyes, or his obvious love of animals.

"That would be wonderful," she answered quickly and gave him her address.

She was dictating directions to her place when his pen abruptly froze, its point pressing hard into the paper.

"Sulphur Springs?" His voice had turned cold. "Isn't Rolling View Farm on that road?"

"Yes, the Gaynors are neighbors of ours."

Chandler scowled. "Loralyn Gaynor was almost my stepmother, if you can imagine such a thing."

"That's an unpleasant thought." Ella Mae rapidly covered her mouth as if she hadn't meant to let that remark slip. "Sorry, but Loralyn and I went to school together and we didn't exactly get along." She picked at a loose thread on her blouse. "She was a bully back then, but I shouldn't put her down. She was your dad's fiancée, so she must have changed, or he wouldn't have wanted to marry her."

Masking his emotions, Chandler shrugged. "You'll be able to judge for yourself. I'm sure she'll be at the gala."

Probably on the hunt for her next husband, Ella Mae thought wryly.

A buzzer sounded and Peggy's voice emitted through the intercom on Chandler's desk. "Dr. Knox, your next appointment is here." A pause followed by a whisper. "It's Mr. Culpeper and he is *not* happy. Says they lost last weekend's race because you didn't give their horse the right medicine. Just wanted you to know you've got a live one waiting for you."

"Thank you, Peggy." Chandler shook his head and gave Ella Mae a small smile of resignation. "These are the charming folks you'll be socializing with Friday night. Pick you up at seven?"

By Friday afternoon, Ella Mae was exhausted. She'd woken early to ensure that she'd be able to bake in The Charmed Pie Shoppe's sparkling new kitchen for a full eight hours.

Crooning along to the country radio station, Ella Mae had tested out every commercial appliance and workspace. The ovens browned perfectly, the mixer blended flour and butter into the perfect pea-sized consistency necessary for piecrust, and the cutting board service of the prep table seemed to welcome having its unblemished surface altered by the knick of the knife. The walk-in freezer was stuffed with balls of dough and dozens of unbaked savory and dessert pies. Rows of fresh, locally grown fruit filled the large refrigerator, waiting patiently for Ella Mae's hands to release their untapped essence.

Singing the latest Carrie Underwood hit with abandon, Ella Mae washed spring greens and halved pecans. She added goat cheese, dried cranberries, and a balsamic vinaigrette to the lettuce and tossed all the ingredients in a large stainless steel bowl. It was time to put her recipes to the test.

Cyrus and the rest of the workmen showed up at noon. Dressed in clean T-shirts and jeans, they sat down at the laminated tables in the dining area and placed napkins demurely on their laps.

"This sure is nice of you, ma'am," Cyrus said, removing his baseball cap in deference. "No one's ever cooked for us before."

"Maybe you should make it a stipulation of your contract." Ella Mae twirled in a circle around the pie shop, her arms outspread. "Look at this place! You guys did this! It's exactly how I dreamed it would be. Warm, inviting, fun, casual. I think people will want to linger here."

One of the men nodded. "It sure is cozy." Then, instantly embarrassed by the remark, he added, "But the smell is what's gonna drag folks in from the streets. My stomach started rumblin' like a monster truck from a block away."

His colleague reached over and poked the soft rise of flesh that pulled the fabric of the NASCAR T-shirt taut. "You're not gonna waste away any time soon, pal."

"Not if I can help it," Ella Mae declared and fetched their lunches.

The men were treated to glasses of iced tea flavored with a twinge of mint, Ella Mae's mixed-green salad, and a sampling of two of the savory items from the regular menu. The first was a bacon, Gruyère cheese, and onion tart and the second was a tomato and feta cheese quiche.

For dessert, she served coffee and a selection of sweet treats, including a slice of chocolate peanut butter tart, a piece of apple caramel pie, and a rectangle of triple berry crostata.

The men ate every morsel on their plates, showering Ella Mae with compliments. She pleaded for constructive criticism, explaining that she wouldn't truly be prepared for next week's grand opening until she found something to improve upon.

"The only thing I have to say is that you can't cook, take orders, serve drinks, and bus the tables by yourself," Cyrus said. "This place is gonna be busier than a mall on Black Friday. You need another pair of hands. Or two."

"I put an ad in *The Daily*," Ella Mae said. "I just hope I can find the right person."

Cyrus wiped his mouth with a paper napkin and gazed around the shop with proprietary affection. "This shop'll let you know who's right. It was just waiting for you to come along and fill it up with folks talking and laughing and enjoying home-cooked food. This is gonna be a merry place, the heart of the whole town. Wait and see." He cleared his throat, stood, and gave Ella Mae a deep bow. "You brought it to life, Ella Mae, and now it's going to bring you to life. We're honored to have been a part of it all. Thank you for the wonderful meal."

Moved, Ella Mae felt her eyes turn moist. She took in the shining black-and-white floor tile, the café au lait walls, the pristine white crown molding, and the shining glass display cases.

Already, the room had begun to fill up with light. The aromas from the kitchen, the banter of the workmen, and Ella Mae's sense of pride and belonging stretched forth and laid claim on the little cottage. Before long, Ella Mae would be welcoming Reba, her mother, and her aunts to lunch for the very first time. During that occasion, another memory would bloom within the pie shop's walls, bursting forth with the same heady brightness of the roses climbing up the porch columns. Soon, the space would overflow with stories, old and new.

And yet, a shadow remained. It waited, carefully concealed, as tense as a big cat poised to spring. There was still a killer in Havenwood. It was impossible to cover the taint of murder with butter, flour, and sugar. The stolen rolling pin, the threat penned on the back of Sloan's letter, the sense that someone didn't welcome her return—these things would rob Ella Mae's fresh start of its luster if she couldn't help restore justice. And soon.

This knowledge tempered some of the joy she felt over

having served a successful first meal in The Charmed Pie Shoppe, but the traces of gloom couldn't keep their purchase as Ella Mae loaded the dishwasher and swept the kitchen floor. The shop was too sun kissed, too replete with cheer.

Smiling at the gleaming kitchen, Ella Mae locked up and dropped the keys in the pocket of her cherry-print apron. They jingled all the way home, as vibrant and rhythmic as a human heart.

Hearing the doorbell, Ella Mae checked her reflection once more in the mirror and then descended the stairs in a whisper of mint-hued tulle. The strapless vintage gown, delivered on Friday afternoon by Aunt Dee, had been wrapped in tissue paper inside a cardboard box. Removing the lid, Ella Mae peeled back the tissue paper, inhaling the traces of honeysuckle escaping from the folds. When she ran her hand over the delicate lace trim on the shelf bust to the tulle of the flirty skirt, she heard a soft whoosh, like sand being shifted by the wind.

She laid the exquisitely tailored dress on the bed and admired the way the light shimmered over the fabric and wondered where Dee had worn it.

The dress fit Ella Mae perfectly and she couldn't help but notice how the rich pale green gown complemented her bronze skin and whiskey-colored hair, which fell in loose curls over her shoulders.

Chandler took one look at her and fell speechless, mutely offering her a bouquet of long-stemmed pink roses. "Not that you need any," he finally said when he managed to find his tongue. "You live in a sea of roses."

"Those are my mother's. I wouldn't dream of cutting them," Ella Mae answered, accepting his gift. "You look very handsome."

Smoothing the lapel of his tux, Chandler grinned. "I'm

just a penguin. You're the swan. The most beautiful woman in Georgia will be on my arm tonight."

On the way to the gala, which was being held in a banquet room at the Lake Havenwood Hotel, Ella Mae did her best to find out what kind of man Chandler Knox was.

During the short ride, she learned that he'd had a carefree childhood, loved all animals, and had wanted to follow in Bradford's footsteps ever since his father had taken him along on a house call. A mare was having a difficult labor but Bradford managed to save the day and Chandler was able to witness a live birth. He'd never forgotten the wonder of that moment and vowed to become an equine veterinarian like his father.

"I'm no horse whisperer," Chandler admitted without guile. "And I know people think my dad was more skilled, but I'm using state-of-the-art equipment and techniques. I can only gain the experience he had over time."

Ella Mae folded her hands over her purse, which contained the list of those who'd attended Bradford Knox's memorial service. One of the gala guests could be a suspect. So could Chandler, for that matter. Hadn't Peggy said that Bradford hadn't been willing to take his own son on as a full partner? Surely, that kind of paternal rejection must have wounded Chandler to a degree. Ella Mae knew exactly how a wound like that could fester. After all, had her mother called her once in the seven years she'd been married to Sloan?

"So did you and your daddy split the workload at the practice? Were you both equal partners?" she asked innocently.

Chandler's brow furrowed. "He didn't think I was ready to take over, but then he met Loralyn and suddenly changed his tune. It was like he wasn't as interested in the daily goings-on at work anymore and he left me in charge of everything but the thoroughbred house calls. That woman . . ." He paused, the muscles of his jaw tightening. "She bewitched him, I swear."

Ella Mae touched him lightly on the arm. "I'm sorry, I didn't mean to bring up a painful topic. Do you have siblings? Someone to help you out during this tough time."

"A baby sister. Ashleigh. But she wouldn't lift a pinkie to help me. Never worked a day in her life, that one, but she still wants to spend money like she's married to Midas."

After telling Chandler that she'd met a few women similar to Ashleigh back in New York, Ella Mae asked, "Did your dad spoil her?"

Chandler snorted. "All the time. He gave her money, especially after her latest husband moved out. Regular payments, as if she was an actual employee. Now she wants me to take up where Dad left off, but I think it's high time for her to earn her own living." He ran his hand through his hair and shot Ella Mae a quick, abashed glance. "Do you think I'm a total jerk right now?"

She shook her head. "Not at all. You sound like you have too many worries and could *really* use a mint julep."

He laughed and the sound bubbled around the car cabin like a fast-moving river. "That's certainly true. Oh, I am so glad you walked into my office the other day. I'm feeling pretty worry-free at the moment."

The air between them changed abruptly. The casual feeling was supplanted by the weight of the desire in Chandler's brown eyes. Ella Mae flashed him a quick smile and then faced forward. She didn't want to acknowledge Chandler's yearning. Not only was he a possible suspect—though she was reluctant to view him as one—but she also wasn't interested in romance.

Involuntarily, she thought of Hugh Dylan. If there was anyone in the world she'd take a leap of faith for, it was Hugh. But she'd blown that chance. She'd never even returned his phone call. Too embarrassed to talk to him, she hoped it would be some time before they ran into one another in town.

I don't want to have to protest my innocence when I see him again, Ella Mae thought. *I want to prove it. Irrevocably. Maybe then I'll have the courage to reschedule our coffee date.*

Chandler pulled up to the front of the hotel and a valet raced around to his side and opened his door. A bellhop opened Ella Mae's and wished her a pleasant evening as he helped her out of the car. Dapper men in tuxedos escorted women in sequined gowns and floor-length dresses into the lobby. From there, the gentry of northern Georgia were filtered into the ballroom.

Upon entering, each partygoer was given a sterling julep cup filled with the signature cocktail. Ella Mae was pleasantly surprised to find a table of nametags and saw that all the guests had stopped to collect theirs.

"Don't you all know each other?" she asked Chandler.

"Mostly, but there are people from all over the country here tonight. If they're not local, their home state will be printed below their names." He gazed around the room, a glint of boyish eagerness in his eyes. "The crème de la crème of the racing world under one roof."

The room was sparkling like sunshine on calm water. The women's diamonds, Waterford chandeliers, sterling julep cups, and gold-plated flatware fought to surpass one another in brilliance.

Chandler wasted no time introducing Ella Mae to the other guests. Most of them were familiar with Dee's work and wanted to claim the honor of being the first client to have one of their horses transformed into a metal masterpiece.

However, the more Ella Mae spoke with the owners, the more she saw that the animals in their stables served a singular purpose: to earn money. She met six couples who'd attended Bradford Knox's funeral and yet appeared completely disinterested in him. However, two other couples exhibited odd behavior when she casually inserted his name into their conversation.

The first pair, a Mr. and Mrs. Hollowell, were very friendly and animated right until the moment Ella Mae asked if their racehorses had been treated by Bradford. Shooting a nervous glance at her husband, Mrs. Hollowell had pretended to spot an acquaintance. Apologizing to Ella Mae, the couple hurried toward the bar. Ella Mae ducked behind a potted palm and watched as the Hollowells huddled together away from the other guests, exchanging anxious murmurs. Their bodies were rigid with tension and their shifting eyes betrayed their fear.

Circling their names on her list as being worthy of further investigation, Ella Mae slipped the paper back into her purse and sought out the Malones. According to Reba's gossip chain, the Malones had faced a racing slump that threatened their reputation as a prominent and lucrative stud farm. Ever since they'd switched veterinarians and began receiving visits from Knox, their thoroughbreds had captured several first- and second-place purses over a remarkable short period of time.

Armed with this information, Ella Mae located the couple at the same moment the dinner gong sounded. Chandler was in the restroom and she didn't dare hesitate in case her quarry escaped, so she took a seat at one the tables next to Mr. Malone, a debonair gentleman in his seventies with wavelets of silver hair and a splendid mustache. He eyed Ella Mae appreciatively and began a flirtation with her. Judging from his breath, Mr. Malone had consumed his token mint julep and had graduated to gin and tonics. Shaking his empty glass, he waved a waiter over and ordered another.

Once his drink had been delivered, Ella Mae showed him Dee's brochure. He immediately passed it to his wife, his attention already divided between his cocktail and Ella Mae's décolletage.

"I'm fascinated by thoroughbred racing," Ella Mae lied, leaning conspiratorially toward her neighbor. "Is it true that the jockeys of competing stables often get into fistfights off the track?"

"And on it too," Malone said, his forehead rippling in ire. "We lost a good horse because one of our wetback riders cut off another taco eater around a tight curve. He didn't have the room, that fool. He took out the other guy, sure, but our Max's Millions would never race again after that day."

Shocked, Ella Mae struggled to ignore the racial slurs. Instead, she asked, "What happened to your horse?"

Malone took a slug of his drink. "When they can't earn out anymore, they have to go. I'm a businessman and I don't fill my stable with charity cases."

A middle-aged woman with a kind and weathered face, who'd joined the table during the tail end of their conversation, picked up her bread knife and pointed it at Malone. "What he means to say, dear, is that the horses who turn lame or are just too slow or too old get turned into dog food. Or glue."

This was not what Ella Mae wanted to hear. Still, she needed to press Malone further. She pivoted, pretending to be hanging on his every word, but he was staring down the newcomer with obvious dislike.

Ella Mae touched his arm in order to reclaim his attention. "You must have some secret," she purred. "To have become so successful. I mean, you practically glow with power. So tell me." She inched in closer. "What's your secret? An incredible trainer? Special feed? Powerful medicine?"

At the mention of medicine, a prideful gleam appeared in Malone's eyes. "We do have a magic potion of sorts."

The woman, whose freckled cheeks were flushed pink from too many juleps, slurred, "You weren't the only ones Knox was supplying. Plenty of snakes in the grass in your own backyard with their share of magic potion. I guess one of you wouldn't stand for that kind of competition, huh?"

Ella Mae turned to the woman, her eyes round with mock innocence. "Bradford Knox? Wasn't he the victim of a horrible tragedy?"

She nodded. "It's a real shame. Once upon a time, he was a decent man." She gave her mint julep cup a wistful glance. "Racing isn't what it used to be. The purity's gone. In the beginning, people lived for the thunder of hoofs against the brown dirt track. Horses were treated like royalty. Now, they're like slaves. It's all tainted by drugs and greed and—"

"Don't pay that old hippie any mind," Malone growled menacingly.

Ella Mae was just about to ask the woman her name when Chandler appeared at the table. "I'm sorry," he said, touching Ella Mae on her bare shoulder. "I can't stay at this party another second."

Chandler's features were pinched with anger. Ella Mae rose to her feet and pulled him aside. "What's wrong?"

"Loralyn Gaynor just showed up, acting for all the world like she didn't just lose the man she supposedly loved." He swallowed hard. "I can't sit here, eating filet mignon and crab cake, while my father's fiancée shames his memory by fawning all over her new man."

Curious, Ella Mae's gaze flitted around the room. "I understand completely. Show me where she is so we can leave without walking too close."

"There, to the right of the stage with her stud boyfriend."

Ella Mae spotted Loralyn immediately. She flaunted a form-fitting white gown and a stunning necklace of diamonds and pearls. Her mouth stretched into a wide, white-toothed smile as she poked the mint spring from her glass into the buttonhole of her date's jacket.

The room suddenly turned so cold that Ella Mae felt her heart freeze beneath her ribcage. The most important muscle in her body felt brittle, like a hunk of ice threatening to shatter should she dare breathe.

"Do you know that guy?" Chandler asked.

She nodded, stricken.

Loralyn had come to the gala on the arm of Hugh Dylan.

Chapter 12

Loralyn let her hand linger on Hugh's chest and then she scanned the room, her eyes glittering with a joie de vivre incongruent with that of a woman grieving over the loss of a fiancé. Chandler watched her fixedly. His anger was a living thing, charging the air with red heat. Ella Mae could almost smell something burning.

"Come on," she said. "Don't let her get to you."

But Loralyn had spotted them. With a haughty smile, she crossed the dance floor, the disco ball throwing starlight onto her white dress. Dozens of guests turned from their meals to stare as the blonde beauty glided from one end of the room to the other.

Without missing a beat, Loralyn threw her arms around Chandler and kissed him noisily on the cheek. "It's lovely to see you."

Chandler was vibrating with rage. "Don't touch me," he growled, unceremoniously pushing her away.

Aware of how many sets of eyes were upon her, Loralyn remained perfectly poised, her face glowing with self-assurance. These were her people. She was at home in this jeweled and tailored crowd.

On the other hand, Chandler was just a veterinarian—a man whose living depended on winning the approval of the esteemed guests in this room. Should any of them denounce his skills as a veterinarian, his career would be reduced from treating thoroughbreds to inoculating farm animals and petting-zoo ponies.

Ella Mae knew she had to protect his future by getting him out of there.

"We have to run," she said in a light, carefree voice. "You look stunning tonight, Loralyn. Enjoy the gala." She offered Chandler her arm. "Ready?"

But Chandler could not stop glaring at his father's fiancée. He didn't even blink. It was as if Loralyn's face had gone Gorgon and had turned him into a block of stone. Only Hugh's appearance, which had been delayed because he opted to skirt the perimeter of the room in lieu of crossing the dance floor, interrupted the staring match between the two.

"Ella Mae." Her name rolled from Hugh's lips like a warm whisper against her skin. "You're beautiful."

What she would have done to freeze time, to remain the center of Hugh's attention, his eyes drinking in the sight of her, clearly liking what he saw. But Loralyn's mouth curved into a scythelike smile and she gestured at Ella Mae's gown with an elegant finger.

"Is your dress old? Looks like it just came out of a steamer trunk in the attic."

There wasn't a trace of scorn in her voice, but it swam in her eyes like a barracuda moving through the shallows.

"How could you?" Chandler hissed, refusing to let Loralyn focus on anyone else but him. "How can you show up and act like my father wasn't murdered? That he wasn't bashed on the head and left to burn?" His voice wavered. "Didn't you care about him at all?"

"Of course I did, sugar. But I'm not dead. I'm young and alive and ready to seize life by the throat. I'm sorry about your daddy, but he and I were more partners than passionate lovers." She was on the verge of an Oscar-winning pout. "You can't be angry with me forever," she sulked. "Can't we be friends?"

Chandler struggled with his reply. Ella Mae knew he had to remain civil to Loralyn as long as people were watching them. He nodded and then took Ella Mae's arm. "Shall we?" he asked her.

Hugh took a step toward Ella Mae. "Wait. Why didn't you return my calls? I thought we—"

"Hugh, darling." Loralyn touched his elbow, a hint of reprimand in her fingertips. "We'd better mosey on over to our table. I haven't eaten all day and am feeling a touch light-headed."

It was like a switch had been flipped in Hugh's brain. He wished Chandler and Ella Mae a pleasant evening and immediately pivoted his body toward Loralyn's, giving her fingers a stronger claim on his arm.

Chandler waited for the valet to collect his car and then he drove Ella Mae home without uttering a word. When he parked in her driveway, she thanked him for giving her the opportunity to hand out Dee's brochures and told him that she'd had a nice time despite Loralyn's arrival.

"I shouldn't have dragged you out of there. It was childish of me. It's just that my parents had such a loving relationship and so, when Loralyn entered the picture, it felt like an offense against my mom's memory. To see her tonight, completely untouched by my dad's death . . . it was too much." He looked chagrined. "I'm going to put your aunt's pamphlets out at the office, but is there anything else I can do to make up for your having to leave the ball before midnight?"

Ella Mae returned his brief smile. "I met a woman who made several remarks about the inhumane treatment of thoroughbred racehorses. I believe she adopts some of the, ah, retired horses."

Chandler nodded knowingly. "Annie Beaufort. She's got a farm between here and Little Kentucky. It's part government subsidized because she takes on troubled teens to help her run the place. It's got a flaky name. Relaxing Ranch or something. But don't set your sights on her. She barely has enough feed for her horses. I doubt she'll be ordering a sculpture anytime soon."

Opening her door before Chandler decided he wanted to prolong the evening, Ella Mae said, "Probably not, but she seemed like an interesting person."

"You do too, Ella Mae. I'd like to get to know you better."

She smiled. "Then come to the grand opening of The Charmed Pie Shoppe. You'll see me in my truest form. Oh, and bring everyone you know!"

"I will," he promised, unable to disguise the flicker of disappointment over her hasty exit.

Ella Mae waited until he was gone and then opened the front door to release Chewy. He leapt around her knees, fervently licking her hands, wrists, and ankles. After a quick visit to the edge of the woods, she and Chewy wandered through her mother's gardens.

Once her restlessness had subsided, Ella Mae sat on the stone bench where the young lovers she'd met at the police station had gotten engaged and reviewed the list from her cocktail bag. She made notes detailing her observations of both the Hollowells and the Malones, writing by the light of the new moon, while Chewy chased fireflies and white-winged moths.

"Annie Beaufort seems to know all about the dark underbelly of the racing world," Ella Mae mused while fingering the soft petals of the rosebushes behind her. As usual, the ones in the center of the path bore only tight, secretive buds. Not a single flower was in bloom. "And she mentioned

Bradford Knox too. We'll have to pay her a visit once we're done hiring our first employee."

The rose she caressed released a heady vanilla scent. Ella Mae closed her eyes and inhaled, recalling every word Hugh Dylan had spoken, the movements of his body, and the way the intensity in his eyes had instantly faded at Loralyn's command.

"Never mind," she told herself and scooped up Chewy, placing him on the bench beside her. "The only man I'm looking for has to wear an apron, carry an order pad, and have enough charisma to talk the most disciplined dieters into a wedge of dessert pie."

Two days later, Ella Mae was sitting at a table at The Charmed Pie Shoppe waiting for the first applicant to arrive to be interviewed for the position of server/cashier. That's how she'd advertised the position in *The Daily*, knowing full well that whomever she hired would have to wear more than one hat.

The appointment had been set for two in the afternoon and it was nearly two thirty. A second applicant was scheduled for three o'clock.

Glancing at her watch, Ella Mae paced back and forth in front of the display cases. She'd set out doilies on each shelf and had printed placards waiting to identify each pie, tart, or specialty item. Her daily specials would be written on a whiteboard near the cash register while the regular menu items were printed on a sign positioned on the back wall behind the display cases. The signage company had delivered exactly what Ella Mae requested—a menu that could be read from across the room while still retaining a vintage diner feel.

Two thirty came and went and Ella Mae began to get angry. She could be doing something useful. Instead, she alternated between pacing, examining the time, and flipping through pages of *Bon Appétit*.

At five minutes to three, she picked up her pen and put three black lines through the applicant's name in her notebook.

"Let's see if Meg Singer can manage to show up," she told Chewy, who was napping behind the counter and didn't stir at the sound of her voice.

Ella Mae needn't have worried. With a minute to spare, the pink raspberry front door opened to the merry jingle of sleigh bells. A young woman entered and momentarily ceased chewing what must have been an enormous piece of gum in order to gape at the bells hanging from the inside doorknob.

"Cool," she said, shifting the gum around again. "Like Christmas." Approaching Ella Mae's table, she thrust out a hand whose fingernails had been chewed right down to the beds. The cuticles were dirty and every finger sported a cheap silver ring. "Hey. Meg Singer."

She's not fond of complete sentences, Ella Mae thought and struggled to tear her gaze away from Meg's hands.

"It's a pleasure to meet you. I thought we'd just chat a bit about your employment history. Have you ever worked in the food industry before?"

"Nope." Meg twisted one of her rings and slid it to the end of her finger, revealing a circle of dirt on her skin below the knuckle. "But I'm bored at the job I have. None of the guys are hot."

Ella Mae asked a few more perfunctory questions and then thanked Meg for stopping by. Meg blew an enormous bubble, popped it crookedly so that it clung to her top lip, and used her filthy fingers to pry the gum free and place it back into her mouth.

The next applicant was a sweet elderly lady whose tongue wagged tirelessly. Despite her friendly demeanor, she moved with the alacrity of a tree sloth and was adamant in her refusal to handle the cash register.

"Those contraptions aren't for me," the woman declared. "Anythin' that needs button pushin' is the work of the devil."

That ruled out the register as well as every one of the state-of-the-art commercial kitchen appliances.

Sighing, Ella Mae proceeded to interview a retired army officer who was interested in earning extra cash. He and Ella Mae struck up an easy rapport and just when she thought her search for an employee was over, the sergeant let her know what he expected to be paid and Ella Mae nearly fell off her chair. Head chefs in top Manhattan restaurants didn't make that kind of money, let alone the wait staff.

By the end of the day, her pool of potential candidates had run dry. Not one of them fit the picture she'd formed of her right-hand man or woman.

Dejected, she whistled for Chewy and led him out to the front porch. She sat on the stoop, inhaling the perfume of her mother's roses and wondering how her mother had bred a flower that smelled faintly of warm sugar and vanilla.

"You look like your ice cream just fell outta your cone," Reba said, appearing from around the side of the building, a white shopping bag in her hand. "Your mama did a good job with the patio garden. The way she blended basil, rosemary, and lavender plants with the clusters of geraniums and black-eyed Susans—it's as cheerful as a kindergarten room."

Ella Mae made a gesture that encompassed the entire eatery, from its butter yellow clapboard to its sparkling windows to the tables shaded by pink and white striped umbrellas on the patio. "It's a slice of heaven, there's no doubt about it, but I won't be able to keep this place open long if people have to wait thirty minutes to be served."

"No luck finding suitable help?"

"None." Ella Mae gave Reba a quick rundown of the applicants.

Reba started giggling when Ella Mae told her about Meg

and her less-than-hygienic appearance. "I'm glad you're amused. This is the one thing I've got going for me and it's on the verge of falling apart."

Pulling a licorice twist from inside her purse, Reba picked up the notebook and held the candy poised over a blank page. "Well? Do I look the part?"

Ella Mae couldn't help but grin. "You'd be the world's best waitress, Reba. You're neat, fast, friendly, have a great memory, and could coerce people into stuffing themselves silly."

"Does that mean I'm hired?"

"As if." Ella Mae's smile faded. "You've been with my mother for decades. She'd never let you go."

Reba's eyes were twinkling with mischief as she pulled a gift-wrapped package from the shopping bag. "She already has." Reba handed the present to Ella Mae.

Perplexed, she ripped open the box and drew forth a custom-printed apron. It was a pale peach and had a rolling pin embroidered in the center. Above the graphic was the name of the shop. Below was the phrase, "That's How I Roll."

"I came up with the slogan," Reba stated proudly. She'd taken one of several aprons from the shopping bag and tied it around her tiny waist. "It's a mite big on me. I guess your average waitress isn't quite so vertically challenged." She touched her nut brown hair, which was styled into an interesting wave cresting over from her forehead. "Good thing I can add a few inches with a dozen sprays of Aqua Net."

Ella Mae pressed the apron to her chest. It smelled of roses and strawberries. Reba and her mother. "Do you really want to do this? I still have time to find a server. You don't need to—"

"I'm sick of cleaning a house that barely gets dirty. It's like a museum in there. This girl's ready for some excitement, a little flirting, and a change of scenery. I want to go home with tired feet and a brain stuffed with conversation and colors and scents. I might not be a young filly, but I defy you to find someone who could do this job better."

"Not possible. And I'd love to have you at my side. It'll be just like the old days when we used to cook together."

Reba opened her arms and invited Ella Mae in for a hug. "You've gone way past my level, honey."

The two women held one another for a long moment and then Ella Mae stepped back and asked, "Who'll take over for you at Partridge Hill?"

"Remember Kelly, that sweet gal you met at the police station? Your mama hired her. Noel got a raise at his job and it won't be long before the two of them can buy that little house they've been dreaming of." She examined her apron with obvious pleasure. "Things have a way of working themselves out, don't they?"

"Maybe this place truly is charmed," Ella Mae turned and smiled at the façade of her eatery. "If only I could work some magic and solve Bradford Knox's murder."

"One enchantment at a time, milady," Reba said with a crooked smile. "Now let's call up your aunts and set up a practice run. For me, that is. You could do this job in your sleep."

Ella Mae reached for her cell phone. "How does an old-fashioned chicken pot pie sound to you?"

Reba considered the question. "If Verena's coming, you'd best make two."

With the pie shop's opening only two days away, Ella Mae found herself with nothing to do. The kitchen was loaded with supplies, the tables had been set, the menu posted. She'd taught Reba how to use the cash register and *The Daily* had run a front-page article announcing Saturday morning's ribbon-cutting ceremony. Her mother would drop by on Friday with bud vases containing greenery and a single rose matching the shade of the café's butter yellow clapboard.

And while she was prepared, she was not in the least relaxed. Ever since Sloan's letter had been crammed into her mail slot, Ella Mae had felt uneasy. Whether she was working alone in the pie shop, taking Chewy on a bike ride, or running errands around town, the weight of Bradford's murder hung over her like a thundercloud.

"I'm not going to give up!" she boldly announced to the rose-covered façade of The Charmed Pie Shoppe and then had spent the morning making a dozen pies. They were now safely loaded into her mother's Suburban. It was Ella Mae's intention to drive out to Annie Beaufort's ranch and worm more information out of the horse lover in exchange for the pies.

Reba, ever a font of local knowledge, had written detailed directions to Annie's place in her spidery hand. As she drove farther and farther away from Havenwood, Ella Mae was grateful to have a guide, for Respite Ranch was located off a trio of unmarked roads. Nestled at the base of the green hills that eventually gave way to a line of proud mountains, the ranch looked like an oasis.

The fenced paddocks sprawled for miles, anchored by a collection of stables and a log cabin–style home. An addition that resembled a college dormitory had been tacked onto one wing without the slightest attempt to match the current architecture. Despite this boxy structure, the overall impression was of deep tranquility. This was a place made more beautiful by its surroundings, borrowing colors and scents from the hills and glades.

Ella Mae parked the truck in front of the double-car garage. Unlike the Equine Center, the fields of Respite Ranch were deserted. No horses whinnied a greeting or grazed beneath the shade of the oak and ash trees.

Leaving the pies for the moment, Ella Mae wandered behind the main house, admiring the enormous vegetable garden. She remembered Chandler mentioning that Annie received a stipend from the government for helping troubled teens and wondered if the vegetables were used in the kids' meals.

Signs of the ranch's self-sufficiency were everywhere. There were rain barrels scattered across the property, a wall of chopped firewood ran the length of one of the stables, and an herb garden was tucked between the kitchen and a sunny courtyard fenced in by blueberry bushes. Adjacent to the courtyard was an outdoor kiln and drying racks for pottery. Farther up the hill, apple trees had been laid out in neat rows and the dense branches of raspberry and blackberry bushes formed a natural border between the grassy field and the orchard.

"This is heaven," Ella Mae said to herself, her gaze drifting up to the blue green mountains and the cloudless skies. As she stood admiring every view, voices tripped down the hills. Companionable shouts and the sound of male laughter erupted from the trees to the far left of the ranch, and before long, a line of horses and riders could be seen winding their way down the slope.

One by one, the riders reached the bottom and immediately set forth toward the ranch at a relaxed gallop. As they drew closer, Ella Mae saw that they were teenage boys of all size, shape, and color. They all wore hard hats and leather gloves and seemed at ease in their western saddles. Annie Beaufort, who was clad in jeans, a Cheerwine T-shirt, and a John Deere baseball cap, brought up the rear.

"Who are you?" demanded the first teen, drawing his horse far too near to Ella Mae for her liking. She took a step back, nervously watching the animal's restless hoofs.

"I'm here to see Annie." She smiled at the young man in what she hoped was a placating manner. "I brought you all some pies."

He frowned. "We're not charity cases. We do our own cooking."

"Hey, I'm all for that." Ella Mae waited while another boy brought his mount in line with the first rider's.

"Chill, dude," the second teen chided. "She doesn't look like she's here to mess with us." He looked fixedly at Ella Mae. "Are you?"

Wishing Annie would ride up and defuse the tension, Ella Mae shook her head. "I met Annie a few days ago at a party. I wanted to come out here and see the ranch."

"You a rich lady?" the first boy asked, his tone still antagonistic. "Comin' out here to size us up before you write a check? See if we're worth the money?"

Thankfully, Annie shouted for the boys to head to the stables, and to Ella Mae's surprise and relief, they obeyed instantly.

"Howdy," she said, dismounting with the ease and quickness of a woman half her age. She handed the horse's bridle to one of the teens and shooed him away. "Don't tell me I forgot an appointment. Your face looks familiar. . . ."

Ella Mae explained who she was and where they'd met. She opened the back of the SUV in order to show Annie the freshly baked treats and couldn't help but mention that she'd be opening her own pie shop in two days. "I won't try to sugarcoat my reasons for coming out here," she said. "I was hoping to exchange these for information on Bradford Knox."

Annie's face became instantly guarded. She was silent for a long time, her gaze on the stables where the teens could be seen removing saddles and bridles from the horses. They stowed the gear neatly and then collected brushes from a tack box.

"I love to watch them groom the horses." Annie's voice was full of affection. "When they first come, they're so ripe with anger you can barely talk to them. They hate everybody and everybody hates them. At least that's what they believe. But a horse, especially a horse that's been rejected because he isn't deemed good enough anymore, can heal these kids. It takes time. The boys need to come back again and again. Some of them get carted here from Atlanta, others come down from the Carolinas. The horses take away their anger and give them hope."

"And the young men stay with you?"

"For one or two weeks. They have chaperones—usually boys who were in their shoes once. When they arrive, the kids think they're going to be miserable. They have to harvest and prepare their own food, wash their clothes, and do chores. For a day or two, they wish they were anyplace but here." She smiled. "By the time they're supposed to leave, they don't want to go. They hug me and we all cry like big babies."

Ella Mae watched the particularly abrasive boy brush his horse. His movements were slow and deliberate and the animal was obviously comfortable and content in his care. "This place is amazing."

Annie nodded. "Amazing and in trouble. The government's decided not to provide a cent of funding starting next month and I don't know how I'm going to keep the ranch afloat. I spend all the extra money I have rescuing horses."

Both women observed the teens for a few minutes. The sounds of nickers floated from the stables, mingling with the gentle cooing of the boys.

"Are you worried that if you talk to me about Bradford, you'll lose someone's patronage?" Ella Mae hazarded a guess.

"I'm already somewhat of a pariah in the racing community, but if I tell you what I know, the few owners who make donations on the sly will freeze me out. Not only that, but they won't even offer me their spent horses. They'll just send them away to be . . ." She trailed off, unwilling to verbalize the fate awaiting a washed-up thoroughbred.

Ella Mae hadn't expected to be confronted by this complication. How could she ask Annie to jeopardize this sanctuary for young men and horses? How many living creatures had been saved because of the goodness of the woman standing beside her?

"What's all this to you anyway?" Annie suddenly asked. "Did you know Bradford?"

"Not at all," Ella Mae admitted. "But the police consider me a suspect in his murder."

"That's ridiculous." Annie dismissed the notion immediately. "Why do they think that?"

Ella Mae briefly explained how she'd become entangled in the investigation. She told Annie about the rolling pin at the crime scene and how it seemed someone wanted to frame her for Bradford's murder.

"I came to you so I could clear my name." Ella Mae said. "I figured you'd know whether Bradford was being paid to administer illegal drugs to the racehorses, and if so, which owners were involved. If I could give the police a viable lead, I might be able to get them to cross me off their list." She sighed. "But I can't ask you to do anything to put this place at risk. It's too important."

"Thank you," Annie replied after a long pause.

Gesturing at the Suburban, Ella Mae said, "I still want you to have the pies."

Annie picked up a pie, peeled back the aluminum foil tent protecting its crust, and took a whiff of apple caramel. Straightening, she put two fingers in her mouth and whistled. A teenage boy wearing an apron appeared in the doorway of the dormitory building.

"Yeah?"

"Grab a few bodies and come unload this truck. This nice lady brought us a bunch of pies!" Annie shouted.

The boys didn't need to be told twice. They raced into the yard, grabbed the pies—thanking Ella Mae very courteously—and disappeared back inside.

"I'd like to bring you regular deliveries," Ella Mae said. "If that's okay."

Annie touched her on the arm. "I can't make it to your restaurant opening because this group will still be here, but will you be at the shop on Sunday? At about three? Maybe there's a way for me to help you without folks knowing about it."

"The Charmed Pie Shoppe is closed on Sundays, so that would be the perfect time for us to meet. We could have a cup of coffee and you could sample any pie you'd like," Ella Mae answered. "If you're sure this is what you want to do."

"I'm not sure, but I'm coming anyway."

Annie walked off toward the stables. The horses whinnied at her, their ears pivoting and their snouts reaching forward in search of a lump of sugar, an apple, or perhaps with even more yearning, the touch of a loving hand.

Chapter 13

The Charmed Pie Shoppe opened to much fanfare on a bliss-fully mild June morning. By exerting her considerable influ-ence, Verena had convinced all of her acquaintances in Havenwood and a host of journalists and food buffs from across the state to attend the ribbon-cutting ceremony.

Her husband, known to the locals as Mayor Buddy, addressed the crowd from a mahogany podium positioned on a square of red carpet. Though his speech was rather dull, focusing on the economic growth of the business dis-trict and the increase in tourism during the previous quarter, it was also short. After reminding everyone of the upcoming Row for Dough boat race, he bragged about Ella Mae's culi-nary training and read the menu aloud with such enthusiasm that the crowd actually began to press forward, centimeter by centimeter, until they threatened to sweep him aside.

"Homemade food created with fresh, local ingredients," he concluded, smiling at his niece. "Like it used to be. We get so busy that we often neglect the delight of gathering together around a table to enjoy Georgia's bounty. Peaches picked from the Ellisons' farm find their way into one of Ella Mae's pies, eggs from the McCartles' farm are whisked together to make a lemon chiffon tart, and herbs from Adelaide LeFaye's famous garden add spice to the quiches! Boy, am I hungry! So without further ado, I'd like to ask my lovely bride to cut the rope and then we'll all go inside and stuff ourselves silly!"

There was a roar of applause, but just as Verena opened the golden blades of the ceremonial scissors, a voice from the crowd called out, "Mayor Hewitt! What about the murder of Bradford Knox? Isn't Ms. LeFaye considered a person of interest by the police? Should we be concerned about her wielding a rolling pin?"

Buddy shot a quick look of command to one of his assistants, who dashed off in search of the questioner. Buddy then switched the microphone back on. "I would like to direct all inquiries regarding that incident to Havenwood's police chief. All I can say is that Ms. LeFaye has given the authorities her full cooperation and is not a suspect. This is a time of celebration and of fellowship and there will be no further comments on that particular matter. Thank you. Now, Verena darling, let them have pie!"

Verena winked at Ella Mae, allowing her a moment to scuttle inside the shop before she severed the shiny length of yellow satin cordoning off the front porch.

"Ready?" Reba asked from behind the counter. She had an order pad and a row of pens tucked into the front pocket of her apron. Her brown eyes were glittering with anticipation.

Ella Mae took a deep breath. "Someone just asked whether or not I was a murder suspect. It's thrown me off my game." She glanced nervously around the eatery. "I feel like I've just been set adrift and I can't reach out and grab on to anything to bring me back to the shore."

"Why should folks order your chocolate bourbon pecan pie?"

Startled by the question, Ella Mae gestured at the row of
dessert pies inside the display case. "Every bite is layered
with flavor. First, your fork will crack through a crisp bark
of pecans, sinking into milk chocolate made smooth and
richer by a splash of bourbon, and then the tines will strike
the buttery bottom crust. One mouthful and you'll believe
it's Christmastime. You'll want to laugh too loudly and make
toasts. Warmth will spread from your fingertips down to
your toes. It will shine from your eyes like a lighthouse
beacon."

Reba put her hands on her hips. "You're ready, honey. It's
a good thing too, 'cause here they come!"

The bells chimed a merry greeting. Buddy and Verena
entered first, arm in arm, and exchanged hugs with Sissy.

"*Best* seat in the house," Sissy declared, showing them a
two-top table overlooking the side garden. Reba took their
drink orders and immediately hustled to the next table. Ella
Mae's mother, Sissy, and Dee came out from where they'd
been waiting in the kitchen. Just for today, her mother had
volunteered to help Reba deliver food and drinks to the
dine-in customers, Dee offered to man the counter, and Sissy
was willing to seat customers and clear away dirty dishes.

Within minutes, the shop was filled to capacity and a
long line of people placing to-go orders formed at the counter. While patrons tried to decide on whether to bring home
a savory or dessert pie or both, Ella Mae began to fill the
orders Reba brought to the kitchen. She arranged a generous
wedge of pie alongside a mound of salad, her fingers moving
with the fluent grace of a skilled pianist. Never before had
she felt so calm, so at ease in her environment.

Reba picked up a plate containing a mixed-green salad
and a wedge of bacon and spinach quiche with one hand
and grabbed a second bearing a fragrant slice of tomato
basil tart and a rounded heap of apple, walnut, and goat
cheese salad. "You're doin' great, Ella Mae."

In what seemed like minutes later, her mother entered

the kitchen and waved an order ticket in front of her daughter's face. "I hope you've got more apple caramel pies back here. Dee's boxed up so many takeout orders that we're running out."

Ella Mae took a precious second to glance at the wall clock mounted above the swing door leading to the dining area. The Charmed Pie Shoppe had already been open for two hours. Where had the time gone?

She finished filling an order for Reba and then checked the wire racks lining the back wall. "I have three left but I need to keep two for dine-in dessert orders. Everyone is having dessert with their lunch today!"

"That won't always be the case," her mother advised. "But it was smart of you to bake extra for the grand opening." She examined the pies on the rack. "I'll have to convince people to opt for the triple berry or the fruit medley tart. The contrast between the blackberries and the vanilla custard is most seductive."

Dee pushed through the swing door and announced, "We're out of banana puddin' pies! The manager of Peachtree Bank just took the last four to bring to his employees as a special surprise. Is anything in the walk-in or the oven?"

"Six more chocolate bourbon pecans should be ready in about five minutes," Ella Mae said, wiping her forehead with the corner of her apron. She hadn't expected to sell out of a single item, let alone nearly every dessert pie on the menu.

After giving her a quick thumbs-up, Dee returned to the front room. Verena was the next to come bursting through the door. She pushed it with such exuberance that it nearly came off its hinges. "Ella Mae! You won't believe what people are saying! I heard phrases like 'utterly divine' and 'even better than Grandma's.'" Verena was rosy-cheeked with pride. "Adelaide, our girl has knocked this opening right out of the park! The reporters are having trouble finding enough flattering adjectives for their articles!"

"It's the truth," Reba said. "And no one wants to leave. People are huggin' one another and extending their lunch breaks as if this was their last day on earth."

Someone knocked on the back door. Ella Mae's mother opened it, exchanged a few words with the person on the other side, and turned to face the room, her hands cradling a cut-glass vase stuffed with sunflowers.

"Aren't those gorgeous?" Verena boomed. "Do you have an admirer, Ella Mae?"

Ella Mae was too busy slicing a pancetta and Gruyère tart to respond. "Will someone read the card?"

Her mother complied. " 'Best wishes on your opening day. Yours, Chandler Knox.' "

The noises in the kitchen abruptly ceased. Only the twang of a Patsy Cline song floating through the radio speakers permeated the silence.

"Knox?" Verena examined the card over her sister's shoulder. "I guess *he* doesn't view you as a suspect!"

"Interesting," her mother remarked just as another knock sounded on the door. This time, she accepted a large, beautifully etched crystal vase filled with bloodred roses. "Not even a trace of scent. Hothouse flowers." She eyed the offending blooms with disdain. "Utterly devoid of passion. Not a single remnant of the journey from seed to blossom."

Verena snatched the card from the center of the rose cluster. "But they *are* red!" She tore open the envelope. " 'Congratulations, darling. You did it! I am so proud of you! Call me. We need to talk. Love, Sloan.' "

"I could have told you who sent those flowers without even opening the card," her mother murmured darkly. "He probably let the florist pick this arrangement. Not an ounce of personal thought went into this."

Ella Mae waved at the roses. "Why don't you put them on the front counter near the register? But leave the sunflowers near the sink. They're like a burst of energy."

Reba entered to collect the lunches Ella Mae had just

prepared. "What's going on? Is this a flower stall or a pie shop?" She sank onto one of the kitchen stools. "I'm about due for a Twizzlers break."

Verena picked up the dishes from the counter. "I'll get these. Mr. and Mrs. Fergusson are on the Parks Preservation Board with me. They'll get a kick out of having me as their waitress. After all, when I'm carrying food, it's usually for me!"

After her aunt's boisterous departure, Ella Mae loaded the dishwasher and leaned back against its stainless steel surface to drink thirstily from a glass of cool sweet tea. Her eyes roamed over the flour-encrusted worktable, the pies browning in the oven, and the depleted baker's racks. She let loose a sigh of satisfaction that welled up from her very core.

"That's what it feels like to meet your destiny, take it by the hand, and jump off the cliff with it," Reba said from her perch on one of the kitchen stools. She pointed at Ella Mae with a licorice stick. "Mighty empowerin'."

For the third time, a knock sounded on the kitchen door.

"There's no one left to give me flowers," Ella Mae protested good-naturedly and went to see if the visitor was indeed the delivery boy from the local florist. But no one was waiting on the other side of the door. Instead, a white note card sat squarely in the middle of the stoop. Ella Mae opened it and grinned.

"Somebody scored, huh?" Reba asked, hopping down from her stool. "What's it say?"

"Nothing." Ella Mae showed Reba the card. There was no writing inside, but someone had glued a pristine four-leaf clover in the center of the white paper.

Reba brought the card to her nose and closed her eyes. "I can practically smell the secluded meadow blanketed by sunshine. Don't know who this boy is, but he's a keeper."

Ella Mae laughed. "Boy? It could be from anyone. One of the construction workers or a rep from the restaurant supply company."

"No." Reba sniffed the clover again. "They would've given it to you firsthand. Somebody searched high and low to get this for you but wasn't ready to show his face. It's been ages since I saw one this big." She handed Ella Mae the note. "Put this in a frame and hang it near the register. This is a true gift."

Setting the card aside, Ella Mae turned her attention to the beeping oven. "What makes a shamrock so special anyway?"

"One leaf for love, one leaf for hope, one leaf for faith, and one leaf for luck. The fourth leaf is a teeny bit smaller than the other three. That's how you know it's real." Her eyes grew distant. "For more years than this town's been standing, people have looked to clovers to ward off evil spirits."

Ella Mae frowned. "Well, I can use all the help I can get keeping them at bay."

At that point, Dee poked her head through the swing door and motioned for Reba. "Table five just left you a very generous tip. And their compliments to the chef," she added for Ella Mae's sake.

Sissy joined her sister in the threshold. "It's a good thing you've got tomorrow and Monday off. You'll have to bake for *hours* before your next business day. People are already talking about coming back on Tuesday."

"And the cash register's so stuffed I can barely close it," Dee declared happily.

Ella Mae's mother pushed her sisters aside and entered the kitchen with a new order ticket. "You'd better use that money to hire another employee."

Reba plucked the ticket from her fingers. "Let her put it in the bank. I'm not sharin' my tips with anyone, right, Ella Mae?"

But Ella Mae wasn't listening. Noises poured in through the open door. The murmur of relaxed voices, the clink of flatware, and the sweet, light music of laughter floated in on a stray air current. This rainbow of sound, this vibrant spectrum of merriment and pleasure, was precisely what Ella Mae had been dreaming about for years.

"Honey, you're crying! What's wrong?" Verena shouted in concern.

Ella Mae touched a finger to her cheek, catching a tear as it slid toward her chin. "This is joy. Maybe I should add it to a pie."

"Maybe you should," her mother suggested.

The next morning, Ella Mae couldn't wait to get her hands on *The Havenwood Daily.* While Chewy scampered around the yard chasing chipmunks, she drank coffee and poured over the article on The Charmed Pie Shoppe. Verena wasn't exaggerating when she'd said that the reporter had used a host of complimentary adjectives to describe her cooking, but it was the secondary story that made Ella Mae nearly splutter coffee out of her nose.

"EIGHTY-YEAR-OLD DOES CARTWHEELS DOWN MONARCH STREET!" proclaimed the headline.

Mr. Jefferson Baxter performed multiple cartwheels in front of a crowd of afternoon shoppers and merchants. Baxter, who has walked with the aid of a cane for the past seven years, claims that he experienced a surge of joy so compelling that he felt the need to express it through movement. When asked how he was able to display such remarkable agility, Baxter was unable to provide an explanation. His only comment was that the pie he'd had for dessert at The Charmed Pie Shoppe had made him feel like a boy again, if only for a few minutes. Perhaps Ms. LeFaye is using water from the Fountain of Youth in her recipes. Or perhaps her pies truly are enchanted.

Ella Mae dropped the paper on the garden bench and drummed her fingers on the side of her mug. "Is it possible?

Do I have some sort of gift?" She stood up and began to meander down the path leading down to the lake, her mind churning.

Chewy followed, a stick clamped between his jaws, tail wiggling madly.

"I should be angry with you," she scolded the terrier. "My favorite sandals look like a straw and leather bird's nest."

Rolling his eyes, Chewy dropped the stick and barked.

She stroked his soft ears, instantly contrite. "You're right. What did I expect? You're just a puppy. Tomorrow we'll visit Canine to Five and look into enrolling you in doggie day care. Mama's going to be working quite a bit." She hurled the stick into the shallows and Chewy dashed forward to retrieve it, his mouth curved into a toothy smile.

Ella Mae reached out to touch the sparkling skin of the water, fracturing the diamond glitter with her hand. Sunlight freckled her palm instead as she continued to reflect on the newspaper article. Had Jefferson Baxter eaten the last dessert pie of the day? She'd poured her joy into the filling as if it were tablespoons of pure vanilla extract. Did she really have the power to transfer emotions into the food she made?

"Impossible."

She removed her hand from the water and stood up. Chewy bounded onto the bank, shaking droplets all over her legs. She laughed, kissed his nose, and sent the stick high into the cerulean sky. The shade was the same blue base as Hugh Dylan's eyes but lacked the striations of lagoon green.

Thinking of Hugh stirred things in Ella Mae's heart she did not wish to have awakened. There was too much work to be done at the pie shop and in unraveling the riddles surrounding Knox's murder. Perhaps Annie Beaufort held the answers. Ella Mae was meeting Annie for coffee later and wanted to make a pie that would prove her worthy of the older woman's trust. Throwing the stick one more time, Ella

Mae headed back to the guest cottage where her recipe box waited inside the kitchen cupboard—a treasure chest full of riches.

"Oh, my, my, my!" Annie exclaimed after swallowing the first bite of Ella Mae's creamy lemonade pie. "It makes me think of one of the trails at the ranch. It leads to my private place—a field in the middle of a ring of trees. The air is as sweet as syrup and big, whipped-topping clouds hang down so low you feel like you could reach up, scoop out a piece, and take a bite of heaven."

Ella Mae topped off Annie's coffee. "Respite Ranch is amazing. You're amazing. Have you always spent your life helping, for lack of better phrasing, broken spirits?"

Annie nodded. "That's accurate enough. And, no, I had to have my eyes opened first. I ruined a horse before realizing what it really cost that animal to be a winner." She put her fork down and stared out the window of the empty café. Locking her eyes on the wall of hollyhocks lining the picket fence in the patio garden, Annie's face tightened with the pain of unwanted memory. "Bradford Knox had to euthanize that horse after I rode him to the ground. My pride killed that graceful creature. My pride drove him beyond what he was meant to endure. I was like most of these thoroughbred owners. All I cared about was becoming a name in the racing world. We were the ones wearing blinders, not our horses."

"Did you know Bradford well?"

Blinking, Annie returned to the present. "Once, that pride of mine caused me to treat him like an underling, but over time, I saw that he had a gift with the horses and I came to admire him. However, toward the end . . ."

Sensing that they'd reached the purpose of Annie's visit—the information that could put Respite Ranch, the chance for troubled boys and horses to heal, and Annie's own life at risk—Ella Mae remained silent. As much as she wanted to be in the clear, she didn't want to cajole the information from Annie. Even when prepping the creamy lemonade pie, Ella Mae's thoughts had returned again and again to Annie's ranch and the feelings of safety and serenity the place evoked.

"In the end, Bradford became what I once was. He chose money over the creatures he was supposed to care for." She sighed lugubriously. "I can't show you a lick of proof, but I heard talk from a half dozen different stable hands. Bradford was injecting injured thoroughbreds with cobra venom."

Ella Mae's lip curled in repulsion. "Cobra venom?"

"It's a painkiller. An injection can block the nerve, giving a horse one last race or two before his injuries are so severe that . . ." She trailed off. "You can guess the fate of a crippled thoroughbred."

"Is cobra venom illegal?"

"It's one of many substances banned on race day. If anyone could have proved what was going on, there would have been repercussions for both Knox and the horse owners. First, they would have had to answer to the racing authorities and, after that, to a district court judge. No hand slapping. We're talking serious penalties."

Pouring herself some more coffee, Ella Mae could easily imagine such a scandal permanently destroying the reputation of an elite thoroughbred farm.

Annie cut another piece of pie with her fork but didn't raise it to her mouth. "You know, Bradford wasn't interested in tending to the horses before a race until this past year. He'd preferred to maintain his dignity by treating only those patients who came directly to the clinic."

"But if these people were all using cobra venom, why would anyone kill Bradford? He was helping them win and they were paying him for his assistance."

Annie shrugged. "The stuff isn't cheap. Maybe Knox didn't pay his suppliers on time. Maybe one of the owners didn't want to share his or her advantage over the other racehorses. When you're talking about hundred thousand–dollar purses, every advantage counts."

A buzzer sounded in the kitchen.

Ella Mae pushed back her chair. "Those are pies for you to take back to the ranch. Let me just put them on a rack to cool."

"Take your time, honey. I'm going to sit here and try to remember the name of the company who sold Knox the cobra venom. One of the hands saw it stamped on a box inside of Knox's medical bag. It sounded Latin. Or Greek maybe . . ."

Thoughts of snakes and racehorses seemed incongruent inside the kitchen. Ella Mae opened the oven door and welcomed the breath of buttery dough. The scent of baked peaches and brown-sugar-crumb toppings stilled the questions battling one another to take precedence in her mind. Pulling on oven mitts, she began to transfer pies onto the metal racks, smiling at the thought of Annie's boys devouring the treats after their evening meal.

While she was moving the sixth out of a dozen pies, the bells hanging from the front door chimed. Ella Mae paused. Had Annie stepped out of the shop? Did she want a closer look at the patio garden? Or had a prospective customer failed to notice the closed sign hanging from the window and entered in hopes of acquiring a snack?

"Whoever it is, they'll have to wait," Ella Mae informed the cheerful kitchen. Curls of cinnamon-laden scent nuzzled the skin of her neck and sank into her hair follicles and she started to hum as she drew forth the last two pies from the oven's hot mouth.

The bells chimed again and the music died in Ella Mae's throat. Something was wrong. The bright sunlight in the room became dull and the ribbons of warm aromas dissipated as if they'd found a safe place to hide.

The feeling of another presence inside the shop was overwhelming. It stretched into the kitchen like a long shadow, and though Ella Mae sensed she should be afraid, she was enraged over the invasion of her sanctuary.

"I'm coming, damn it!" Ella Mae shouted and yanked off her oven mitts. She slammed them on the worktable and burst through the swinging door.

No one was there.

No one but Annie, that is.

Yet Annie's posture made no sense. It took a long moment for the information Ella Mae's eyes absorbed to be processed by her brain. Annie Beaufort was bent over the table, her face completely submerged in the creamy lemonade pie.

Annie looked like a zealous participant of an eating competition.

With one exception.

She never came up for air.

Chapter 14

Ella Mae paused for only a fraction of a second, but it felt as if she'd delayed too long, that in that blink of time in which she'd stood still, trying to comprehend what she was seeing, she had robbed Annie Beaufort of any chance of survival.

When she did move, she crossed the room in a flash, lifting Annie's face from the creamy slop that had once been a lemonade pie. She cradled Annie's limp head against her chest and began to scoop the whipped sugar and cream from her mouth. Ella Mae flung the pale yellow filling on the floor and it struck the black-and-white tiles with sickening thwacks.

This process stole away more precious seconds and then Ella Mae sacrificed five more grabbing her cell phone from the counter and dialing 911 as she felt for a pulse in Annie's neck.

She put the phone on speaker and set it on the table alongside the ruined pie. It had been caved in by the weight of Annie's head. The bottom crust had separated in violent fissures and exposed the celadon-hued ceramic dish underneath.

Ella Mae did not wait for the emergency operator to pick up before placing her lips over Annie's slack mouth and blowing air into her throat. Her chest did not inflate. Ella Mae's breath was obstructed by a blockade of moistened crust and filling.

"Nine-one-one. What's your emergency?" a voice inquired though the cell phone speaker.

"I need an ambulance at The Charmed Pie Shoppe! There's a woman . . . She's not breathing! *Hurry!*"

The operator cautioned Ella Mae to remain calm and asked for the address. She then made assurances that paramedics were en route and suggested Ella Mae try breathing into Annie's nose instead of the mouth.

Putting her lips on Annie's lips had been odd enough. They'd been supple, unresisting, and laced with sugar. Covering the older woman's mouth had been a necessary intimacy, but it felt both distasteful and invasive to press her lips over another person's nose, to form a seal of flesh over the nostrils and send forth a burst of warm, desperate breath into Annie's nasal passages.

Once again, the air found no place to go. A wisp of Ella Mae's breath escaped from the narrow tunnels inside Annie's nose, only to be instantly whisked away by the gentle downdraft created by the ceiling fan.

"It's not working!" Ella Mae called out, the last word sounding more like a hiccup that a pair of syllables. Centipede legs of panic crawled up her spine.

"Keep trying," the operator responded in calm, even tones that managed to increase Ella Mae's distress.

But she kept trying.

Her breaths were wasted. Ella Mae knew it was over, but she wouldn't give up until someone told her to stop.

Beneath her mouth and her hands, Annie Beaufort felt flaccid. It was as if her muscles had gone to sleep, allowing the bones to fall any which way, making her limbs as floppy as a marionette's.

Ella Mae could sense the quietness of Annie's body. Her chest did not rise and fall, her fingers didn't twitch, the wrinkles on her face didn't crease in laughter. All the dozens of little actions the body makes within the space of a minute were stilled.

And Annie's eyes . . . They were the worst. The lashes were clotted with pie filling and the corneas were coated with a sparkling layer of tiny sugar granules, as if they had been touched by Jack Frost.

Ella Mae shut her own eyes and concentrated on her task, silently pleading for a measure of air to be transferred from her lungs into Annie's.

The minutes dragged on, stealing all hope away. Ella Mae's tears dripped onto Annie's cheeks and the cheerful café was filled with her exhalations and mutterings of "please" and "come on, breathe."

She didn't hear the bell hanging from the front door tinkle. Her mind was on autopilot. She blew air in, waited, and blew again. It took a strong, male arm to pull her gently away from Annie.

"Let us take it from here," a voice said from miles off.

Ella Mae felt like she had been treading water for hours. Her limbs were stiff and heavy and could no longer support her weight. She sagged where she stood, fully expecting to slump onto the ground, but the man with the arms of stone kept her from slipping all the way down.

Instead, he eased her carefully onto the tiles and wrapped something soft and blue around her shoulders. A blanket. Ella Mae couldn't look anywhere but at Annie, whose body was being hastily placed onto a gurney. One EMT performed chest compressions while the other searched for evidence of a heartbeat using a stethoscope. The paramedic pressed the round disc against the tanned and freckled skin stretching over Annie's breastplate. The shiny metal caught the late afternoon light. It flashed once. A bright, searing white glow. Annie was saying good-bye.

"Are you okay? Would you like some water?"

The man's words floated somewhere above her head. Ella Mae stared at the floor. She put her hands out, palm down, like twin starfish, and pressed them against the tiles. Their coolness brought her back to herself and she looked up just in time to see Hugh Dylan walk through the doorway.

"Ella Mae!" He rushed over, dropped to his knees, and looked at her from head to toe with an agitated gaze. "What happened?"

As much as Ella Mae wanted to lose herself in the blue grottos of Hugh's eyes, she remembered how he'd acted like Loralyn's obedient dog at the Mint Julep Gala.

"What are *you* doing here?" she asked, her voice sounding harsh and unfamiliar. "There's no fire."

Hugh winced a little and the hand he'd been extending toward her shoulder fell away. "I heard the call come in over my radio. Volunteer firefighters never turn them off, and when the dispatcher recited the address, I had to find out if you were in trouble."

Ella Mae swallowed hard. "Is Annie alive?"

Hugh obviously didn't want to answer and focused his attention on the action beyond the display window. "They're working on her."

"Is she alive?" Ella Mae repeated, her fingers stretching forth and burying themselves into the cotton fabric of Hugh's sleeve. She scrunched her hands into fists, certain that if she did not grip him this way, she would float out of the room like a child's balloon.

"It doesn't look good," Hugh answered softly. "I'm sorry, Ella Mae."

She continued holding on and he put his hands under her elbows to offer extra support.

"I'm right here," he whispered. "It's going to be all right."

Ella Mae shook her head. It would not be all right. She

pointed at the walkie-talkie attached to his utility belt. "You need to call the police."

Hugh seemed reluctant to move. "Why?"

"Because this was no accident. Annie didn't just collapse face forward into my pie. Someone pushed her into it. Held her down." She hated to continue but she did just the same. "Her mouth was stuffed with filling. It was far more than one bite."

"She probably choked."

Bit by bit, Ella Mae released her claim on his shirt. Pointing at the sleigh bells suspended by ribbons above the front door, she said, "They rang twice. I should have paid more attention to them because the shop is closed."

Hugh followed her glance, his forehead creasing in confusion.

"Those bells rang to say that someone came in. And then again, about two minutes later, when they went out," Ella Mae explained. "And I can guess what happened in those two minutes."

"But who?" Hugh asked. "Who went in and out?"

Ella Mae drew the sea blue blanket tighter around her shoulders. "Annie's killer."

Ella Mae decided that death had a way of manipulating time. It could grab hold of a single moment and pull, stretching it lengthwise until sixty seconds were as long and elastic as newly spun taffy.

She didn't remember leaving the dining area of the pie shop and retreating to the kitchen but was grateful to enter a quiet space. The scent of the freshly baked pies rolled over her like a lullaby. She shrugged off the blanket and, setting it on a stool, recalled how Reba had perched there the day before.

"Reba," Ella Mae whispered as if she could summon her from thin air.

But she was alone.

Her finger traced a wobbly line through the flour dust on the worktable and, without thinking about what she was doing, Ella Mae pulled on a pair of yellow latex gloves and began to clean.

To her, time continued to stretch out. It yawned, slowed to a belly crawl.

Ella Mae wiped down counters, loaded the dishwasher, and mopped the floor. She thought of nothing but ridding the room of every trace of flour or speck of dough.

She still had a four-foot square to finish when two policemen strode through the swing doors.

"Watch it!" Ella Mae held out a hand to prevent them from taking another step across her clean floors.

At first, Officer Hardy looked contrite. Like a little boy scolded by his mother, he did a little hop backward until the swinging door, still in motion, slammed against his hip. He frowned, embarrassed, and began to pummel Ella Mae with questions.

She couldn't take in everything he said, especially with the noises from the front room sweeping into the kitchen. Radios crackled, chairs were pushed around with protesting squeaks, and authoritative voices issued commands. Hardy's inquiries rose above this din and then his partner, Officer Wells, the man who'd interviewed her during her most recent visit to the police station, added his voice to the cacophony.

Ella Mae heard the words "murder" and "Annie Beaufort." She glanced at the gleaming countertops and scrubbed worktable and tried to focus, but time had switched gears again. Now it was moving too quickly, like floodwaters rushing through a narrow canyon. She suddenly remembered a lesson on measures of time from her high school science class. The world was spinning inside her head faster than a millisecond. Maybe even a microsecond: one millionth of a second.

She couldn't grasp a single coherent thought or lucid word. Everything was a blur.

"Hey!" Hardy shouted and gently shook her shoulders. "Snap out of it!"

Jerked back to the present, Ella Mae sighed wearily and said, "I know this looks bad, but I'd never hurt Annie. She actually came here today to help me." Gesturing at the pies on the cooling racks, Ella Mae pleaded for the policemen to believe her. "Someone came into the shop while I was back here taking these pies out of the oven. By the time I got them all onto the racks and returned to the front room . . . Annie . . . Her face was . . . submerged. I tried to save her. I *tried*!"

"We'll talk more down at the station," Wells said without a trace of emotion.

Defeated, Ella Mae nodded. "Can we go out the back door?"

Hardy cocked his head. "You afraid people will see you? Everyone knows this is your shop. They'll put two and two together soon enough."

Imagining the crowd that had already gathered in the wake of the ambulance and fire engine, Ella Mae shrugged. "I know all about Havenwood's gossip chain. A dozen insane rumors will be spread about me before suppertime. There's nothing I can do about that right now. It's just . . . I don't want to see where she'd been sitting. Annie. I want to remember her as she was before this happened. Like when I saw her on horseback at Respite Ranch. She was so full of life. I don't think she wasted a minute of it."

There it was, she thought. *That theme of time again.*

Had Annie known that hers was about to run out? Had she turned and recognized her killer? Had she seen a sinister reflection in the nearest display case or had she been betrayed by someone she'd viewed as a friend?

"Let's go," Hardy commanded and took Ella Mae by the elbow.

Flanked by the two officers, Ella Mae walked past the Dumpster, across the rear parking lot, and around the corner. The officers were unable to load Ella Mae into their sedan, however, for Hugh was planted in the middle of the sidewalk, arms folded over his chest, legs spread in a defensive stance. He was deliberately blocking their path.

Sunlight cascaded through the waxy leaves of the magnolia tree above Hugh's head, streaking his molasses brown hair with caramel. But his eyes were dark, like a body of water reflecting a bank of thunderclouds. "Is she under arrest?"

"Not yet, Dylan," Wells replied easily, clearly on familiar terms with the firefighter.

Hugh didn't move. "Be sure to listen to the recording of the nine-one-one call. She did everything she could to resuscitate Ms. Beaufort."

Hardy nodded. "Will do. Are you heading over to the kennel? My boys might need to stay a few extra hours." He began to steer Ella Mae around Hugh. Though he handled her gently and Ella Mae didn't feel the slightest bit mistreated, a quiet anger surfaced in Hugh's eyes.

"Treat her well," Hugh cautioned.

Hardy caught the look and nearly stumbled off the small edge of the sidewalk. The mild-mannered dog lover and civil servant had suddenly transformed into a stone-faced colossus with the clenched jaw. It was obvious to the officer that Hugh felt intensely protective of their suspect, but that was not Hardy's concern. The only thing he cared about was catching Havenwood's killer.

Ella Mae felt waves of powerful emotions coursing from Hugh's body toward hers. She sensed frustration and guilt and a deep, unspoken longing. Their eyes met, and for just a moment, a miniscule fraction of time, she imagined what it would feel like to be held by him.

"I'll be waiting," Hugh said, as if he'd read her mind.

As the police cruiser pulled away from the curb and

inched through a knot of curious townsfolk and tourists, Ella Mae closed her eyes and focused on Hugh's words. She didn't know whether he'd meant that he'd wait at the station until her interview was over or that he was ready to touch her the moment she extended an invitation. The question was, with her stalled divorce and her involvement in two murders, would she ever be ready to explore the naked want she saw in his eyes?

Chapter 15

Wells and Hardy took turns grilling Ella Mae until she nearly burst out in tears. The shock of Annie's death combined with their relentless and repetitive questions had her at the breaking point. Finally, frustration and exhaustion won out and she ceased to be the courteous, cooperative woman they'd driven to the station.

"I've told you all I know!" she shouted two hours into their interview. "Why don't you track down the people involved in the horse doping? I've given you owner's names, the drug used, and repeated every word of what Annie told me verbatim. What more do you want?"

Neither man answered so Ella Mae continued her rant. "I don't benefit from Annie's death. Someone obviously wanted her to keep quiet about the cobra venom." She put her hands over her eyes, hoping to give them a rest from the sight of the stark room and the sickly glow of fluorescent lights.

Hardy consulted his notes while Wells offered Ella Mae a bottle of water. She drank thirstily, welcoming the sting of cold water on the back of her throat. The small sensation allowed her a fresh surge of anger. "Are you going to charge me with murder or not? Because I have nothing else to tell you! If you're going to charge me then go ahead and do it! At least I'll get to lie down on a cot, even if it's in a jail cell."

Wells studied her curiously. "We're waiting for you to provide us with some tangible evidence, ma'am. So far, you've claimed that someone stole a rolling pin from your mother's house and used it to incapacitate Bradford Knox. A few weeks later, this unknown individual then sneaks into your place of business and suffocates a woman in one of your pies. And yet, you insist that you have no intimate knowledge of either victim. You never met Bradford Knox and you had only a passing acquaintance with Annie Beaufort."

"That's the truth, as crazy as it sounds," Ella Mae insisted.

Leaning forward, Wells jabbed the cover of a file folder sitting on the table with his index finger. "There hasn't been a murder in Havenwood in decades and now we've got two of them. And *your* name shows up again and again in both reports. Why? How do you fit in?"

Sensing this was a rhetorical question, Ella Mae stared at the policeman in hostile silence.

Wells held her gaze. "That's what I'm trying to work out. What is your connection? What are you keeping from us?"

"Nothing! It's not my fault that you aren't doing your job. Instead of wasting time with me, you should be questioning these racehorse owners, digging through Bradford's financial records, or looking over the names of the companies supplying drugs to his clinic! But what are you doing? Wasting hours with someone with no motive!" Ella Mae reined in her temper with a sigh. "I demand to be allowed to see my attorney. I'm done talking."

Hardy shot Wells a fleeting look of disapproval.

Ignoring him, Wells shrugged and rose from his seat with agonizing slowness. "I'll phone Mr. Templeton right away."

Once he was gone, Hardy fiddled with the label from his

water bottle, peeling it into small strips. He avoided making eye contact with Ella Mae. "We went over Knox's financial records a dozen times. Both those of the clinic's and his personal accounts too. Even though Knox took out a heavy loan against the equine center, the folks at the bank told us that he was planning to put on an addition and that the business was growing nicely. Everything adds up and that's why my partner is unconvinced by your story."

"Because there's no money trail," Ella Mae said and then threw out her arms in exasperation. "It's not like I've got a safe deposit box stuffed with cash, so why focus all your energy on me?"

Hardy collected the scraps from the label and stuffed them inside the empty bottle. "Shoot, you didn't even have a bank account until your mother and aunts bid on the pie shop property. I hear you're in a rush to establish residency so you can file for divorce six months from now."

"Exactly! I told you that I'm living on the generosity of my family and the money I brought with me from New York." She sighed. "Look, I know Loralyn had an alibi, but isn't it possible she had an accomplice?"

Tossing the bottle into the garbage can in the corner Hardy said, "Such as?"

"Knox's daughter, Ashleigh. I was told she's always in need of money. Or his son, Chandler." Ella Mae felt a prick of guilt over mentioning him. "He wanted to be a partner in the practice long before Knox was killed."

Hardy dismissed her theories. "We spoke with Ashleigh. She's a greedy one, mind you, but why would she bump off her daddy when he was writing her checks? And Chandler admitted that despite hoping for the partnership years ago, he realized that he wasn't ready and came to respect his father's decision to wait."

Ella Mae reached over and grabbed Hardy's hand. "Just look for a cobra venom supplier in Knox's records. Please. I saw an invoice on the office manager's desk for twenty grand." She told him of the bill and the Post-it note bearing a question mark that she'd seen on Peggy's desk.

"And you can't remember the name of the company?"

Ella Mae's shoulders dropped in defeat. "No. It was Greek or Latin. A single word. That's all I can remember. Trust me, I wish I could rattle it off for you. But one of the thoroughbred owners, Mr. Malone, told me that Bradford had been supplying him with a magic potion. I don't know much about racetrack regulations, but I'd bet that 'potion' is illegal."

"I'll look into it. In the meantime, try to stay out of trouble." Hardy pulled his hand free as the door to the room opened and August burst inside, red-faced and out of breath.

"My client is to be released immediately. I am most disappointed in this department, Officer Hardy." August filled the threshold like a man twice his height and beckoned for Ella Mae to join him. She was so glad to see the rotund attorney that she flung her arms around him. "There, there," he soothed, giving her a fatherly pat on the back. "Come along, my dear, I'm taking you home."

The moment Ella Mae entered the guest cottage, Reba flew at her, enfolding her in an embrace of strawberries and love.

After thanking August by calling him the finest gentleman in all of Havenwood, Reba politely shooed him away. "I should have been there!" she cried when he was gone. "It's my job to protect you."

Ella Mae took note of the gleaming countertops and spied a bucket and mop resting near the sink. She was too wrung out to console Reba. "You've been cleaning?"

Reba pulled a licorice twist from the package in her pocket, examined it, and then wound it around her finger. "I tidy up when I'm at my wit's end. You know that."

"This is not your fault, Reba. Someone came in and—"

"Shot Annie in the neck with enough tranquilizer to fell an elephant and then stuck her face into your pie."

Gaping, Ella Mae sank into the nearest chair. "How do you know that?"

"August. He and the ME are good buddies. It'll all be in the official report. Those jackass cops are gonna realize that Annie got a dose of the kind of tranquilizer used on big four-legged creatures, like, say, *horses*, and then they might finally start sniffin' around the right places."

The mention of "sniffing around" had Ella Mae searching for her dog. "Where's Chewy?"

"Sound asleep in your mama's sunroom." Reba filled up the teakettle. "Your mama said he's been out of sorts ever since you left this mornin'. It was like he was trying to warn her that somethin' was about to happen." She put the kettle on to boil and then began opening and closing cupboards, pulling out cups, the sugar bowl, and a jar of honey. "But your mama thought he was actin' unsettled because of tonight's new moon."

Ella Mae was too tired to try to sort out this reasoning. She thought animals were sensitive to only full moons. "I'm glad Chewy wasn't there today. I almost brought him because I wasn't expecting customers. What if he'd gotten hurt?" She watched Reba sort through a variety of tea bags through heavy eyes. "I don't suppose my mother is too concerned about what I went through, seeing as she's not here."

Reba stopped what she was doing. "She and your aunts are having a powwow about your trials and tribulations this very minute. A serious war council." She smiled, obviously pleased with her choice of imagery. "I wouldn't mess with those four, not for all the Twizzlers in Walmart."

Ella Mae watched Reba place five teacups on the table. Just as the kettle began to shriek, her mother, Sissy, Verena, and Dee entered the guest cottage. All four women looked solemn but determined. Ella Mae's aunts paused to give her a quick hug or peck on the cheek, but her mother hurriedly sat down next to her and seemed to be examining her for signs of trauma.

"You poor thing!" Verena exclaimed. "Do you need a few aspirin? A shot of booze? A warm washcloth for your head?"

"Having all of you here is the best medicine." Ella Mae gazed at the faces around the table. "But I don't see what you can do to get me out of this mess. There are no witnesses to back up my claim that someone else killed Annie, and the police might not have enough evidence to arrest me, but folks in this town are going to judge me one way or another. If they think I'm guilty, then they won't come to the pie shop and everything will be ruined." She swallowed hard. "I could have been just as miserable without bothering to leave New York."

Sissy shook her head vehemently. "You didn't have *us* in New York. And we've been busy. Tell her, Dee."

Dee produced a notebook from a straw purse that looked like it had been used as a scratching post by a dozen cats. "I visited the horse owners who raised red flags in your mind at the Mint Julep Gala under the pretense that I was viewing the horse they wanted to have immortalized in sculpture. The first farm is in the clear. The horses are well treated and the trainers are good people who don't use illegal pharmaceuticals to influence race-day results."

Adelaide looked dubious. "Then how are they thriving in this economy?"

"Mostly as a stud farm," Dee answered patiently. "They have an impressive lineage that dates back to the turn of the century."

"And the other two crooks?" Verena demanded, blowing heartily on her steaming cup of tea.

Dee dropped two sugar cubes into her cup. "The Hollowells and Malones are a different story. I made a cat sculpture for one of the stable hands working for the Hollowells and a rooster piece for the Malone's cleaning lady, and both of those folks told me horrible things."

"Someone wanted a sculpture of their rooster?" Reba asked but no one paid her any heed.

"Those two couples would do anything to their animals in exchange for victories. Both of the staff members said that Bradford had begun coming to the farm a few days before each big race. The owners and trainers would be pretty agitated until he showed up. Afterward, they were relaxed and confident."

Ella Mae took a sip of strong tea. "He delivered the cobra venom. The magic potion."

"But if Knox was providing a service for these people, *why* kill him?" Sissy asked.

"Peggy told me that someone had been arguing with Knox the day before he was murdered," Ella Mae said. "Maybe one of the owners offered to pay Knox *not* to provide the other farms with venom."

Her mother nodded. "A feasible motive. If a competing farm repeatedly lost the chance to win their share of a big purse, not only would their profit margins shrink, but their reputation would suffer."

Sighing, Ella Mae ran her hands through her hair. "I keep thinking about the rolling pin. Why did the person who wanted to frame me choose that object? Why not a kitchen knife?"

"Everybody in town knew you were gonna open a pie shop," Reba said. "You were bound to put your prints on that rollin' pin."

"There's got to be more to it than that," Ella Mae insisted. An unformed idea played at the edge of her thoughts but disappeared before it could become solid, like a phantom burned away by the dawn light.

The women drank their tea in silence for a few minutes. The kitchen had grown cozy and warm—replete with the sound of the women's mellifluous voices and the aroma of tea and roses.

"So what do we do now?" Sissy said.

Verena put her cup down with enough force to shatter the sturdy ceramic, causing a flake of celery-colored glaze to flutter onto the table. "We exert our sizable influence! I'll whisper in Buddy's ear and he'll whisper into the police chief's! They need to turn over some rocks at these horse farms and see what kind of vermin has been hiding from the law."

"The thoroughbred owners will see the cops coming from a mile away," Ella Mae argued. "The authorities need help. If only I could get my hands on a single piece of evidence . . ."

Dee watched her niece closely. "You know where to find one, don't you?"

"Maybe. There was a bill for twenty thousand dollars on Peggy's desk." She closed her eyes and willed herself back to that day in the equine center. It was easier to think in this pleasant space with the support of the women she loved wrapped around her like a hand-knit shawl. "The company logo was a triangle with sunbeams shining behind the tip. Damn it, I still can't remember the name."

Sissy motioned for Dee to pass over her notepad. "Let's think of synonyms for snakes. Maybe we can jog your memory."

The women began calling out words like serpent, reptile, cold-blooded, legless, slither, viper, poisonous, rattler, and scaly until Ella Mae's skin prickled with unease. She could almost hear hissing from underneath the table.

"Wait," her mother declared, holding up a hand. "Was the triangle a pyramid? With the sun glinting off the capstone?"

"Yes!" Ella Mae's anxiety was forgotten. "It looked Egyptian."

Her mother exchanged looks with Reba, and without a sound, Reba was out the door and racing across the lawn into the main house. She returned two minutes later carrying a large tome called *Egypt: The Land and Its Legends* and dumped the heavy volume in front of Ella Mae.

As Ella Mae flipped through pages of color illustrations

and photographs, her mother lowered her face closer to the open book.

"I can smell his cologne," she whispered almost inaudibly.

Sissy put a hand on her sister's forearm as the atmosphere in the kitchen changed. Adelaide's memories pressed in, crowding the small space. Ella Mae was about to ask about her father, a taboo subject, when an image in the book caught her eye. It was of a tomb painting showing a pharaoh in profile. Another view showcased the king's headdress, drawing attention to the sacred serpent curling above Pharaoh's brow. A caption identified the symbol by name.

"Uraeus!" Ella Mae cried. "That's the company's name!"

Sissy leaned over Adelaide and examined the illustration. "It's a cobra, symbolizing the goddess Wadjet, serpent goddess of time, justice, heaven, and hell." She looked at her niece. "For these thoroughbreds, Wadjet is *definitely* hell."

Verena produced a cell phone and began typing on the touch screen. "Here they are. Uraeus Pharmaceuticals. They operate out of Cameroon but there's a U.S. distributor in Atlanta."

Ella Mae traced the cobra head with her forefinger. "I need to get my hands on that bill. What if Knox never paid up? Maybe some thugs from Uraeus came to collect their money."

"How are *you* going to get a copy of that invoice? Break into the clinic at night?" Sissy asked.

"Not exactly. I was planning to borrow a set of keys from Chandler without him realizing it."

Reba's mouth formed a sly grin. "Seducin' a man for his keys, eh? I like it. Afterward, you and I can sneak in after dark."

Adelaide frowned. "This is not wise. Let August tell the authorities about Uraeus and both of you keep clear of the whole affair. Ella Mae, you have a business to think about."

Ella Mae glanced at her watch and sighed. "Speaking of

which, I'd better go to bed. I have to get up early to open the shop and do the day's baking. I just hope I have some customers after what's happened."

"You'll be as stuffed as a Christmas stocking!" Verena declared exuberantly. "There's nothing people like more than visiting the scene of the crime. Believe me, you're going to need plenty of rest, honey. And an extra pair of hands too."

Reba cleared the teacups and set them gently in the sink. "I have a feelin' we might end up with a very special volunteer tomorrow." Refusing to say anything further, she coaxed Ella Mae to head upstairs, promising to walk Chewy before letting him back into the guest cottage for the night.

Ella Mae complied and crawled into bed. She closed her eyes and pictured Chewy racing over the wet grass and pine needles, envying her little dog his freedom. She could only hope to find a similar escape in her dreams.

Ella Mae jerked awake a few minutes before midnight. She turned over and tried to go back to sleep but couldn't. After stroking Chewy's fur for a bit, she drank some water from the glass on her nightstand and then stood up and walked to the window, her eyes lifted toward the sky.

The Milky Way was spread out like the train of a wedding dress and the edges of the galaxy glowed indigo before eventually giving way to black. The new moon was an insignificant sliver, its illumination weak in comparison to the twinkling stars.

Sliding a window open, Ella Mae invited a waft of floral scents into her bedroom. Wild rose vines, jasmine, and oleander clung to her white nightgown, infusing her with tranquility.

Groggy once more, she began to turn away from the window when a white yellow light glowing above the back garden caught her attention. The beam was too wide to have come from a flashlight and it pulsed like a giant's heart.

"What on earth?" Ella Mae whispered, more fascinated than alarmed.

It was at that moment that she became aware of a figure dressed in a white robe and cowl standing on the garden path. The figure raised both arms, beckoning to the radiant mass hovering above the circle of Luna roses.

As Ella Mae watched, the light began to descend toward the stone bench and the bush in the center of the circle.

Two more figures were present. From their shapes, Ella Mae assumed that they were a man and a woman. They stood immobile, hand in hand, focusing on the tight buds of the Luna roses.

The cloud of light throbbed and shifted and Ella Mae recognized the source of illumination. Gripping the windowsill in astonishment, she stared as hundreds of fireflies drifted downward. Within seconds, they completely obscured the surface of the rosebush. A blinding light shot from the core, reminding Ella Mae of the orb she'd seen the night of the celebratory dinner at Le Bleu with her mother and aunts.

She blinked once and the flash was gone. The man and woman were lowering forearms that had been raised to shield their eyes and were now gazing directly ahead again.

The fireflies began to rise. No longer glowing with surreal luminescence, their blinking lights were weak and sporadic. They climbed toward the rooftop and then lazily dispersed like a crowd of spectators leaving a stadium.

What they left behind, however, was a rose unlike any Ella Mae had ever seen. Infused with golden light, the single bloom sparkled in the dark garden. Its petals flickered like a candle flame, beautiful and dangerous.

Though she knew nothing of this flower, Ella Mae sensed that it had the power to change a person. Perhaps it could heal a wound. Perhaps it could create one too.

With a nod of the head, the robed figure invited the couple to step forward. After a brief hesitation, they touched the rose at the same time. The second their flesh made contact with the fiery petals, the light captured within was immediately snuffed out, plunging the garden into shadow.

Ella Mae strained her eyes, searching for the human shapes below. She saw a flash of white robes and then, nothing.

"Am I dreaming?" she wondered aloud and stood at the window for several more minutes. But the garden felt deserted.

Ella Mae climbed onto the bed next to Chewy. He raised his head and sniffed her fingertips, his eyes half-mast. Rolling onto his back, he let all four paws dangle in the air and instantly drifted back to sleep, his mouth curved into a contented smile.

She kissed the top of his head and then looked outside once more. There was no movement, no color, not even a glint of lingering light.

"What the hell goes on in that garden?" she murmured, her words stretched out by a wide yawn. "I'll find out tomorrow. Tomorrow," she whispered and then snuggled up against her dog.

Chapter 16

As much as Ella Mae wanted to hang around Partridge Hill so she could ask her mother what had transpired in the garden the night before, she needed to get to town to do her week's shopping and make dozens of piecrusts for the pie shop's freezer. The day passed in a flash and her mother was out by the time she got back home.

On Tuesday morning, Ella Mae considered waking her mother up to ask her about what she'd seen, but decided against it. Assuming she'd have customers to serve in a few hours, she loaded Chewy in her bike basket and began the long trek to work.

"I've got to buy a car," she said upon reaching Swallow-tail Avenue.

Though the summer sun had yet to climb over the horizon, the air was far from cool. The humidity had already descended upon Havenwood and it wasn't long before tendrils of hair began to stick to the back of Ella Mae's neck. The shade in The Charmed Pie Shoppe's patio area was heavenly and she couldn't help but take a moment to rest at one of the umbrella tables. Drinking in the scents and colors of the garden, she marveled over her mother's ability to blend a dozen different varieties of red and golden flowers with lush clusters of herbs. The aroma on the patio was both sharp and sweet.

"A little early for a coffee break, isn't it?" a male voice teased, startling both Ella Mae and Chewy. The terrier bared his teeth and growled until Hugh Dylan dropped to his knees and held out his hands, palms up, for Chewy to inspect. "Sorry, little man. I didn't mean to scare you."

Ella Mae watched her dog smelled Hugh's fingers with interest. After issuing a sniff of forgiveness, he pivoted his body, inviting Hugh to pet him.

Hugh smiled at Chewy and then looked at Ella Mae. "Since you weren't able to visit Canine to Five, I thought I'd come and invite him to spend the day with Dante." He waved at the shop. "I know you've got an enclosure behind the kitchen, but today's going to be a scorcher. He'd be better off at the center. The staff will take great care of him."

"That's really sweet of you," she said. "I've been dumping poor Chewy on my mother too much, but every time I thought about heading over to Canine to Five . . ." She trailed off. "Let's just say that things haven't been going as planned."

Hugh rose to his feet and moved across the patio. He took the seat opposite her and glanced around at the garden, his expression somber. "I heard about Annie Beaufort from a kid who works at Canine to Five. He went to her ranch and will tell anyone how Annie and the horses saved him. She made a difference in someone's life every day. I wish I could be more like that."

Ella Mae felt a rush of sorrow. "Me too. And I'm worried about the fate of Respite Ranch. How will it survive?" She stared woefully at the border of marigolds at the edge of the patio.

"Maybe Annie's sister will take over." Hugh's gentle tone

coaxed Ella Mae into meeting his brilliant blue gaze. "Hey, now. You can't blame yourself."

"Sure I can," Ella Mae retorted more sharply than she'd intended. "I put her life at risk the day I drove to her place and pressured her to talk to me. It was total selfishness on my part. I figured that if she had information that could clear my name, then I had to do anything in my power to get it."

"Was she able to help you?"

Unsure of how much to divulge to Hugh, Ella Mae sighed heavily. "Clues. Theories. I shared them with the police last night, but still I'm not off the hook. Annie was killed in *my* shop. Right on the other side of that pink front door."

Glancing beyond the riot of climbing roses, Hugh said, "Are you allowed to open for business today?"

"Yes. There wasn't much evidence to be gathered, I'm afraid."

Stretching his arm farther across the table, Hugh took her hand. He wrapped his fingers around hers and squeezed, his eyes becoming electric with intensity. "If you're scared to go inside, I'll come with you." He stood up and pulled her to his feet. "In fact, why don't you give me an apron? I've decided to be your shadow until closing time. Just give me five minutes to run Chewy over to Canine to Five so he can go swimming and make some new friends."

Ella Mae readily accepted his offer. Hugh scooped Chewy into his arms, held the dog out so she could kiss him good-bye, and then strode off to a mud-encrusted Ford Explorer parked along the curb.

"I hope I can concentrate with him in the same room," Ella Mae murmured, her heart going rabbit-fast as she pictured Hugh rolling out piecrust, his strong hands covered in flour, bare forearms flexing as he caressed the dough, coaxing it into the pan and running his fingertips over its delicate skin. "Get ahold of yourself," she said and unlocked the kitchen door.

Switching on the overhead lights and the radio, Ella Mae

retrieved ingredients from the walk-in and began to press chilled balls of pie dough into pans.

Outside the kitchen window the sky turned a dusty lilac. The scent of butter floated through the room, intertwining with tart fruit aromas and the sharp tang of aged cheddar and Parmesan. The shop had shrugged off the shadows of the previous day and Ella Mae felt her flagged spirits being restored by the kitchen's warmth.

She sang while pressing dough into pie pans, influenced by the theme of fearlessness running through the morning's selection of songs. Just as she threw back her head to hit a particularly high note, which ended up coming out rather flat, Hugh walked in the back door.

Instead of laughing at her, he joined in. Grabbing her flour-dusted hands, he pulled her toward him. He didn't seem to notice that her apron was covered in flakes of dough, fruit juice, sprinkles of dill, and bits of shaved cheese as he waltzed her around the worktable as if they were at a ball.

For a heartbeat, Ella Mae was in heaven. This was her prom dream come true. True, she wore Keds and khaki shorts instead of a gown of shimmering green, but the boy she'd longed to dance with was dancing with her. He smelled of apples and the cool water of the swimming hole, and his hand melted perfectly into the small of her back. It was as if her body had been formed specifically for one man, this man, to be able to hold her like this.

Heaven.

But the thought of proms brought Loralyn to mind. Ella Mae spun away from Hugh, putting the commercial-sized mixing bowl between them.

"Why did you really come today?" she asked, her eyes going gray with suspicion. "It wasn't just for Chewy, was it?"

Hugh was clearly taken aback by her abrupt change in mood. "I wanted to do something to help you."

"Aren't you with Loralyn?"

"She's my friend. We're not a couple." He picked up a

pomegranate from the colander in the sink and examined it
quizzically. Lightly juggling the fruit from hand to hand, he
continued talking. "She and I go way back. Just like you
and I do, but I never got to know you when we were younger,
Ella Mae. You kept to yourself. Loralyn was my first crush
and you never really forget that person. They always own a
piece of your heart." Two pink spots bloomed on his cheeks,
transforming him into the boy Ella Mae had wanted so badly
for such a long time. "She and I sometimes end up . . .
together. But it's never serious and she's never between husbands long." He put the fruit down and locked eyes with her.
"Was your husband your first crush?"

It was no surprise that Hugh knew she was married. After
all, they lived in a very small town. But Ella Mae was so
crestfallen by his raising the subject of her husband that she
couldn't answer for a moment. Lining a pie shell with apple
slices, she wondered if she should tell Hugh the truth—that
she'd been in love with him since she was thirteen years old.

"No," she answered eventually. "Sloan was my ticket out
of here." She sprinkled cinnamon over the apples. "Wait,
that came out wrong. I didn't use him. I loved him, but there
was always something missing between us. But that doesn't
matter anymore because it's over."

Hugh gave her a little smile. "Now that we've cleared the
air on our exes, can you give me a job so I don't feel completely useless?" He brandished the pomegranate. "Just don't
ask me how to get the seeds out of this. That's way beyond
my abilities."

Ella Mae would have liked to bluntly ask Hugh if he
wanted to be her friend or if he was interested in something
more, but she wasn't sure if she was ready to hear his answer.
Besides, she had to concentrate on cooking.

"Could you fry some pancetta and ham for me?"

Hugh looked perplexed. "Pancetta?"

Handing him a package and gesturing at the bouquet of

shining pots hanging from a ceiling rack, she said, "It's Italian bacon."

He smiled. "My favorite food group. I can't guarantee you'll have any leftovers, but I promise to take home the bacon, fry it up—"

"Don't even finish that line!" Ella Mae ordered with a laugh and smacked at his thigh with a kitchen towel.

He feigned injury. "So *this* is how you treat your staff? And I thought cleaning up dog poop was degrading."

The pair worked together for the next two hours. Ella Mae told Hugh about culinary school and life in Manhattan and he spoke of his travels. After graduating from college, he'd become interested in genealogy and had visited the homelands of his ancestors. His wanderlust satisfied, he returned to Havenwood and became a firefighter. Four years after he joined the department, he rescued Dante from a burning house. Dante's owner was too badly injured to care for the dog and Hugh and the Harlequin Dane had been together ever since.

As they compared childhood memories of school, the swimming hole, and town landmarks, the kitchen filled with golden sunbeams, laughter, and the scent of baking pies.

"Hey!" Hugh exclaimed shortly before Reba was due to arrive. "Am I dreaming or are you mixing together ingredients for a shoofly pie?"

Picking up a bottle of King syrup, Ella Mae nodded. "I couldn't make it like your granny did using molasses. I had to send away for some northern syrup."

Hugh abandoned his task of washing lettuce and stepped next to her. He was so close that their shoulders brushed when Ella Mae moved her arms.

"Can I watch or will it break the spell?" he whispered.

"I'll do my best not to mix in any eggshells," she murmured, her voice becoming deep and husky against her will. Luckily, the filling was an uncomplicated blend of syrup, water, baking soda, eggs, cinnamon, and cloves. The traditional shoofly pie recipes didn't always include the last two ingredients, but Ella Mae wanted to add an extra burst of flavor to Hugh's pie. As she stirred, she could feel a tide of desire flow from her body into the grain of her wooden spoon.

Adding measures of flour, brown sugar, and butter to the bowl of her food processor, she pulsed the mixture until it had formed the perfect crumb topping. Scooping the crumbs with her fingers, she spread them across the surface of the dark brown filling. It was difficult to keep her hands steady when all she wanted to do was look into Hugh's eyes. Would she find a reflection of her own need in his blue green pools?

As though sensing her longing, Hugh slipped directly behind her and placed his hands on her shoulders. "I could watch you bake all day. It's hypnotizing."

Now she did turn. Their bodies were so close that only a sliver of air and light separated them. The edge of the worktable dug into Ella Mae's back, encouraging her to press a centimeter nearer. Hugh placed a rough palm against her cheek and then let his fingers slowly travel down her jawline to the tip of her chin, igniting her skin. "I've been wanting to do this since I first saw you," he murmured and then leaned in to kiss her.

Hugh's warm, wet mouth found hers and she felt a tingle of heat spread over her lips. She closed her eyes, welcoming the slow burn that had sparked within her chest and was now sweeping across her shoulders, down the staircase of her spine, over the slope of her hips, and between her thighs.

Suddenly, the heat intensified, assaulting her nerve endings with a jolt of pain. She jerked back and so did Hugh. They stared at one another in astonishment, lips swollen from kissing, their shallow breaths falling into the space that now stretched like an abyss between them.

Ella Mae had no chance to ask Hugh if he'd felt the same pain, for the sound of Reba's whistling preceded her entry through the kitchen door.

"Howdy!" she greeted the flummoxed pair, acting unsurprised to find Hugh Dylan at the pie shop. She hung her purse in the closet where the cleaning supplies were kept, tied on her apron, and began to scrub her hands at the sink. "I hope your baker's racks are full, my girl," she called over the sound of the water. "You've got folks lined up already. Looks just like openin' day out front."

Smoothing the fabric of her own apron where it had bunched together against Hugh's cotton T-shirt, Ella Mae tried to release the electricity coursing through her by grabbing the shaker filled with ground cinnamon and sprinkling the surface of the shoofly pie with it, but she could still feel the friction of Hugh's body. Each crystal of sugar was charged with lust, landing on the pie's crumb topping one by one until the pie pulsed with a sheen of abandoned inhibition. Ella Mae slid it into the oven and set to work pouring the shoofly filling into a dozen more shells.

Reba was right. Not only were curiosity seekers waiting to have breakfast at The Charmed Pie Shoppe, but patrons who'd eaten there on Saturday had also returned to sample different dishes.

Hugh offered to play hostess and to handle the takeout orders. According to Reba, he responded to lighthearted ribbing from the townsfolk about trading in his fireman's uniform for a "woman's" apron with good-natured wisecracks. However, when a sour-faced matron asked him how he felt about working alongside a potential murderer, Hugh's expression darkened and his peacock blue eyes flashed dangerously.

"If your intention is to blacken Ella Mae's name, Mrs. Buckland, you can turn right around and leave. I'd be more than happy to sell this sweet, succulent strawberry pie to another customer."

Reba was grinning from ear to ear as she recited this story. "That hag fell all over herself apologizin' and ended up buyin' two pies! After that, our friendly fireman got rid of two reporters by sayin' that you weren't available until after five, but you'd be more than willin' to talk to them then."

"But we close at four, right after afternoon tea!" Ella Mae said and then laughed.

Reba joined in. "Those newspaper boys aren't too good at research. They didn't even bother checkin' the sign in the window. Our hours of operation are right there. What jackasses."

"Hugh's been . . . amazing. He took Chewy to doggie day care too." Ella Mae cut a slice of tomato basil quiche and added a bowl of triple berry salad to a plate, garnishing the fruit with a sprig of fresh mint. "You told me that a special volunteer would show up today." She placed the finished plate onto Reba's tray. "How did you know?"

"Call it woman's intuition," Reba replied airily. "You never returned the man's calls and I bet that made him curious. Not too many women ignore a man who looks good enough to eat." She picked up the black tray and paused. "Be careful with that boy, Ella Mae. He's not for you."

"And why not?" Ella Mae felt her cheeks flood with color. Reba had obviously recognized the charge in the kitchen air when she'd first arrived. She could tell that something had happened between Ella Mae and Hugh. "Is it because I'm still married? I told him that Sloan and I are done."

Reba shook her head. "Not until the papers are signed, you're not. And it's more than that, sugar. Hugh's left a trail of broken hearts as long and wide as the Mississippi. He's not available even though he acts like he is. Trust me on this one. He's not for you. He can never be free to be the man you need him to be. He'll always be bound to another."

The words hung around well after Reba left to serve her customer. Ella Mae tried to ignore them and focus on the next order ticket, but they hovered like persistent wasps until she wished she could swat them from the room.

When Reba next appeared, there was a marked bounce

in her step. "Remember that plan you mentioned about usin' your feminine wiles to get Chandler's keys?"

Still irritated, Ella Mae answered with a curt, "Yeah?"

"No need!" Reba declared and then triumphantly flourished a set of keys. "He's out there havin' lunch and lookee what he dropped bending over to help an old lady pick up her cane."

Widening her eyes, Ella Mae forgot that she was annoyed. "How will we know which one unlocks the clinic?"

"How about this one?" Reba pulled a brass key from the ring. "Says 'clinic front door' clear as day." Grinning slyly, she dropped the key into her apron pocket, winked at Ella Mae, and disappeared through the swing doors with one of the dozen shoofly pies lined up on the wire racks.

Ella Mae was glad that she'd reserved a pie for Hugh, because by the time the lunch rush had ended, there were none left. She came out to the front room and presented him with a white bakery box tied with red-and-white-striped string while Reba was back in the kitchen loading the dishwasher.

With the exception of a young couple lingering over slices of peach tart, the pie shop was empty. Ella Mae felt suddenly uncomfortable and shy as she handed Hugh the box and thanked him for his help.

"This isn't much of a payment considering how hard you worked today," she said.

He held the box under his nose and inhaled. "Smells just like Granny Glattfelder's. If it tastes anything like hers, then I came out ahead."

Feeling like an awkward teen, Ella Mae shifted her weight from one foot to the other. "I'll pick up Chewy after we close. Will you be there to give me a tour?"

He shook his head. "No, but the staff will take good care of you." Smiling at her once more, he said good-bye and walked out the front door, the bells chiming in his wake. Ella Mae was tempted to rip them down. Their sound had heralded the death of Annie Beaufort and now the swift departure of a man she'd kissed with more passion than she had ever known. It left her hungry for more.

"Oh, dear," Reba said as she entered the front room to deliver the bill to the young couple in the window seat. "We always want the ones we can't have."

After locking up the shop, Ella Mae pedaled over to Canine to Five to collect Chewy. The doggie day care was thirteen thousand feet of canine bliss located directly behind the firehouse. Ella Mae was astounded by the nonslip rubber flooring, the play equipment, the exercise pool, the resting areas, and the outdoor space. Everywhere she looked, happy dogs were being trained, groomed, or given physical therapy while others were engaged in swimming games, eating, or resting in one of the dozens of unique dog beds.

Chewy was curled up in the middle of a pack of dogs in the small breeds room. He was the picture of contentment but still had the good grace to show Ella Mae that he'd missed her by leaping to his feet and covering her cheek with wet kisses.

"He's definitely teething," a Canine to Five staff member informed her. "And he's also really smart and very social. He's made tons of new friends today and we treated him to a massage and grooming session. Mr. Dylan wanted this little guy to have the star treatment. Not that he had to convince us to do anything extra. Charleston Chew has won us all over with his good manners and sweet smile. He's been a perfect gentleman today."

Ella Mae felt a rush of pride and wasted no time enrolling Chewy in the day care program.

Pedaling home in the late afternoon heat drained Ella Mae of every ounce of remaining energy. She still wanted to ask her mother what had transpired in the back garden last night but could manage only to drink a large glass of sweet tea, take a brief shower, and settle down on the sofa with a book. She read about five pages before her eyelids drooped closed.

Hours later, the combined sounds of a rumbling engine in the driveway and Chewy's barking woke her. Groggily, she sat up and stumbled to the front door. Reba's Buick was parked outside.

"Good thing you had a catnap!" Reba sauntered in and went straight into the kitchen. "You were probably as wrung out as a dish towel. Now come sit at the table and eat your supper. Oh, and this package was at the door." She placed a cardboard box on the table.

While Reba fixed a plate of fried chicken, okra, and corn and poured two glasses of iced tea, Ella Mae opened the box from the restaurant supply company. She'd ordered another marble rolling pin to replace the one taken from her mother's kitchen, and when she freed the pin from its layers of bubble and plastic wrap, she began to examine it carefully.

"I sure wouldn't want to be clobbered on the head with that," Reba remarked.

Ella Mae nodded, cradling the marble pin in her right palm. Her memory took her back to the sight of the smoldering façade of the nail salon, and she could almost smell the smoke and the harsh, acrid scents of chemical fumes. She pictured Hugh moving through the wreckage, ax in hand, searching for the tiny orange sparks burrowing deep into the heart of the charred wood.

She was so absorbed by the image that she lost her hold of the rolling pin when Chewy barked at a squirrel racing up the tree outside the window. The pin hit the floor with a crack, breaking neatly in the middle.

Ella Mae swore and bent over to collect the two halves. She peered into the hollow inside the pin and showed it to Reba. "Maybe this helps answer part of the mystery of the rolling pin."

"Why?" Reba shrugged. "What would somebody put in there? Cobra venom?"

"I don't know," Ella Mae admitted. "I haven't puzzled it all out yet, but look, see how these handles unscrew? You could slide something inside and replace the handles and no one would be the wiser."

Reba took one of the halves and held it up to her eye, spinning it like a kaleidoscope. "I could put a whole pack of Twizzlers in there. Now eat up. We've got places to break into, people to incriminate."

She consumed several licorice twists while Ella Mae ate, chatting about the day's customers and marveling over the generous tips she'd received. "I'll wash up," she said after Ella Mae had finished every scrap of food, leaving only a tidy pile of stripped chicken bones on her plate. "You'd better change into darker clothes. I don't want to get caught because somebody saw those white pants and thought you were a ghost."

"I feel as transparent as one," Ella Mae said glumly. "Until these murders are solved, I won't be welcome in Havenwood. People will see me as the woman who grew up here and left the town behind for bigger and better things, only to return bearing a curse."

"Folks don't think that. Not the ones comin' into the pie shop anyway." Reba shrugged. "And if they ain't payin' customers, I don't give a fig what they think. Now scoot upstairs and change so we can get our hands on that snake bill."

Ella Mae insisted on driving. She couldn't handle Reba's reckless speed or wild curve hugging on a full stomach. By the time they crossed into Little Kentucky, the sky had morphed from a dark pewter to a bruised blue black and millions of stars glittered above the fields of the equine center.

"It's a good thing people are spread out in this county," Ella Mae remarked. "This car is not stealthy."

Reba gave the dashboard an affectionate pat. "You can't

beat a real American-made engine. Those foreign tin cans might save on gas money, but they don't have a shred of personality."

Parking behind the largest barn, it occurred to Ella Mae that someone might be bunking with the horses, especially if one of the clinic's patients was recovering from surgery, but there were no other cars in sight.

"I hope this place isn't wired with some fancy alarm system," Reba muttered as she pulled Chandler's key from her pocket. "We won't have much time to rifle through drawers with a siren ringin' in our ears."

Ella Mae peered in through the glass double doors. "I don't see anything mounted on the wall. What would people steal? It's not like they have lots of cash on hand."

"What about drugs?" Reba countered. "Aren't they the cause of this whole mess?"

"Good point," Ella Mae conceded and held her breath while Reba fit the key into the lock, turned, and opened the door a crack.

No alarm sounded. In fact, the center was preternaturally quiet. Expecting to hear muffled noises from the horses in the barn or those recovering from surgery inside the clinic, Ella Mae was spooked by the heavy silence.

Unperturbed, Reba switched on her flashlight and directed the beam at Peggy's desk. "Where'd you see that bill?"

After a quick examination of Peggy's papers and file folders, it was clear that the bill was no longer in her possession. Ella Mae couldn't find a single reference to Uraeus Pharmaceuticals nor was there a hanging folder for the Malones or Hollowells in Peggy's file cabinet. There was no paper trail indicating that Bradford Knox had ever treated any of their animals.

"This is going from bad to worse," Ella Mae murmured morosely.

"Don't go all doom and gloom on me," Reba ordered and

flipped Peggy's desk calendar over. "Well, well. Looks like Peggy spent her coffee breaks fantasizin' about the Boss Man."

There, taped to the cardboard of the calendar, were candid shots of Bradford Knox surrounding a photo of Peggy and Bradford taken in front of the clinic. Balloons were tied to the door and Bradford appeared to be much younger, so Ella Mae deduced that it was from the equine center's grand opening. The two were laughing and had their arms wrapped around each other's waists and Peggy had drawn a red heart around the photo.

"Poor Peggy. I wonder how long she carried a torch for him." Ella Mae passed the flashlight beam over the pictures again. "According to his children, Bradford was devoted to his wife. A few years after she passed away he took up with Loralyn Gaynor. That must have torn Peggy's heart in two— to have been passed over like that."

"I thought you said that Peggy spoke kindly of Loralyn," Reba remarked.

"She did. I certainly didn't detect any animosity. Peggy actually defended Loralyn by saying that she wasn't a gold digger."

Reba replaced the calendar. "This just gets weirder and weirder. Let's go root through Chandler's office."

Chandler wasn't nearly as organized as Peggy. Ella Mae couldn't see how he functioned among such dishevelment, but then recalled a college professor telling her that some of the world's most brilliant people had their own unique classification system. Still, it made finding the incriminating bill impossible. The pair searched for nearly an hour but found nothing useful.

"We'll be here all night," Ella Mae complained, watching as Reba fanned the pages of a *Journal of the American Veterinary Medical Association*. Tossing it on top of a teetering stack of similar publications, Reba turned her attention to the slim center drawer of Chandler's desk.

"Locked."

Ella Mae slammed a file cabinet drawer in exasperation. "We've got to see what's in there."

Reba unzipped her purse and produced a small utility knife. Selecting the nail file, she inserted the blade into the keyhole, turned, and smiled as the lock disengaged with a click.

"Is there anything you can't do?" Ella Mae asked in amazement.

Reba shrugged. "I can't curl my tongue. Other than that, I'm damned near perfect."

Inside the drawer was a single file folder. Ella Mae whipped it open and discovered that the equine center was mortgaged to the hilt. Underneath this bank statement were several bills from Uraeus Pharmaceuticals. Apparently, an order for cobra venom had been placed six months ago. Vials containing powdered venom were delivered in a timely fashion, but no payment had been received by Uraeus. The company sent several letters addressed to Bradford Knox requesting that the outstanding balance be paid. Interest was added to the amount due until Knox was in debt to Uraeus Pharmaceuticals for tens of thousands of dollars.

"Bingo!" Reba whispered.

Ella Mae pointed the flashlight beam into the drawer and spotted a piece of white paper stuffed to the back of the drawer. She did her best to flatten the wrinkles and then read the typed missive aloud, "We're coming for our money. Have it ready or your center will burn. And there's no telling who will be inside this time."

Below that was a date and time.

Ella Mae and Reba exchanged horrified glances.

"That's today's date," Ella Mae rasped and checked her watch. "We only have a few minutes to get out of here!"

Reba's eyes were dark and wide with dread. "Too late. Someone's comin'."

Chapter 17

At first, the only sound Reba and Ella Mae could make out was the rumble of a car engine. In a panic, they replaced the folder, shut the desk drawer, hit the lights in Chandler's office, closed his door, and raced across the hall to hide in the small kitchen. As they panted in the dark, the jingle of keys and the squeak of rubber-soled shoes against the lobby flooring indicated that someone had come inside.

"Did you grab a copy of one of the bills?" Reba whispered.

"Yes," Ella Mae answered and then took a quick, anxious peek down the hall. The lights were on in the lobby and she could see Chandler. He had his back turned and was staring fixedly out the front door. Moments passed and he didn't move but stood like a sentinel on the rectangular mat just inside the door.

When an abrupt flash from a pair of powerful headlamps illuminated the glass, Chandler shielded his eyes and uttered a low curse. His voice held both anger and anxiety.

Tires crunched over gravel and two car doors slammed

shut. Ella Mae heard Chandler gasp. Wondering if he'd recognized his late-night visitors, she ducked her head back into the kitchen before the newcomers could spot her.

There was a whoosh of air as the pair entered, altering the silence. Before, when it had just been Ella Mae and Reba inside the clinic, the building had felt poised on the brink, as if it were waiting for an inevitable event to occur. Now the atmosphere was cold with dread. Gooseflesh erupted on Ella Mae's arms and she resisted the temptation to grab hold of Reba's hand. Instead, she edged closer to the smaller woman, drawing comfort from the warmth of her body and her strawberry scent.

Two sets of footfalls crossed the threshold. The first was heavy and distinctly male while the other was the light and graceful tread of a woman.

"You!" Chandler hissed loudly, echoes of indignation reverberating down the corridor.

"Were you expecting hit men dressed in black? A carload of tattooed thugs with brass knuckles? Sorry to disappoint," a female voice scoffed.

There was a pause and Ella Mae could almost visualize Chandler struggling to accept the identity of the Uraeus representatives. It had to be Uraeus, Ella Mae reasoned. The company had sent someone to collect the money owed to them by Bradford Knox. And since the note threatened that the center could be burned, Ella Mae also had to assume that the two people standing before Chandler had had a hand in torching Loralyn's nail salon. It was also possible that this pair had struck Bradford with a marble rolling pin, started a fire, and left him in the salon to die.

She shuddered at the thought.

"Who's the woman?" Reba's whisper was barely audible. "Is it Peggy? The woman scorned? Knowin' what office managers get paid, she probably wouldn't say no to some extra spendin' money either. Sounds like a double motive to me."

Ella Mae didn't have the opportunity to answer because Chandler began to speak again.

"The only reason I came tonight is to find out who dared to send me a note referencing my father's murder." His voice was a dangerous growl. "And it turns out *you* sent it. That *you* knew what happened to him all along. You disgusting, greedy, little bitch."

There was a tinkle of derisive laughter from the woman followed by the deep bass of a man's voice. "We're not here for drama, Chandler. Just give us the money."

"Look, mister." Chandler's tone changed abruptly as he addressed the stranger. "This center isn't turning over enough profit to pay you the full amount. You can look over our books if you don't believe me. I've brought all I could afford from my personal savings, but this money is not for *her*; it's to serve as the first payment toward my father's debt." Chandler was clearly struggling to remain calm. Icicles entered his voice when he spoke next. "I can't believe he got involved with illegal doping, but did you have to kill him for *this* amount of money?"

"It's no small amount to our company," the man answered.

"I'm not talking to you, *sir*. I'm talking to the spoiled waste of breath standing to your left," Chandler said acidly.

Ella Mae pressed her mouth close to Reba's ear. "I don't think the woman is Peggy."

"Did you go to a firin' range in New York? Keep your shootin' skills up?" Reba whispered in return.

"What? *No*." Ella Mae had no time to consider the odd question before she felt the cold metal of a small revolver pressed into her right hand.

"It'll come back to you. It's like ridin' a bike. All muscle memory."

Shifting her hand so that it closed around the grip, Ella Mae's index finger felt for the trigger while her thumb located the hammer. It would take approximately three seconds to aim, pull back the hammer, and fire. She knew better than to ask Reba whether the gun was loaded. Its cool weight felt solid in her hand, instilling her with a sense of calm. No one would be striking Chandler on the head and leaving him to die while the equine center burned down around him. Not if Ella Mae could help it.

She forced herself to concentrate on the conversation in the lobby. The tension between Chandler and the malevolent woman was obviously escalating.

"How could you let him die?" Chandler was asking, grief and rage billowing into the air like smoke. "Did you watch it happen or did you hit him? Are you that evil?"

"Oh, stop it, Chandler. Do you think I'd attack him with a rolling pin? I wouldn't even know how to hold one. I've never been much good in the kitchen." She chortled. "My associate from Uraeus, Dirk, did that, but it was kind of by accident, wasn't it, Dirk? If Daddy had just given us the cash he owed, none of this would have happened. But he wouldn't. Dirk was forced to grab the rolling pin out of his hands and then Daddy rushed for the door. He was trying to call the cops on his cell, and obviously, Dirk couldn't let him make that call." There was a pause, and in the lull, Ella Mae realized that she recognized the speaker's voice.

"That's Ashleigh Knox," she muttered in horror. "Chandler's sister."

Ella Mae could feel Reba's body grow tense in response. She was like a wild cat preparing to spring, her blood simmering with unspent adrenaline. Ella Mae was also drawn as taut as a wire. Her hand was tight on the gun's grip and she stood with her knees slightly bent, intent on leaping forward any moment. She didn't pause to consider the danger she might face. Even though she was trapped in the clinic with two people who'd resort to violence to get what they wanted, Ella Mae was determined that this was to be the end of the line for Ashleigh and her sidekick, the man named Dirk.

Chandler must have been looking at his sister through

eyes tinged red with rage. "I wouldn't give you a dime, Ashleigh. You leeched off our parents and a bunch of rich, weak men who were dumb enough to marry you. You've never mucked a stall or filled a feed bag. You've never so much as chipped a nail doing manual labor. You are owed *nothing* because you've earned *nothing*."

"Why should I have shoveled shit?" Ashleigh sounded shocked by the notion. "Daddy always told me that I was meant for more—that our family was going to rise higher than his parents had ever dreamed. He sent me to finishing school and I married well and I moved up with every divorce. *That* was my job. I did what was expected of me!" Ashleigh spat.

"Our parents expected you to become a *lady*," Chandler retorted. "Instead you cheated on three husbands, maxed out dozens of credit cards, and gambled away any cash you could get your filthy hands on."

After this short speech there was a brisk, heated exchange between Ashleigh and her partner. Dirk demanded that they take Chandler's money and go without any more chitchat, but Ashleigh clearly didn't care to be told what to do and had a few choice words for her associate before focusing her malice on Chandler again.

"Dirk here didn't exactly score an eighteen hundred on his SATs, but he's got a point. We should get going. I'll allow you to walk out of this dump on two conditions. First, give me the pittance you brought. Second, find me the rolling pin Loralyn took from the nail salon and we'll forgive the rest of the debt."

If Ella Mae was surprised by the second part of the offer, Chandler was even more so. "Who cares about this rolling pin? It's too late to clean off any fingerprints and the cops have it, not Loralyn. I guess you and your buddy Dirk made a serious mistake."

"Dirk's prints weren't on that rolling pin. He wiped it off with alcohol, thank you very much. Too bad the fire department got there before it had a chance to burn, but the cops still have nothing on us," Ashleigh declared triumphantly. "And we didn't make *any* mistakes the second time."

The significance of Ashleigh's phrase "the second time," hit Ella Mae like a blow to the stomach. Chandler had seized on that statement as well. "Annie Beaufort . . . that was your handiwork?"

"She was going to tell that nosy pie girl everything! I charged a few of our clients an extra fee to take care of Bleeding Heart Beaufort. And the best part? My weapons were totally free. The tranquilizer Dirk shot into Annie's neck came from your supply room." Ashleigh laughed with delight, causing Ella Mae to clench her jaw so tightly her teeth hurt. "All that's left is getting the rolling pin from Loralyn. It's taken me a little while to figure out that she switched the two pins, but I won't let that stand in my way. You're going to be my errand boy, Chandler."

"Get ready," Reba whispered. "The storm's about to break."

"Go to hell, Ashleigh," Chandler said and Ella Mae sensed that he had begun to move away from the front doors. Perhaps he was trying to reach the phone on Peggy's desk. "You've manipulated people all your life, but you won't get your way this time. I'm not one of your husbands or lackeys. I'm the man who's going to make sure you get locked up until you're old and gray. And as soon as the judge's gavel falls, I will sell every possession in that Atlanta mansion of yours and give the proceeds to Annie's ranch."

Ashleigh shouted, "Put that phone down! *NOW!*" Less than a second later, the shout escalated to a shrill shriek. "Dirk, stop him!"

In unison, Ella Mae and Reba sprang into the hallway, guns cocked, barrels pointed dead ahead.

"Freeze!" they yelled simultaneously.

A stocky, pug-faced man went slack-jawed in surprise,

the Beretta in his hand dipping slightly toward the floor. Ella Mae had enough time to register the silencer attached to the end of the sleek firearm before Chandler struck out with his foot, knocking the Beretta to the ground. The gun slid across the laminate floor and Ashleigh lunged for it.

Ella Mae raced forward, launching herself at Ashleigh Knox. The two women were about the same size, but Ella Mae's athleticism combined with momentum gave her the advantage. She slammed into her opponent, forcing Ashleigh off balance. With a snarl, Ashleigh fell.

Pressing her father's Magnum mini against her opponent's temple, Ella Mae commanded Ashleigh to put her hands behind her back. She then sat on the other woman's rump and looked around for something to use to bind her wrists.

The action on her side of the room had taken all of fifteen seconds. During that time, it was obvious that Reba and Chandler had subdued Dirk. Chandler had not escaped unscathed, however. The flesh around his left eye was turning a deep plum and blood trickled from his nose. While Ella Mae caught her breath, Reba tied Dirk's hands to his ankles using a horse lead and a series of intricate knots.

"Call the cops and then throw Ella Mae the phone cord," she told Chandler. "I'm sure she doesn't want to perch on your sister's ass for the rest of the night, though I reckon that girl's long overdue for a servin' of humble pie." Having trussed up Dirk like stuffed chicken ready for the oven, Reba pulled her cell phone from her pocket and used the camera function to snap a picture of Ashleigh.

"Your ex-husbands are gonna love that pose," she taunted.

Ashleigh began to swear, spittle hitting the floor as she vented her rage. She struggled to be free of Ella Mae's weight, bucking and kicking like an unbroken colt. Chandler hurriedly completed his phone call and then ripped the phone cord out of the wall.

Reba helped Ella Mae bind Ashleigh's wrists and then,

with a gleam of genuine pleasure, yanked the Hermès scarf from Ashleigh's neck and used it as a gag.

Chandler watched in horror as his only sibling rolled back and forth on the floor, her muffled screams of hatred and wrath reverberating throughout the lobby. The anger in his eyes was slowly giving way to sorrow as the truth set in. His sister had been an accomplice in the murder of her own father. She had committed the most grievous sin in exchange for money, and the full impact of her wickedness was washing over Chandler in a wave of palpable anguish. Ella Mae noticed the color drain from the undamaged flesh of his face and steered him into the kitchen.

She held him by the elbow as he vomited into the sink. He retched over and over until there was nothing left but empty heaves.

"Are you okay out there?" she called to Reba.

"Right as rain. You just look after the good doctor."

Easing Chandler into a chair, Ella Mae poured him a glass of water and then searched in the freezer for something to put over his swollen eye. She found an ice pack, wrapped it in a dish towel, and placed it gently against his skin. He grabbed her wrist and held it as though it were a lifeline until she sank into the seat next to him.

"I'm so sorry, Chandler," she whispered, feeling an ache in her chest as she witnessed the pain overtaking him. It appeared like a cloud in his good eye, but she knew that it had permeated throughout his whole being, creeping through every cell like a dark fog.

He nodded, too shell-shocked to speak.

The minutes crawled by and Ella Mae used the heavy silence to wrap her mind around all that had happened. She should have felt a measure of relief. After all, Bradford and Annie's killers had been caught and the police were on the way. In a few hours, Ella Mae would no longer be considered a suspect and she could finally focus on the pie shop and her fresh start in Havenwood.

But she didn't feel the slightest inkling of relief. Only numbness.

Chandler lowered the ice pack and looked at her. "I don't mean to sound ungrateful, but what were you two doing here at this time of night?"

Ella Mae removed the Uraeus bill she'd stuffed into her back pocket and handed it to him. "Reba helped herself to your keys during lunch today. We let ourselves in and searched your office." She tried to meet his gaze, but his left eye was now swollen shut and shame forced her to look at the table instead. "I wanted to find out what happened to your father and to Annie. Whether I liked it or not, I was involved. The cops certainly believed I had something to do with his death and I had to prove them wrong."

Chandler just stared at her.

"My prints were on the rolling pin the cops found at the nail salon," she continued. "A detail that still makes no sense. Why would Ashleigh ask you to get it back? And what's all this stuff about Loralyn? She was in Atlanta when this happened."

"Why a rolling pin?" Chandler asked in a monotone, gazing off into the middle distance. He didn't seem to be directing the question at Ella Mae. "It's not something people carry around in their pockets. If it hadn't have been in the nail salon in the first place, maybe my father . . ." The words died in his throat.

Ella Mae thought of the broken rolling pin sitting in her kitchen. Ashleigh said that her father was supposed to have been carrying money. He entered the salon carrying a rolling pin—one that had a hollow interior.

That's where the money was hidden, she realized with a jolt. *But clearly it wasn't inside. Ashleigh wants Chandler to get it back from Loralyn. Loralyn!* Ella Mae's hands balled into fists. *I knew she wasn't innocent!*

Looking at Chandler, Ella Mae's resolve to seek justice

exacted doubled. "We'll make it right," she said with feeling. "I promise you. They'll pay for what they've done."

The shrill cry of multiple sirens cut through the night. Ella Mae imagined the tan cruisers from Little Kentucky's sheriff's department racing up the long drive followed by at least one Havenwood police car. She realized that this might be her only chance to interrogate Ashleigh about the rolling pin. Once in police custody, Ashleigh would lawyer up. She was exactly the type of person who believed that a crafty defense attorney could see to it that she'd serve no jail time.

Terrified by the thought, Ella Mae advised Chandler to stay where he was until the police entered the building and moved to leave, but he reached up and grabbed her by the arm.

"Thank you for saving me," he said.

"We only helped. That was a well-aimed kick." Ella Mae gave him a shy smile. "Does this mean you're not mad at me for breaking in?"

He shook his head. "You were searching for the truth. I was too. I should have known what was going on right under my nose, but my father kept me so busy with other facets of the practice that I never took care of the star thoroughbreds or saw any of the billing paperwork. The latest Uraeus bill was addressed to me and I left it on Peggy's desk with a big question mark, but she didn't know what the products were." He sighed. "She called Uraeus and they refused to tell her anything, insisting that they'd only discuss the matter with me. But I put it off. Between my father's death and my trying to keep the lights on around here, I didn't have time to deal with them."

The sirens were getting closer. "Chandler, you did the best you could during a really difficult time." She removed his hand from her arm and squeezed it gently. "You're not going to go through this alone. I'll stay with you as long as you need me. Why don't you wait here? I'll be back in a few minutes."

Her words recalled the promise made to her by Hugh on Sunday morning. She felt a rush of warmth as she visualized him wearing a Charmed Pie Shoppe apron and pressing close to her in search of a kiss. The memory of their lips meeting glimmered in her eyes like tinsel, and the corners of her mouth turned up in a smile.

But then, she recalled how their kiss had gone from being warm and passionate to intense and oddly painful. Reba had warned her away from Hugh, saying that he wasn't free— that he was bound to another just like Ella Mae was still bound to Sloan.

Once I put this mess to rights, Ella Mae thought. *I'm going to figure out the mystery that is Hugh Dylan.*

In the lobby, Reba sat in one of the waiting room chairs, a magazine open on her lap, her gun pointed at Dirk's chest. She chewed a licorice stick and flipped through ads of horse products as if she was waiting for an appointment with her hair stylist.

Stooping by Ashleigh's face, Ella Mae removed the silk gag. "If you shoot your mouth off, this gag goes right back on," she warned. "I want some answers."

"You'll regret interfering in a family matter, Pie Girl." Ashleigh's voice was a dry hiss. Lying on her belly, she twisted from side to side like a serpent and Ella Mae almost moved away, but she held her revulsion in check, listening to the sound of tires displacing the gravel outside.

"Why the nail salon?" she asked, knowing there was a good chance Ashleigh wouldn't play along.

"That little slut was supposed to deliver the money. I had no idea she'd end up in Atlanta that night. Somehow she got Daddy to come instead. And then my fool of a father shows up and tells me he didn't bring the money. God, I wish it had been *her.* I wish his tramp had died that night."

Ella Mae tried to ignore the multicolored lights flashing through the lobby's glass doors. "The original meeting was supposed to be with Loralyn?"

"Yesssss," Ashleigh answered in another snakelike rasp. "And I was going to make it clear that she wasn't welcome in our family."

Some of Ella Mae's confusion ebbed away. "It was always your intention to burn down the salon that night. You wanted to scare Loralyn into breaking it off with your father."

Ashleigh had noticed the strobe from the light bars of the four cop cars. "Daddy promised to pay Uraeus's cut and what I'd earned in commission with bearer bonds he'd bought years ago. I opened doors for him from Atlanta to Kentucky. I *did* work for that money. But Daddy showed up that night with that stupid rolling pin and big talk about how his slutty fiancée was going to help us expand our business and elevate our family name to a whole new level. He asked us to be patient a little while longer while she set up a plan." She snorted, her eyes blazing with hatred. "As if her plans were better than mine! He picked her over *me*!"

"Your father brought the rolling pin with him? It was supposed to contain those bearer bonds, but it was empty, wasn't it?" Ella Mae muttered seconds before a gang of uniformed men entered the clinic.

A sheriff's deputy reached her in two strides. "Please step away, ma'am," he commanded and she promptly obeyed.

The looks she received from Officers Wells and Hardy when they saw her standing in between two people with bound wrists and ankles might have once terrified her. Now, however, she was too caught up in Ashleigh's tale about the night Bradford Knox died to pay the grim-faced policemen much attention.

"Dr. Knox is in the kitchen," Reba explained in a chipper tone utterly incongruent with the scene. "Dirk over there has a serious right hook. The poor doc is gonna have a hell of a shiner, but maybe he can tell his clients he got kicked by a horse." She laughed at her own joke while the cops blinked at her in befuddlement.

Chandler suddenly appeared in the hallway and the four

lawmen immediately tensed, their hands flying to their holsters.

"That man and that woman"—Chandler pointed at Dirk and Ashleigh without so much as a glance at his sister—"are responsible for the murders of my father, Bradford Knox, and Annie Beaufort." He then gestured at Ella Mae and Reba. "These women came to my rescue when it became apparent that I was going to be the third victim."

Ashleigh and Dirk had remained quiet, but when Wells squatted down next to Ashleigh and asked for her name, she called him a dumb pig and spit in his face. While Wells wiped the spittle from his nose and cheeks, Ashleigh cursed everyone in the room.

"Please get her out of here," one of the deputies said to Hardy. "You can Mirandize her outside."

Hardy and Wells lifted Ashleigh to her feet and half dragged her into the night. She struggled and alternated between howling like a rabid wolf and threatening the officers with a bevy of lawsuits.

"Jesus, the mouth on that one," a muscular deputy with a buzz cut remarked in amazement. "And I thought I heard the worst that could be heard in the corps."

Dirk departed with much more dignity and was escorted to one of the deputy's cars. The deputies waited in their vehicles and Wells stayed with Ashleigh while Hardy returned to the clinic. He asked for a brief synopsis of the evening's events, and Ella Mae was more than happy to remain silent while Chandler did all the talking.

"So Ms. LeFaye and her companion were breaking and entering?" Hardy inquired at one point.

"We entered, but there wasn't a lick of breakin' involved," Reba interjected, her hands on her hips. "And I've already given the key back to Dr. Knox. He won't be pressin' any charges. After all, we saved his hide."

Hardy raised a quizzical brow but then pivoted to face

Chandler again. "Sir, it seemed like you knew the female assailant. Can you tell me her name?"

The air deflated from Chandler's lungs. He looked at Ella Mae, his eyes entreating her to speak on his behalf.

She walked up to Hardy, moving as close to him as she dared. He smelled surprisingly pleasant. She detected pine needles and spearmint, but Hardy stiffened as she invaded his personal space.

"Officer, her name is Ashleigh Knox," she whispered. Despite her soft tone, she could sense a wave of grief and shame rolling off Chandler. His hurt collided with the lobby's air molecules like some devastating tsunami and Ella Mae's eyes grew wet with tears.

Hardy nodded and Ella Mae knew that he was aware of Chandler's pain. "I see," he answered with deliberate gentleness.

But Chandler needed to lay claim to Ashleigh, regardless of the cost. Undoubtedly, he felt he deserved this agony for failing to save his father from his tragic fate. Following a ragged inhalation, Chandler straightened his shoulders and said, "Ashleigh's my sister. God help me, but she's my sister."

Chapter 18

Ella Mae would have done anything to avoid another two- or three-hour stint in The Havenwood Police Department, but it couldn't be helped. She recited her role in the night's events but omitted her theory about the bearer bonds and the rolling pin. Unbeknownst to Bradford Knox, Loralyn must have switched pins, simultaneously implicating Ella Mae in the crime and allowing her to walk away with her fiancé's nest egg. That meant Loralyn was just as responsible for Bradford's death as Dirk and Ashleigh were, and Ella Mae was determined to make her pay. The police wouldn't be able to prove Loralyn's culpability. They had no evidence against her and Loralyn would simply lie and play the part of the grieving widow. Not only that, but Ella Mae had yet to find the holes in Loralyn's alibi.

"Let's review your statement," the young female officer interviewing her said.

Ella Mae recounted the details again and again until she finally put her head on her forearms and closed her eyes, too exhausted to repeat her testimony another time.

"Just type up whatever you want and I'll sign it," she told a young female officer. Apparently, Wells and Hardy had bigger fish to fry. "Seriously," Ella Mae moaned. "You can blame the whole thing on me if it means I can go to bed."

The officer pushed back her chair and came around the table. Ella Mae heard a click as she turned off the recorder. Then the woman touched her lightly on the shoulder. "I think we have enough. You can leave now."

Ella Mae nodded gratefully. "If you need to find me, I'll be at my pie shop bright and early. I'll even make something special for you."

"In that case, I might just drop by to go over a few things." She winked and then busied herself at the computer. A few minutes later, she handed Ella Mae a printout of her statement. "Sign here and here." She collected the papers and said, "I'm especially keen on desserts with nuts."

"There'll be an almond and apricot tart on tomorrow's menu, assuming I can stay awake long enough to do any baking."

The woman opened the door and gestured for Ella Mae to step out into the hall. "I know all about sleep deprivation. I've had the night shift for the past two years."

Ella Mae was just about to ask after Reba when she appeared in the corridor, looking utterly unfazed by the whole experience. "Come on, sugar. Time to go home."

The Buick's cracked bench seat couldn't have felt more welcoming had it been made of kid leather. "You rest now," Reba ordered. "We can rehash this crazy night in the mornin'."

For once, she obeyed the speed limit. The car rocked and swayed as it hugged the curves and climbed over gentle hills, lulling Ella Mae to the edge of sleep. She had no memory of arriving at Partridge Hill, putting on her nightgown, or curling up in bed with Chewy. Only the shrill call of her clock alarm sounding in her ear could lift her through a fog of exhaustion.

Reba was already dressed and sitting in the guest cottage's cozy kitchen when Ella Mae stumbled down the stairs. Her whiskey-colored hair was tangled, her complexion wan, and her gait stilted, like that of a newly minted zombie. She'd even put her T-shirt on inside out.

"Coffee." Reba handed her a thermos. "You can drink it in the car."

Ushering Chewy into the backseat, Ella Mae examined Reba in amazement. She looked well rested and immaculately groomed. Her hair was gelled into a high waves and her makeup was flawless. "Did you stay in the main house last night?"

Reba nodded. "I've got a change of clothes there. I caught your mama up on our little adventure and then slept a bit. You know I've never needed much shut-eye. I was born with caffeine in my veins." She turned on the Buick's engine and tossed a newspaper onto Ella Mae's lap before peeling out of the driveway, gravel spraying into the air. "That front page will wake you up. Take a gander."

Ella Mae had expected the headlines of *The Daily* to center on the arrest of Ashleigh Knox, but the news had apparently occurred too late to make the small town paper's deadline. The feature story was sufficiently shocking and Ella Mae bolted upright, her seat belt digging into her breastbone.

"What the hell?" She brought the photograph occupying the front page closer to her face. "Are these people wearing any clothes?"

"Naked as babies in the tub," Reba said cheerily. "But not quite as innocent. Start readin'."

Below a headline asking, "Havenwood: A Nudist Colony?" the local reporter had written:

> *Several businesses kicked off the workweek by becoming the setting for acts of spontaneous nudity. Whether influenced by the heat, something they ate, or a temporary lapse*

in sanity, three of Havenwood's residents and a pair of
vacationers claimed to have felt an inexplicable urge to
remove their clothes and make a physical connection with
another person. Mabel Johnston of Woodbury, Minnesota,
selected her husband as the source of her affection, but
Havenwood native Mr. Edward Dobbs went farther afield
to seek out the source of his devotion. He strolled down
Queen Street, entered the public library, and attempted to
coerce a kiss from Miss Lillian Pettigrew, the reference
librarian.

Ella Mae's mouth fell open as she read about the other
locals who stripped their clothes and tried to seduce members of the opposite sex. One man grabbed a cashier's mike
at the Piggly Wiggly, dropped his trousers, and recited a
Shakespearean love sonnet to the dumbfounded store manager. An elderly Sunday school teacher pulled off her dress
and began scattering rose petals at the feet of a Mr. Andrews,
an employee at Hogue's funeral home.

"They completely lost control of their inhibitions." Ella
Mae put the paper down. "Is this town going crazy?"

Reba shot her a sidelong glance. "What's it gonna take
for you to see, girl? What happened to that old man who did
cartwheels down the street? How did your aunts cry blue
tears? Why did those folks get so turned on that they felt
like their clothes were on fire and had to shuck them off like
husks from a corncob?"

"It can't be my pies that—" The protest died on Ella
Mae's lips. "It's impossible."

"Says who?" Reba snorted. "People have all sorts of gifts.
Maybe yours just comes on a little stronger than most. But
you've gotta be careful. If those newspaper folks sniff
around too much, the world will wanna dissect you like a
frog in biology class."

Ella Mae shook her head in protest, but even as she did
so, her mind returned to the pie shop kitchen and she saw

Hugh standing before her. Her fingers tingled, recalling the feel of his wavy, dark hair, and a surge of heat coursed through her body as she remembered how they'd melted into one another. She could almost feel the burning again, as if the electricity generated by their desire had gone beyond any normal physical sensation. Pain alongside pleasure.

"The shoofly pie," she murmured, her voice embarrass-ingly sultry. "Every cell in my body wanted Hugh. That's what I was feeling when I mixed the filling. After he kissed me, I sprinkled sugar on the top of the pie. My blood was pounding and I felt like a fire was lit under my skin. I swear the crumbs sparkled."

Reba reached over and patted the newspaper. "I reckon those folks had a slice of that pie. Lucky devils. 'Course I don't need any help from your pies to get the urge. It comes on quite regular, thank you very much."

She careened into the parking lot behind the pie shop and screeched to a halt. "Better get some of that coffee down your throat or your customers are gonna fall asleep at the table. And that's no good because they might be too tired to reach into their wallets for my big, fat tip."

The summer morning grew in strength, filling the kitchen with sunbeams as Ella Mae prepared the regular menu items and then added an almond tart to the dessert list. Despite having only five hours of sleep, her movements were fluid. She felt like one of the dancers from Sissy's school as she chopped, sliced, and stirred in time to the piano sonata play-ing on the radio.

Reba took charge of the salad preparation and then read-ied both the indoor and outdoor eating areas. Chewy was stationed on the front porch, his leash tied to one of the rails. The town was still slumbering at this point, but the terrier amused himself by snapping at insects or barking out a greeting to the paperboy or occasional jogger.

Ella Mae was grateful to have so many tasks on which to concentrate. She didn't want the image of Chandler's anguished face or the bitter sound of Ashleigh's cutting words to influence her baking. If her feelings were somehow being transferred into her food, she'd have to be careful not to let the negative ones take over while she was prepping her pies. And this morning, that meant pushing aside the puzzling aspects of Ashleigh's confession.

At half past eight, Reba offered to bring Chewy to Canine to Five. Ella Mae glanced at the sausage browning on the cooktop and back at her dog with regret. The devoted parent in her wanted to deliver Chewy to day care herself, but she didn't want to neglect the sizzling meat or chance running into Hugh. She wasn't ready to sort out what their kiss had meant. Not today. Not yet.

"Have a great day, Charleston," she said, holding her little dog in her arms. She fed him a piece of chicken breast and ruffled the fur behind his ears before Reba led him outside.

Ella Mae had just transferred the sausage crumbles to a plate covered with paper towels when someone knocked on the back door. Pausing the mixer, which had been beating the eggs for the breakfast quiche, she peered out the window over the sink and instantly recognized Chandler's car.

"Hi," she said, stepping aside. "Come on in."

Chandler looked like hell. His bruise had turned the same hue as a prune and the skin beneath his good eye was gray with fatigue. His hair stuck straight out on one side of his head and stubble had sprouted across the lower half of his face.

"Have you been up all night?" she asked, taking him by the elbow and leading him to a stool.

He shrugged with the slow weariness of the grieving. "It feels longer than that. Years longer."

"I've got fresh coffee. Let me get you a cup and then we'll talk."

She pushed through the swing doors and filled two mugs embellished with The Charmed Pie Shoppe's logo with a strong Colombian brew. Grabbing a sugar bowl and a small pitcher of cream from the tiny refrigerator below the counter, Ella Mae was surprised by how much she wanted to comfort the man waiting in her kitchen. It was a completely different feeling from the complex and powerful hunger she felt for Hugh or the dull ache that overtook her whenever she thought of Sloan. This was a calm, governable attraction— something she could handle after everything that had happened over the tumultuous past few weeks.

"Drink this," Ella Mae commanded gently, placing the mug in front of Chandler. "And you're going to eat something too." He began to shake his head but she wagged a warning finger at him. "No arguing. Trust me, my food will make you feel better."

A row of individual breakfast tarts made with eggs, cheese, avocado, crème fraîche, Capicola, and chives were baking in the oven. When there were only two minutes of cook time remaining, Ella Mae grabbed a bowl of grated provolone and opened the oven door. As she sprinkled the cheese over golden, buttery puff-pastry squares, she did her best to conjure up images that made her feel hopeful. She let her memory drift back to the simple pleasure of shopping for new school supplies every August, listening to Dick Clark broadcasting the New Year's Eve countdown, and the sight of fireworks igniting the sky above Lake Havenwood.

She didn't know whether it was a trick of the light, but the cheese shimmered as it fell onto the baking pastry squares. The twinkle was gone in a blink, and by the time she'd placed a tart on a plate with a sliced strawberry garnish, she began to doubt it had been there at all.

"Now we can talk." Ella Mae served Chandler the tart. She then sharpened a large knife and began to cut cucumbers into delicate slivers. "I hope you don't mind my working. I'm running a bit behind today."

Chandler pinched the strawberry between his thumb and index finger and stared at it as if he'd never seen the bright red fruit before. "I'm sorry, I don't mean to get in your way. It's just that you're the only one who knows what I'm going through. You were there and, well, you were amazing." He put the strawberry back onto his plate.

"You were pretty fearless yourself," Ella Mae said with an encouraging smile.

With a crooked grin, Chandler pointed at his bruised cheek. "Yeah, you should see the other guy."

Ella Mae laughed. "I'm glad you haven't lost your sense of humor. Most people would be home in bed with the covers pulled over their heads after what you've been through."

Absently gripping his fork, Chandler cut through the breakfast tart and speared a mouthful with the tines. He didn't eat, however. "Couldn't sleep if I tried. There are things that still don't make sense about what's happened. It's bad enough that my own sister had a hand in my father's murder—it'll take me years to deal with that—but I have questions." He sighed. "And until they're answered, this isn't over."

That was the last thing Ella Mae wanted to hear. More than anything, she hoped that the taint from the deaths of Bradford Knox and Annie Beaufort would fade as quickly as possible. She knew the pall cast by two murders would linger, forever staining her homecoming and the opening of the pie shop with a dark and ragged shadow, but at least the townsfolk would know that she had no part in the violence that had ridden into Havenwood on the shoulders of Ashleigh Knox.

"Take the rolling pin," Chandler continued. "Why would my father show up at a meeting in a nail salon carrying one? Did he go out and buy one? My mom's was made of wood. She never had the marble kind. What is the significance of the damn rolling pin?"

Without warning, Ella Mae's knife skittered sideways,

coming within a centimeter of her exposed palm. Surprised by her sudden clumsiness, she swept the cucumber slices into a bowl and salted them.

"I'd wager this shop that the rolling pin was Loralyn's idea. She and I have always been enemies and she didn't want me sticking around town. She was furious when she found out we'd outbid her on this property." Wiping her hands on her apron, Ella Mae took a sip of tepid coffee. "I know it sounds crazy and I've been trying to sort out whether I'm blindly prejudiced against Loralyn or if the only rational explanation for the use of the rolling pin was to plant it at the scene so I'd become a suspect." She went on to explain that her prints were on the pin the firemen found and that someone had stolen that same pin from her mother's kitchen.

"Being a suspect would keep you in Havenwood," Chandler pointed out. "If Loralyn wanted to get rid of you, why get you involved in a murder investigation?"

Ella Mae considered his question. "Maybe because she knew there wasn't enough evidence to build a case against me. Just enough to get me to hightail it back to New York as soon as I was free to leave."

"Or maybe she hoped you *would* take the fall. In a town this small, that would have an impact on your entire family." His eyes were full of pain. "God knows my practice will fold as soon as people hear about my twisted sister and that my father was doping injured racehorses."

Though she sympathized with Chandler's fear about the future of the equine center, her thoughts were focused on his first point. The Gaynors and the LeFayes had been at odds for generations. Perhaps Loralyn was striking out at Ella Mae's mother and aunts too. If Ella Mae had been charged, the enrollment in Sissy's school would have dropped dramatically; Verena would no longer influence the politicians and Havenwood's upper crust; the garden center would cancel orders for her mother's roses; and someone might finally confront Dee about the number of animals in her care.

"If we're right about Loralyn planting the rolling pin, then she believed there was a good chance my father would die that night." Chandler directed this mournful statement to his plate of food. "She led him into a volatile situation while making sure she had a nice, neat alibi. But how could she know things were going to go sour? Did she tell my dad to carry the rolling pin so he could look tough?"

Ella Mae pulled up a stool and sat so close to Chandler that their knees nearly touched. "The answer must lie with the money. That's what went wrong. Loralyn must have convinced your father not to pay Ashleigh or Uraeus a single dollar. He was supposed to deliver a bunch of cash in the form of bearer bonds, but when Ashleigh went to collect them, he tried to run. He also tried to call the cops."

"Those bonds had been in his safe deposit box for decades. They were his retirement fund. All his other cash had been sunk into the clinic. He was going to take out a second mortgage to buy Loralyn that tanning salon. The cops showed me his financial records." Chandler shook his head. "And where are the bonds now? We're talking about well over two hundred thousand dollars!"

That kind of money could save the equine center, Ella Mae thought. "Uraeus didn't get it and neither did Ashleigh, so all signs point to Loralyn. The police have no grounds to question her, but she might let something slip if I confront her. She's never resisted the chance to brag about a victory to me, whether it was a blue ribbon in dressage or being crowned Homecoming Queen." She patted Chandler on the arm. "I'm going to be insulted if you let that tart get any colder."

As always, it gave Ella Mae immense satisfaction to watch another person eat her food. Chandler put the first forkful in his mouth, mechanically chewing without interest as he glanced around the kitchen. However, as the combination of the farm-fresh eggs, creamy cheese, and the sweet, nutty flavor of the avocado caressed his taste buds, Chandler's eyes widened in unexpected delight.

"This is delicious," he mumbled before hurriedly shoveling in another bite.

Ella Mae waited for a sign of hopefulness to blossom across Chandler's features, but nothing happened. He ate his breakfast, asked about the day's menu, and mustered up a smile every now and then.

"I didn't think I'd feel like eating, but that was just what I needed. I came here in search of comfort and I got it. Thank you, Ella Mae." He grabbed her hand and squeezed it firmly to emphasize his gratitude, and she couldn't help but feel the tremor running through his fingertips. She couldn't imagine what it felt like to lose a parent and be betrayed by a sibling within such a short stretch of time.

"You'll make it through this and so will the equine center," she assured him. "Remember when you told me about accompanying your father to that difficult birth? How he rewrote the fate of that colt? How you saw the magic of that newborn horse rising to life on wobbly legs?" Chandler nodded, lost in the memory. "Hold on to that feeling," she advised. "Picture that foal as your dream. Feed it, care for it, and encourage it to grow. Don't let it fade away."

Chandler bolted to his feet, shrugging the lethargy from his body as if slipping off a coat. "You're right! I can still honor the Knox name by being the best horse doc in the region." He carried his empty plate to the sink, drained the rest of his coffee, and kissed Ella Mae on the cheek. "And I'm not going to waste another second. Thank you for everything. Wish me luck!"

Grinning in wonder over his change in demeanor, Ella Mae led him to the door and opened it just in time to see Reba getting out of the Buick. Reba cocked her head inquisitively as Chandler jogged to his car, the morning sun burning a path of light beneath his feet.

"What'd you do to him?" Reba asked in astonishment once she and Ella Mae were back inside the kitchen. "He looks like he's ready to run a marathon carryin' a refrigerator on his back."

Ella Mae indicated the breakfast tarts waiting on the baker's racks. "I gave him one of those. I tried to put a sense of hope into the cheese I sprinkled on top." Her cheeks turned pink. "Listen to me, Reba! Do I sound sane? My words influenced him, not my food."

"Maybe it was a bit of both, but you definitely enchanted that boy."

The bells on the front door chimed and Ella Mae shot Reba a questioning glance. "Did you hang out the open sign before you left with Chewy?"

"Nope. We've got another thirty minutes before the mornin' rush. I haven't even finished makin' the fruit salad, so I suspect we've got a few LeFayes in our midst."

As if on cue, Verena, Sissy, and Dee rushed through the swing doors and flew at Ella Mae, assaulting her with hugs, kind words, and questions. Shooing all of her aunts into the dining room, Ella Mae gave a brief explanation of the previous night's events while Reba served coffee and breakfast tarts.

"You're in the clear!" Verena shouted. "Buddy talked to the chief of police while the roosters were still crowing and said that they had a signed confession from a man named Dirk Ridley. From what I gather, this Dirk fellow was Ashleigh's contact at Uraeus. He also bashed Bradford Knox over the head with the rolling pin, so his hands are very, very dirty! Naturally, he jumped at the chance to make a deal with the DA. In exchange for copies of all of his communications with Ashleigh Knox, he'll get a reduced sentence. When Ashleigh heard that her boy Dirk sang like a bird, she wanted to confess too. This nightmare is over! Let's mix up some mimosas to celebrate!"

Sissy jerked her thumb toward the front porch. "Not until the feeding frenzy is past. If you wanted free advertising for The Charmed Pie Shoppe, you've got it. *Again*."

Ella Mae peered out the display window and was annoyed to find the street's prime parking spots occupied by television vans.

"Even ESPN sent someone," Dee said quietly. "This is big news for fans of horseracing."

Groaning, Ella Mae rubbed her throbbing temples. "I am too tired to deal with this. I just want to hide in the kitchen and then go home and sleep for two weeks."

The women made soothing noises and Reba tried to cheer Ella Mae by telling her that her mother would be joining them as soon as she'd gathered fresh flowers for the table's bud vases.

Verena threw her arms out and exclaimed, "Wait! I've got it! Invite the media inside, feed them, and answer a few, safe questions. They'll mention the shop in their articles and you can have them out of the way before your paying customers arrive. Brilliant, right?" She popped a piece of tart in her mouth and rolled her eyes in pleasure. "Oh, divine!"

Dee and Sissy agreed with Verena's plan and once again offered to serve as Ella Mae's honorary wait staff. They gobbled up their tarts, donned aprons, and invited the press inside.

"No cameras!" Verena bellowed once Sissy had issued a genteel invitation to the group waiting outside.

Ella Mae prepped a dozen plates in the kitchen and then, smoothing her hair and dusting some of the flour and pastry dough from her apron, provided the reporters with a short and heavily edited version of Dirk's and Ashleigh's arrests. She was careful to avoid mentioning why she and Reba were in the clinic after business hours and played up Chandler's bravery in the face of his sibling's treachery and betrayal.

Beyond that, she refused to elaborate, stating that she didn't want to risk jeopardizing the case by repeating important details to members of the press.

"And you don't think Chandler Knox had any prior knowledge of the horse doping?" one reporter asked dubiously once she had finished.

"Absolutely not," Ella Mae declared, her eyes flashing. "He would never inject an injured thoroughbred with cobra venom so it could run another race or two. He is devoted to his patients and runs a safe and ethical practice. People shouldn't judge him by either his father's or sister's actions."

She answered one last question and then thanked the reporters for joining her for breakfast. Most of them chuckled and offered to pay for their meals, but she waved away their cash. "This time, it's on me. But if you come back, I'll definitely take your money."

They filed out quickly, intent on tracking down Chandler, Peggy, and Officers Wells and Hardy. One young woman remained behind, lingering near the counter where she prevented Reba from busing the dirty dishes into the kitchen.

She showed Ella Mae her press card, revealing the name of an infamous gossip rag. "Are you and Chandler Knox romantically involved?"

Ella Mae looped her index finger through the handles of three coffee cups and shook her head. "No, we're not. And now I need to get to work. If you stay any longer, I'll ask you to wait tables. Have a nice day."

Thus dismissed, the reporter departed. The moment the bells rang out their good-bye, Reba muttered, "You and Chandler might not be involved yet, but it's gonna be a long six months, Ella Mae. By the time you're free of Sloan, you'll be ready to jump the bones of the first man you see."

"I certainly hope not," Adelaide announced. She'd passed through the kitchen's swing doors without a sound, her arms laden with stunning lavender-hued roses. "Ella Mae has to be very careful who she chooses to date."

"Because Havenwood's such a small town?" Ella Mae asked, putting her nose into the flowers and drinking in their scent of warm currants, dewdrops, and elderberries.

Her mother snapped off a single blossom and tucked it into her daughter's hair. "Because there's no one else like you, Ella Mae. You were born to do amazing things."

Ella Mae smiled. "Like opening this pie shop?"

Glancing around the inviting dining room, redolent with enticing aromas and the glimmer of memories yet to be made, her mother nodded with satisfaction, though something mysterious and slightly calculating flitted through her eyes.

Holding a rose out to the light, she watched the velvety petals shimmer beneath the sun's caress and said, "This, my dear girl, is just the beginning."

Chapter 19

Two days later, Ella Mae and August Templeton were settled at one of the cast iron tables on The Charmed Pie Shoppe's front porch. The pair sipped from tall glasses of pomegranate-flavored iced tea and discussed the fate of Ashleigh Knox.

"Word from my source inside the courthouse is that she tried to retract her confession. She began to boast that the authorities had nothing substantial on her, and that while Dirk Ridley, her shady associate, has a string of prior misdemeanors, she's a veritable pillar of society. She's positive that no one will listen to him and she'll have the last laugh at the trial."

"A trial? Oh." Ella Mae's heart sank. The last thing she wanted to pencil in on her wall calendar was the date she'd need to go to court to and testify. "Will you coach me, August? The defense will want to know why my prints were on the murder weapon."

Folding his handkerchief into a neat triangle, August shook his head. "In actuality, the smoke was the murder weapon and Mr. Ridley graciously provided the Havenwood police with the location of the plastic gas canister he used to start the fire in the nail salon. His prints are on the canister, and so are Ashleigh's. She claims she always kept it in the trunk of her car for emergencies, but I doubt any jury would fall for that."

"She left her own father inside a burning building," Ella Mae declared angrily. "I don't care what piece of evidence trips her up, as long as she gets her comeuppance."

August crossed an ankle over his opposite knee and waved cheerfully at a passerby. "Ashleigh's attorney is no fool. He's accepting the DA's terms as we speak. Ms. Knox faces a charge of accessory to commit murder at the very least. I expect her to be sentenced to ten to fifteen years in a remote correctional facility loaded with some real dangerous women. She could be released in eight years on good behavior, but since she's not *exactly* Miss Congeniality . . ." He chuckled. "Oh, I do feel sorry for her future cell mate."

Ella Mae couldn't help but grin, but she quickly became solemn again. "Have the missing bearer bonds been located? Chandler could really use that money. The equine center is barely limping along."

"Don't know, my dear. I'd guess they were inside the rolling pin Ashleigh left at the scene, there was a switcheroo, and someone walked away with a tidy sum of money."

"I'd swear the culprit is Loralyn, even though she was in Atlanta. It would have been easy for her to take the rolling pin from my mother's kitchen, but how could she switch that pin with the one Dirk used on Bradford if she was fifty miles away?" Ella Mae fell silent. Loralyn could have made it back to the nail salon in an hour if she'd been driving above the speed limit. Had Loralyn had the opportunity to switch pins once the fire department was on scene? Could Hugh possibly have been involved?

What if he's been on her side all along? she thought miserably. *What if he's been spying on me? Is that why he spent the day with me? Is that why he kissed me?* Her throat suddenly dry, she reached for her tea.

August rose to his feet, smoothed his suit jacket, and patted Ella Mae on the hand. "Stop churning this over or your mind will look like a tub of butter. If there were a clear solution to the matter of the missing bonds, the police would have made an arrest, but they are simply untraceable. You need to focus on your own affairs, my dear. Don't let the past drag down your future."

She simply nodded in reply.

"How about selling me a boxful of your cheeky cherry hand pies?" August asked hopefully. "I cannot get enough of those little darlings."

Ella Mae packaged a half dozen hand pies—crescent moons of folded pie dough coated with a healthy sprinkling of confectioners' sugar. They'd been such an immediate hit that she knew she'd be baking twice as many tomorrow morning. Perhaps she'd fill the next batch with fresh peaches. A bike ride to the farm stand would make for a nice afternoon outing. It had been too long since she and Chewy had had any fun.

On the way to Canine to Five, she paused at the intersection of Emperor Street and Painted Lady Avenue, her attention drawn to the enormous television screen hanging above the bar inside the Wicket Pub. Through the pub's spotless window, she could easily see the screen.

"I'll be damned." Ella Mae instantly recognized the mustached face of Mr. Malone, her debonair table companion at the Mint Julep Gala and one of the horse owners she'd suspected of being involved in illegal doping. The footage showed him exiting a courthouse, head bowed, eyes downcast. The screen flickered and a commercial for men's antiperspirant came on.

Ella Mae locked her bike to a parking meter post and studied the pub's large wooden archway, which had been constructed to resemble a real door but didn't actually

function as one. A smaller door with the same arch, an aged
metal handle, and curlicue embellishments made of brass
offered entrance into the pub. When Ella Mae was a child,
the door within a door had fascinated her. She'd imagined
that the large door was a gateway, a portal that could grant
entrance to magical creatures like unicorns and griffins on
certain nights of the year.

She stepped into the Wicket and was greeted by a delightful waft of cold air and the smell of hops. The bar was empty
save for an older man in a tattered baseball cap nursing a
tumbler of whiskey.

"What'll it be?" the barkeep asked.

"A whiskey daisy," Ella Mae answered. "And could you
turn the volume up on the TV, please?"

The man, whose face was covered with a grisly beard
and eyebrows resembling black tumbleweeds, paused in the
act of pouring Wild Turkey into a shot glass and adjusted
the volume. Ella Mae listened, fascinated, as ESPN reported
on the charges brought against the Malones, the Hollowells,
and a dozen other thoroughbred farms in Georgia and eastern Tennessee.

"Bradford really racked up the mileage," Ella Mae mused
quietly and then smiled at the bartender as he served her
drink. The cocktail, a blend of whiskey, lemon juice, grena-
dine, and soda, was sweet and refreshing. She drank it
eagerly, absorbed in ESPN's coverage.

She listened raptly as the anchorman explained that the
police in Havenwood, a bucolic town in northwest Georgia,
had discovered a detailed list of horse farm owners who'd
purchased cobra venom from veterinarian Bradford Knox
at least once over the past six months. Ella Mae was shocked
to learn that not only had thoroughbreds been subjected to
doping, but a host of quarter horses as well. The list included
the date of purchase, the amount of venom delivered, and
the method of payment. In some cases, the foolish owners

had paid Knox by check, creating a paper trail that would be difficult to dispute.

The camera switched views, zooming in on a grim-faced man in a well-cut suit. The caption identified him as Mike Hegarty, the executive director of the Georgia Horse Racing Commission. He issued a brief statement, asserting that both his counterpart in Tennessee and the governor of Georgia were personally investigating the allegations.

"It is not a crime to possess cobra venom," he stated with a small shake of his head, as if someone had made a big mistake by not making the substance illegal. "But it is a felony to inject it into a racehorse. We will charge anyone found guilty of this action with a felony per animal based on the crime of interfering with a domestic animal or race fixing or both. Guilty parties may face prison sentences."

An equine vet from Kentucky was given thirty seconds to explain how cobra venom could be administered and its usefulness as a painkiller. After another series of commercials, the coverage concluded with a quick statement from an agent from the Federal Bureau of Narcotics. He tersely stated that Uraeus Pharmaceuticals had cooperated fully with authorities, and because they'd shipped legal goods to a licensed veterinarian, the company would not face criminal charges.

The final sound bite was provided by a tearful young woman who claimed to have seen one of her family's thoroughbreds injected by their trainer shortly before a race. The horse won the day and a handsome prize purse and then collapsed a few hundred yards past the finish line, injured beyond the point of treatment. As soon as the stands had cleared of spectators, the magnificent animal was put down.

Ella Mae's eyes grew moist as she listened to the anguish in the young girl's voice.

"Don't worry, gal, the two crooks responsible for that are behind bars right here in Havenwood," said the man in the baseball hat.

"Yes, I know," Ella Mae replied. "Hopefully, there'll be an end to such abuse."

The man grunted in assent, picked up his drink, and toasted her with his glass. "Same color as your hair, darlin'. Here's to you. And to those scumbags gettin' what they deserve."

Ella Mae saluted him in return. "I'll drink to that."

Three whiskey daises later, Ella Mae got back on her bike and rode in a rather wobbly fashion to Canine to Five. She collected Chewy and then, showing a marked lack in judgment, headed for the second of Loralyn's two nail salons, Perfectly Polished Too.

As was typical during the warmer months, all the parking spots on Painted Lady Avenue were occupied and someone had even parked in the loading zone directly in front of the salon. Ella Mae took a moment to examine the lipstick red convertible.

"We don't see many of these babies in Toronto," said a man wearing a fanny pack and a Blue Jays T-shirt. "Guess some hotshot wanted to drive around a town whose streets are all named after butterfly species, eh?"

Ella Mae walked to the back of the car, keeping Chewy on a tight leash so he couldn't jump up and scratch the shiny red paint. Glancing at the Georgia vanity plate, which read SIREN in bold block letters, she grinned wryly at the tourist and said, "This little gem belongs to a local. A woman."

The tourist whistled in admiration. "She must be doing something right."

Eyes narrowing, Ella Mae thought of the missing bearer bonds. This thought was quickly replaced by the image of Annie Beaufort riding out of the woods at Respite Ranch, her face aglow with purpose and contentment. "She's about to," Ella Mae said and, filled with a simmering rage, breezed by the befuddled man and entered Loralyn's salon.

"May I help you?" a petite brunette inquired as soon as the door shut behind Ella Mae. The girl then spotted Chewy and frowned. "We don't allow dogs in here."

Having never been inside either of Loralyn's salons, Ella Mae discovered that they offered more than manicure and pedicure services. According to the menu board, the nail technicians were also trained to give facials, massages, and a variety of tortuous waxing procedures. She was amazed to see that clients occupied every chair and three more women were flipping through fashion magazines in the waiting area. The popularity of the business explained why Loralyn wanted to open a tanning salon.

"I have an urgent message to deliver to Loralyn," Ella Mae told the girl manning the front desk. "If she doesn't get it right away, she will be *very* upset."

This gave the young woman pause. Apparently, upsetting her employer resulted in serious consequences. "You can't go back now. She's testing out a new massage therapist who specializes in hot stone massage and you'll have to wait until she's done." Recovering her poise, she pointed at the door. "And your dog needs to go outside. Now."

Being bossed around by the pint-sized, twentysomething brunette stirred Ella Mae's smoldering anger, igniting it into something red, orange, and palpable. "He stays with me," she said, the slight slurring of her words making her sound unstable. "And we're going back now. If you have a problem with that, then you're welcome to try to stop us."

The young woman gaped at her, openmouthed, and then chose to pretend Ella Mae didn't exist. She blithely called out the name of one of the waiting clients and directed her to a vacant pedicure chair.

The spa rooms had been given ridiculous names like Oasis, Shangri-La, and Xanadu. It was easy to determine Loralyn's location, for Ella Mae could hear her remonstrating with the new technician from the other side of Shangri-La's closed door.

"Those are too hot!" Loralyn shouted. "There's a difference between warming the muscles and giving our clients first-degree burns."

Ella Mae didn't bother knocking. She turned the knob, pushed open the door, and pointed at the masseuse, a fresh-faced girl of eighteen or nineteen. "Out!" she commanded in a tone that echoed Verena's in volume and authority.

The girl fled. Ella Mae's next orders were directed at Chewy. She told him to sit and stay and then she locked the door while Loralyn tried to flip over onto her back without losing hold of her towel. Ella Mae smiled. Her nemesis looked like a flounder in the bottom of a fisherman's pail.

"Nice car," Ella Mae said, sitting in the technician's stool as if she had every right to be there.

Loralyn's eyes flashed but she rapidly gained control over her emotions. "Do you like it? It's a small step above the little ten-speed you've been pedaling around town. Did you forget how to drive while you were in New York?"

Unfazed by Loralyn's patronizing tone, Ella Mae made a sympathetic noise. "Maybe you should consider how to spend your latest windfall. After all, the bearer bonds you stole belong to Chandler Knox."

"How do you figure?" Loralyn widened her eyes in affront. "Except for Bradford and maybe a few of the fine people at Uraeus Pharmaceuticals, I'm the only one who's actually worked for that money. I wasted valuable months with Knox. I even agreed to marry him if he would stick with my plan. All he had to do was take advantage of my family connections to sell that lovely reptilian product to area horse farms, but he got cold feet. I didn't even get the tanning salon he'd promised me as proof of his willingness to follow my lead." She pouted. "After this I am only pursuing men with no children. Knox was so wrapped around Ashleigh's finger that he couldn't think straight."

Ella Mae was tempted to shake the smugness out of Loralyn. She clenched her hands to keep them still. "Go on.

Admit that you told Knox to put the bearer bonds in the rolling pin and then you switched that pin with the one from my mother's kitchen—that you went through all that just to get me to leave town."

Loralyn shrugged and examined her nails. "It was a two-birds, one-stone kind of thing. My darling fiancé didn't want to go on with the doping scheme so I needed to break it off with him. I figured I might as well collect some cash for the months I'd worked talking him up to the bigwigs in the equestrian world. Ashleigh thinks she was responsible for that, but it was all my doing. As if anyone would listen to some no-name housewife from Atlanta. Old names and old money are what make the horse world go round, and our farm has been rising in prominence since the turn of the century." She sighed. "Now that you've interrupted a perfectly unimpressive massage, I might as well get dressed."

Standing, she locked eyes with Ella Mae and dropped her towel to the floor. She paused a moment, giving Ella Mae ample time to gaze at her swimsuit-model body before slowly drawing on a cloud white robe. Chewy growled lowly and Loralyn curled her lip and growled right back at him.

"It's all right," Ella Mae reassured her dog.

Loralyn rolled her eyes. "As for scaring you off, view my warning as a favor. You don't belong in Havenwood. Not anymore. You've been gone far too long and we don't care for outsiders."

"Who's 'we'?"

Pulling off the elastic holding her hair in place, Loralyn shook out her locks. They cascaded down her shoulders and back like a golden waterfall. "My family," she answered tersely.

Ella Mae frowned. "Don't play coy. I bet you stuck that paper boat in my mail slot too, but I'm still here."

"That was a neat trick, wasn't it?" Loralyn's voice was giddy with pride. "The paper was as dry as the skin on your elbows. A few minutes in the oven and it was as good as new. And I can't believe you ripped up Sloan's check. You should have taken it—used the funds to pay for therapy sessions or, at the very least, some new footwear. Only professional athletes wear sneakers every day of the week, and you couldn't even pass the presidential fitness tests in grade school. Weak. You've always been weak."

Again, Ella Mae fought back the urge to strike Loralyn. How wonderful it would feel to just slap her once on the cheek. Once. Hard enough to leave a mark on the skin.

As if reading Ella Mae's mind, Loralyn examined her face in the closest mirror. "Anything else?" Her tone was meant to convey boredom. "I need to head over to my other salon and see how the restoration work is coming along. The fire was an unpleasant event, but in the end, that Dirk fellow got rid of Knox more efficiently than I could ever dream of doing. I'd only counted on a permanent falling out between Ashleigh and her dear daddy after he refused to pay up. I never thought she'd let him roast like a pig on a spit. Very poor taste, that."

Ella Mae made a noise of disgust, but Loralyn continued before she could be interrupted.

"I knew that Ashleigh was going to torch my salon. I've been bribing her housekeeper for months. She's been listening to Ashleigh's phone calls and was able to share several juicy tidbits with me. Including the arson plans. Frankly, I was delighted. Now I get to buy all new equipment with the insurance money and the story alone will have women lining up around the block."

"You haven't changed." Ella Mae seethed. "You're still the twisted narcissist you were when we were kids. A man *died*, Loralyn. Annie Beaufort *died*. These were not accidents. These people were *murdered*."

Loralyn rolled her eyes. "Spare me the drama. Annie might have been innocent, but Bradford wasn't. He knew the risks of supplying competing horse farms with cobra venom." She smiled coldly, her eyes dark with malicious satisfaction. "It's all worked out splendidly for Gaynor Farms. We're one of the few places in northern Georgia without a stained reputation. Imagine how profitable these unfortunate events will be for my family."

Ella Mae was struck dumb. Why hadn't she considered the effect the downfall of a dozen competing thoroughbred stables would have on the Gaynors' horse farm? That had been Loralyn's scheme from the start. Bradford Knox had no idea that he was engaged to such a duplicitous woman. All the while she was recommending his services to horse owners around the area and convincing him to administer cobra venom, she was setting Knox and the other horse farms up for ruination.

"How did you get my rolling pin into the salon before the police came?" she asked to cover up her stupidity. "You were in Atlanta when the fire began."

Loralyn opened the door and shooed off the young technician cowering in the hall. "I have many talents, Ella Mae. One of them is my ability to seduce men. Including men with big hoses." She raised her brows at the lewd suggestion.

"Hugh?" Ella Mae could barely speak his name. The air felt too thin to breathe.

"Such a beautiful creature," Loralyn spoke wistfully. "But far too easy to manipulate. No challenge at all. If you're interested in Hugh, go for it. He falls for the damsel-in-distress routine every time." Removing a white Rolex from her robe pocket, she slipped in onto her wrist, fastened it, and sighed. "Now unless you plan on having your nails done, and Lord knows they could use some attention, you need to run along, Ella Mae. I have a future husband to research."

Ella Mae stood her ground. She had no intention of simply walking away, leaving Loralyn to gloat in triumph. "You won't get away with this," she announced firmly.

Loralyn uttered a haughty laugh. "No one can prove that I switched the pins or took the money. You've got nothing on me, Ella Mae. It's just like old times." She lowered her voice to a whisper. "I win. And you're still a loser. Have a nice day."

"Actually, I have plenty to hold over your head." Ella Mae took a seat on the padded stool near the door and crossed her legs. Gesturing for Chewy to relax by her feet, she folded her hands on her lap as if she had all the time in the world to chitchat with Loralyn. "For example, I can support Ashleigh's claims against you. If I back up her story and tell the police that you admitted to switching the rolling pins— bragged about it even—then they're going to take a longer, closer look at you. And your family. So will the press. How do you think the Gaynor name and sterling reputation will handle such an examination? What will happen to your stables? If people link you to this scandal, you won't sell a single foal."

Her lips curling into a snarl, Loralyn said, "What do you want?"

"I'm here to tell you exactly how you're going to spend that two hundred grand." Ella Mae gestured at the massage table. "Why don't you take a seat? You need to listen very carefully."

A few minutes later, Ella Mae and Chewy left the salon, feeling the quizzical stares of the pampered women on her back. And though the whiskey's warm buzz began to recede, Ella Mae felt as if she were floating on champagne bubbles. She'd forced Loralyn's hand, and though she couldn't prove her enemy's guilt to the authorities, she could help remedy some of the pain Loralyn had caused.

Ella Mae pedaled into the sultry evening, Chewy's toothy smile encouraging her feelings of giddiness in her victory over Loralyn Gaynor. Skipper Drive was bursting with the scents of honeysuckle and ripe blackberries. A breeze from the lake kicked up dust from the road and a million insects buzzed from the underbrush as she passed.

By the time she got home, Ella Mae was covered in dirt and sweat and wanted nothing more than to take a cool

shower and then relax in front of the TV with a large glass
of wine.

But when she opened the front door, she discovered
that the guest cottage wasn't empty. Her mother was inside,
futzing over an arrangement of coral and cream-colored
roses. Chewy raced into the kitchen and nuzzled against her
calves. She laughed and bent down to kiss the terrier's black
nose.

"Your roses needed some freshening up," she said with
a welcoming smile. "Long day?"

Nodding, Ella Mae poured two glasses of wine and sat
down at the kitchen table. She waited for her mother to finish
with the roses and then told her what she'd learned from
August. After a moment's hesitation, she also recounted her
visit to Loralyn's salon.

"You did well. One might argue that you could have told
the police how she took the bonds and switched the rolling
pins," her mother stated matter-of-factly. "But they wouldn't
have been able to act on that information. There's no evidence, Loralyn would have lawyered up or lied through her
teeth about the entire affair, and the bonds aren't traceable.
If she's smart, she'll do exactly as you've instructed and will
cash them in Atlanta."

"What if Hugh Dylan comes forward and tells the authorities that Loralyn took the rolling pin from his truck?"

Her mother gazed into her wineglass as if she were a seer.
"He won't. Firstly, because he may have no idea that Loralyn
stole evidence, and secondly, because Hugh displays a rather
blind loyalty when it comes to Loralyn."

Hugh had confessed as much to Ella Mae the day he'd
helped at the pie shop, so why did it create an ache in her
heart to hear further proof of an unbreakable connection
between the high school sweethearts?

"One day, people will see her for what she is," Ella Mae
declared passionately. "A harpy."

Her mother threw back her head and laughed, a musical

sound echoing the wind chimes in the garden. "You don't know how accurate that statement is. And her mother is no prize either. Opal and I have been at each other far longer than you and Loralyn. But you're home now. We're together and things will change for the better." She reached across the table and stroked Ella Mae's cheek. "All those years ago, when you left with Sloan . . . I didn't want to let you go. I regret how I handled that, Ella Mae, and I hope that you can forgive me. I've lost so much time with you and I don't want to lose any more. Your return has taught me that it's never too late to begin again. That family is forever."

Ella Mae conjured up an image of Dee, Sissy, Verena, Reba, and her mother as they'd all gathered on the opening day of The Charmed Pie Shoppe. Such beautiful, intelligent, gifted women. And she was one of them.

She raised her glass, thinking no obstacle could stand in her way with such a troupe of exceptional women guiding her forward. The fatigue of the past two months dissipated like winter's last frost. She felt unburdened, almost weightless, as if the promise of the days to come would enable her to drift out the window like one of her mother's rose petals.

And yet, she didn't want to travel beyond this moment. After seven years, her mother had finally apologized, and Ella Mae had forgiven her in an instant.

She clinked her glass against her mother's and whispered, "Family is forever."

Chapter 20

Ella Mae's days began to take on a predictable rhythm. She woke to a lavender sky, loaded Chewy into her bike basket, and pedaled into town. Her skin was tanned, her arms freckled, and her hair streaked with filaments of auburn and gold. She was also in the best shape of her life. Between the commute to Havenwood and a workday spent entirely on her feet, her body felt stronger than it had in years.

"The town should put your face on a billboard," Reba teased one morning as she tied on her peach apron. "If the tourists think they'll look like you after a long visit to Havenwood, spas around the country will be empty as tombs."

"Thanks, but the last thing I want is more media attention," Ella Mae had responded.

Helping herself to one of the plump, red raspberries drying on the counter, Reba nodded. "True. And we've already got more customers than we can handle. Folks are askin' for delivery service, so you might wanna hire a nice, strappin' young man to carry your pies all over the county. Somebody real easy on the eye."

"I'll make sure to include that requirement in the classified ad." Ella Mae flicked Reba with a dish towel.

Reba popped the raspberry in her mouth and then her eyes grew wide. "Speakin' of newspapers, guess what I read in *The Daily* this mornin'?"

Ella Mae shrugged. "Your horoscope predicted that a tall, handsome stranger is about to walk into your life?"

"Don't I wish. I know just what I'd do with him too," Reba said, wiggling her brows suggestively. "But this is almost as good. Annie Beaufort's sister is gonna take charge of Respite Ranch. The sister's from Texas, has two teenage boys, and has won a pile of rodeo trophies, so I reckon she knows a thing or two about kids and horses."

Ella Mae was delighted. "That's the best news I've heard in ages. But what about money? Can the ranch stay afloat?"

Reba nodded. "Thanks to your aunt Dee it can. She's raffled off a custom-made sculpture to the highest bidder. Raised enough cash to keep the place in hay and frozen pizzas for a long, long time. We're talkin' six figures."

"Aunt Dee is amazing." Ella Mae shook her head in awe.

"It's always the quiet ones that get the job done," Reba observed, taking a licorice twist from her apron pocket. "Everybody underestimates them."

Ella Mae grinned. "Let me have one of those. I want to see if they'll make me as chipper as you."

"There's nothing magical about this candy," Reba said and then bit off the end of a Twizzlers. "But it sure tastes like there is." She then fluffed up her hair and went back to work.

In the middle of another busy Saturday, one of the pie shop's regular patrons suggested that Ella Mae offer a customer pie or pastry of the week. Ella Mae agreed that it was a wonderful idea and the patron, a Mrs. Sandra Gregoire, informed her that lime pie had always been her favorite.

"Drop by on Monday," Ella Mae told her. "And you'll see your name and pie written on the chalkboard."

After closing the shop, Ella Mae mounted her bike and slowly made her way south on Emperor Street. She was relieved to be able to skip the trek north to Canine to Five to pick up Chewy as her mother had decided to keep the terrier with her on Saturdays.

"He's the perfect grandchild," she'd informed Ella Mae. "He's independent, an excellent eater, and chases off the rabbits before they can get to my vegetable garden."

Turning left onto Painted Lady Avenue, Ella Mae noticed a narrow pillar of black smoke twisting into the summer sky. As she crossed over Monarch and headed toward Red Admiral Street, she saw a crowd of people gathered around what appeared to be a burning garbage can.

Ella Mae nudged her bike through a knot of pale-legged vacationers until she could see the façade of Perfectly Polished Too. Smoke was rising from the steel trash can outside the salon's front door and a Havenwood fire engine had already arrived on the scene.

Her curiosity piqued, Ella Mae dismounted and then stopped short upon hearing Loralyn's voice, which was raised in a harsh shout. If Ella Mae hadn't seen her with her own eyes, she wouldn't have believed Loralyn capable of such a screech. As long as she'd known her, Loralyn had been gifted with a lovely and musical voice. Even when she was angry or used cutting language, the words were delivered melodically, like a song.

The recipient of her disharmonious ranting was Hugh Dylan. He appeared completely unmoved by her tantrum and barely looked at her as he tried to maneuver the engine's heavy hose around her feet.

"What kind of moron starts a fire in a garbage can? It's got to be one of our chain-smoking townies. Find the culprit, Hugh!" Loralyn demanded, the cords of her neck taut and angry. "I'm losing business every second this drama occurs outside my salon!"

Hugh reeled out the hose line with calm, deliberate movements. "It's a garbage can, Loralyn. Relax."

"I've already had one torched salon, thank you very much. I don't need another. Hurry up before this somehow spreads!" Loralyn put her hands on her hips and waited.

Dropping the hose with a thud, Hugh turned on her and spoke in a low rumble. "Go back inside, Loralyn. I can't concentrate when you're this close to me."

Loralyn was aghast. Ella Mae could tell that she was unused to being dismissed by Hugh. "You . . . you never talk to me like this. What's come over you?"

Hugh jerked his hand at the engine. "This is my job, Loralyn, and I need to get back to it. Please go."

A wicked smile spread across Loralyn's face and her voice returned to its customary timbre. Gone were the petulant shrieks, replaced by a tone as rich and smooth as melted chocolate. "Just see to it that my customers can still get into my shop."

Having delivered her command, Loralyn stormed off, shoving aside anyone not clearing a path for her quickly enough.

Ella Mae scanned the faces of the crowd and recognized one of the onlookers.

Standing between a man in a Bud Light T-shirt and a woman wearing a bikini top and denim cutoffs was Peggy. Waving, Ella Mae caught the older woman's eye and walked her bike toward the receptionist.

"How are you?" she asked.

Peggy's smile was like a ray of sunlight. "Good. Really good! Did Chandler tell you that we got an anonymous donation at the equine center? For two hundred grand! Can you believe it?"

"No!" Ella Mae pretended to be surprised. "How wonderful!"

"It sure is. Chandler, um, Dr. Knox, can relax a bit now. We've got enough funds to launch a media campaign and restore our image. The clients are already starting to trickle back in. Everything's going to be okay."

Ella Mae sighed in relief. Loralyn had followed her instructions to the letter. "And what about you? Are you recovering?"

"I am." Peggy's cheeks flushed a pretty pink. "Something unexpected and completely marvelous happened."

"Oh?"

Peggy's gaze grew dreamy. "My neighbor, Ernest Jenkins, is a widower. He and I have always been friendly. We chat whenever we're outside and he's borrowed the occasional cup of milk or sugar while I've borrowed hedge clippers or a socket wrench. And then, one day, everything changed." She put both hands over her heart. "Ernest came to my door carrying the biggest armload of red roses I've ever seen. They smelled like warm honey."

My mother's Sweet Love roses, Ella Mae thought. "Go on," she prompted.

"Well, he dropped to his knee and said that he loved me—that he'd loved me from that first day when I pointed out the crabgrass growing around his mailbox bed."

Ella Mae grinned. "And do you feel the same about him?"

"Not right away," Peggy confessed. "I'd only had eyes for Bradford for so long and the grief was too raw, but Ernest has won me over and now I only have eyes for him."

"I'm so glad," Ella Mae said and the two women embraced.

Over Peggy's shoulder, Ella Mae could see that the thin, gray beanstalk of smoke had dissipated. The summer sky was a brilliant blue sapphire once more.

"I have you to thank for my happiness," Peggy added. She took a step back, keeping a hand on Ella Mae's arm. "Ernest said that we owe everything to you and your shoofly pie—that he was inspired to tell me how he felt after just one bite."

Ella Mae waved off the idea. "It wasn't my pie that sent him to your door, Peggy. It was you. But either way, I can't wait to meet your new beau. Bring him to see me at the shop."

After promising to do just that, Peggy said good-bye. Her step was light as air, a little smile played at the corners of her mouth, and she hummed like a woman who'd found exactly what she'd been looking for. And even though Ella Mae was delighted that both Peggy and the Equine Center were headed in a positive direction, there was still one more issue Ella Mae had to address. She needed to know if Hugh had helped Loralyn switch the rolling pins.

Gathering her courage, she watched as he started to reel the hose back into the truck. She didn't want to make a fool of herself by pushing through the remaining crowd of bystanders in order to talk to Hugh while he was still working, so she stood in place and focused her mind on sending forth a single thought.

"See me," she whispered, willing the air the move her words across the space that divided her from him.

The noise of a second fireman emptying the smoldering contents of the trash can and that of the murmuring spectators faded. Ella Mae pictured Hugh standing before her in the pie shop's kitchen. She felt their kiss again.

"See me," she repeated, willing her gaze to touch the skin on Hugh's back like cold snow.

Straightening as if he'd been pinched, Hugh swung around and saw her.

He let the hose drop from his hands and strode toward her. His protective gear and massive boots gave him the lurching gait of a hunting giant and there was something fierce and wild in his eyes.

"I felt you," he said, his voice a caress. "Like you were standing right behind me."

She wanted to reach out to him, but she kept her hands at her sides. "I know this isn't the right time or place, but I need to know, Hugh. If you and I are ever going to be any-thing, I need to ask you something."

He nodded wordlessly.

"What happened to the rolling pin you and the other firefighters discovered the night Bradford Knox was murdered?"

Hugh was clearly taken aback by the question, but he immediately looked off into the distance, forcing his mind to return to that moment. "Another guy on my crew, Jay, bagged it and put it in the truck along with some other stuff. We weren't sure how stable the building's structure was at that point and we wanted to remove anything that might be relevant to our fire investigator."

"Was it locked up?"

"I don't know," Hugh replied. "It wasn't in our possession very long. Maybe an hour, an hour and a half tops. And we were pretty busy." He glanced back at his crewmembers. "Why are you asking me about the rolling pin, Ella Mae? I thought that case was closed."

Ella Mae couldn't detect any deception in Hugh's words. His face was open and guileless and she believed his version of events. Loralyn had swapped rolling pins without Hugh's aid, and that gave Ella Mae an immeasurable amount of relief.

"I'll tell you all about it later." She hesitated and then plunged ahead. "When do you think you'll be done here?"

Hugh glanced at his watch and then adjusted the band, pivoting the watch face so he could read the time. As he did so, Ella Mae noticed a tiny tattoo on the inside of his wrist. She recognized the shape instantly. It was a shamrock. A four-leaf clover identical to the one she'd been given on The Charmed Pie Shoppe's opening day.

"I like your tattoo," she whispered.

He smiled at her. "The real thing is better. Only a special person deserves something so rare, so special."

Then she knew for certain that he'd given her the

shamrock affixed to the plain white card—the one she'd had framed and had mounted above the cash register. Deciding to thank him later for the incredible gift, she gestured at his heavy coat and pants. "I imagine you'll be hot and tired after this. Wouldn't it feel lovely to dive into the swimming hole?"

A light surfaced in his eyes and he smiled widely. The radiance of his gaze nearly knocked Ella Mae off her feet. "It sure would. The only thing that could make it better is if you'll meet me there."

"I'll be waiting for you," she promised and he turned to finish his work.

Ella Mae got on her bike and rode away thinking, *I've been waiting for you for a long, long time.*

Ella Mae only made it a block farther before the vision of Loralyn's license plate made her pull over onto the sidewalk and pause. She thought of how Loralyn had always been able to sweet-talk her way out of any fix. And her vanity plate had read "Siren." Was it possible that Loralyn possessed a special vocal gift? Was it anything like her own ability to transfer her emotions into the food she made?

For weeks, Ella Mae had been dismissing the unusual and implausible things that had been happening around her and to her, but now she wanted to understand why she was different in Havenwood than she had been in New York.

Reba had told her more than once that names had power. Perhaps the answer was hidden in the meaning of her name. Ella Mae pushed her bike the short distance to the corner of Painted Lady Avenue and Soldier Street and stepped into the Cubbyhole, Havenwood's bookstore.

Normally, she would have happily tarried in a shop crowded with new and used books, plush reading chairs, and sleeping cats, but she felt driven by a need for answers. She purchased a book of baby names and then pedaled home. After setting the coffeepot to brew, she took a quick shower and then sat down at the kitchen table and cracked the spine of the thick pink and blue paperback.

Pen and paper at the ready, she decided to look up her aunts' names first.

"Let's start with Verena." She flipped to the *v*s and began to read. "Verena means 'true' or the 'detector of truth.'"

Ella Mae took a sip of coffee and jotted a note. "Sounds like Verena. She always knew when I was lying. And neither Buddy nor her sisters ever bothered trying to deceive her. I wonder if she can differentiate between lies and truth with everyone. Is that her gift?"

She turned to the *c*s. "Sissy's full name is Cecilia. Cecelia is the patron saint of music." Ella Mae remembered how Aunt Sissy had told her to be inspired by the sight of her students dancing, by the sound of the music filling the school. Sissy had always supported the arts. She played five different instruments, sang like a nightingale, and floated like she walked on airy, musical notes instead of solid ground. "She inspires people through music. Okay, these are pretty accurate so far."

Next up was Aunt Delia. "Named for Delos, the birthplace of Artemis, goddess of wild animals." Dee definitely had a connection with animals, and the way she could bring life to those sculptures was beyond anything Ella Mae had ever seen. A spark of life had flowed from Dee's fingertips into the metal dog. If that wasn't goddesslike, then Ella Mae didn't know what was.

Her mother's name, Adelaide, meant noble and her middle name, Salena, stood for the moon. Ella Mae thought of the white-robed figure in the back garden. The couples who'd visited during the full and new moons. The fireflies and the Luna roses.

And Reba? Reba's full name was Rebekah. "To secure, to bind, to protect." The last definition reminded her of Reba's anger over not being present when Annie Beaufort was killed. Reba had always been there for Ella Mae. She'd walked her to the bus stop, tended to her childhood injuries, and stared daggers at anyone who glanced at her sideways, especially a member of the Gaynor clan.

It was Ella Mae's turn.

"Okay, there's nothing mind-blowing about Mae. It's the fifth month of the calendar and honors the Roman Earth goddess."

Ella Mae put the book down and sighed. "This is so stupid." She drank more coffee and scanned her notes. Finally, she turned to the *e*s and found Ella. "What am I? A 'torch, bright light, beautiful fairy, enchanted, and other.'" The last word gave her pause. "Other? Other what?" But the baby name book had nothing more to offer.

Frustrated, she left her pen and coffee behind and went into the living room. Her mother had transferred a selection of Ella Mae's favorite girlhood books over from the main house to this room. She reached for a beautiful coffee-table book on magical creatures and glanced at the stunning color plates of goblins and witches, mermaids and nymphs, and ancient gods and goddesses. She stopped when she reached the section on Arthurian legends.

"Morgan le Fay," she whispered, tracing the fiery hair of a beautiful and terrifying woman casting a spell on Merlin. "Sorceress, priestess, half faerie, other."

There was that word again. Other. And she, Ella Mae, shared a surname with Morgan le Fay. Her mother and her three aunts were all LeFayes, and neither of the two married sister's had taken their husband's surname. "There's power in a name," she echoed the statement Reba had uttered weeks ago.

More confused than ever, Ella Mae slammed the book shut and marched into the kitchen. She tied on an apron and took a ball of pie dough from the freezer. While the dough defrosted in the microwave, she put random pieces of fruit and cheese on the counter. She grabbed a handful of spices without glancing at the labels and began to mix eggs, sliced fruit of every color, and shredded cheese in a stainless steel bowl. "Show me what I am!" she repeated over and over as she stirred. "Show me," she commanded as she sprinkled nutmeg and dried mustard and paprika and cardamom over the mixture. "Show me!" she shouted as she pressed the dough into a pan and poured the filling inside. Covering the unappetizing mess with a top crust, she shoved the pie into the oven and set it to broil. Pacing around the kitchen, she ignored the conflicting smells coming from the oven and mumbled her refrain again and again.

When crust had turned golden brown, Ella Mae removed the pie and set it on a trivet to cool. She poured the rest of her coffee down the drain and searched for some wine or something even stronger, but she'd forgotten to restock her liquor supplies.

Filled with restless energy and a sense of desperation, she jogged across the back lawn into her mother's house. She heard laughter from within and discovered Reba, her mother, and her aunts sipping lemonade on the sunporch. The women were all wearing gauzy white sundresses, and for a moment, they looked like debutantes before a ball.

"It's spiked!" Verena shouted upon spying Ella Mae. "Want one?"

"Absolutely," Ella Mae replied, reaching for the pitcher. She poured herself a glass, drank it down without pause, and refilled the glass. The taint of vodka and orange liqueur did nothing to calm her nerves.

Reba gestured at her apron. "What are you cooking?"

"Answers!" Ella Mae snapped, feeling as though the world were unraveling. "You see, I have the power to put my emotions into food and I don't get how that's possible, so I've made a pie that's going to define what the hell I am. Want a piece?"

Exchanging curious glances, the women rose and followed Ella Mae to the guest cottage. Ella Mae walked next to her mother. "Ever since I was little, I've known that your ability to grow things isn't normal. Your roses can be the size of dinner plates and their fragrances are so powerful that they move people. They influence people. And then there's this business with the couples in your garden. I've seen them. Somehow, you use a special rose to tell them something. What is it they want to know?"

"If they're well matched," her mother answered simply. "The rose is a symbol. A messenger if you will."

"So you're like some kind of oracle?" Ella Mae was stunned. "How is that possible?"

Her mother opened the door to the guest cottage. "Let's see what else is beyond the realm of possibility."

The tiny kitchen smelled of the deep wood after a thunderstorm and of a wildflower field, as wide and endless as the sea.

"The pie is moving," Dee whispered in awe and pointed at the counter.

Indeed it was. Beneath the top crust, something pulsed, straining against the baked dough.

"Are you going to let it *out*?" Sissy asked, and despite the surreal situation, Ella Mae noticed that the sight of a writhing pie didn't alarm the women in white in the slightest.

Her mother picked up a pair of potholders. "Grab a knife. We'd better take this to the garden."

Ella Mae followed, her eyes riveted on the cracks forming in the piecrust. "Do you know what's inside?"

"Your answer, I imagine," her mother said as though they were discussing a commonplace item on The Charmed Pie Shoppe's menu. "But I have no idea what form it's taken."

"Only one way to find out." Reba handed Ella Mae a butter knife. "Ask your question once more and then cut the crust."

It took a moment for Ella Mae to move. Did she want to know what was inside? Did she really want to hear the answer to her question? She looked at her reflection in the blade of the knife. "What am I?" she asked for the last time and then stuck the knife into the pie, slicing it neatly down the middle.

Butterflies burst from within. Hundreds of butterflies in every color. They were striped, speckled, iridescent, and monochrome, and there were species of fantastic beauty that Ella Mae had never seen before. Their wings were like tissue-thin stained glass painted by the afternoon light.

Instead of flying away, the winged insects began to gather on the garden path. They jostled one another as if in a rush to get to the correct place, and Ella Mae gasped when she realized what they were doing.

"They're forming letters," her mother said, her eyes wide with wonder.

The women watched, spellbound, as butterflies continued to rush out of the pie. In a rapid blur of color and fluttering wings, they completed their word and then, as if they'd been frozen in time, held perfectly still.

Ella Mae read the message, but the word was foreign to her. She didn't even know how to pronounce it, let alone decipher its meaning.

"Draíocht." The rest of the women spoke in unison, their voices hushed and reverent.

Ella Mae searched their faces, noticing how timeless they suddenly appeared and how the sun had formed soft halos around the crowns of their heads. "What does it mean?"

"It's the Gaelic word for magic," her mother replied, taking her daughter's hand. "That is what you are, Ella Mae. You are Other. You are magical."

On the ground, the butterflies were trembling and Ella Mae no longer wished to make them prisoners of her desire. She glanced over her shoulder at Verena, Dee, Sissy, and Reba, noting the flush of pride and happiness reflected in their eyes. She didn't need magic to know that they'd been waiting for this moment for years.

Dozens of other questions fought one another in her

mind, but Ella Mae shoved them aside. She inhaled, drawing the signature of roses and sunshine into her body and spread her arms wide.

Something had broken free inside of her and she felt a giddy sense of elation. Her gaze rose to the blue hills beyond the lake and the part of her that had just been awakened yearned to seek the heart of the forest, but there would be time for that later.

For now, she wanted to celebrate. Standing in an ocean of blooms, encircled by the love of five extraordinary women, Ella Mae believed she was the luckiest girl in Georgia. She felt reborn. The magic that had been lying dormant inside of her until the past few weeks now sang through her blood. Every sense was heightened. It was like no feeling she'd ever known and she could not stop smiling with the joy of it.

Ella Mae looked down at the butterflies, glistening like jewels at her feet.

"Thank you," she whispered, her heart rising as the insects began to flutter their wings. "Now fly."

En masse, the butterflies rocketed into the summer sky and hung suspended for several seconds—a rainbow of sparkling confetti. Ella Mae watched them, knowing that her future was much like the swirl of colorful creatures. Fragile. Unpredictable. And utterly amazing.

Recipes

Charmed Piecrust

2 ½ cups all-purpose flour, plus extra for rolling
1 cup (2 sticks) unsalted butter, very cold, cut into ½-inch
    cubes (to make the butter cold enough, put in freezer for
    15 minutes before use)
1 teaspoon salt
1 teaspoon sugar
6 to 8 tablespoons very cold water

Combine flour, salt, and sugar in a food processor; pulse to
mix. Add butter and pulse until mixture resembles coarse
meal and you have pea-sized pieces of butter. Add ice water
1 tablespoon at a time, pulsing until mixture begins to clump
together. Put some dough between your fingers. If it holds
together, it's ready. If it falls apart, you need a little more
water. You'll see bits of butter in the dough. This is a good
thing, as it will give you a nice, flaky crust.

Mound dough and place on a clean surface. Gently shape into 2 discs of equal size. Do not overknead. Sprinkle a little flour around the discs. Wrap each disc in plastic wrap and refrigerate at least 1 hour.

Remove first crust disk from the refrigerator. Let sit at room temperature for 5 minutes or until soft enough to roll. Roll out with a rolling pin on a lightly floured surface to a 12-inch circle (Ella Mae uses a pie mat to help with measurements). Gently transfer into a 9-inch pie plate. Carefully press the pie dough down so that it lines the bottom and sides of the pie plate. Use kitchen scissors to trim the dough to within 1/2 inch of the edge of the pie dish.

Roll out second disk of dough and place on top of the pie filling. Pinch top and bottom of dough firmly together. Trim excess dough with kitchen shears, leaving about an inch of overhang. Fold the edge of the top piece of dough over and under the edge of the bottom piece of dough, pressing together. Flute edges by pinching with thumb and forefinger. Remember to score the center of the top crust with a few small cuts so that steam can escape.

Charmed Egg Wash

To achieve a golden brown color for your crust, brush the surface with this egg wash before placing pie in oven.

    1 tablespoon half-and-half
    1 large egg yolk

Note—if you're short on time and decide to use the premade piecrusts found in your grocery store's dairy section, then use the egg wash on the crusts to give them a homemade flavor.

Charmed Chocolate Bourbon Pecan Pie

(makes two pies)

1 Charmed Piecrust recipe
¾ cup white granulated sugar
1 cup light corn syrup
½ cup salted butter
4 eggs, beaten
2 tablespoons bourbon
1 teaspoon pure vanilla extract
6 ounces semisweet chocolate chips
1 cup chopped pecans

Preheat oven to 325 degrees. In a medium saucepan combine sugar, corn syrup, and butter. Cook over medium heat, stirring constantly, until butter melts and sugar dissolves. Cool slightly. In a large bowl blend eggs, bourbon, and vanilla. Mix well. Slowly pour sugar mixture into egg mixture, whisking constantly. Stir in chocolate chips and pecans. Pour mixture into pie shells. Bake in preheated oven for 50 to 55 minutes or until you spot a lovely golden bark.

Charmed Banana Puddin' Pie

1 Charmed Piecrust (recipe makes 2 crusts so you can freeze the extra for another time)

FILLING:

¼ cup cold water
2 ¼ teaspoons unflavored gelatin (1 package)
2 cups whole milk
4 large egg yolks

⅔ cup sugar
¼ cup cornstarch
¼ teaspoon salt
1 teaspoon pure vanilla extract
3 large, very ripe bananas, peeled and sliced

WHIPPED TOPPING:

1 cup heavy cream
2 tablespoons confectioners' sugar
1 teaspoon dark rum
1 teaspoon vanilla extract

GARNISH:

6 ounces semisweet chocolate, shaved into curls using a vegetable peeler

Transfer dough to a 9-inch pie dish. Trim and flute the edge. Using a fork, pierce the dough several times, then line with aluminum foil and freeze for 30 minutes. Preheat oven to 450 degrees. Place the dough-lined pan on a baking sheet and fill the foil with pie weights. Bake for 12 to 15 minutes. Cool and then remove the foil and weights.

Pour cold water into a small bowl and add gelatin. Let gelatin firm up for about 10 minutes. Next, pour milk into a medium saucepan and warm over low-medium heat until hot (about 10 minutes) but don't allow it to boil. In a large bowl, whisk the egg yolks and sugar. Add cornstarch and salt and blend until there are no lumps. Gradually add the hot milk to the egg mixture, stirring constantly. Add the gelatin to the mix and blend thoroughly. Return entire mixture to saucepan. Cook over medium heat until mixture begins to bubble, whisking constantly. Remove from heat and immediately add vanilla.

Line the banana slices along the cooled piecrust and then spread the custard on top. Put a piece of plastic wrap directly onto the surface of the filling, piercing the plastic a few times with a knife. Cover and refrigerate for 2 to 4 hours.

To make the whipped topping, place a large stainless steel bowl and blender beaters in the freezer for 10 minutes. Remove from freezer and add cream, rum, vanilla, and sugar into chilled bowl. Beat on high speed until stiff peaks form. Spread the topping over chilled pie and garnish with chocolate shavings.

Sandra Gregoire's Charmed "Customer of the Week" Lime Pie

9-inch graham-cracker crust
3 egg yolks, lightly beaten
21 ounces (1 ½ cans) sweetened condensed milk
¾ cup fresh lime juice or key lime juice
2 cups whipping cream
⅛ cup sugar (2 tablespoons)
Green and blue food coloring (if desired for greener effect)
Fresh lime slices or candied lime slices for garnish

Whisk together the egg yolks, sweetened condensed milk, and lime juice. Add food coloring, if desired. Pour into crust. Bake at 350 degrees for 15 minutes. Remove from oven and cool on a wire rack. When cool, cover and refrigerate for at least 4 hours.

Place a large stainless steel bowl and blender beaters in the freezer for 10 minutes. Beat whipping cream in chilled bowl at high speed with an electric mixer until foamy. (Note: Start slowly and increase speed in increments over several seconds.)

Gradually add sugar and continue beating until soft peaks form. Spread whipped cream over well-chilled pie or pipe on with a cake decorator. Garnish with fresh or candied lime slices.

Charmed Shoofly Pie

1 Charmed Piecrust (recipe makes 2 crusts so you can freeze the extra for another time)
1 cup flour
⅔ cup dark brown sugar
3 tablespoons butter
1 cup molasses
1 large egg, beaten
1 teaspoon baking soda
¼ cup boiling water

Preheat oven to 375 degrees.

Make Charmed Piecrust. Roll out crust and place on bottom of 9-inch pie dish (Ella Mae recommends a glass pie dish for this pie). Trim off extra dough and pinch sides of dough.

Mix together first three ingredients until butter is integrated (using the pulse button on a food processor works nicely). Reserve ½ cup of crumb mixture.

Add molasses, beaten egg, and baking soda into mixture. Then add boiling water and mix well. Pour the filling into pie dish. Scatter reserved crumb mixture evenly atop pie.

Bake for 18 minutes, then lower temperature to 350 degrees and bake another 20 minutes until the crust is golden and center of pie is only a bit wobbly. Cool for 1 hour.

This pie is very rich and Ella Mae recommends that you serve it with vanilla ice cream or whipped cream.

Charmed Pancetta and Gruyère Tart

Butter and flour for prepping tart pan
1 Charmed Piecrust (recipe makes 2 crusts so you can freeze the extra for another time)
1 Charmed Egg Wash
2 teaspoons vegetable oil
3 ounces pancetta or any other type of bacon, cut into small pieces
5 eggs, lightly beaten
½ cup mascarpone cheese, at room temperature
2 cups shredded Gruyère cheese
3 green onions, thinly sliced
½ teaspoon ground pepper

Preheat oven to 400 degrees. Butter and flour the bottom and sides of a 9-inch tart pan.

Place piecrust in the tart pan. Carefully press crust into the bottom and sides of the pan. Trim excess crust using kitchen scissors. With the tines of a fork, prick the pastry a few times. Using a pastry brush, coat the crust with Charmed Egg Wash. Put the pan on a baking sheet and bake for 10 minutes or until the egg wash has set. Allow the crust to cool.

In a medium skillet, heat the oil. Add the pancetta and cook until brown and crispy (like regular bacon). This will take 8 to 10 minutes. Transfer to a plate covered with a layer of paper towels. Let drain.

In a medium-sized mixing bowl, combine the beaten eggs, mascarpone cheese, Gruyère cheese, green onions, pepper, and pancetta. Mix gently. Pour filling into the piecrust and bake until the mixture has set and the top has a nice, golden bark—18 to 20 minutes. Cool tart for 15 minutes before removing from tart pan.

Note: For a meatless tart, substitute mushrooms for the pancetta.

Turn the page for a preview of Ellery Adams's
next Charmed Pie Shoppe Mystery. . . .

Peach Pies and Alibis

Available from Berkley Prime Crime!

"There's nothing like a wedding to ruin a perfectly good Saturday," Mrs. Dower declared to the pie shop's empty dining room. She dropped the newspaper she'd been reading on the table, leaving the radiant faces of new brides to stare at the ceiling.

Ella Mae LeFaye studied her first customer of the morning. Mrs. Dower was gray. Her clothes, her hair, and the cloud above her head were all a shade of dark gray. She sat alone at one of the café tables, rumbling like a thunderhead. With every breath, she seemed to expel an invisible vapor of gloom. It gathered around her and then spread across the pie shop like a low fog, blotting out the light, muting the twang of the country music being piped through the radio, and squelching the pleasant aroma of baking pies.

"Nothin' like a challenge before you've even got your eyes open," said a pixielike woman with nut brown hair. She examined Mrs. Dower through a crack in the swing doors leading from the kitchen into the dining room and shook her head. "It's hopeless, Ella Mae. You'll never make her smile. For a half century, that woman has been swallowin' up all traces of joy like she was a human bog."

"What's her story?" Ella Mae asked as she moved away from the door to stand behind her worktable.

Reba smirked. "She's been playin' the organ at the First Baptist church since before I was born."

Ella Mae pressed a ball of dough flat and picked up her rolling pin. She paused, the flour-dusted pin poised in the air. "You're kidding, right?"

"Of course!" Reba laughed, a sound like the tinkling of tiny bells, and tied her apron strings behind her back. "She only acts like she's older than dirt. Shoot, she's probably younger than I am."

"I don't know what to believe about the people of Havenwood anymore!" Ella Mae replied heatedly. "You try discovering that you're able to transfer emotions into food, thereby directly effecting other people's behavior, and see how muddled your thoughts become."

Waving in surrender, Reba glanced out through the crack again. "I know you've been thrown for a loop, but you'll be all right. The LeFayes are tough." Her eyes widened. "Wish me luck, I'm goin' out to take her order."

Ella Mae waved the rolling pin at Reba and then pressed it into the center of the dough, releasing a burst of buttery scent. She maneuvered the wooden tool up and down, side to side, and up and down again until the dough had been manipulated into a flat circle. Folding it in half, she gently transferred the piecrust into a glass dish.

"She wants a breakfast pie," Reba announced as she re-entered the kitchen, the swing doors flapping in her wake. "But not the one on the menu. Says she doesn't care if she has to wait an hour for her order. She wants what she wants."

Ella Mae pushed a stray lock of hair out of her face, covering her cheek and the edge of her ear with flour. "Then I suppose it's a good thing she showed up before we're officially open. What exactly would she like?"

"I see that twinkle in your eye," Reba said, holding out a warning finger. "You think you're gonna charm her into smilin', but even your mojo isn't that powerful. All jokin' aside, Ella Mae, you don't know how to control your gift just yet. You'd best rein it in for now."

"How am I ever going to control it when no one will give me straight answers about how I got this way!" Ella Mae snapped. "How any of us got this way. What makes me and you and my mother and aunts different?"

Reba shook her head. "I told you, sugar. You have to find your own path to the truth. It's one of the rules."

"Made by whom? Another mystery none of you will explain to me." Gesturing at the pie plate, Ella Mae said, "Forget it. Just tell me what Mrs. Dower wants for breakfast."

Relieved to change the subject, Reba reached into her apron and pulled out a pack of red licorice twists. "Her mama used to make a pie full of cheese, hash browns, bacon, and somethin' crunchy on top. Mrs. D. doesn't remember what made the crunch—probably the bones of small children who lost their way in the woods—but she said if you're as good as folks say, then you'll figure it out."

Ella Mae walked over to the pantry and examined her supplies. She glanced at the tidy jars of dried fruit, passing over the cherries, apricots, cranberries, raisins, prunes, figs, and quince until her gaze rested on the collection of nuts. But she wasn't looking for pecans, almonds, macadamia, walnuts, hazelnuts, pine nuts, pistachios, peanuts, or cashews. What she needed wasn't in her kitchen.

"Just sprinkle a few dead beetles on top," Reba suggested. "She'll think it's some kind of exotic nut."

Ignoring the jumbo tubs of sugar and flour, the canisters of spices, and the clumps of dried herbs hanging from the wire shelves, Ella Mae turned to Reba. "Can you run over to the Piggly Wiggly for a box of Corn Flakes?"

"Ah ha." Reba tapped her temple. "You're a clever girl. Be back in two shakes of the devil's tail."

After Reba left, Ella Mae took eggs, bacon, and cheddar cheese out of the walk-in refrigerator. Once the bacon was sizzling on the stovetop, she shredded the cheese and sliced the potato until she had a mound of thin, white strips on the worktable. When the bacon was crisp, she removed it from the frying pan and dumped the potatoes in the hot fat where they jumped and jerked like a child being tickled. By the time Reba returned, Ella Mae had blended all the ingredients together with a cup of cottage cheese. Seasoning the mixture with salt, pepper, and a pinch of paprika, she poured it into the pie shell and then opened the box of Corn Flakes.

"You said that Mrs. Dower's an organist. Have you ever heard her perform?"

Reba nodded. "People are so glum when she plays the offertory hymn that they can barely pull out their wallets, let alone pry them open and stick a bunch of cash in the collection plate. And that woman can make a bridal march sound like a funeral procession." She pointed toward the dining room. "You heard what she said. She hates weddings. Hates happiness in general."

"And her mama? The one who made her favorite pie?" Ella Mae shoved her hand into the cereal box, her fingers caressing the small, stiff flakes.

"Passed on years ago. Why?"

Ella Mae scooped up a handful of Corn Flakes and held them over the pie. "I bet she misses her mother—that she's never gotten over losing her. I need to help her believe that her mother wouldn't want her to spend the rest of her life moping. I need to help her stop feeling so . . . gray."

Reba frowned. "Not blue?"

"Blue doesn't describe loss. Grief robs the world of color. Turns it heavy and gray." At the mention of grief, Ella Mae thought of her failed marriage and of how she'd left New York before completing her final semester of culinary school. Shoving the memories aside, she glanced at Reba.

"Give Mrs. Dower some more coffee, please. I want to add something special to her pie."

"You should save your superpowers for an emergency, like making that hunky UPS man fall madly in love with me. Instead, you're gonna waste them on that sourpuss." With a scowl of disapproval, Reba left the kitchen.

Ella Mae closed her eyes and traveled back in time. In her mind's eye, she was a little girl again. It was summertime and her thin limbs were bronzed and freckled by the sun. There was a kite in her hands. It was shaped like a butterfly and had been made from a rainbow of bright nylon hues. Ella Mae had tied the kite to the basket of her bicycle and sat perched at the top of a steep hill, ready to propel herself forward.

Letting out a holler of anticipation, Ella Mae pushed off with her bare feet, launching the bike into the air. She picked up speed instantly, her whiskey-colored pigtails lifting from her shoulders, the kite shooting into the cerulean sky. She'd looked up at her kite, watching the sunbeams illuminate the reds, blues, yellows, and greens until the fabric seemed to shimmer with life.

Here, in her warm kitchen, Ella Mae relived that moment of light and joy. She saw the colors and felt the wild freedom of her downhill plunge. And she willed those feelings into the cereal flakes as she scattered them over the surface of the pie. "Be happy," she whispered. "Let go of your grief."

By the time the pie was done, Mrs. Dower had finished reading the paper and was glaring at the other customers who'd entered The Charmed Pie Shoppe in search of breakfast. Ella Mae noticed the woman's agitation and quickly handed the treat to Reba to deliver.

"Made-to-order 'specially for you, Mrs. Dower." Reba put the plate down with a flourish and then moved to the next table to take the customers' drink orders.

Ella Mae carried a pair of ginger peach tarts through the

dining area to the rotating display case in the café's front window. Out of the corner of her eye, she watched Mrs. Dower take a bite of pie. Then another. And another.

The older woman chewed slowly at first, but then her jaw moved with more gusto. Slowly, so slowly that Ella Mae wasn't certain it was there, Mrs. Dower's mouth began to curve upward into the tentative beginnings of a smile. By the time Ella Mae went back into the kitchen and returned with two coconut cream pies for the display, she barely recognized the woman in gray.

Mrs. Dower, who'd been licking the crumbs from her fork, reached out and grabbed Ella Mae as she passed close to her table. "Your pie," she began and then faltered. She touched her cheeks, which had grown flushed and rosy, and lifted a pair of meadow-green eyes to Ella Mae. "It was delicious," she whispered, the blush on her face spreading over her neck and arms, infusing her sallow skin with a healthy pink glow.

Ella Mae put a hand on the woman's shoulder and grinned. "Come back again, you hear?"

"I most definitely will," Mrs. Dower promised. She then lifted a sugar packet from the bowl of sweeteners on her table and pivoted it in the light. "What a pretty yellow. Reminds me of buttercups." She then looked down at her gray blouse and gray skirt and frowned. "I like yellow," she told Ella Mae.

"I bet you look lovely in it too," Ella Mae said and couldn't help but giggle as Mrs. Dower shouldered her purse and hustled out of the pie shop, dropping her gray scarf in the trash can bordering the sidewalk.

Reba handed Ella Mae an order ticket. "Where do you reckon she's going?"

"Shopping," Ella Mae replied. "Look out, Havenwood. Mrs. Dower is on the loose."

"Well, at least she'll be dressed like a peacock when she goes into credit card debt." Reba gave Ella Mae a stern look.

Ella Mae held out her hands. "I was just trying to brighten her day. The rest of my pies will be totally normal, I promise. After all, I can't make something special for every customer."

As it turned out, Ella Mae barely had time to think, let alone infuse her food with specific feelings. In the months since she'd opened the pie shop, she'd worked five days a week. Nearly six if she counted Mondays, because even though the shop was closed, Ella Mae used that time to make a week's worth of pie dough.

Her days were long too. She was on her feet for ten hours straight and, after locking the front door at four o'clock each afternoon, she'd say good-bye to Reba, clean the kitchen, and wearily pedal her bike to Canine to Five, Havenwood's doggie day care, to collect her Jack Russell terrier. And yet, no matter how tired she was, her dog's kisses of greeting gave her the energy she needed to manage the uphill ride home.

Charleston Chew, or Chewy, as Ella Mae had taken to calling the impish puppy after he'd succeeded in shredding most of her handbags, belts, and shoes, would perch in her straw bike basket, brown eyes gleaming and tongue lolling, as she made the trek to Partridge Hill, her family's historic house. Ella Mae would dismount in the garage and gratefully step into the lovely and tranquil carriage house. Her cozy refuge from the world.

It still seemed unreal that only a few short months ago, Ella Mae and Chewy had been living in a Manhattan apartment with Sloan Kitteridge, Ella Mae's husband. For seven years Ella Mae had been content as Sloan's wife, but after she'd caught him in flagrante with the redheaded twins from 516C, she grabbed Chewy and took three planes to her hometown of Havenwood, Georgia. She returned to her beloved aunts, her daunting mother, and to Reba, the housekeeper who'd practically raised her. And she'd finally fulfilled her dream of opening her very own pie shop.

"Stop gatherin' wool and plate me some sausage pie," Reba ordered and slapped three more order tickets on the counter. "I sure wish that sweet girl you hired to work the register and handle the takeout side of things didn't have to go back to Georgia Tech. She made my life easier, even though I hated sharin' my tips with her."

"I was hoping to find a nice high school kid to take her place, but no one's responded to my ad." Ella Mae placed a sprig of mint on top of a small bowl of sliced kiwis and fresh strawberries, plated an egg and mushroom tart, and took a bacon and onion quiche out of the oven. She tore off the potholders and quickly filled four more orders, wondering if today would be as busy as yesterday.

The rest of the morning passed by in a blur of baking, plating, and dish washing. The breakfast rush merged into brunch and before Ella Mae knew it, the lunch crowd had arrived.

With a loud "Yoo hoo!" Ella Mae's aunt Verena strode into the kitchen, a glass of pomegranate iced tea in hand. Verena, who was clad in a black and white checked dress and a pair of cardinal-red pumps, settled onto a stool and drank her tea down in three gulps. Verena was famous for her hearty appetite. As she surveyed the heaps of dirty dishes in the sink and the pies cooling on wire racks, her fingers marched across the worktable and snagged a blueberry from a bowl of fruit salad. "Full house again, I see!" She popped the berry into her mouth.

Ella Mae cut a tomato basil pie into even wedges and wiped a hunk of dried dough from her forehead. "Are you still glad you invested in this place?"

Verena rolled her eyes. "Of course!" she shouted. Verena didn't have an indoor voice. Whenever she spoke, it was as if she was addressing a large crowd. Her exuberance was as powerful as her appetite. "But we're all worried about you, Ella Mae. You work all day and then you go home, drink some wine, and fall asleep with a book in your hand. That's no way to live! Where's the fun? The adventure?"

"Has my mother been spying on me?" Ella Mae joked, but she didn't really want to hear Verena's answer.

Grabbing another blueberry, Verena shook her head. "No one's peeking in your windows. We only have to look at you to know that you're in over your head!" She scrutinized her only niece. "Your hair's a tumbleweed, you're too skinny, and I bet you can't recall the last time you ate out or went to the movies. You need help!"

Reba entered the kitchen in time to catch Verena's last sentence. "Amen to that. Our girl needs another employee, a car, and a roll in the hay. And not necessarily in that order."

Shooting Reba a dirty look, Ella Mae said, "I'll run another ad in *The Daily*, okay? If I get a break this afternoon, I can check out the auto listings too. As for the roll in the hay? I should get divorced first, don't you think?"

Balancing three plates on her arm, Reba still managed a shrug. "Sloan didn't let his marriage vows get in his way, so why should you?"

"Hush up! She's going about things the right way!" Verena scolded, grabbed the next two orders, and followed Reba through the swing doors. She came back a minute later. "Dining room's stuffed, patio's packed, and there's a line at the counter!"

Groaning, Ella Mae hurriedly plated two lunches, slipped off her apron, and picked up the dishes that needed to be delivered to a patio table.

Verena was right. There wasn't an empty seat in the shop. Reba was busy boxing a key lime pie for a to-go order while the in-house customers eyed her impatiently. Some were waiting for food and others were eager to pay their bill or have their drinks refreshed.

"This place is a train wreck," Ella Mae murmured. Pasting on a smile, she served lunches to the couple seated by a cluster of black-eyed Susans and pink coneflowers, checked to make sure the rest of the patrons were enjoying their meals, and then went back into the dining room to see to her other customers' needs.

By the time she'd walked around the room with pitchers of sweet tea and ice water flavored with paper-thin slices of lemon and lime, the line at the counter had doubled. Without being asked, Verena volunteered to ring customers on the register. Ella Mae blew her aunt a kiss of gratitude and then hustled back out to the patio to tend to people's empty glasses.

Too preoccupied to bring dirty dishes into the kitchen, Reba and Ella Mae piled them on the counter behind the display cases, well out of sight of the customers eagerly waiting to buy slices of dessert pies and tarts to take home. Ella Mae had just finished boxing a half dozen cherry hand pies when Reba thrust a plate containing a piece of blackberry tart into her hands.

"Take this outside to Mr. Burton. He's sitting by the geraniums. And don't get stuck at his table," she warned. "He's a real talker."

Reba was right. Mr. Burton accepted his tart and before Ella Mae could slip away, he asked where the blackberries had come from.

"There's a lovely swimming hole on the way to my house," she explained, momentarily distracted by the image of the deep pool of water in the middle of a copse of old trees. "On a rise above the water, there's a ridge covered by blackberry bushes. They grow plump and juicy all summer long and are the best I've ever tasted." Her eyes grew distant as she pictured the place. "The sun bathes them all day and at night, cool air from the swimming hole drifts upward and coats the berries in a gentle dew. My mother used to say that fruit and flowers are best picked by moonlight, so that's when I go."

Mr. Burton had yet to sample his tart, but now he lifted

a forkful to his mouth. He closed his eyes and chewed slowly, relishing the sweetness of the berries and the flaky, butter-kissed dough. "I taste them both," he said, his eyes filled with delight. "The sunshine and the moon glow. I think it's about the most magical thing I've ever eaten. Could you box a piece for my wife? She's been feeling poorly lately. It's her hip, you see."

Ella Mae did her best to look sympathetic, but she sensed the tale of Mrs. Burton's hip could go on for quite some time and time was one thing Ella Mae couldn't spare. With an apologetic smile, she interrupted Mr. Burton's narrative and excused herself.

The moment she opened the door leading into the dining room, she was assaulted by an unpleasant aroma. It was strong and acrid—the kind of odor that typically accompanies a fire. Ella Mae stopped and sniffed.

"Something's burning," she murmured and then saw a curl of smoke escape from the crack between the kitchen's swing doors. She began to walk toward the counter, horrified to see another curl and then yet another snake through the tiny opening. The smell intensified.

At first, Ella Mae had found it reminiscent of smoldering wood, but now it called to mind the image of something blackened and charred. Something like a pie. A half dozen meat pies to be exact.

"No, no, no!" Ella Mae cried and rushed into the kitchen.

She was met by a wall of gray smoke that obscured the worktable and countertops. As she moved closer to the commercial ovens, the air darkened from pale pewter to dark charcoal. Ella Mae quickly turned the appliances off and opened the top oven door. Smoke burst out like a puff of dragon's breath coming from a mouth of a cave and Ella Mae waved it away from her face with a potholder. Bubbles of burned cheese and ground beef pooled at the base of six black and unrecognizable shapes. To Ella Mae, the pies looked like charred Frisbees.

"The dinin' room's clearin' out!" Reba shouted, flinging open the back door. "If you wanted a break, you could have just asked. No need for such dramatics."

Ella Mae removed the smoldering pies and dumped them into the garbage can. "I know you're teasing me, but I don't see anything funny about this. By suppertime, everyone in Havenwood will be talking about how I burned an oven full of pies."

Reba slid the window above the sink open. "They didn't exactly stampede out of here. Everybody paid and I gave them all a slice of dessert pie to take home for their trouble. I put up the closed sign too. We're done for today, sugar."

Sagging against the worktable, Ella Mae watched the smoke race out of her kitchen and rise into the clear August sky. "At least the smoke alarm didn't go off."

Glancing at the ceiling, Reba frowned. "I reckon that's not a good thing. Isn't it supposed to yell and scream when the kitchen is close to burnin' down? And what's that little red blinking light mean?"

"A malfunction," a man's voice said.

Ella Mae turned to see Hugh Dylan standing at the other end of the room. He was breathing hard, his chest straining against his navy blue Havenwood Volunteer Fire Department T-shirt. He ran a hand through his molasses-brown hair and looked around. "No flames?"

"Not this time," was Ella Mae's foolish reply. She tried to look away from Hugh's startling eyes, but they were as mesmerizing as always. She tried not to be captivated by their brilliant hue—twin pools of blue-green that made her think of secluded Grecian coves, but she found herself getting lost in them just the same. Eventually, her gaze moved down to his lips, which she had kissed not so long ago, and the strong jawline, which she'd traced with her trembling fingertips.

Ella Mae's face grew warm as she recalled the two of them working together in this kitchen. How he'd had his back to her and then had suddenly pivoted until their bodies had been so close that it had felt completely natural to erase the gap between them. She remembered raising her chin and parting her lips, how she'd closed her eyes and slid her hands over his broad shoulders as he'd bent to kiss her.

She remembered the feel of sparks leaping beneath her skin, of the heat coursing through her veins with such force that she thought she was burning from the inside out.

Even now, despite the smoke lingering in the air, she could detect Hugh's scent of dew-covered grass and sun-warmed earth. Just the memory of it filled her senses. But she could also never forget how quickly those seconds of exquisite pleasure had turned to pain. How she and Hugh had broken off their kiss, baffled and frightened. They'd only been alone together once since that day, but they hadn't touched. And as the summer passed, Ella Mae feared that they'd never find a way back to the moment they'd shared in this room.

Reba cleared her throat, forcing Ella Mae back to the present.

"We're okay," she told Hugh. "Just a bit of smoke. There's no damage."

"Speak for yourself," Reba said and put a hand to her forehead, feigning a swoon. "I feel kinda dizzy. You might need to carry me outta here, young man."

Hugh grinned. Along with everyone else in Havenwood, he knew that Reba was an incorrigible flirt.

"How did you find out about my little charbroil incident anyway?" Ella Mae asked.

Hugh focused his blue-green gaze on her once again. "One of your customers called nine-one-one. The rest of the emergency response crew will be here any—"

The rest of his sentence was cut off by the howl of a siren.

"Oh, no!" Ella Mae shouted and hurried past Hugh and through the dining room. She burst out of the front door onto the wide rose-covered porch in time to see a neon yellow fire truck turn the corner and head down her street, its siren's wail cutting through the peaceful afternoon.

Ella Mae leapt off the porch and raced up the flagstone path lined by snapdragons and purple salvia and frantically tried to wave the truck away.

"They're not going to drive by!" Hugh yelled, clearly amused by her antics. "Someone reported a fire so they have to investigate now." The smile playing at the corner of his mouth suddenly disappeared. He stared at the fire engine, frowning in confusion. "What the hell?"

Ella Mae followed his gaze. It took a few seconds for her mind to register what she was seeing, but when the image became clear, she began to laugh. For there, clinging to the steel handrail on the back of the fire truck, her canary-colored dress flapping in the wind like a ship's sail, was a middle-aged woman.

She was no firefighter. That much was obvious to both Hugh and Ella Mae. In addition to her bright sundress, the woman also wore a pair of blue Converse sneakers and rhinestone-encrusted sunglasses. As the truck drew closer, Ella Mae could also make out a fuchsia headband in the woman's gray hair.

"Why are you laughing?" Hugh asked. "Do you know that crazy lady?"

"It's Mrs. Dower," Ella Mae replied, delightfully awe-struck. "She's the organist at the Havenwood First Baptist church."

Hugh threw out his hands in frustration as the truck drew to a halt and the siren ceased blaring. "I don't care if she's the preacher! She can't just hitch a ride on the back of our engine!"

Ella Mae smiled. "I think she's having a carpe diem moment. It's been a long time coming too, so let her be."

Mrs. Dower hopped off the back of the truck, waved at Ella Mae, and paused by one of the rosebushes marking the far corner of the pie shop's lot. She bent over, drew in a deep lungful of flower-scented air, and then plucked one of the soft purple roses from the bush. Tucking the flower behind her ear, she skipped down the sidewalk in the direction of the church, as agile and carefree as a young girl.

Hugh's shock quickly faded and his eyes twinkled with humor. But then he looked at Ella Mae and his expression changed. She saw longing there. And a reluctant resignation too. "When you first came back to town and I saw you at your aunt's school, I knew you were going to be trouble." His smile was twisted, as if being so close to her was agonizing. "So why is it I keep ending up here? Why can't I stay away from you?"

And then, without waiting for an answer, Hugh walked off to meet his fellow firefighters.

Hurt and confused, Ella Mae turned back to her pie shop. She noticed how the gray-white smoke still hovered over the roof like a pair of wings. She studied their shape, thinking that they didn't resemble the wings of a bird or even an angel. They were wispy and diaphanous, shimmering in the air for a few precious seconds before disappearing completely. Like the wings of a dragonfly. Or a fairy.

DON'T MISS THE FIRST NOVEL IN
THE BOOKS BY THE BAY MYSTERIES FROM

ELLERY ADAMS

A Killer Plot

In the small coastal town of Oyster Bay, North Carolina, you'll find plenty of characters, ne'er-do-wells, and even a few celebs trying to duck the paparazzi. But when murder joins this curious community, writer Olivia Limoges and the Bayside Book Writers are determined to get the story before they meet their own surprise ending.

M769T0910

FROM THE AUTHOR OF *A KILLER PLOT*

ELLERY ADAMS

Wordplay becomes foul play . . .

A Deadly Cliché

A BOOKS BY THE BAY MYSTERY

While walking her poodle, Olivia Limoges discovers a dead body buried in the sand. Could it be connected to the bizarre burglaries plaguing Oyster Bay, North Carolina? The Bayside Book Writers prick up their ears and pick up their pens to get the story . . .

The thieves have a distinct MO. At every crime scene, they set up odd tableaus: a stick of butter with a knife through it, dolls with silver spoons in their mouths, a deck of cards with a missing queen. Olivia realizes each setup represents a cliché.

Who better to decode the cliché clues than the Bayside Book Writers group, especially since their newest member is Police Chief Rawlings? As the investigation proceeds, Olivia is surprised to find herself falling for the widowed policeman. But an even greater surprise is in store. Her father—lost at sea thirty years ago—may still be alive . . .

M896T0511